MARISA DE LOS SANTOS
BELONG TO ME

"Marisa de los Santos's *Belong to Me* is my favorite discovery of the past years: a terrific page-turner that's also poignant, funny, surprising, and deeply heartfelt. *Belong to Me* is the kind of novel you can't wait to share with your friends.
The perfect book club pick."
New York Times bestselling author Harlan Coben

"De los Santos, an award-winning poet, explores what happens when life throws us kinks and crumbles the plans we've so carefully laid out. And as one would expect, there is poetry in her words and all around the world she has created for Cornelia. . . . De los Santos quenches our gossipy sides by giving us what we want—a window into these characters. . . . There are plenty of surprises in *Belong to Me* that will keep you turning the pages."
Richmond Times Dispatch

"De los Santos delivers an interconnected network of compelling little stories. Her writing is both vividly descriptive and surprisingly insightful."
Boston Globe

"Witty and intelligent."
Kirkus Reviews

"[A] hot read for lazy summer days. . . . Marisa de los Santos writes beautifully, and her novels are smart and funny. This is another winner."
Montreal Gazette

W9-CZS-142

"Reading *Belong to Me* was like spending a perfect evening with an old friend; by the end, my cheeks ached from grinning, I had cried off all my mascara, and I felt happy and replete—filled to the brim. With a poet's ear for language, her trademark sharp wit, and a stunning faith in the value and power of love, Marisa de los Santos held me spellbound as the catalysts of passion and parenthood caused strangers to evolve into families. I love this book. You will, too."
Joshilyn Jackson, author of *Gods of Alabama*

"We fall in love with Cornelia and her husband, Teo, as they navigate a new landscape, along with grief, secrets, betrayal and the universal ache to love and belong. Marisa de los Santos's witty dialogue, profound characters and punch-in-the-stomach plot twist keep the book from becoming just a catty novel. We keep cheering for Cornelia as she's discovering who she is—and who to trust."
Minneapolis Star Tribune

"Marisa de los Santos definitely beat the sophomore jinx with her novel, *Belong to Me*. . . . She creates remarkably real characters. . . . The writing is consistently intelligent. . . . It's the three-dimensional men, women, and children who populate her fiction that I'll remember for a very long time."
Nancy Pearl's Picks

"Gracefully written. . . . A good read."
Publishers Weekly

By Marisa de los Santos

LOVE WALKED IN
BELONG TO ME

Forthcoming

FALLING TOGETHER

Belong to Me

Marisa de los Santos

AVON

An Imprint of HarperCollins*Publishers*

AVON BOOKS
An Imprint of HarperCollins*Publishers*
10 East 53rd Street
New York, New York 10022–5299

Copyright © 2008 by Marisa de los Santos
Excerpt from *Falling Together* copyright © 2011 by Marisa de los Santos
ISBN 978–0–06–198385–6
www.avonbooks.com

First Avon Books digest printing: July 2011
First Avon Books mass market printing: July 2011
First Harper paperback printing: April 2009
First William Morrow hardcover printing: May 2008

Avon Trademark Reg. U.S. Pat. Off. and in Other Countries, Marca Registrada, Hecho en U.S.A.
HarperCollins® is a registered trademark of HarperCollins Publishers.

Printed in the U.S.A.

10 9 8 7 6 5 4 3 2 1

For Charles and Annabel,
my sleek brown otters

Belong to Me

ONE

❧

Cornelia

*M*y fall from suburban grace, or, more accurately, my failure to achieve the merest molehill of suburban grace from which to fall, began with a dinner party and a perfectly innocent, modestly clever, and only faintly quirky remark about Armand Assante.

Armand Assante, the actor. If you didn't know that Armand Assante was an actor, don't be alarmed. Had I not caught, years ago, the second part of the two-part small-screen adaptation of Homer's *Odyssey,* I might not have known, either, but whether or not you are familiar with the work of Armand Assante, you are right to wonder how he could have had a hand in anyone's fall from grace, suburban or otherwise. I wondered myself, and, even now, I don't have a clear or satisfying explanation for either of us.

What I know is that I was doing my best. I had lit out for the suburbs in the manner of pioneers and pilgrims, not so bravely and with fewer sweeping historical consequences, but with that same combination of discouragement and hope, that simultaneous running-away and running-toward. I was a woman ready for a new life. I was trying to make friends, to adapt to my new environment, and for reasons that felt entirely out of my control, I was failing.

People like to say that cities are impersonal, that there's nothing like a big city to make a person feel small. And, sure, when viewed from the top of a twenty-story building, I'm an ant, you're an ant, everyone's an ant.

Trust me. I know what it means to be small. I'm five feet tall and weigh about as much as your average sack of groceries, but for years, every time I walked down a city street, I could have sworn I expanded. I lost track of where I ended and the city began, and after a few blocks, I'd have stretched to include the flower stand, the guy selling "designer" handbags on the corner, the skyscrapers' shining geometry, the scent of roasting nuts, the café with its bowl of green apples in the window, and the two gorgeous shopgirls on break, flamingolike and sucking on cigarettes outside their fancy boutique, eyes closed, rapturous, as though to smoke were very heaven.

I loved the noise, opening my window to let a confetti of sound fly in. I loved how leaving my apartment, in pursuit of newspapers or bags of apricots or bagels so perfect they were not so much bagels as odes to gloss and chewiness, never just felt like going out, but like *setting* out, adrenaline singing in my veins, the unexpected glancing off storefronts, simmering in grates and ledges, pooling in stairwells, awaiting me around every corner, down every alleyway.

Imagine an enormous strutting peacock with the whole jeweled city for a tail.

But my peacock days didn't last. They went on for years and years, first in Philadelphia then in New York, before skidding to as abrupt a halt as anything ever skidded, so that by the time my husband, Teo, and I took a left turn onto Willow Street, those days had been over for months, and as we drove through as quiet a neighborhood as I had ever seen, I could not shake the feeling that we were home. I wanted and did not want to feel this way. My heart sank even as my spirits lightened and rose toward the canopy of sycamore leaves, the sleepy blue sky.

What you need to understand is that I had not planned to become this person. I had planned to remain an adventurous urbanite, to court energy and unpredictability, and to remain open to blasts of strangeness, ugliness, and edgy beauty for the rest of my life. Instead, as Teo drove ten miles an hour down street after street, it came from everywhere, from the red flags of the mailboxes and the swaths of green lawn, from the orderly flower beds and the oxidized copper of the drainpipes: the sound of this sedate, unsurprising place calling me home.

"It looks like home," Teo said, and after a mild double take (very mild, since the man reads my mind with unnerving regularity), I realized that he didn't mean "home" the way I'd been thinking it, or not quite. He meant the place where we'd been kids together and where all four of our parents still lived.

My husband and I had grown up, not in a suburb exactly, but in a cozy little Virginia college town, in the same kind of neighborhood we drove through now, beautiful, with houses dating from the early twentieth century, trees dating from before that, not a McMansion in sight. A place where late spring meant hardwoods in full, emerald green leaf, fat bumblebees tumbling into flowers, and a Memorial Day lawn party replete with croquet, badminton, barbecue, and at least five kinds of pie. And although we were years and miles away from that place, that childhood, although it was late morning and Memorial Day had come and gone two weeks ago, I could almost see the children we had been darting through the dusk, could almost smell the rich perfume of grilling meat.

I know how syrupy this sounds, how dull, provincial, and possibly whitewashed, but what can I do? Happy childhoods happen. Ours happened. What came back to me, with lightning-crack vividness, as I looked out the car window, were the clusters of women, at birthday parties, cookouts, standing in yards and kitchens, the air warm with their talking, and how oddly interchangeable we all were, women and children both. The woman who picked us up when we fell down or wiped our faces or fed us lunch or yelled us down from treetops or out of mud (all of it so casually, with barely a break in the conversation or an extra breath) may have been our mother but could just as easily have been someone else's. We hardly noticed. The women merged into a kind of laughing, chatting, benevolent blur, a network of distracted love and safekeeping.

"You're right," I told Teo. A stinging pang of longing shot through me and I found myself on the verge of tears. I wondered if that's what I was up to (because leaving the city had been my idea), if I were doing what so many others have done, upstarts who head off to adventure in the big city only to choose the life their parents had chosen, moving onward and backward at the same time.

As soon as we pulled into the driveway, before the

sunny-faced real estate agent had so much as unlocked the door of the house, I knew we would take it.

The truth is that cities are not for the faint of heart, and I had become the faint of heart. I spent my last days in New York as I had spent the preceding nine months, feeling shaky and so small I was afraid I might disappear altogether. I had lived in cities for over ten years. I had wanted to stay forever. And the day came when I couldn't pack boxes fast enough.

Teo and I had lived in our new house for two weeks, and the dinner party was in our honor. Teo is an oncologist, had just started his new job at a hospital in Philadelphia, and another doctor had thrown the party, although his wife had given me her stage-whispered assurance that it wouldn't be an all-doctor party.

"I've invited a nice mix of people," Megan had said when we'd arrived at her house, "so the evening won't turn into everyone raging against managed care. You know how that is!"

I didn't, actually. Teo and I had been married less than two and a half years, and while we hadn't spent all of that time lovebirding our way around New York City— he'd been working; I'd been taking art history courses at NYU; we'd hit a few bumps in the road (at least one of which was as bone rattling as bumps come)—we had lovebirded as much as we could, which I suppose kept discussions of managed care to a minimum.

"Thanks!" I stage-whispered back, giving Megan a conspiratorial smile.

Megan smiled, too, then stepped back and eyed me appraisingly. "Such a cute dress," she said, which was a perfectly fine thing to say despite the fact that, perhaps because it's applied to me and other small women

so liberally, I'm decidedly un-wild about the adjective
"cute." But there was something about the way Megan
paid me this compliment—a certain glint in her eye
or note in her voice—that caused a tiny red flag in my
head to start inching its way up its tiny flagpole.

A word or two in defense of the dress. I called it
a slip dress, but before you start picturing Elizabeth
Taylor in *Cat on a Hot Tin Roof*, I should tell you that
its only truly sliplike quality was spaghetti straps. It
was fluid and loose, a cross between a late-1950s sack
and a shift, and, yes, it was above the knee, but only
just, and, no, I wasn't wearing a bra with it, but, as everyone knows, one of the few privileges of an almost
complete lack of curves is forgoing the welt-leaving
architecture of the strapless bra. In other words, the
dress was entirely appropriate. Worn with high-heeled,
barely-there sandals as I was wearing it, it was the perfect dress for a late-summer dinner party. Everything
in my life up to that moment had taught me that.

But as soon as Megan led me into the living room
where four other couples stood talking, I understood
that the dress was all wrong. In fact, as far as I could
tell, any dress would've been all wrong because Megan
and every single other woman in the room was wearing pants. Linen pants. Linen pants with sleeveless
silk blouses or cotton sweaters. It was a pastel-colored
prairie of linen pants and sleeveless tops, stretching in
every direction as far as the eye could see. I stood on
its edge and felt myself in my dress turning—subtly,
like an early-autumn leaf or a days-old open bottle of
red wine—from easy and elegant to overreaching and
tarty.

But I realize I'm making this sound very important,
like a major humiliation, and it wasn't. It wasn't even

a minor humiliation, but it did set me a bit off balance. Still, clothes are only clothes, and even in the suburbs, modern America isn't an Edith Wharton novel, right? You don't appear in public with a skirt an inch above regulation length or with the wrong color fan and get thrown out of the social galaxy, for Pete's sake.

So after a pause and a fortifying wink from Teo, I strode into the living room, smile bright, hand extended. The off-balance sensation never quite went away, but I was fine. For a full ten minutes I chatted with a lovely young woman who turned out to be one of the evening's two hired servers, but other than that, I negotiated the cocktail portion of the evening quite nimbly, if I do say so myself.

And then, at dinner, the one-two punch: first, Piper; then, Armand.

Piper was my neighbor. She lived directly across the street, and prior to the dinner party, I had endured two separate encounters with her, two and a half if you count the time I waved at her as her car pulled out of her driveway and she failed, ostentatiously (our eyes meeting for at least three seconds before she slid her sunglasses from the top of her head to the bridge of her nose), to wave back.

I met her two days after we'd moved into our house. I was sitting on my front steps in my junior high gym shorts, grimy and glazed with sweat, gulping bottled water as fast as I could gulp, and feeling sorry for myself the way anyone who's ever unpacked boxes in the middle of August feels sorry for herself, when Piper appeared before me.

In trying my very hardest to describe Piper without exaggerating or editorializing, what I come up with is this: trim, tan, and long waisted, a white polo shirt with matching teeth and nail tips, blue gingham Capri pants with matching blue eyes and espadrilles, and the kind of bobbed, butter-blond flawlessness that proliferates among newscasters and sorority women of the Atlantic Coast Conference. In fact, after one glance, I'd have bet money she'd attended college somewhere in the top half of the state of North Carolina.

Piper's smile started out as dazzling, but quickly developed a pasted-on quality as she surveyed me, her gaze coming to rest and lingering for a few beats too long on my cropped head of hair. Later, I would identify the look on her face as one I hadn't seen in a very long time, since high school or maybe before, that of a person disliking me on sight. But at the time I didn't recognize the look. In fact, it almost didn't register with me. Instead, I thought, *It's beginning,* my heart giving a hopeful hop, *the community of women, the safety net.*

"Hello there!" she'd said, crisply. "Welcome to the neighborhood."

I stood up, eagerly, rubbing my hopelessly filthy hand on my hopelessly filthy shorts, but she made no move to shake it, for which I couldn't really blame her.

"Hi," I said, "I'm Cornelia Brown, and I'm usually much cleaner than this."

I smiled. She didn't. She cocked her head to one side, reflecting.

"Cornelia. Now, that's a different name!"

Different from what? Hephzibah? is what popped into my head, but I didn't say it. I sighed a self-deprecating sigh and said, "Believe me, I know."

"We're the Truitts," she said, although there was no one else with her, "from across the street. I'm Piper."

Piper. Not the undifferentest name in the world. Not quite the pot calling the kettle black, but close.

"Hi, Piper."

"I've come on a reconnaissance mission." Her eyes gleamed with artificial mischief.

"How exciting. Reconnoiter away."

"The Paxtons, who lived here before you, were a professional couple, no kids." Piper pronounced the word "professional" as though it were another word altogether, something more like "pornographer."

"I met them when we closed on the house," I said. "They seemed lovely."

Piper smiled a tight smile. "I wouldn't know. But all of us have been hoping that whoever bought this house would be a real family."

Wondering whom she meant by "us," and even though I didn't really see at all, I said, "I see."

"So, do you?" Piper raised her eyebrows, waiting.

"Do I what?"

"Do you and your husband—at least I assume the man I saw move in with you is your husband"— Piper gave a teasing laugh— "have any kids?"

The question sent a lightning flash of pain zigzagging through my stomach. After asking it, Piper glanced around the yard, as though she suspected I'd hidden my children behind a bush or inside a planter.

"No," I said, "it's just me and my husband, Teo." I thought about adding a breezy "For now!" but decided to leave it, fearing that breeziness might be more than I could manage.

"Huh," said Piper, "just the two of you." And that's when she cocked her head again and gave me a small, puzzled, pitying, faintly disapproving frown, the kind of look one might give a stain on one's blouse or a bearded lady at the circus.

"Shoot," she said, snapping her fingers. "And this is such a great neighborhood for families."

Stunned, I took a short, reeling step backward, and almost tumbled into a defunct-looking hydrangea. The comment, along with the face Piper had made, struck me as exactly the kind of comment and look you do not, under any circumstances, give to a woman whose acquaintance you have made seconds ago and about whose personal history you know next to nothing.

There was a small silence, during which Piper appeared to further consider, mournfully, my childless state and during which I suppressed, barely, my battling urges to blurt out either "I'm sorry" or "Go to hell."

"Well, anyway," Piper said finally, "welcome to the neighborhood!"

"It was nice to meet you," I said, with all the sweetness I could muster, "Pepper."

"Likewise," she said, flashing her teeth at me. Then she turned on her raffia-covered heel, her bob bobbing, and sang, "And it's PI-per!" over her shoulder as she trotted across the street and into her house.

That evening, over mediocre pizza, I described Piper to Teo, including the newscaster/ACC sorority-girl part, the head cocking, and blinding teeth.

"I don't think she liked me," I said.

"I like you," said Teo, smiling, and putting down his pizza.

I didn't tell him what she'd actually said, the part about "real family," the face she'd made when I'd told her we had no children. Teo and I had been in various stages of "trying" since we'd gotten married (full disclosure: since before we got married, but not *much*

before). Why worry him? He had worried enough, we
both had, and in the terrain of peaks and valleys Teo
and I had been treading for the past three years, Piper's
face wasn't even a pothole.

That was Piper encounter number one.

Encounter number two took place a few days later,
when I opened my front door to find Piper and a plate
of cookies. Piper was smiling. The round faces of the
cookies, peeking up at me through the Saran wrap,
seemed to be smiling, too. Despite my best efforts to
hang on to my wariness, I found it slipping out of my
head as the women of my childhood (Mrs. Sandoval,
Mrs. Wang, Mrs. Jackson, Mrs. Egan, Mrs. Romanov,
Mrs. McVey, Mrs. Brown) slipped in, with their firm
voices and gentle hands.

"How nice of you, Piper," I said, taking the cookies.
"Please come in."

Piper's glance swiped the inside of my house, taking
in the heaps of moving boxes, the discarded bubble
wrap and newspapers.

"No, thanks," she said. "Actually, I was wondering if
you might come out."

I set the cookies on the nearest box and walked outside.

"What's up?" I asked.

Piper put her hands on her hips and said, "I was just
noticing what the moving truck did to your lawn."

She walked over to the front corner of our yard and
pointed, shaking her head. I followed her. A deep, tire-
track-shaped muddy rut cut across one corner of the
yard. It was only about three and a half feet long, but
the expression on Piper's face suggested that the rut
was a horror, an abomination, that the rut cut across
our yard and across the corner of Piper's soul as well.

"Oh, yeah," I said, vaguely. What else was there to say?

She reached into her pocket, pulled out a business card, and handed it to me. "Our landscaper is excellent," she said, "just top-notch. A little sod, maybe?"

I took the card and stared at it.

"And that bush." Piper pointed to a bush, wrinkling her nose. "A hydrangea. It's never done well."

"No?" God, who did this woman think she was?

"No. My guy'll yank that puppy right out of there before you can say boo."

Piper wasn't talking about a real puppy, of course. She was talking about a bush, just a bush, and one even I had to admit looked half dead, but the bush was *it,* the final straw. Sparks began to fly behind my eyes, and a smothering cloud of outrage surrounded me.

Before I'd regained my powers of speech, Piper said, brightly, "Anyway. Enjoy the cookies!" Then, smile, bobbing bob, and Piper was gone, crossing the street and slinking back into her lair.

I threw the business card after her, an ineffectual missile, naturally. It fluttered into the center of the muddy rut.

"Loathsome toad," I growled aloud.

"Loathsome toad," I growled to Teo as soon as he'd returned home from his third trip to Home Depot in forty-eight hours. "Loathsome Jane Pauley Tarheel toad."

"You went to an ACC school," Teo said. "You know that, right?" He grinned his curly-cornered grin at me.

"Whose side are you on?" I demanded, although of course I knew the answer. Always, and in every way that mattered, mine. And, when I took the long view, I understood that Teo's serene core, his failure to go ape-shit crazy over all that made me ape-shit crazy was a quality I treasured. But sometimes I take the short view. Right then, I wanted Teo to cut the "core of serenity" crap and call Piper some *names*.

He leaned in to kiss me, but I turned away. "Traitor."

"How can I prove my loyalty?" Teo asked, leaning in again. "Buy you a garden troll?"

"Gnome." I gave him a push. "And I am not overreacting."

"A set of plastic flamingos?"

"I'm serious," I said.

By way of accounting for the depth of my indignation, I considered telling Teo about my first conversation with Piper, but decided not to. It was easier if he thought I was only furious about insolence and insulted shrubbery.

"Plastic flamingos would give old Pepper a seizure disorder, don't you think?" said Teo.

"Teo, it's *our* lawn!" In all my life, it had never occurred to me to want a lawn. In fact, it had occurred to me to *not,* under any circumstances, want a lawn. But now that I had one, I'd defend every last blade of grass in it. "It's our grass," I told Teo.

I had a thought. "Listen, Teo. Walt Whitman said, 'I believe a leaf of grass is no less than the journeywork of the stars.'" Although the line's relevance to the situation at hand was elusive, even to me, I felt a surge of triumph.

"Oh." Teo nodded contemplatively. "Wow. So we'll make it *two* garden trolls."

I held Teo at arm's length and eyed him, his flushed face and clear green eyes, his mouth. One of the many salient facts about my husband is that he has the most perfect upper lip ever invented. I felt myself giving way.

"Gnomes," I said, faintly.

"Hell," he said, "let's go all the way. Three. Three
trolls." I could feel the shape of his shoulder through
his shirt. "Would that show you whose side I'm on?"

I sighed. I shrugged.

"Forty-five minutes of sex among the boxes ought to
do it," I said.

And it did, but the fact that I was thus diverted from
my self-righteous indignation didn't mean I wasn't still
indignant. And the fact that my indignation was self-
righteous didn't mean it wasn't also righteous. Right?

Thus, you can imagine my chagrin when, just as a bowl
of cool gazpacho was being placed before me, Piper
herself came scuttling into the dining room with a man
I presumed to be the unlucky Mr. Truitt in tow.

"Hello, all! Here at last!" cried Piper. "Megan, we let
ourselves in. Hope you don't mind."

"Get me out of here," I whispered into the shining
red depths of my soup.

Apparently, Megan didn't mind that they'd let themselves in. In fact, the expression on Megan's face bespoke pure, near-frantic delight as she flew out of her
chair and across the room to embrace Piper.

"I'm so sorry to be late," said Piper, settling herself
down in the chair Megan's husband pulled out for her.
"We dragged ourselves away from the Lowerys' cocktail hour just as quickly as we could."

The woman seated next to me, whose name was Kate,
tilted her head toward mine and said, "The Lowery,
Lowery, and Lerner Lowerys," to which there was no
possible reply.

"I'd love to see the inside of that house," exclaimed
Kate. "Was it fabulous?"

"I guess it was," said Piper, shrugging. "The party was so boring, I barely noticed."

"Now, Piper," said Piper's husband. "It wasn't that bad."

"It was *dreadful*," asserted Piper, shooting her husband a disparaging glare.

"Only you would call the Lowerys boring, Piper," remarked Megan affectionately, looking a bit surprised afterward, sheepish, as though she hadn't known she'd had it in her to say such a thing.

I glanced at Megan's face as she gazed at Piper and then I glanced at the faces of the other women at the table. Ah, I thought, Queen Bee. Figures.

"Piper, Kyle," said Megan's husband, Glen, "this is Mateo Sandoval, a new colleague of mine, and his wife, Cornelia."

Piper turned to Teo, and I set down my soupspoon and leaned in to watch for the inevitable shift, the unconscious softening of expression that happens to women's faces when they meet my husband. Teo's mother is Swedish and his father's Filipino, which is apparently some recipe for genetic alchemy because Teo is this combination of about ten different shades of golden brown that almost no one can help but notice.

And there it was. The slight parting of the lips. The hand reaching up to touch the pendant on her necklace. The almost-purr in Piper's voice as she said, "Hello, Mateo."

Since I might sound like a jealous wife and since there are few roles more humiliating, I should tell you right now that I'm not. I'm used to seeing people see Teo. The first time I noticed it, at one of those Memorial Day picnics I mentioned earlier, I was all of five years old.

All the neighborhood kids were playing what I still

avow was the longest and best game of freeze tag ever played anywhere, and Teo was it. As he was running, one of the mothers caught him by the shoulder, stopping him cold, stared at his face, and said, "Mateo Sandoval, you are the handsomest child I have ever seen." And while we all stood around panting, slumped with waiting, Teo blushed, ducked his head, gave the mother a polite, upward smile, then took off running as though he'd never stopped. It was a scenario that would repeat itself pretty regularly over the nearly three decades since. Teo looking like Teo; people noticing; then, if Teo even notices their noticing: blush-duck-smile-move along like it never happened.

Really, it hardly registered with me anymore except as a source of amusement at Teo's discomfort. And forget jealous. When I saw Piper's face change, I wanted to hoot "Hallelujah!" and enwrap Kate in a celebratory hug, but I settled for high-fiving myself under the table. If Piper had to be my neighbor, it was good to know she might be human after all.

"I saw Armand Assante in a Starbucks," I said.

We were talking about New York City.

Megan had seen Richard Gere. Glen had seen the guy in *An Officer and a Gentleman* who wasn't Richard Gere, a coincidence that, for about two seconds, sent everyone into a breathless state of cosmic awe. Piper had seen Uma Thurman ("huge feet, no makeup, and dark roots, and I do mean dark"). Kate's husband, Jeffrey, had seen Jill Hennessy from *Law & Order*, but then had, as he was falling asleep that night, suddenly remembered that Jill Hennessy had an unfamous identical twin, and was kept awake by the possibility that the woman he'd seen in a leather jacket walking her dog might not have been Jill Hennessy at all, a story that somehow made me like the guy. Kate had seen "that gymnast, oh, what's her name, the really short one." I had seen Armand Assante in a Starbucks.

"I saw Armand Assante in a Starbucks," I said.

Silence. The kind of silence that thickens the air in the room to the consistency of gravy. For a mad couple of seconds, I wondered if I only thought I'd said, "I saw Armand Assante in a Starbucks," and instead had barked like a seal.

Then, finally, Kate: "The tennis player who used to be married to Brooke Shields?"

Everyone ignored this, although I saw Teo's lips twitch.

Then Piper said, coolly, "I don't think I'd know Armand Assante if I saw him."

"Oh, but you would!" I began.

"I don't think so," interrupted Piper, firmly. "I don't think I'd know him if I saw him. I don't think I know who Armand Assante is."

"But that's the beauty of Armand Assante," I said. "Even if you'd never seen any of his movies, even if you'd never heard the name before, you would look at him and instantly say, 'That's Armand Assante.' He just *is* Armand Assante."

Everyone looked at me. Everyone except my husband, who grinned into his glass of wine.

"What does that mean?" asked Piper, masking, or pretending to mask, her derision with a tight little smile.

"Oh, you know what I mean," I said, laughingly.

"No," said Piper, unlaughingly, "I don't." The corners of Piper's modestly lipsticked, petal pink smile were actually turning white. She's furious, I thought. Holy hell.

"I just mean . . ." I groaned. Not aloud, but inside, every cell of my body was groaning at the top of its lungs. "Well, he had this slicked-back hair, and gold rings, and this suit, and those very European shoes, pointy . . ."

Henry David Thoreau said, "City life is millions of people being lonesome together," and, yes, there came a time when I agreed. But I was beginning to wonder if, when it came to isolation, the city had nothing on this new place, this would-be haven. I wondered if I'd jumped out of the frying pan and into the fire because, for my money, there are few experiences more isolating in the world than picking up a joke that's fallen flat, brushing it off, and then choking the life out of it by explaining it to a roomful of strangers who will never, not in a million years, get it.

"I'm good at dinner parties!" I wanted to shout. "Dinner parties are my natural habitat! I am appropriately dressed and good at dinner parties!"

As far as soul-bruising events go, this one, when taken alone, was relatively minor. Not even in the same soul-bruising-event universe as the time I'd stood on the top riser at the school Christmas concert and thrown up on half of the third grade, midway through "White Christmas." Maybe just a little worse than the time I'd walked into a salon and day spa and said, in a moment of distraction, "I'd like to make an appointment for a pedophile." And compared to my deeper, more recent contusions, it was almost nothing: thumbprint-sized and pale, barely there.

Except. Except I had the sneaking feeling that this wouldn't be an isolated event. That this lonely moment was the first of many lonely moments, so many that if you were to string them all together and look at them from a certain angle, they'd make up not a lonely life, I wasn't feeling *that* gloomy, but at least a lonely epoch in an otherwise unlonely life. The person I'd been for most of that life wouldn't have minded a stint of loneliness, at least not minded much, but I hadn't been that person for a while.

I sat there, with the dinner party droning and burgeoning around me. You chose this, I reminded myself. This is where you live now. These people are your people.

I closed my eyes. When I opened them, I was still there.

TWO

$\mathcal{A}$s Piper sat on a hard, wooden, undersized chair in a brightly lit school library, without warning, from out of nowhere or from out of a past so distant that it felt like nowhere, the memory of the man's back came to her.

There was no way in the world she could remember the man's name (because he had not been particularly important to her, had not even so much been "the man" as "a man," one of many), but there it was, a back Piper hadn't seen in, God, it must be fifteen years. And it was as if she were seeing it at that moment, as though she were not sitting in the crowded library but were instead naked, tangled in sheets on the bed in the man's apartment with the man's back before her, within touching distance of her hands and mouth.

The man's back was tanned and V shaped. Water trickled down the cleft of spine toward the white towel wrapped around his narrow hips. How she had loved damp men, men just out of the shower, gleaming and supple, but also somehow softer than usual. Newly born and fragile.

Piper sat in the library of what would be, in a few

days, her son's school, what technically already was
his school, she reminded herself with satisfaction,
since she'd talked Kyle into bypassing the quarterly
payment-plan option—might as well wear a sign
saying "We don't know if we can really afford this"—
and putting up a full year's tuition two months ago.
Technically, Tallyrand Academy had been Carter's
school for two months. More technically, for two
months, the Truitts had been a Tallyrand family. She
and Kyle had been Tallyrand parents. She and Kyle
were Tallyrand parents.

WELCOME, TALLYRAND PARENTS! proclaimed the
easel-propped dry-erase board by the library door.

Piper looked around at the other parents, many of
them people she knew, noting what an attractive group
they comprised, how tidily turned out and uniformly
tan. The men had expensive but unflashy watches; the
women had expertly summer-streaked hair and manicured toes peeping out of sandals. It was true that three
of the women were less than slender. A ten, a ten, and
a twelve, Piper estimated. But three out of roughly
fifty was certainly not bad, especially when you considered—and Piper never considered this without a
shudder—that the average American woman was a
fourteen.

Just as she glimpsed her husband entering the library,
Piper had a sudden memory of herself playfully slipping on the man's—the other man's, the fifteen-years-
ago, nameless man's—white coat, like a robe, going
into his bathroom to brush her teeth. She could see the
edge of the white coat against her tan, nineteen-year-old
thigh. A medical resident. Or perhaps a fellow. Probably a fellow, since Piper had generally chosen men who
were considerably older than she and as many removes

from her world as possible. An ophthalmologist, she remembered now. He'd made flirtatious jokes—weak but sweet jokes—about looking into her eyes.

Kyle stopped to talk to the headmaster, but met Piper's gaze across the room. He gave her a look that said "Made it!" She gave him a look that said "Just under the wire."

Kyle's job moved in cycles of frantic activity and relative quiet, the vicissitudes of which still eluded Piper, although, a few years ago, she had made one long conversation's worth of good-faith effort to understand them. She remembered with fondness Kyle's almost childlike enthusiasm at answering her questions about this mysterious, intricate ebb and flow, but when he'd gotten out a notebook and begun to supplement his information with chartlike hieroglyphs, she'd tuned out. Consequently, Piper was not entirely clear on the reasons for Kyle's current, prolonged period of busyness, but she found that she didn't need to understand it in order to find it inconvenient and irritating.

Still, now that Kyle had appeared, she registered his appearance with pleasure. The fine cloth and cut of his shirt, his suit-pant cuffs resting on his shoes in just the right spot, the precise and recent haircut. He was the very picture of a man who'd spent the last nine hours performing a lucrative, enviable job in a tastefully appointed office. And she admired the way these indicators of a well-spent day were balanced by the absence of jacket and tie, the smallest whisper of a five o'clock shadow, the gentle ruffling of his hair, as though he'd run a hand through it in the car on the way to the school.

If he'd shown up in full, polished workday regalia, like a couple of the other men had, Piper would have experienced a distaste bordering on repulsion, but

Kyle's note of unstudied casualness, of not trying too hard, was the right note to strike, and Piper loved it when people struck the right note.

This was something Piper kept to herself, knowing that it could make her sound snobbish, which she didn't so much mind, and also shallow, which she minded more, but she also knew that her love of the right note wasn't evidence of snobbery or shallowness, not really. While she would never have put it quite this way, for Piper, appropriateness meant the opposite of chaos; Piper's trust in it was akin to other people's trust in God.

Just two nights ago she'd woken from one of her usual nightmares—Carter sinking into quicksand or her daughter, Meredith, bouncing out of the convertible Piper drove, vanishing, screaming, over the edge of the roadside cliff—and calmed herself by remembering the socks she'd bought that day. Athletic socks, thin but not too thin, rising to just above the knobby bone of her inner ankle for a slimming effect (not that Piper's ankles were thick, but she had to admit—not publicly of course—that they were not her best feature), at twelve dollars a pair, expensive but not ridiculously so.

The crowning glory of the socks was their apparent seamlessness. Ever since Piper could remember, she'd hated the sensation of a sock seam across her toes. Her father used to tell stories of an infant Piper tugging at her socks and weeping, and Piper herself vividly remembered slipping into the cloakroom at school, sometimes three times a day, to remove her shoes and twist her socks back to the least uncomfortable position. These new socks were wholly suitable—perfect for kickboxing class, perfect for step class, perfect for jogging on the treadmill—and recalling their suitability, picturing

them, four pair, white and folded, like sleeping but-
terflies, in her drawer, slowed Piper's racing heart and
mind, chased away her terror.

As Kyle approached, Piper stood to greet him. The
plastic cup of red wine in his hand precluded a hug—
Piper wore white pants—but she smiled at him and
gave his arm a squeeze.

"Hey, pretty wife," he said, "sorry I'm late."

"You're not," said Piper, running a hand along his
arm, restoring the crease in his shirtsleeve where she'd
squeezed it, "not very. A few minutes. Did you say hello
to Bob and Betsy yet? They're over in the corner, near
the early reader shelves. He's wearing a golf shirt."

"I just got here, Pipe," Kyle said, a little wearily.

"A golf shirt," repeated Piper, musingly. "You think
that means he decided to take that early retirement
offer?"

"I don't know. I can ask," said Kyle. His voice grew
vehement. "He'd be a fool not to."

"Because of that golden parachute, you mean," said
Piper, raising her eyebrows and glancing again at Bob
and Betsy. Bob was laughing at something; Piper noticed the pale skin around his eyes, a sunglasses tan.

Kyle looked at Piper. "That, too."

"It means he's expendable, though, which has to
hurt." Piper's gaze drifted over her husband's shoulder.
"Oh, God, there's Tom," said Piper. "I should go talk
to him. He looks like hell." Tom Donahue was Piper's
best friend Elizabeth's husband, and he did look like
hell, although there was nothing remarkable about this
fact. For months, ever since Elizabeth's battle with
cancer had begun, "like hell" had been Tom Donahue's
standard look.

Piper smiled up at Kyle. "Give Bob and Betsy my

best? Tell them we'll do dinner soon. Okay? We'll
throw something on the grill. They're over near the
early reader books." She gave him a tiny push in the
proper direction. "Okay?"

Kyle took a long sip of his wine, and his eyes did
the squinting thing they did when he was thinking of
something else. Fleetingly, it occurred to Piper that
Kyle's eyes had been doing the squinting thing a lot
lately. If she didn't know him better, if she'd been a
different kind of wife, she might suspect that he was
harboring secrets. The thought of Kyle with a secret
life was so preposterous that it made Piper smile. Kyle
noticed the smile, smiled back, and said, "Okay, honey.
Will do."

Piper made her way over to Tom, who still stood
just inside the library entrance, his arms hanging at
his sides, his shoulders slightly hunched, and Piper
couldn't stand it that he stood that way, couldn't stand
the way he drew in breath after deep breath, as though
he were preparing to swim the English Channel instead
of to step into an ordinary room full of people he knew.

For God's sake, thought Piper, *would you pull yourself together?*

All the women Piper knew agreed that Tom Donahue
was a good-looking guy. He had a slightly-too-long, angular face—a face that would look at home under a
cowboy hat in an old Western—offset by big, winsome
blue eyes, baby's eyes almost, with long, thick lashes.
But when Elizabeth got sick—as soon as she was diagnosed, Piper thought bitterly, on the way home in the
goddamn car—he'd begun to lose weight, to appear
almost monstrously gaunt and hollow-eyed and lost.
Defeated, Piper thought. Walking around the house
with defeat written all over him, while his wife fought

the battle of her life, a battle that wasn't over, not by a long shot.

"Tom touches me like I'm made of glass," Elizabeth had told her a few weeks ago.

Piper had followed Elizabeth's gaze out her kitchen window to the backyard, where the sprinkler swept its great fan of water back and forth with languorous grace. Like a dancer, thought Piper, like a manta ray. The sprinkler's beauty made her want to cry.

She'd looked at Elizabeth, wondering if she'd noticed the sprinkler, too. But Elizabeth was running a finger around the rim of her teacup. "Not just like I'm fragile, but like I'm made of something besides flesh and blood. Like I've already turned into something else." Elizabeth paused. "Although he's probably not thinking that. Probably it's just the way he makes me feel."

Suddenly, Piper had felt so angry she couldn't speak. Silently, she'd swooped up their two cups of the vomit-tasting, curative tea some college friend had sent Elizabeth, strode over to the sink, and emptied them with vigor, the green-brown splashes ugly and dramatic against the white porcelain. Piper had stared into the sink for a long moment, then had turned around, smiled at Elizabeth, and said brightly, "Someone had to put that tea out of our misery."

When she saw Tom standing in the school library like a tired, frightened old man, the anger flared again, fresh and hot, but Piper felt people watching. She was aware of all those eyes full of sympathy for Tom. *Poor bastard,* thought the men. *Poor sweet man,* thought the women. Piper could almost hear the words.

"Elizabeth's the one who's sick," she wanted to tell them all, "and she's getting better." She wanted to scream it, but instead she gave Tom a reassuring hug, then took his arm and led him into the room. Piper felt the eyes on her now, imagined the voices saying, "Piper's been a rock for that family," and despite her anger and her huge, genuine worry, she felt a twinge of pleasure.

She walked Tom over to the long table at one end of the room and poured him a cup of wine. Tom thanked her, took the cup, and was about to sip from it when he noticed the poster hanging over the table. An illustration of two pigs in party hats and a parrot hovering between them against a yellow background.

"I recognize that," he said, quietly. "I think my kids have that book."

"Toot and Puddle," supplied Piper. Probably every woman in the room would recognize those pigs, she thought. "And Tulip. The parrot's name is Tulip."

Tom knitted his brows, then shook his head mournfully. "Doesn't ring a bell," he said with heavy consternation.

Piper resisted a strong, sudden urge to punch Tom in the stomach or at least give his upper arm a hard, twisting pinch the way her mother had done whenever Piper had acted up in public. A grown man getting maudlin about a pair of pigs and a parrot. *Lighten the fuck up,* thought Piper.

"No worries," said Piper, with a light laugh. "Kyle wouldn't know Toot and Puddle from the Cat in the Hat. And he might not know the Cat in the Hat."

Tom turned his sad eyes on Piper. "Elizabeth does most of the reading out loud around our house," he said, bleakly. "She does voices and everything."

Piper would've socked him then, she was sure of it, but at that moment the headmaster, Rupert "Roop" Patterson, a short man with a thunderous voice, bellowed cheerfully, "I hate to interrupt this good time, but the prekindergarten teachers have put together a short presentation on what your children can expect over the next year. It'll make you wish you were four years old again, I guarantee it!"

Tom looked at his watch. "How long is this supposed to take?" he asked Piper. "The sitter needs to be home by nine o'clock."

Piper was the one who felt socked. "You got a sitter?" she said, biting out the words, one by one. "Did Elizabeth ask you to?"

There was no sign that Tom had picked up on her tone. "No. I just called her. Abby Lau. We usually use her sister Lauren, but she broke a tooth this morning. She was playing tennis. It's Abby's first babysitting job, but she seems very mature for her age. Has to be home early though."

Grimly, Piper took hold of Tom's elbow and steered him toward the seats.

"How do you break a tooth playing tennis?" mused Tom, shaking his head.

With an intense concentration of effort, Piper loosened her grip on his elbow. "I cannot imagine," she said.

It happened again in the middle of the pre-K presentation. Just as the teachers were beginning to describe the road to reading readiness, the ophthalmologist's back reappeared, pushed its way through years and years to arrive still damp, the muscles finely articulated and breathtakingly symmetrical. So breathtakingly symmetrical that, before she could stop herself, Piper gasped.

Oh, God, thought Piper, trying to shake off the memory with a slight shake of her head, *what is wrong with me?*

This was her first official night as a Tallyrand parent; on one side of her sat her husband in the blue-verging-on-purple shirt she'd bought him for his birthday; on the other side sat the drooping scarecrow who was once the handsome, capable husband of her sick best friend, the drooping scarecrow who had hired a thirteen-year-old to care for his children, as though their mother weren't right there, at home, with them. "You can't be trusted anymore," he might as well have told Elizabeth. "You're already gone." And here Piper sat, almost shaking with longing to touch a man she'd slept with a handful of times ages ago, a man she'd barely known and had never, not for one second, not even in her imagination, loved.

Leave, she told the back, *you have no business being here.*

"Resist the urge to push," one teacher was saying—not Carter's teacher, Carter's was the younger, curly-haired one. Distractedly, Piper noticed that the teacher who spoke was wearing a pair of Taryn Rose sandals. Piper had tried on the same sandal in white at the beginning of the summer and had nixed it as too expensive. The teacher had chosen the red patent. Piper would never have chosen the red patent. The teacher continued, "What's most important at this stage is getting them to feel at home with books."

Listen to this, Piper told herself, reading readiness is important. Reading readiness is *crucial.* She tried to think of her son's face, the cornflower blue eyes she found unspeakably beautiful. Whenever Piper read to him, she'd look down to find him watching her. "Look at the book, sweetheart," she'd prompt him, gently. "What do you think that pig there is thinking?" Or sometimes, "This letter's an *A.* I think it looks kind of like a tent. Do you think it looks kind of like a tent?"

Carter was intelligent, Piper knew that. But his intelligence wasn't the kind that drew attention to itself. He wasn't a show-off. Piper believed that Carter knew all his letters by sight, but, honestly, there were moments when he'd regard the alphabet refrigerator magnets so blankly, she couldn't be positive. When the Tallyrand acceptance letter had arrived, she'd gone into the walk-in pantry and sobbed with relief. Whenever Piper thought about this moment, she would touch a hand to her ribs, remembering how the sobbing had made them ache.

"Let them know that books are their friends," the teacher was saying, and Piper repeated the words under her breath.

Piper didn't discover the reason for the ophthalmologist's back's sudden appearance until the following afternoon. She and Elizabeth were sitting in the big sunroom off Elizabeth's big dining room, an unusual spot for them. Their usual spot was the kitchen, of course. As with all of Piper's adult friendships, hers and Elizabeth's took the form of a long string of conversations in kitchens. On playgrounds and at poolsides, too, but everything real, everything monumental between them had happened in kitchens. And Elizabeth's kitchen was gorgeous since the remodeling last year. They'd knocked down a wall, gutted the old butler's pantry, and gone high-end with everything: Sub-Zero, Viking, hardwood cabinets, Italian tile, and magnificent black granite countertops. The custom, built-in wine cooler loomed almost six feet high.

Piper and Kyle had been privately skeptical of the expense. Supposedly, kitchen improvements paid for themselves at resale, but Piper and Kyle had their doubts. Still, Piper couldn't argue with the kitchen's beauty, especially the new windows—nearly the whole back wall was windows—the way the abundance of light deepened the honey color of the floors and set the countertops flashing with secret glints of pearl and blue. At certain times of day, the light appeared to billow into and expand the room, like air filling a balloon. If Piper had been in the habit of taking inventory of such things, she'd have realized that Elizabeth's kitchen was her favorite place on earth.

But when she'd arrived at Elizabeth's house that afternoon, Elizabeth's "Come on in, Pipe" had come from the sunroom instead, a room that, despite its name, was rather dim and cool due to the enormous (and, in Piper's opinion, ridiculously, even horrifyingly, overgrown) rhododendrons that bordered the exterior of the room on two sides.

Elizabeth reclined in a white armchair, her hair—the hair she'd been so grateful to keep—unbrushed and loose on her shoulders, her feet propped on the matching ottoman. The chair and ottoman represented an overstuffed style of furniture that Piper had always disliked, finding it bloated and mushroomy. Elizabeth looked frail in the huge chair, but as soon as Piper noticed this, she reminded herself that a fat, stupid chair like that would make anyone look small. She felt a twitch of annoyance, two twitches, one at Elizabeth for owning such a chair, and another at Elizabeth for sitting in it.

"It's a gazillion degrees out there, Betts," Piper said. "If I don't have iced tea running down my throat in two minutes, I will pass out."

Elizabeth smiled wanly and gestured in the direction of the kitchen. "Go for it."

"Okay, well, come on," said Piper, her annoyance mounting. "Come with me and have some, too. I'll grab a handful of that mint out of the backyard."

Piper extended her hand to help Elizabeth out of the chair, and Elizabeth took it, but she didn't pull herself up. She just held Piper's hand in hers and looked at Piper with an uncommonly sweet, tired affection in her eyes. Somehow, it was the last kind of look Piper wanted to see. No, she thought. She wanted Elizabeth out of that chair. She wanted Elizabeth to have iced tea in the kitchen. She gave her hand a tug, but Elizabeth shook her head.

"You go ahead," she said in a quiet, firm voice. *That's more like it,* thought Piper, releasing her friend's hand. Elizabeth was famous for her stubborn streak.

When Piper got back with her drink, Elizabeth was sitting up in the chair with her legs Indian style instead of stretched out on the ottoman and with her hair smoothed back into a ponytail. Piper felt like singing at the sight of her. She set the glasses of iced tea down on the coffee table, then pulled the ottoman several feet away from the chair, out of Elizabeth's reach, and sat down on it, crossing her own legs.

"Crisscross applesauce," she said, giddily.

"I have a bone to pick with you, lady," said Elizabeth, narrowing her eyes. "You've been holding back about our new neighbor. Time to come clean."

"What do you mean holding back?"

Piper had told Elizabeth about the cocktail party, about Cornelia's ludicrously skimpy black dress and condescending jokes, the way she'd thrown her supposed sophistication in everyone's faces. "And she had Carter's exact haircut, I swear to God. And four-inch-high 'do-me' shoes." "Fuck-me" is what she'd meant, but Piper only ever swore in her head. If she had been being completely honest, she'd have had to retract the bit about the shoes. Yes, they were high, but they were understated enough in other ways, little pale gold sandals with thin straps. But Piper could tweak a detail here and there if she felt like it, couldn't she? She wasn't a reporter for the *New York Times*, was she?

"I *mean* the hunky husband! What else would I mean?" Elizabeth removed the lemon wedge from the lip of her glass and threw it at Piper. "Holdout!"

"Oh, him," said Piper, laughing and, in a single motion, scooping the lemon wedge off Elizabeth's antique Persian and tossing it in the wastepaper basket in the corner of the room.

"Yes, him. Parvee Patel-Price nearly had a heart attack this morning. She dropped off some food for us on her way to work . . ."

"Don't tell me," interrupted Piper. "A casserole." Parvee Patel-Price was famous for her dinner parties, which the unsuspecting attended fearing or hoping for exotic Indian fare, curry or maybe some of that homemade cheese, and at which she invariably served American dinner-table cuisine circa 1972.

"Baked tuna-cheddar spaghetti, God bless her, chock full of cream of mushroom soup," said Elizabeth, grinning. "And a bag of groceries along with it, which she somehow managed to drop on the way up my front walk, just as the new hunk in town was coming back from his early-morning run. He helped her pick up the groceries and carry them in. The man was in my kitchen!"

"Mateo," said Piper. "Although he seems to go by

Teo. Dr. Teo Sandoval. He's an ophthalmologist."

"Huh," said Elizabeth, frowning. "I heard he was an oncologist."

Piper flushed. *Oh,* she thought, *oh my.* She took two sips of iced tea.

"That's what I meant to say," she said, finally. "I'm not sure I'd call him a hunk, though."

"Really? Parvee was practically hyperventilating."

"Oh, he's certainly attractive. Kind of tall and modely looking. Blondish brown hair and tan skin and green eyes. Or maybe they're blue." Green. Definitely green.

Elizabeth snorted and rolled her eyes. "Oh, one of those tall, model-y types."

"You know what I mean. Almost too pretty? And sort of exotic. Not my type." She shrugged, dismissively. It was true, at least officially. Her official type had always been WASPy and solid and corporate, even in high school, even in *junior* high. Men like Kyle, whose handsomeness was foursquare and daily. Unofficially, secretly, her tastes leaned toward the gorgeous and glowing. Her secret men had always been formidably beautiful, another quality that marked them as happily separate from her real, day-lit life.

Piper felt unsettled by the idea that Cornelia's husband had triggered the memory of the ophthalmologist's back. But the ophthalmologist and all the others were from a very long time ago. It wasn't as though she wanted them now. It wasn't as though she were jealous of anything Cornelia had.

"Is his wife beautiful, too?" asked Elizabeth.

"Oh, she's got a pretty face, I guess," said Piper, her tone undercutting the assessment. "But she's the size of an eight-year-old and built like one, too, and her eyes are too big for her face, and her head's too big for her body."

"A Powerpuff Girl!" crowed Elizabeth.

"Exactly," said Piper. She loved it when Elizabeth talked smack about people. They looked at each other and burst into giggles.

When their laughter dwindled and Piper was wiping her eyes, she found Elizabeth smiling at her, some of that wistful sweetness from earlier creeping back into her gaze.

"I love you, Pipe." Elizabeth almost whispered it. Piper held her breath. She and Elizabeth did not say "I love you" to each other.

"The cancer's spreading." Elizabeth said the words as though they were any words. Almost before she had finished saying them, Piper was shaking her head, firmly.

Piper stopped shaking her head, let her breath out, and said coolly, "The cancer is not spreading."

"Piper."

"Did Dr. Firestone tell you that? The man is seventy if he's a day. They took out your ovaries, Elizabeth, *and* your uterus. Remember?" Elizabeth flinched, but Piper wasn't about to stop talking.

"There's nowhere for the cancer to spread from or to. You've been on chemo for months." Piper felt her voice getting louder and harder. "The *cancer* is *gone*."

"They did a scan. I had pain in my hip, so they did a scan." There was a pleading note in Elizabeth's voice now.

"I knew you should've gone to Penn. Or Hopkins! What were you thinking, dealing with these local yokels?" Piper stood up, nodding her head decisively. "We are calling Hopkins *today*!"

"Piper." Elizabeth closed her eyes. "Piper, please sit down."

"So, tell me," Piper said, acidly. "What does your Dr. Firestone propose to do about this?"

There was a long silence. Elizabeth leaned her head back and looked at the ceiling. When she looked back at Piper, there were tears on her face. *Oh, stop it,* Piper thought. *You stop that.*

"It's a team, Piper. They have a cancer team. And they said we could try a more powerful protocol along with radiation. But—" She broke off and took a deep, sobbing breath.

"But what?" snapped Piper.

"They said it might buy me a few months." Elizabeth's voice was suddenly quiet and steady. "They said the side effects could be severe. I told them no."

Piper felt as if her breath had been vacuumed out of her body with a *whoosh.* In her chest, where the air used to be, a bird was beating its wings as hard as it could. She tried to speak and, after a moment, discovered that she was opening and shutting her mouth. *Like a goddamn fish,* she thought, *like a goddamn fish out of water.* She clamped her lips shut.

Elizabeth sat perfectly still and upright in her chair. The circles under her eyes were as dark as bruises, and Piper had a crazy urge to get her makeup bag out of her purse and cover them up. The dark circles, Elizabeth's thinness, the way Elizabeth sat, waiting for her to say something, all of it made Piper furious.

"Oh, so you're giving up? Is that it?" Mean. Piper felt so mean. She started to walk out of the room.

"Piper," said Elizabeth in a voice that was almost a wail. When Piper turned toward her, she saw that Elizabeth's hand was stretched out, reaching for her.

"Do I have to remind you that you have two children who need you?" said Piper. She stood in the doorway to the room and pointed a finger at Elizabeth. "You are such a coward, Elizabeth. And you are *not* giving up."

Piper walked as fast as she could to Elizabeth's front door, and before the door had even slammed shut behind her, she was running.

THREE

... [T]he human species is by no means the pinnacle of evolution. Evolution has no pinnacle and there is no such thing as evolutionary progress. Natural selection is simply the process by which life-forms change to suit the myriad opportunities afforded by the physical environment and by other life-forms.

—MATT RIDLEY,
*Genome: The Autobiography
of a Species in 23 Chapters*

*D*ev Tremain wasn't Sarah Chang or Gregory R. Smith or Toby "Karl" Rosenberg. He sure as hell wasn't Pablo Picasso or Wolfgang Amadeus Mozart or Bobby Fischer. And forget about A.E., whose name he couldn't even bring himself to say because it was one he'd been called way too many times in way too many tones of voice. Privately, Dev felt kind of sorry for A.E. because he'd gone from being the flesh-and-blood guy who pretty much figured out what made the whole physical universe tick to being a metaphor: the generic, universal symbol for genius. Like flesh and blood didn't matter. Like the theory of relativity wasn't enough.

Dev Tremain wasn't a genius, not a genius-genius, although from the way Lake was acting, you wouldn't have known that. Lake Tremain was Dev's mother, and from the way she'd loaded up the car and taken off like a bat out of Hades, you'd think he was Sarah, Gregory R., and Toby "Karl" rolled into one; you'd think he'd gotten into Juilliard at the age of six, graduated from college at the age of thirteen, and learned to write Japanese from a sake bottle before he turned five years old. Those kids were freaks (Japanese from a sake bottle? *A sake bottle?*) and Dev wasn't a freak, definitely not freak material, not even close.

When he thought about those kids being freaks, though, he immediately also thought, *No offense,* because those kids couldn't help being so freakishly smart or gifted or whatever, the same way Dev couldn't help being highly, but unfreakishly, smart. He didn't know how it had happened to them, but he did know that not one of them had asked for it.

But at the moment, as he sat in the backseat of his mom's 1988 Honda Civic, thirteen years old, deep into his Discman, Green Day pounding into his head, fingers drumming hard on the book in front of him, more than smart or anything else, Dev was mad. It had been a pretty rotten year for him. A crap year. Seventh grade. Seventh grade was at least partly why he and his mother were wherever they were—Kentucky, maybe?—instead of back in their little apartment in their little nowhere California town.

Even though Dev had lived most of his life in that town, leaving it was not what made him angry. Dev was glad to leave, more than glad. The truth was that

it had taken a full one hundred miles for Dev to finally unknot, a hundred miles for him to breathe like
a normal person again. He'd just been sitting there in
the car when he'd felt this opening sensation, like there
was suddenly more space between each of his ribs, and
although he hadn't changed position, his slouch suddenly felt like a slouch, true and easy. So he'd looked
up to check how far they'd gone and, weirdly enough,
it'd been one hundred miles exactly.

Dev amused himself with the idea that the town, or
more specifically, Dev's school had a kind of atmosphere of tension and dread around it that stretched
out a hundred miles in every direction and that Dev
had escaped, punched out of that atmosphere like a
rocket into clear, breathable air. This wasn't true, of
course, although Dev didn't rule out that there might
be some real reason for the one hundred miles, and
that if Dev had more information about space and
time or maybe about physiology, he might be able to
figure the reason out.

Anyway, Dev would love it if he never saw that town
again. He wasn't mad at Lake for taking them out of
the town. He wasn't even mad that she'd given him less
than two weeks' notice that they were leaving, because
if she'd tossed his duffel bag to him in the middle of
dinner one night, said, "We're out of here," and headed
for the door, he would've gladly gulped down his milk
and gone.

Dev was mad, Dev was *fuming* because his mother
wouldn't give him a straight and complete answer to
his question of why they were leaving, and he was
fuming because she wouldn't give him any answer at
all as to why, with the whole country spread out before
them, they were making a beeline for some suburb of

Philadelphia, as small and random a black dot as there was on the entire map. For Dev, the more mysterious and complex an idea the better; he loved unpacking a difficult theory, working to understand how it all fit together. But Dev wanted two things in the world to be as utterly straightforward and unmysterious as possible: one was music, the other was his mother.

Dev glanced down at the open book on his lap, at the sentence under his thrumming fingers: "Evolution has no pinnacle and there is no such thing as evolutionary progress." The music in his head didn't grow fainter, but it slipped slightly into the background to clear out a space for the sentence. Evolution, now there was an idea you could really sink your teeth into. Dev's list of heroes was fairly constantly rearranging itself, but Charles Darwin was definitely up there, way up. What thrilled Dev about Darwin was that he hadn't employed esoteric equations or fancy gadgets to accomplish what he'd accomplished, but had done what all human beings do, more or less. He'd walked around the world looking at the things in it, but because of what he'd chosen to look at and because of the kind of attention he'd paid, he'd come up with an idea so rich and dazzling, it had made everyone see life in a new way.

But if you tried to trace Dev's seventh-grade trouble to a single source, that source would be Darwin. To be precise, the source would be the idea that lay strong and still under Dev's beating fingers, that evolution wasn't moving toward any pinnacle or toward anything at all. But blaming that idea wasn't entirely fair because trouble had been waiting for Dev; he'd felt it as soon as he'd walked through the door of his new junior high. Trouble had been like a ten-ton sleeping monster curled up somewhere in the vicinity of Dev's locker; the theory of evolution had just been the noise that woke it up.

It had happened at the start of the second week of school, the first week of real school, since the first calendar week had been a combination of getting-to-know-you games, passing out gym uniforms, and seething chaos. On Monday of the second week of school, Mr. Tripp had entered Dev's biology class, tossed his books dramatically on the desk in front of him, turned his back to the class, and written EVOLUTION on the chalkboard in letters nearly a foot high.

Then Mr. Tripp had spun around and demanded, "Do you people know why we can sit in this room today and talk about the theory of evolution?"

Dev considered saying something about the separation of church and state, but decided that Mr. Tripp probably wanted to answer his own question.

Mr. Tripp turned around and smacked the word on the board, then boomed, "Evolution!"

Like the rest of the kids in the room, Dev wasn't sure if Mr. Tripp was answering his own question or if he was just repeating part of the question, so, like the rest of the kids, Dev kept quiet.

"Evolution is why we're able to sit here and discuss evolution!" Mr. Tripp went on. "Monkeys can't discuss evolution. Goldfish can't discuss evolution. You know why?"

Of course they all knew why. Everyone knew why goldfish couldn't discuss evolution. Probably every kid in the room, at least every kid who'd stayed tuned in up to this point, was listing the reasons in her or his head: hard to talk underwater, no books about evolution available to goldfish. Just for starters. But no one opened her or his mouth. Clearly, the guy was on a roll; no one was stupid enough to get in his way. Yet.

"Because they haven't evolved enough! Human beings are the most evolved animals on the planet—and we *are* animals, make no mistake!" Mr. Tripp's finger was stabbing the air and his forehead was beginning to glisten. He took a deep breath. "Human beings are the *pinnacle* of evolution!"

And even now, even after everything that had happened afterward, Dev was glad he'd ignored all the signals—and the signals were as loud and clear as spinning red lights and that repeated foghorn-type blaring that Dev assumed happens in nuclear plants at the start of a meltdown—that he should keep his mouth completely, possibly permanently shut. Even now, he was glad he'd spoken up. Because this was *Darwin* they were talking about.

Still, he had hesitated before raising his hand because he'd felt a little bad for Mr. Tripp. What Dev would figure out very soon thereafter was that all that bluster and drama, that bad imitation of Robin Williams in one of his inspiring-mentor roles stemmed from the fact that Mr. Tripp was a self-important, histrionic, humorless jerk. A class A windbag. But Dev didn't know this, yet. Just then, the possibility still existed that Mr. Tripp was honestly trying to inspire them, and one look around the room told Dev that none of the students in it was going to be jumping on top of a desk to spout poetry anytime soon, himself included. Still, this was *science* class. If no one spoke up, all the kids who were paying attention to Mr. Tripp would walk out of science class thinking something was scientific fact that wasn't.

Dev raised his hand, although from the startled, pained expression on Mr. Tripp's face you would've thought Dev had thrown a spitball at him instead.

"Do we have a question?" asked Mr. Tripp.

"Well, not really a question," said Dev. "But I don't think that's right, what you said."

"Excuse me?" Mr. Tripp walked around from behind his desk and stood just a foot or two in front of Dev. Dev noticed that Mr. Tripp's short-sleeved button-down shirt was getting dark under the arms.

"I mean, definitely, the part's right about humans being the only species that can formulate an idea like the theory of evolution. If Darwin had been a goldfish, forget about it." Dev smiled at Mr. Tripp, as a few other kids in the class laughed, but to put it mildly, the smile and the laughter didn't lighten up the atmosphere in the room. Dev felt his own palms starting to sweat, but he kept talking.

"Well, you can sort of see how people might think that humans are the pinnacle of evolution because we have high reasoning and creativity and supercomplex brains. I think a lot of people think that, in fact."

"But not you," said Mr. Tripp sarcastically. "And you would be?"

"Dev," said Dev, suddenly feeling exhausted. "But, okay, the goal of evolution isn't complexity or high reasoning. Evolution is about having certain traits that enable you to survive changes by adapting to them, period. That's a huge simplification, but if you want to talk about winners and losers in evolution, the winners are the ones who survive change, not the ones who have the most complex brains or who communicate with language. Or whatever."

Now, every single person in the room was paying

attention, and not the kind of attention people pay to someone who is saying something interesting. The kind of attention people pay to the guy who falls in the shark tank.

"And you know this because you spent your summer reading *The Origin of the Species*?" Mr. Tripp had raised his eyebrow and looked around the room at the other kids, as though they were all sharing a joke. But what Mr. Tripp said hit a nerve for Dev, a big nerve, and suddenly he surged way past caring what they all thought. For the record, he wouldn't *stay* past caring; but at that moment, he'd only been able to think about Darwin.

"No, see, that's just it. It's not *The Origin of the Species*. Not '*the* species.' Just species. All species. It's not about us. We think we're the center of everything because we're smarter than other animals, but even that's not fair because we invented the whole idea of 'smart' and we decided smart means the thing that we are. When you think about it, whales are smarter than we are when it comes to surviving in the deep ocean, right?"

Dev had felt himself getting increasingly worked up, and some small part of him was aware that getting worked up about biology was not a way to make friends, not in the seventh grade anyway. But some things were more important than people liking you. Darwin, humility, and respect. Dev had been thinking about all this stuff a lot, and as corny as it sounded, he felt a kind of team spirit, a connection with all the survivors, with every living thing that had gotten this far. Team spirit mattered, right? Dev believed that it did.

"Well, I see that at least one of us has decided that smart is the thing that he is," said Mr. Tripp, which made Dev hate him. Mr. Tripp looked down at his roll book. "Aha. Deveroux Tremain."

And then Mr. Tripp had done a shocking thing. In front of the whole class, he'd said, "Oh, I was warned about you, Mr. Tremain. We all had a little sit-down about you before school started." Mr. Tripp had begun walking around the room, addressing the other students in the class. "Mr. Tremain's mommy and his elementary school principal decided to come on out and tell us all how special Mr. Tremain is, about how he deserves special treatment." He'd circled the room and come back to stand in front of Dev again. "Now maybe I'm not as smart as you are, Dev. I didn't reread the Constitution on my summer vacation, and no doubt you did." What Dev saw in the teacher's eyes was pure hatred. "But last time I checked, this was a democracy. Which means no one, not even Mr. Einstein here, I mean Mr. Tremain, deserves special treatment."

Naturally, that had been it for Dev, the end. He knew Mr. Tripp had been way out of control, that saying what he'd said in front of everyone was not only evil, but maybe also against the rules, some kind of violation of Dev's right to academic privacy maybe. Dev knew that if he'd reported Mr. Tripp, the man might have gotten into some kind of hot water. But Dev felt defeated in a way he'd never felt in his life; no matter what they did to Mr. Tripp—and Dev didn't think they'd actually fire him—the hour in that classroom had doomed Dev.

So instead of telling on Mr. Tripp, Dev had retreated, folded in on himself every weekday from eight thirty to two thirty. At home, he felt pretty normal, and he'd finish his homework in no time and then would read and talk to Lake about what he'd read. Sometimes, in the evenings or on weekends, he'd go to a playground nearby and play pickup basketball with older guys who didn't care about anything except that Dev was tall and had a knack for catching even the wackiest, from-out-of-nowhere passes.

At midterm, without ever opening his mouth in class except to answer questions directed specifically at him, Dev had earned all As, an achievement in which he took no pride. It bugged him, in a way, how easy it had been. Even Mr. Tripp had given Dev an A, probably because even Mr. Tripp knew he'd crossed a line that first day. Probably Mr. Tripp didn't want to get into any official trouble, and grades were official.

But after Dev got back from winter break, he found he just couldn't do it anymore. All of it—memorizing capitals in social studies, doing algebra problems he could've solved years before, reading a story in his reading book and answering the accompanying questions— felt pointless, and the pointlessness started to make Dev feel a weird, dull anger accompanied by a weird, lonely ache in his chest, and he stopped doing his homework. He read his own books in class, doodled during tests, and became such a bad student that even his teachers noticed.

It took them a while, though, so that it wasn't until the school year was nearly over that Dev found himself spending an excruciating hour in the office of the school psychologist, Leslie Winkle, who told him she'd been observing him without his knowledge in order to assess his needs. In fact, Dev had known she'd been watching him, mainly because she'd sat on the side of the room during several of his classes, staring at him

and taking notes, not that he'd cared or altered his behavior. But in her office, he'd said, "You mean, you
were spying on me?"

And she had turned red and said, "I was not spying
on you. I was observing you without your knowledge."

"Which is totally different from spying."

Then the psychologist had asked, "Do you think
people spy on you a lot, Deveroux?"

So when Leslie Winkle called Lake into her office to
tell her that, in Leslie Winkle's opinion, Deveroux had
attention-deficit/hyperactivity disorder and needed to
start eating Ritalin for breakfast, lunch, and dinner or
whatever, Dev was only surprised that she hadn't said
paranoid schizophrenia and Haldol. Surprised and relieved. But the biggest relief was at what he saw in his
mother's face and heard in her voice. Lake was furious.
Lake was taking charge.

That afternoon, after spending a couple of hours
online, Lake called a child psychologist all the way
in Berkeley who was so fancy and expensive that Dev
couldn't get an appointment for almost two months.
Then, when they finally went, they had to spend the
night in a motel because the testing went over two
days. Dev worried about the expense, but he enjoyed
the tests, which weren't much like tests at all. More like
games. Dev sat in the doctor's beautiful, elegant office
and played games and thought about his mother waiting outside in her jeans with her wild hair and hopeful, worried face. He gave the tests his all, his A game.
Because of his disastrous school year, and especially
because he had kept from Lake just how disastrous it
was, he figured he owed her. More than that, he wanted
to make her happy.

But when the test results finally came, they hadn't made Dev's mother happy, Dev could tell that much. Lake had read the letter and the fat sheaf of papers, and then, ignoring Dev's questions, she'd gone into her bedroom, shut the door, and called the Berkeley psychologist.

When she came out of her room, she was wearing what Dev immediately recognized as her post-roller-coaster-ride face, a scared-eyes smile: part "God, I hated that," part "I'm just fine, Devvy." Until that moment, Dev hadn't known his mother had a post-roller-coaster-ride face, or he hadn't realized he'd known. And until that moment, Dev, who was crazy about roller coasters, hadn't realized that his mother was afraid of them, maybe even hated them. What he figured out right then was that the only reason his mother rode roller coasters at all was to be with him. He felt like touching her arm or hugging her or something, but he didn't. Instead, he gave her a half grin.

"So, what'd they say?" he'd asked. "What's my major malfunction?"

"Nothing, baby," said Lake. She kept smiling, but stared right into his eyes as though she were trying to find something in them. "You're fine." She patted his cheek. Then she'd paused and said, "But I'll be damned if you're going back to that school."

Then she'd made dinner and they'd eaten, and she'd told Dev a funny story about a customer at the restaurant where she worked who'd accidentally spilled a martini down his date's blouse, how the date had fished out the two olives and stuck them in his ears before she walked out.

But that night, when she thought Dev was asleep,

Lake had come into his room, crying softly, and
touched his hair, and said, "I'm so sorry, Devvy. I'm
so sorry."

And a couple of weeks later, without telling Dev
what he'd gotten on the test, even though anyone would
say he had a right to know, without telling Dev much
of anything at all, Dev's mother had sublet their apartment, loaded the Honda, stuck Dev's bike on top of it,
and sped off for some little black dot on the other side
of the country.

In the backseat, Dev stopped tapping his fingers, closed
the book, and looked at his mother, at her fierce, de-
termined eyes and set jaw and at her hands gripping
the steering wheel, and wondered if the little black dot
was ready. Dev thought that if the black dot could see
what was heading straight for it at seventy-one miles
an hour, it might inch toward the coast, slip off the map
altogether, and let itself drift out to sea.

FOUR

Cornelia

Chicken Soup for the Soul. You've heard of these books, am I right? We've all heard of them. But I wonder if you're aware of just how many *Chicken Soup* books exist on the planet. No offense, but I doubt it. I doubt it because in the time it would take you to come up with a number, the number would have become obsolete. Even as you read this, in some quiet, fecund place, another *Chicken Soup* book is being born.

I've never actually opened one of these books, but I have a soft spot in my heart for the supposition underlying the series: that souls are highly specific, that they come in a multiplicity of shapes and permutations, that one cannot assume that what heals the NASCAR soul would do diddly for the horse lover's soul.

If there's ever a volume titled *Chicken Soup for Cornelia Brown's Soul*—and clearly, it's only a matter of time—what will appear on page one won't be an inspirational story but a full-color, inspirational—ideally, scratch-and-sniff—photo of a plate of pasta. Preferably heaping and preferably spaghetti alla puttanesca, the smellier, fierier, and fishier the better.

So it wasn't surprising that a month after the Piper-Armand dinner-party debacle, I found myself in a little Italian bistro tucking away spaghetti alla puttanesca as though my life depended on it and inhaling the scent of garlic, anchovies, olives, and capers as though it were rare Alpine air. But how I came to be in that particular bistro was surprising, was enough to make anyone believe in, at the very most, guardian angels, and at the very least, pure, sweet, dumb luck.

Finding a sublime plate of spaghetti alla puttanesca in New York or Philadelphia is as easy as falling off a log; in the suburban town I now called home, however, not so easy.

There were plenty of decent restaurants around—a good-sized handful anyway—and even a few fine ones with wine lists as long as your arm, and therein lay the problem. The restaurants were a little too fine and decent because, truth be told, spaghetti alla puttanesca is a wee bit indecent, a rather lowly dish. Life-alteringly, soul-healingly scrumptious, but lowly. In fact, for reasons best left obscure, "puttanesca" derives from an Italian word for "whore."

So, after days of searching in vain for a plate of it, and despite the fact that I find comfort food far more comforting when it's prepared by someone else, I ended up in a cavernous grocery store, a recipe ripped from *Gourmet* clutched in my hot little hand. I'll say this for the suburban grocery store: it may be blindingly lit, it may make you feel like a mouse in a maze, but it is *loaded* with stuff. Before long, I'd found everything I needed, and was just tossing a bottle of capers into my cart when I heard a voice say, "Puttanesca sauce!"

I whirled around to find a tall woman with startling blue eyes and a wondrous, untamed wilderness of dark hair. She waved her hand over my cart and smiled at me. There was the tiniest gap between her two front teeth. "Puttanesca. Am I right?" One black eyebrow shot up in a steep, almost-Gothic arch and she gave me the once-over. "The dish of Neapolitan prostitutes?"

"Watch it, lady," I said, huffily, "I'm a respectable married woman." Then I smiled. I liked this person. I liked her even more when she tilted her head back, sending her curls avalanching, and laughed a deep, throaty laugh.

"You laugh exactly like Garbo," I told her.

"But there," she sighed, "the resemblance ends." She pointed her chin in the direction of my cart. "So come on, was I right or was I right?"

I handed her the page from *Gourmet*. "Comfort food," I said. "Just what the doctor ordered."

"What the doctor ordered for you, maybe." She wrinkled her nose. "I drown my sorrows in something less garlicky. Like Häagen-Dazs."

I wrinkled my nose back and shook my head. "Not so original of you."

"I know it. A chick-flick cliché." She handed the recipe back to me. Her hands were remarkable: long, strong looking, and broad across the palms. A potter, I thought, or a musician, and I was picturing her at the cello, hair electric, eyes blazing, when she said, "The chef at the restaurant where I work makes a mean puttanesca."

"You're kidding," I gasped. "Which restaurant is that?"

"Vincente's." The woman's voice chilled, just a tad. "I'm a waitress." Her use of the word "waitress" instead of "server" seemed deliberate. Since, despite my fairly high-grade educational background, I'd spent years managing a coffee bar, I recognized the defiance in her gaze. "I am not a pastry chef. I do not own the place. I am a waitress," said the gaze. "Got something to say about it?"

The only thing I had to say was "Vincente's? But I stopped in and asked at Vincente's. No puttanesca."

"Ah," she said, relaxing, "but that's the menu for customers. Every afternoon, between lunch and dinner, Vinny makes a meal for the staff. The puttanesca is on *that* menu."

"Oh." It was a forlorn "Oh" for sure, but at least I didn't do what I felt like doing, which was bleat like a lost lamb.

"Look," the woman said, smiling, "I work the lunch shift. Weekdays. Tell me when you're coming and I'll pull some strings."

"I could just—hug you," I told her, and it was true. In five glorious minutes, this woman had promised me my pasta and laughed out loud at my joke. I could have hugged her and the kid stocking shelves behind her and the guy at the fish counter and then danced a jig afterward.

"I'm Cornelia," I said. I held out my hand. It looked undersized and flimsy compared to hers, like a little, breakable starfish, but she didn't just shake it. She took it between both of hers and gave it a squeeze. It was the friendliest thing to happen to me in weeks.

"Hi, Cornelia," she said, "I'm Lake."

* * *

Two days later, I sat avidly absorbing an ungodly huge plate of spaghetti alla puttanesca and talking about *The Women* with Lake, a combination that wasn't just soothing my soul but was elevating it. In fact, if both the eating and the conversation hadn't been abruptly and tragically derailed by the entrance of the very last person in the world I wanted to see, I probably would have been lifted bodily into heaven, fork in hand, lips gleaming with olive oil.

We hadn't started out talking about *The Women*. We'd started out talking about the sorrows I was drowning or, to be more accurate, smothering under some three pounds of carbohydrates, and while the shift from my suburban life to the cattiest catfight film ever made might seem a natural one, it wasn't really, because while that film isn't exactly a flattering depiction of female friendship, it's about female friendship and funny. And my life in suburbia was friendless and dull. At that point, having Joan Crawford snatch my husband or Rosalind Russell stab me in the back was looking pretty good; at least, they snatched and stabbed with aplomb.

On a recent rainy Monday, I'd tried imagining the last month and a half of my life as a feature film, a game I play, secretly, fairly often, and that I'm convinced other people play, secretly, too. (I'm so convinced of this that I consider imagining your life as a feature film to simply be part of human nature. If I'm wrong, don't tell me; I do not want to know, and I wouldn't believe you anyway.)

The imaginary film's title was either *Cornelia in the Wilderness* or *Babes in Lawnland,* neither of which are fabulous titles, but both of which were several thousand times more intriguing than the film itself turned out to be. Because in imagining the imaginary film, I came to realize that—apart from the time I spent with Teo, which wasn't much, given his new job—the plotline of my recent life was completely flat. The rising action refused to rise; except for an occasional hiccup, it just lay there, bored into prostration.

The closest thing to a climax I could come up with was the time Piper had stopped by to say she was on her way to the local farmers' market and wondered if I wanted her to pick up some mums for us. Despite the fact that the offer had been accompanied by her gesturing wincingly toward two empty concrete planters (the previous owners had left them and we'd allowed them to remain empty for over a month) as though they were two steaming piles of elephant dung, I'd been touched by the offer. Touched enough to put aside my dignity and, apparently, every shred of good sense I'd ever possessed and say, "Would you like some company?"

Needless to say, I'd regretted those words as soon as they were out of my mouth, maybe regretted having said them almost as much as Piper regretted having heard them. But this line, followed by the regret-filled silence, is not the scene's dramatic high point. The dramatic high point came a minute later, after Piper had eked out a reluctant "Why not?" (to which there were too many answers to count), after I'd gone inside and pounded my head against the wall three times on the way to get my handbag, and as I was preparing to open the passenger door of her mammoth SUV.

Climactic Scene's Dramatic High Point:

> PIPER (sounding utterly unembarrassed): Oh, this is so embarrassing.

CORNELIA: What's wrong?

PIPER: Would you mind sitting in the backseat?

CORNELIA: Oh. Sure. I mean, no. I wouldn't mind. I guess. Why?

PIPER: It's just that I can never remember how to disable the air bag. How embarrassing is that? My own car.

CORNELIA: Disable the air bag?

PIPER: Air bags are a hazard to children twelve and under, and, well, plenty of twelve-year-olds are bigger than you are, wouldn't you say?

CORNELIA: I don't know if I would say that. I never *have* said it. I don't think *anyone's* ever said it.

PIPER: No?

CORNELIA: No.

PIPER (perkily): Well, safety first!

See? As far as dramatic high points go, not so high, and, as far as climactic scenes go, not so climactic. As you know, when you're imagining the film version of your life, you have to stick to bare, unembellished fact. That's the rule. And without embellishment, my facts made for pretty slim pickings. One paltry, isolated humiliation after another does not a movie make.

It probably doesn't even make for particularly scin-
tillating conversation, although Lake was as engaged
a listener as anyone could ask for. We were able to
talk because I'd arrived at Vincente's at 11:10 A.M. on
the dot, ten minutes after they opened (standing panting at the door when they came to unlock it would
have been too pathetic) and was their sole customer
for a good half hour. Vinny, who bore a startling resemblance to Oliver Hardy (minus the Heil, Hitler
mustache), had pulled out the chair across from me
and guided Lake into it, saying, "Sit, darling, don't
let this lovely little girl eat alone," with such kindness
that I forgave him the "little" on the spot.

At Lake's encouraging, and it didn't take much, I
poured out my tale of woe—okay, not of woe exactly,
but at least of embarrassment and dislocation—and her
vehement, beautifully timed interjections of "Tell me
you're joking!" and "She did *not!*" were music to my
ears. By the time I got to the air-bag story, I was well on
my way to being head over heels in like with Lake, and,
when I got to the line "Safety first!" the horror-struck
expression on her face—jaw dropped, eyes widened,
eyebrows leaping—cemented it.

So that when the subject of *The Women* came up,
when she *brought* the subject of *The Women* up, I
thought at first I hadn't heard her correctly. I'd fallen
passionately in love with classic films when I was fourteen and saw *The Philadelphia Story* for the first time.
That this woman had, during our first real conversation,
mentioned a George Cukor film and that she'd done so
wholly unprompted by me seemed too good to be true.

This is how it went.

She said, "What about the men? Are the men any
better than the women?"

I said, "Men? There are no men. You hear about them, but you never see them."

She said, "Ah, like in *The Women*."

I held my breath.

"Over a hundred and thirty speaking roles," she said, "and not a single man."

I stared at her. Spaghetti alla puttanesca, great listening ability, a sense of humor, and hair that looked nothing like a newscaster's. All this and Cukor, too?

Vinny called from the kitchen, and Lake stood up.

"Wait," I said, setting down my fork, "*The Women*. Best line."

She thought for about one and a half seconds before saying, "'Any ladle's sweet that dishes out some gravy.'"

My cup ranneth over.

While it was still running, about two minutes later, Piper walked in. Piper *breezed* in, with Kate hot on her heels, and even though I'd left the eighth grade behind years ago, I still wished Piper had shown up a few minutes earlier, back when I was sitting with a friend, deep in conversation, or maybe right at the moment when the entire bistro was reverberating with the friend's Garbo-like laughter at an extremely witty remark I'd made. Really, when you encounter your nemesis, it's nicer not to be adrift in the center of an empty restaurant, skating your fork across your nearly empty plate, entirely alone and with the scent of whore pasta reeking from your every pore.

But when, despite my best efforts to avoid it, Piper caught sight of me, she suddenly didn't look at all like a woman with the upper hand. For one thing, she blushed, the pale raspberry stain showing through her makeup and traveling into the irreproachable roots of her blond hair. And for another, her eyes took on a nervous, almost stricken look, like Tippi Hedren's eyes when she first begins to think the birds are after her.

I smiled my best bare minimum, only-just-qualifies-as-a-smile smile, then turned my attention to the inside of my handbag. Handbag rummaging is one of the lamer avoidance tactics, I know that, not nearly as impressive as turning your attention back to, say, the volume of un-translated Simone de Beauvoir lying open on the table before you, not even as impressive as flipping open your cell phone and dialing, but I'd forgotten my cell phone, couldn't read French, and anyway, I figured that Piper would leap at any excuse not to approach me. So it was with surprise and a sinking heart that I heard her la-dylike low-heeled shoes tap-tap-tapping their ladylike way across the hardwood floor in my direction.

In order to put off the awkwardness as long as pos-sible, I waited until the tapping had ceased completely to look up, with a startled expression that I hoped said, "Oh, my, I was so absorbed in my fascinating and very important rummaging that I'd forgotten you existed."

"Hi, there, Cornelia," said Piper. I waited for the con-descending gaze, the imperious, closed-mouth smirk, but Piper was still pink faced, and her smile was tentative, even shy. She looked a lot like what she could not possibly be: a person hoping to ingratiate herself to me.

"Hello," I said.

She looked at my plate. "Did you enjoy your, um, your . . ."

"Pasta," I supplied. Did she think just saying the word would cause immediate, irreversible weight gain? "Yes. I did enjoy it. Thanks for asking."

"Listen, I was wondering." Her pinkness intensified. Very soon, she would be magenta.

"Yes?"

"I was wondering when a good time might be to catch your husband at home?"

"Teo?" I was so taken off guard at the idea of her wanting to see Teo that for a second it seemed possible I had another husband, one Piper might more plausibly drop in on.

"Teo. Yes." She nodded. Then she took a deep breath, straightened her watch so that its face was precisely in the center of her wrist, and said, "I, well, I was hoping to discuss something with him, and I wasn't sure, since he's a physician, if he kept regular weekday hours or if he worked, um, evenings, or if maybe weekends were good. I just sort of thought if we had an appointment or, you know, set a date to talk, it might work well for, well, for all of us because, really, I hate the idea of interrupting your family time . . ."

The woman was rambling. Actually, the woman was just this side of incoherent, and I realized how very much it must be costing her to ask a favor of a person whom she so disliked. I also toyed with the idea that maybe mixed up in all that stammering was a bit of guilt at having been consistently and unabashedly unfriendly to me. But possibly that was giving her too much credit. In any case, the rambling had to be stopped.

"Piper," I said sharply. She stopped talking. "Teo has tomorrow afternoon off. Why don't you come then? Around four?"

"Around four," she repeated. "Around four sounds fine." In a flash, an overbright smile materialized on her face. She cocked her head like a chickadee, chirped "Perfect!," spun around, and walked briskly back to her table, where Kate's round eyes had been peering at us over the top of a menu, watching the whole exchange.

Piper seated herself, whipped open her napkin, and draped it over her lap. "Gosh, I feel like a salad," she told Kate in the same chirpy voice. "Don't you?"

Of course she does, I thought to myself. *Kate feels exactly like a salad because Kate is a fucking salad.* And even though this insult was unspoken, meaningless, and directed at a person with whom I wasn't even angry, it helped me get my bearings.

As Lake handed me my check, I rolled my eyes toward the table, made an anguished face, and mouthed the word "Piper."

After an almost imperceptible lift of an eyebrow, Lake strode over to Piper's table, smiled warmly at the two women, and said, "Hello. I'm Lake and I'll be your server today."

"Lake," said Piper, flapping her lashes. "Now, that's a different name!"

Lake swept her gaze around the restaurant, as though to make sure no one was listening. Then, in a loud, conspiratorial whisper, she replied, "Actually, it's my middle name. My first name is ridiculous. Just god-awful. I don't know what my parents were thinking."

"Oh, tell us what it is!" burbled Kate.

"Yes, do." Piper made it sound like a command.

Lake didn't pause to blink or swallow; the words slipped off her tongue as innocently as you please. "Piper," she said, "can you imagine?" If Kate's gasp hadn't been so loud, my gasp would've echoed through the restaurant like thunder. Lake handed Piper the wine list. "Piper. Like 'Viper' with a *P*."

The next day turned out to be the first day of fall, one of my favorite days of the year. I'm not talking about the actual autumnal equinox, which had come and gone a week earlier and had felt pretty much like all the summer days preceding it. What I mean by the first day of fall is that day when you suddenly understand with your whole body that the season has changed. When the air feels snappier against your skin and the sky's blueness turns wistful, and the humming of insects shifts pitch, and you just know like you know your own name that summer is over.

I'd planned to do what I'd been doing for over a month: set up housekeeping, a job I enjoy and prefer to do slowly and thoughtfully, a method that works only if you don't mind living in disarray for a while, which Teo and I didn't.

A few days before, Teo had surprised me by bringing home six black-and-white photographs, matted and framed, the sort of photographs you know are exquisite before you have any idea what they're of. My best friend Linny—who'd toyed with the notion of law school for a few years before rediscovering photography, an old passion—had taken them and sent them to me as a housewarming gift. Sent them from San Francisco, sadly enough, the city to which she and her boyfriend Hayes had relocated five months ago, despite my pleading, no-holds-barred pouting, and relentless warnings about gray skies and earthquakes. As I watched their car disappear into the distance, I suffered a kind of earthquake of my own, chandeliers swinging and paintings falling off the walls of my inner life.

That day's tasks were supposed to be hanging Linny's photographs and then sorting through the piles of graduate school applications (material culture, art history, decorative arts) that were beginning to take over my desk and the floor around it, but when I stepped outside to water my mums, which were thriving despite their inauspicious arrival, the first-true-fall-day feeling hit me, and I knew spending the morning indoors was impossible.

If I'd been a runner, I would've run, but since just thinking about running causes me to pull several hamstrings at once, I threw on jeans and my obnoxiously bright, very complex-looking running shoes—which I bought because the irony of me in complex, obnoxiously bright running shoes pleased me—dragged my bike out of the garage, and took off.

I rode for over two hours, first through our neighborhood, then through other neighborhoods, and then through a park full of squirrels and tattered sunlight. When I got back, I was red faced and starving and happy and ready to fall into the arms of my husband, which is exactly what I did. I fell, then let go of him, then whipped us up a pair of turkey club sandwiches, which we devoured like birds of prey.

The glow from all of this was the kind that sticks with you for a while and that allows you to temporarily forget anything that might cause the glow to dim. It stuck with me for so long, in fact, that it wasn't until I happened to glance at the clock as Teo and I were hanging Linny's photos that Piper's impending visit suddenly loomed up out of the glow, casting its tidy, Pilates-honed shadow over my home and its inhabitants: 3:45. Oof. I watched my husband blithely trying to drive hooks into the wall without destroying the plaster, touchingly oblivious to the blond freight train hurtling toward him.

"Maybe she's in love with you," I mused.

"Linny?" Teo mumbled around the hook he held between his teeth. "Of course she's in love with me. Can you remember a time when Linny *wasn't* in love with me?"

"No," I said. "Teo, that's too high. How will anyone see it?"

Teo took the hook out of his mouth and sighed. "Cornelia, as it is, every mirror in the house gives me an excellent view of my chest."

"It's a nice chest," I told him, even though I knew men didn't come more flattery proof than Teo. He ignored me.

"Could I possibly enjoy our artwork without getting down on my knees? Is that too much to ask?"

"Fine," I said. "Heightist."

"What?"

"You're a heightist. Don't try to deny it either. And I was talking about Piper. Maybe Piper's coming over to tell you she's in love with you."

Teo shook his head. "No chance. If she were in love with me, she would have invited me to her house. That's how it's done around here. She would have waited until I was mowing the grass and then asked me over for a nice tall glass of lemonade."

"Don't be crazy," I scoffed, "Piper would never interrupt a man in the middle of lawn care."

Teo acknowledged the irrefutability of this with a shrug, then said, "But if she were in love with me, she'd probably leave her kids at home." He nodded toward the window, and there they were, two generations of Truitts marching resolutely toward our front door, autumnal afternoon sunlight glancing off all three yellow heads.

I sighed a full-body sigh. Teo turned to me, grinning, and teased, "Stiff upper lip!"

"Easy for you to say," I snapped. "And what does that even mean? Why upper lip? When people start to crack, their lower lip is the one that does all the moving, isn't it? Their lower lip quivers, while their upper lip remains more or less motionless. And can a lip even *be* stiff? Either lip? That's my question." Teo still refused to view the Piper Posse's rejection of me in a sufficiently serious light. I understood that this refusal arose out of his respect for my ability to handle my life, combined with his belief that, given time, I could thaw even the coldest shoulder, but with Piper standing on my very doorstep, I could have used a little more support.

I opened the door. The two children stood on my doormat, shuffling and stamping. "Just like this," the little boy was saying to his sister in a solemn voice, "so all the mud comes off." They were holding hands. Great, I thought, they're adorable. The fruit of Piper's loins. I was ready for them to be Satan's spawn—I was *rooting* for them to be Satan's spawn—and they were adorable.

"Hey, guys!" I said, crouching down. "I'm Cornelia. You're doing such a nice job of wiping your feet."

"Thank you," said the boy. The girl smiled shyly, then turned to bury her face in her mother's legs.

I stood up. "Hi, Piper," I said, "come on in."

If I'd been expecting the Hitchcock victim who'd approached me at Vincente's (and while I hadn't been expecting her, exactly, I'll admit I *had* been hoping for her), I'd have been disappointed. Chin lifted, eyes scornful, leather portfolio tucked under one arm, this was Piper in full Queen Bee mode, and, in her skinny, dark-wash jeans and black ballet flats, as stylish as I'd ever seen her.

"Hello, hello," she said airily. Then she turned to Teo. "Thank you so much for taking the time to talk with me, Teo. I know how busy work must keep you."

She looked at the unpacked boxes in the corner and the empty picture hooks in the wall. "And it looks like you've still got plenty to do here, too!"

"Yeah," Teo said, smiling, "I guess we like to take our time."

"Would you like to sit down?" I asked. "Can I get you a drink or something? San Pellegrino? Cranberry juice?"

"Oh, nothing, thanks." Piper fished a Tupperware container and two tiny bottles of spring water out of her Coach tote and handed them to me. "Pretzels," she explained. "Trans fat free. For Carter and Meredith. And water, but only if they ask." She dropped her voice. "Meredith's working on toilet learning."

I stared down at the pretzels and water, the phrase "toilet learning" buzzing around inside my head like a fly.

Unexpectedly, Piper laughed a nervous, rippling laugh, a laugh that made her slick surfaces suddenly crackle like old porcelain. This was one tightly wound woman. "Oh, look at your face! Did you think I'd leave you without supplies?"

"Are you—leaving?" I asked, bewildered.

"We'll just be in the next room," she said, patting my arm consolingly and laughing the odd laugh again. "I need to speak to Teo privately. You don't mind, do you?" Before I could answer, she reached into her tote again and pulled out a couple of books. "Would you mind pointing to each word as you read? Carter is this close to being reading ready. And no television, please. Oh, and no sweets!" She shook a finger at me, playfully.

I was getting angrier at Piper by the second, but part of me watched her with a fascination that was almost admiring. Even as she pawned her children off on me as though I were the hired help, Piper's perkiness was intensifying. As a matter of fact, her perkiness was getting downright creepy. It came to me: Doris Day. An evil Doris Day. And then, because I remembered that the real Doris Day has always struck me as evil, my next thought was simply *Doris Day.*

"Anything else?" I asked.

Piper frowned and gazed skyward, thinking hard. Teo's eyes met mine.

"Hey, Piper," he said, "you remind me of a friend of my sister's from college. Did you go to Duke, by any chance?"

Duke. The Harvard of the Atlantic Coast Conference. I could have kissed him. My husband, he insists on seeing me as a woman who doesn't need rescuing (and he's right most of the time), but he knows when to slip a girl a little help.

"Duke?" said Piper, startled. "No. I went to Wake Forest, though, right down the road in Winston-Salem." Then she added, quickly, "I considered Duke. Duke, UVA, or maybe an Ivy. But my dad grew up in Winston-Salem. He's a Wake alum!"

Not a Tarheel after all, but pretty darn close. In the brief lull that followed "He's a Wake alum!" I let my smile spread slowly across my face.

"So. You're a Demon Deacon," I said, drawing the words out. And though I've never been sure what a Demon Deacon is, at that moment, calling Piper one was so sweet, it felt almost like revenge.

Piper and Teo were gone—behind the closed door of our den—for slightly less than fifteen minutes. The meeting's brevity was a bit of a letdown, really. After so much buildup, I'd expected something bigger, longer, maybe

along the lines of a UN summit. Besides, I'd been enjoying Piper's kids, who'd spent the fourteen minutes first
playing with an empty packing box, a game they christened Box, then carefully divvying up the pretzels into
three tiny piles, one for each of us.

"Some for Mommy?" Meredith had asked her brother.

"No," he'd said, "Mommy doesn't eat pretzels,"
which I could have told her, followed by, "And this is
Cornelia's house, so she gets to have some." He said my
name "Cuh-nelia."

It had been some time since I'd eaten crunchy, miniature pretzels (in my Philly days, I'd eaten more than
my share of the soft ones, hot, chewy, and clutch-purse-
sized), and maybe it was because of the company or the
utter absence of trans fat or both, but they tasted divine.
Somewhat less divine when swallowed whole, however, which is how I consumed my third one because,
just after I'd popped it in my mouth, I heard the den
doorknob turning and didn't want to be caught snatch-
ing food from the mouths of Piper's babes.

It turned out not to matter, though, because when
she emerged from the den, Piper was so unsettled, I
could've been using her children to mop my floor and
she wouldn't have noticed. She was stuffing papers back
into her portfolio with the urgency one would use to put
out a grease fire, and when she looked at me, her face
was crimson, her eyes were wild, and, if a smile can be
hysterical, Piper's was.

"I just remembered something I left on the stove,
Cornelia." Her voice was uncharacteristically high and
thin. "Could you watch the kids for a minute? I'll be
back in two shakes." And she was gone.

"What's up?" I asked Teo, in a low voice, as soon as
I'd reignited the kids' interest in Box.

"She's got a sick friend who started a new course of treatment a few weeks ago and wants to discontinue. Piper wanted my opinion." He ran a hand through his hair and sighed. "No she didn't. She wanted me to tell her that her friend should keep going with the treatments."

"Did you?" I asked. I took Teo's hand. His face was suddenly so tired.

Teo shook his head. "No. I told her that in my highly unofficial opinion, the friend should stop. Today, if she wants."

A shudder ran through me. "Oh, God, Teo, you don't think the friend is really Piper, do you?"

"Piper had a copy of the woman's medical records; the name on every sheet was blacked out, but, no, whoever this woman is, she's too sick to hide it."

I watched Carter pop up like a jack-in-the-box, watched Meredith fall on the floor laughing. Absently, I lifted Teo's hand and kissed it. "Thank God."

Teo watched the kids for a second, then said, "The friend has two children, too."

I didn't say anything because there was nothing to say. Then, eerily, somewhere in our house, music began to play. Even before Meredith and Carter began singing the words, I recognized the song. The theme from *Sesame Street*.

"Piper's cell phone," I said. Teo walked back into the den and came out carrying the Coach tote.

"Where's Mommy?" Meredith's eyes filled, but she didn't burst into tears. Instead, she sat down on the floor and rubbed her eyes with her two fists like a child in a movie.

"Your mommy will be right back," I told Meredith.

Carter stood very still for a moment, then sat down beside Meredith.

"Your mommy will be right back," he told her.

But ten minutes and four missed cell phone calls later, Piper still wasn't back. Because I began to worry that someone was desperately trying to reach Piper and because each time the *Sesame Street* theme song played, Meredith came closer to dissolving into sobs, I picked up the tote and walked across the street.

Even before I got to the front steps, I heard it. A wretched, unloosed, primeval keening. A sound that couldn't possibly be coming from a human being, except that it was. I stood on the front porch, hearing the sound. I stood there. I even started to open the door. The knob was in my hand. Then I turned around and walked back home.

FIVE

The discovery of a complete unified theory, therefore, may not aid the survival of our species. It may not even affect our life-style. But ever since the dawn of civilization, people have not been content to see events as unconnected and inexplicable. They have craved an understanding of the underlying order in the world. Today, we still yearn to know why we are here and where we came from.

—STEPHEN HAWKING,
A Brief History of Time

*D*ev was figuring things out.

Of course, Dev was *always* figuring things out, or trying to. Figuring things out was an essential property of Dev the way impenetrability is an essential property of matter or oddness is an essential property of the number three. Nothing unusual about the figuring-out part.

But the *things* part? Unusual. In fact, if Dev had a list of the things he'd been figuring out lately, the only typical, unsurprising item on it would have been string theory. And string theory was hanging on to its place on the list by the skin of its pointy teeth because string theory was proving to be a very tough nut to crack, so tough that Dev was beginning to suspect that impenetrability might be one of its properties, too.

But Dev didn't mind. For one thing, when it came to theories, hard was good, nothing wrong with hard, and even the guys who came up with string theory didn't seem to get it, not completely. For another, Dev was too happy to mind, too happy and too astonished. If you'd told him a few months ago that pretty soon he'd have worked out more about being happy at school than about string theory, he'd have told you, in his polite Dev way, that you were stark, raving nuts. While it was true that before he'd tumbled into the nightmare of seventh grade, Dev had sometimes been happy in school, mostly it had been coincidence: Dev happened to be happy, and he happened to be within the walls of a school.

Now, though, if happiness were a fire, school was what fed it. School—*this* school, Liberty Charter—was feeding Dev in ways no other school ever had. And even though Dev still didn't know what was written on them, he knew that the papers from the Berkeley psychologist had somehow made it happen. Lake had waved the papers like a wand (or faxed them, more likely, since she'd set it up from California), and they'd worked magic.

Magically, a Dev-size space had opened up at a quirky hybrid of a school the likes of which Dev hadn't known existed: you had to apply, but it was free, a regular public school with basketball, band, and chess club, but also with something called "Non-Age-Specific Grouping." As far as terms went, Non-Age-Specific

Grouping struck Dev as clumsy and patched together, but as far as ideas went, NASG rocked. NASG meant that kids like Dev—and NASG seemed to be based, at least in part, on the idea that there *were* other kids like Dev—could take pre-calc with juniors and advanced bio with seniors.

Seniors. Liberty Charter had them, too. Seniors, juniors, SAT prep, prom, and homecoming because Liberty Charter was a *high* school, and that meant the Berkeley papers must have worked magic on Lake, too, because after years of swearing Dev would skip grades over her dead body, during their second night in their new town house, she'd said, "Let's jump you up. Ninth grade. What do you think?" And her body, as she sat in that taut, waiting, coiled-spring way of hers, was the total opposite of dead.

So suddenly school was a place where, in English, Dev found himself reading a poem by a guy named Wallace Stevens that ended: "For the listener, who listens in the snow, / And, nothing himself, beholds / Nothing that is not there and the nothing that is," which in itself seemed unreal, just too good to be true, a teacher handing out a piece of paper with words like those on it.

But more unbelievable was that when Dev raised his hand, took a deep breath, and said, "The first thing I thought of was Charles Darwin. Which might sound kind of weird. But he started out believing in God. Then, after he discovered so much about how nature works, he had to, you know, let God go. I remember he said something like, 'There are parasitic wasps whose whole existence is about breeding inside the bodies of caterpillars. No god would create a creature like that,'" nobody, not one person in the class, rolled his eyes or faked gagging herself with her finger.

In fact, when Dev continued by saying, "I personally think that you can believe in God *and* evolution, but Darwin didn't. He had to decide between truth and God and he picked truth, and that's kind of like seeing the nothing that's there, like God got replaced by nothingness. And even if you don't, like, think Darwin was right, it was still a pretty brave thing to do," another kid in the class shot his hand up.

"Yeah, totally brave," the kid said, nodding, "like Galileo. Back then, saying the earth wasn't the center of the universe was like saying God is nothing, but Galileo wouldn't keep his mouth shut. The dude got arrested for saying that!"

The teacher, Ms. Enright, didn't sneer and say, "Did you losers spend your summer vacation reading *The Origin of the Species* and some book by Galileo?" She didn't even say, "This is English, not science class, guys," in that reminding voice teachers use. She didn't say much of anything, but definitely she didn't sneer. Ms. Enright let the class talk, and then, the next day, she brought in copies of a Robert Frost poem called "Design" and said, "What Dev said yesterday made me think of this poem. I'd love it if you all would read it and talk about it. There's an 'if' in the last line that just chills me to the bone, always has." So that the rest of the day, Dev walked around with the sentence "What Dev said yesterday made me think of this poem" stretched over him, like a rainbow only he could see.

Yeah, school was on the list of things Dev was figuring out. Friendship, too. The Galileo kid turned out to be a sixteen-year-old soccer star and entrepreneur named Aidan Weeks, facts Dev found out during a conversation that started with Aidan setting his tray down next to Dev's at the lunch table and saying, "You obviously know a lot about Darwin, but what do you know about cutting grass?" and that ended with Aidan asking Dev to be his business partner.

"My old partner Ritchie got a C in physics and quit on me. First C of Ritchie's life, and his dad makes him quit his very lucrative job to study more." Aidan stood up. "Cutting grass, raking leaves, shoveling snow." He emphasized each task by slapping the table with one cinnamon-colored hand. "Think about it."

"I will," said Dev. What he really meant was that he had to convince Lake. If it were up to him alone, he would've said "You got yourself a partner" as fast as he could get the words out.

As Dev was putting his tray on the tray-conveyor belt, he heard Aidan's voice again, shouting, "Hey, Dev!"

Dev turned around. Aidan stood near the door of the cafeteria. "Yeah," shouted Dev.

A bunch of kids in the cafeteria were looking at Dev now, and the expressions on their faces made Dev understand that Aidan Weeks was *somebody* at Liberty Charter.

"Did I mention the job is very lucrative?" shouted Aidan, grinning.

Dev shouted, "Uh, yeah, I think you did," and the smile that suddenly cut across his face was so big and real, he turned back toward the conveyor belt so that he could keep it to himself.

That night, Dev sat at the dinner table wolfing down white bean and chicken chili, his favorite, and tried to come up with the best way to spin the job idea so that Lake would go for it. Actually, he was 99.9 percent sure Lake was spin proof. Lake didn't just have a built-in bullshit detector, she had a state-of-the-art, atom-splitting bullshit annihilator. So mostly Dev spent dinnertime just getting his nerve up.

But before his nerve was anywhere close to as high as it needed to be, as Dev mopped up the last of his chili with the last of his corn bread, his mother said, wryly, "Well, it doesn't seem to have affected your appetite much."

Crap.

Dev took his time chewing and swallowing the corn bread before he asked, "What?"

"Whatever's on your mind," said Lake.

"Oh," said Dev. Crap, crap, crap, crap, crap.

His mother gave him her ice blue, laser-beam stare. How did she do that? Could it be good for a person to stare like that? Didn't her eyeballs start to dry out?

Dev didn't point out this potential health hazard. Instead, he said, finally, "Did you know that the two main theories all of modern physics is based on are totally incompatible?"

Lake threw back her head and laughed.

"It's true," Dev said, relieved. "Relativity and quantum mechanics. On their own, they're full proof, the solidest theories around. And they explain pretty much everything. But they cancel each other out; no way can they both be true."

"Sounds like a problem," said Lake, nodding, the laughter still hovering around the corners of her eyes and mouth.

"Yeah. It is. Or it was. Have you ever heard of string theory?"

"Nope." This struck Dev as funny because if anyone seemed to be made up of zillions of tiny vibrating strings, it was Lake. Dev remembered how one of the books he was reading talked about the "resonance" of the ultramicroscopic strings, how they vibrated like the strings of a musical instrument. Dev looked at his mother and imagined her strings making tense, layered, glittering music, like those Bach fugues she listened to all the time. Music so complicated you could hear the math in it.

"Well, string theory just might be the unified field theory everyone's dying to find," said Dev. "String theory makes the other theories compatible. Some people call it the theory of everything."

"Wow," said Lake, raising her black eyebrows. "The theory of everything. Sounds like one theory worth looking into. Tell you what, you loan me a book on string theory, and then we'll talk about it together. Deal?" She gave Dev a smile.

"Deal."

Dev slid his gaze down to his empty bowl and held it there for a few seconds. Then he slid it back up and met his mother's eyes.

"Okay," he began, "I met this kid at school."

She said yes. There was a wide, empty, cavernous moment when Dev knew she was going to say no. But then she walked around the table, hugged him from behind, and pressed her cheek to his.

"Yards only," she said. "I don't want you going inside any strange houses. And you ride your bike. After I get to know this kid, *maybe* he can pick you up, but no highway driving. Neighborhood roads, and that's it. Got it?"

"No strange houses. No highways," said Dev. "Got it."

She didn't let go; Dev's face could feel her smiling,

the lift and nudge of her cheekbone. He knew she was glad about Aidan.

"Mom, your hair's tickling me."

"Oh, gosh, so it is. Sorry about that."

"Mom, I can't breathe."

"Hmmm. That's no good. Let's hope you don't lose consciousness."

"Mom!" Dev started laughing then, which was what Lake had been waiting for, what she always waited for, so after one more squeeze, she let him go.

Aidan Weeks was a talker.

"I'm a talker," he told Dev. "Most of these yards, I could do on my own, but listening to nothing but leaves rustling and birds chirping drives me bananas."

Without meaning to, Dev let out a laugh that was more like a snort.

"What?" asked Aidan, pretending to freeze, midrake.

"Bananas?" said Dev, trying not to snort again. "Sorry, man. But, who *says* that?"

Aidan grinned and got back to raking. "I told you, I'm a talker. When you talk as much as I do, you basically end up using every word out there."

It was Saturday, the kind of tricky October Saturday that contains equal parts hot sun and cool air, so that you keep taking off your sweatshirt and putting it back on, taking off, putting on until, pretty soon, you're laughing at yourself. When the sun was out, the leaves caught in Dev's rake were the reddest and goldest things he'd ever seen, so much color rubbing up against itself on the surface of each leaf, Dev imagined he could smell smoke.

"You live in this neighborhood?" Dev asked Aidan.

"It's a great neighborhood." It *was* great. Dev couldn't remember being in a neighborhood he liked more: big trees, the houses close together, old, spacious, and interesting, all stone or brick with roofs made of gray, blue, and pinkish slates, a sunporch or a sunroom pulling light into every house.

"Nah," said Aidan, sheepishly. "You notice the neighborhood you rode through to get here?"

Dev had noticed it. You'd have to be blind not to notice that neighborhood. The houses were newer than these and huger and each sprawled like a section of storybook village across the center of an enormous, pool table–green lawn. Dev gave a low whistle.

"Yeah," said Aidan, shaking his head, "I know. My dad's one of those guys who can make money in his sleep. He says it's a knack, like he can't really take credit for it."

Dev gave Aidan's rake a push with his own. He grinned. "Guess he's not giving it to you, though."

"Nope," chuckled Aidan. He ran the back of his hand across his forehead and pretended to shake off the sweat. Then, he jerked a thumb toward the largest pile of leaves. "What do you think? Bag?"

As they took turns shoving leaves into a black trash bag large enough to hold a giant panda ("Construction-site bags," Aidan informed him. "The best of the best, don't settle for less"), Aidan said, "So you wanna hear my story?"

"Is it interesting?" asked Dev, giving him a skeptical look.

Aidan shrugged. "I'm a black kid with two white parents. Most people think that's interesting. I like to explain it up front, before people find out and do the 'uh-that's-your-mom-then-act-all-shocked-then-feel-bad' routine."

"A preemptive strike," said Dev, nodding. "Good strategy."

It turned out that Aidan's mother was Irish from Ireland ("Hence, the name. Aidan: it's Irish, not girlish"), and that she swore like a street punk ("f-bomb this, f-bomb that, when she's not even mad"), which maybe all Irishwomen did, maybe just her and Aidan's grandma (called Mammo, like ammo), Aidan wasn't sure, but she was pretty nice anyway, and his dad, the money-in-his-sleep dad, was the only dad he'd ever known.

"Not a case of 'biological didn't bother,' though. My biological dad—the African-American dad—bothered as long as he could. Then he went to work at this new job at some fancy engineering firm in New York?" Aidan paused for effect. "Dropped dead. Aneurysm. Imagine that? Twenty-eight years old; new, handsome, genius son at home; first day on the job and wham."

Right then, Dev and Aidan both stopped what they were doing and looked at the ground and the sky for a few seconds because even if death happened to someone you never knew sixteen years ago, it still deserved a pause. You couldn't just keep jamming leaves into a bag, not if you were Dev and Aidan. If Dev had been wearing a hat, he would've at least considered taking it off. As it was, he stood, quiet, feeling the burn of fresh, cold air in his chest.

"Sorry about that," he said finally. "I mean, sorry for him."

"Yeah," said Aidan, picking up an armful of leaves. "Pretty interesting story, right?"

"Pretty interesting," Dev agreed. Then he said, "But it still doesn't explain 'bananas.'"

After Aidan finished throwing armfuls of leaves at Dev and they'd raked the leaves back up, and after Mrs. Finney, the elderly woman whose yard they were working in, came out with giant blue mugs of very hot chocolate, Dev told Aidan, "I never knew my dad either."

It wasn't something he told people. He didn't care if they knew; he just didn't tell them. For a simple statement of fact, the sentence was surprisingly hard to say, and immediately, weirdly, Dev felt older and somehow remote, like a stranger, a guy the real Dev might see sitting alone at a bus stop or something and feel sorry for. To bring himself back to himself, Dev did the first dumb kid thing he could think of, which was to take a searing gulp of hot chocolate and yelp, "Yow!" The lonely stranger vanished, but just for good measure, Dev hung out his tongue, Saint Bernard fashion, and fanned it with his hand.

"Hence the name: hot chocolate," said Aidan, dryly. "So what happened? He walk out or something?"

Dev wished he had a tidy, prepackaged story like Aidan's to hand over, all the edges worn smooth with use. He thought about what his mom told him when he was worked up and trying to tell her something: begin at the beginning.

"Okay. My mom? She's really smart, like crazy smart," began Dev.

"Smart DNA?" joked Aidan. "You?"

"Shut up," said Dev, "and drink your cocoa. Seriously, she grew up in this tiny, nowhere town in Iowa, and she was the smartest kid to be born in that town in, like, a thousand years. She got a scholarship to Brown

University, which was so amazing because hardly anyone in her graduating class even went to college."

"Old geezers sitting on their front porch saying, 'You hear about that little Tremain girl? She's taking her genius self to the big leagues,'" said Aidan.

"Her name wasn't Tremain yet, but right. And she did. She went. But then, at the end of her sophomore year, she and this guy from back home . . . Her high school boyfriend. Uh, he would come visit her. And, well, she got, like—" Dev broke off, red-hot embarrassment flooding his face and running down his neck, which was stupid because, come on, Aidan's mother and everyone's mother had done it with some guy at some point, right?

"Pregnant?" supplied Aidan. "In the family way? Knocked up? *Avec bébé?*"

"Yes," said Dev, "all of the above. She couldn't go home because everyone was mad and disappointed and whatever. So she and my dad, Teddy Tremain, they ran away, went someplace out west, and got married."

"And Teddy couldn't take the desert heat and ran home."

"He didn't run," Dev said. "Well, he probably would have, but she ran first. Not home, though. Just away."

Aidan swirled the nearly black circle of liquid at the bottom of his hot chocolate, then said, quietly, "Was he a bad man?"

Dev had wondered this himself, wondered so much that, years ago, he'd finally asked his mother. He told Aidan what his mother had told him. "Not a bad man. Not a man, though. Teddy Tremain was a child. My mom said it wasn't that he didn't want me, exactly; he just didn't want to grow up. So right after I was born, she took off."

"Whoa," said Aidan, after a pause. "And that was that. You never see him?"

"No," said Dev. "It's not a big deal, though. I mean, sometimes I wish I had *a* dad, but not necessarily *that* dad. It'd be easier for my mom if there was another person around to help."

"Easier for you, too?" asked Aidan. His eyes were kind, lucid, and so dark they appeared to be without pupils or else looked like they were all pupil, which, with Aidan, seemed more plausible: windows, wide open, so the light could pour in.

"Anyway, I don't even know where he is," said Dev, and abruptly he jumped up and brushed off his jeans. He needed to get away from the conversation fast, not because he'd told too much truth, which was probably what Aidan thought, but because he hadn't told enough.

Aidan had befriended Dev and given him a job. Lying to this good, funny, clear-eyed kid was like getting invited to a clean, bright house and stomping all over it with muddy shoes, and that last sentence, the one about not knowing where his father was, Dev was pretty sure it was a lie.

It happened the way Dev imagined all theories happened: first, there were pieces, scattered and separate; then someone figured out that the pieces *were* pieces; then someone put the pieces together.

The first piece was the secret itself. The why of their being in that particular town at that particular time, a why that, for a while, had taken a few baby steps back from the forefront of Dev's mind, because no matter what had brought them to it, the town felt more right than any other place ever had. So why ask why? At heart, though, Dev was anything but a "Why ask why?" guy, and if moving to the town was a gift horse, eventually Dev, being Dev, would not only look it in the mouth, but would also perform a CAT scan on it and a DNA analysis.

What he was positive of was that the secret was big. Monumentally big. Lake wouldn't guard it so closely if it weren't big because while Lake wasn't especially a teller—a talker, yes, a teller, not especially—generally, she only kept secrets that belonged to her (and she was keeping secrets; you could just tell), which was fine with Dev. But, in all fairness, this particular secret belonged to Dev, too, and when it came to Dev, Lake was fair. Until this secret came along, Lake was as fair as moms get.

The second piece was the town house. The town house was nice. Not fancy, but with three bedrooms, a real dining room instead of just a kitchen, and with floors made of a blond wood that sunlight slid across like melted butter. And it wasn't in some cut-off, gated "community" like town houses Dev was used to, but sat on a quiet tree-lined street, the last house in a row of ten. Even if Dev hadn't seen the rental agreement, he would've known that the town house was way more than they could afford, even though Lake, who always worried about money, didn't seem worried now.

But Dev might not have thought of the town house as a piece of anything at all if he hadn't found the envelopes. Two envelopes, big ones. They came from schools, one in Miami and one in Los Angeles, and inside were fat, slick brochures full of pictures of kids: kids in white lab coats, test tubes and beakers gleaming around them; kids in front of enormous computer screens; kids playing violins; kids reading books under palm trees. Not just any kids, but gifted kids, because that's who these schools were for. The crème de la crème, according to the Los Angeles brochure, and the too-rich phrase made Dev queasy.

Dev could tell from the pictures, from the weight and gloss of the brochures and the thick, creamy paper of the applications, that the schools were expensive, probably superexpensive, that even with a "partial, need-based scholarship" Dev wouldn't be able to go. Not that he wanted to go. He didn't want to be at the Melton School, which had "an aura of specialness that emanates from the children themselves," and he didn't much care about "maximizing his unique gifts." (Neither brochure even mentioned basketball.) He wanted to stay where he was.

Besides, he couldn't imagine himself or Lake living in either of those cities, under all that hard sunshine with suntanned rich people everywhere you turned. The Berkeley papers must have done a heck of a number on Lake for her to even consider it.

The Berkeley papers. The secret. The bigness of the secret. The town house. The schools.

Dev stared at the brochures for a long time, feeling the pieces inching toward each other, feeling a theory take shape. Lake had dragged them to a town Dev had never heard of for no reason she would share. She was breaking all her own rules, dipping into their tiny savings to pay rent. She was making crazy-expensive plans.

And then Dev had it. Lake must be expecting to have money, and she was expecting to find the money here. If Lake, who never took a dime from anyone, was expecting money, it must be money someone owed her. Or money someone owed Dev.

Belong to Me   87

Dev touched his hair, spread his hands open in front of him, ran a finger along his eyebrow, and thought about his cells, every cell containing a nucleus, every nucleus containing two strands of DNA, the double helices coding Dev, Dev, Dev. He thought about Aidan saying "biological didn't bother." Did strands of DNA make someone owe? Did people belong to people because of what lay tangled in their cells?

Dev didn't know what he thought about these questions, but he thought he knew what Lake thought. He was almost sure.

But the night after the day of raking leaves with Aidan, Dev wasn't thinking about these questions. He wasn't thinking that somewhere in the dark town outside his room, among all the squares of light, was a square belonging to his father. He had thought about it, a lot. But that night Dev lay stretched out in his bed, letting gravity pull his pleasantly aching body down, down into the mattress, and he thought about the poster hanging over his headboard, a photograph of the Milky Way swirling its shining arms.

In large ways, Dev had always felt located. Many times he'd stood on a sidewalk or a patch of grass and felt his place in the universe: third planet from the sun, on the Orion arm of the Milky Way galaxy, two-thirds of the way out from its center, in the Virgo supercluster, in the continuum of time and space. He'd planted his feet and closed his eyes and tried to feel the motion of the earth.

But now, Dev realized he felt located in small ways, too: in school hallways, and sitting on the hard ground in Mrs. Finney's yard talking to Aidan, and falling asleep in his bed with Lake in the next room, reading. Dev belonged to these places; he fit. He imagined he could hear the click of himself snapping into place.

He pictured the black dot on the map again. Not very long ago, Dev had believed in the dot's randomness, but now the dot was houses, friends, trees, poems, fiery leaves snagged in his rake, his bike wheels on asphalt. He imagined the dot grown larger and printed with the words on his Milky Way poster: YOU ARE HERE.

"I'm here," Dev thought, and then he fell asleep.

Six

*W*hen Piper turned eight years old, Piper's grand-mother—the good grandmother, her father's mother—had given her a box. The box was made of wood, glass-smooth and dark, was lined with strawberry-colored velvet, and in the center of its heavy lid was a silver rectangle engraved with Piper's initials. Piper bore a breathless love for the box and never touched it without reverence. Even though Piper understood that she was too old to believe in magic, Piper believed that it was a magic box, and that the magic lay in the sound it made when she shut it. Not a click but a soft, smoky thunk, like the sound of a moth hitting a window, a toe shoe on a wood floor.

While the box was meant to hold jewelry, almost as soon as she got it, without planning it out beforehand, Piper made the box a container for anger, sorrow, and wishes. For example, if Piper got mad at her mother, as she often did, she'd go to her room, open the box, whisper her rage into it, close her eyes, and—sliding her fingers slowly out from under it—let the lid fall. As soon as she heard the sound, the sound that meant the box was as closed as anything ever got, as closed as a pharaoh's tomb, she could walk away, lightened and able to love her mother as a daughter should.

In utter secrecy, Piper performed this ritual for years—"leaving it in the box" she called it—and then, in her early twenties, she made herself stop. When she left her parents' home for good, she left the box behind.

Now, boxless and facing the unbearable sadness of losing Elizabeth, Piper had a word.

Fine.

Fine. Fine. Fine. *Fine.*

If, over the years, Piper had not developed a vehement and frequently professed contempt for all things New Age (a heading under which she corralled crystals, chiropractors, ESP, yoga, Dr. Andrew Weil/ Deepak Chopra (in her mind they were, literally, the same person), aromatic candles—excepting cinnamon and vanilla holiday candles—echinacea, singer/ songwriter music, and the entire country of India), she might have called "Fine" her mantra. In fact, she didn't call "Fine" anything at all, but she said it, sometimes audibly, sometimes under her breath, many times a day, her top teeth digging hard into her lower lip with each *F* sound, and every time she said it, she felt its power.

Before anything else, before it held grief or anger, the word held guilt.

It was Piper who had talked Elizabeth into giving the new protocol a try. "At least a try," Piper had said, and moments later had admonished, "Give yourself a fighting chance, Elizabeth." Afterward, Piper had felt ashamed of having said this, of having implied that Elizabeth wasn't a fighter, but at least she'd stuck to her resolution not to add, "You owe it to your children."

In fact, Piper hadn't breathed a word about Elizabeth's children, although they were as present as if they'd been sitting in the room, side by side, their round hazel eyes full of listening. The only other person actually sitting in the room had been Tom, and Tom hadn't mentioned the children either. The three of them had sat at one end of Elizabeth's long dining room table, speaking in calm, reasonable tones. Even Tom had shrugged off his tragic demeanor and had brought a steady voice, a nearly neutral face to the discussion. His boardroom face, thought Piper, approvingly, and the whole conversation had the tenor of a business meeting, except that they were discussing the body of one of the participants, what its chances were, the level of suffering it could be expected to endure.

"We know it might make you sick," Tom had said gently. "The doctors have told us that's likely. But there's also the chance that it won't be so bad. And you could stop. At any time, if it's too much, you could just say, 'Enough.'"

But no matter how quietly they addressed one another, no matter how mellow and civilized the room appeared—the artichoke-print fabric of the window treatments, sun resting on the russet-colored walls—the fact remained that it was two against one.

A couple of weeks later, in a moment far removed from that conversation, Elizabeth, clenched with nausea, would raise panicked, confused, wholly unaccusatory eyes to Piper—the eyes of an injured animal—and rasp through cracked lips, "I feel like a battered wife," and names for what Piper and Tom had been in that dining room would come to Piper on an ice-cold wave of guilt: "Bullies." "Thugs."

It was this same wave of guilt that had swept Piper into Cornelia's house to have Teo confirm Piper's greatest fear: that Elizabeth's new protocol and its attendant misery were pointless, had always been pointless, and should end.

The night after her conversation with Teo, Piper was wrenched awake by the sound of her own gasping sobs, and as she sat up, methodically smoothing her hair in the dark room, turning the ends under with shaking fingers, the single word had arrived suddenly, like a small, heavy object placed in her hand. Not "Everything's fine," a phrase to soothe a child. The magic of the word was not transformative; "fine" made nothing fine. However, the word was capacious, a receptacle— like a trap in a drain—for every emotion that made moving out of one moment and into the next impossible for Piper.

Piper said it, whispered it into the darkness, then again in the direction of her husband, who lay sleeping with his back to Piper and didn't stir. Her hands went still and dropped from her hair to her lap. Then, Piper turned, slid her cold feet into her boiled-wool slippers, got out of bed, and descended two flights of stairs to the basement in search of a cardboard box.

When Piper walked to Elizabeth's house the next morning, the cardboard box contained an expensive and hard-to-find brand of stainless-steel cleaner; a cellophane package of sponges; a five-pound free-range chicken, uncooked; a sack of miniature Yukon golds; fresh rosemary; a lemon; and two vast, sweet Walla-Walla onions. The box was heavy, but Piper stepped with certainty, shoulders squared under her quilted jacket. Meredith walked a few steps ahead, carrying, with exquisite care, a second lemon.

When the two of them arrived at the Donahues' back door, through the wall of kitchen windows shining like a waterfall in the morning sun, Piper caught sight of Elizabeth's son, Peter, sitting at the table in a blue vinyl art apron, gluing pieces of colored felt onto other pieces of colored felt. Next to him sat what appeared to be an ordinary middle-aged woman, but who, Piper had reason to know, was, in fact, a coup, a gem, a bona fide *goldmine* of a babysitter: a fit, college-educated, native-English-speaking, nonsmoking, fifty-year-old retired art teacher. A grandmother whose daughter had recently remarried and packed the grandchildren off to Cleveland.

Piper had reason to know this because she had initiated and carried out the Donahues' search for a sitter herself. Piper had discovered Ginny Phipps. Ginny Phipps. Even her name was perfect: sensible but fun, like Mary Poppins. Now, as Piper peeked through the window, she saw Ginny touch a finger to Peter's nose. Peter giggled.

I did this, Piper thought. *At least I did* this *right.* Then she looked at Meredith, smiled, and said, "Okay, then." Still smiling, Piper kicked lightly at the French door with the toe of one red driving moc.

"Hands full!" Piper explained cheerfully as Ginny answered the door. "Thanks a million, Ginny!"

Ginny smiled and made a move to take the box, but Piper said, "No, no. I'm fine. You shoo."

She settled the box on the kitchen counter, lifted out the chicken, and walked to the refrigerator, pausing to examine the expanse of stainless-steel door and to

cluck once with annoyance before opening it and settling the chicken on the bottom shelf. Then she washed
her hands, soaping them copiously and scrubbing her
fingers, consciously setting a good example for the
others, in case they were watching.

With a crisp motion, Piper ripped off one square of
paper towel and almost dropped it, surprised by its
coarseness, its flimsiness. Not Elizabeth's usual brand.
Piper drew in a breath, feeling a headache, silvery and
flickering, like a Fourth of July sparkler, begin to sizzle
behind her eyes. She and Elizabeth were of one mind
about paper towels: they should be as close to cloth
as any paper could be. She stared at the towel for a
moment, then crumpled it in one hand.

With the other hand, she slid open the trash can disguised as a cabinet and tossed in the towel. "Fine," she
said, and shoved the trash can back out of sight.

"Sorry. Did you say something?" Ginny asked.

Piper turned toward her, briskly slapping her palms
on the fronts of her thighs, feeling the sting through
her jeans. Ginny was leaning over, settling Meredith
into a second booster chair. A wing of Ginny's hair fell
forward, and, absently, Piper noticed that the hair, gray
and gleaming, nearly matched the kitchen's stainless-
steel appliances. It was shinier than the appliances.
Meredith reached out one hand and gently batted it.

"Well. I think I'll just run up and say hi to Mrs. Donahue." Piper looked down at Meredith. "Is that okay
with you?"

"Oh, fine," said Ginny, with a reassuring wave of her
hand. "Not to worry. I'm happy to watch them both."

Piper had been speaking to Meredith. Abruptly, she
shifted her gaze to Ginny, then blinked. "Oh," she said
after a beat. "Super! I so appreciate it."

As she walked up the stairs toward Elizabeth's bedroom, a grand master suite with room for a love seat, an armchair, and the delicate mahogany secrétaire that had been in Elizabeth's family for generations, Piper felt her headache's hard glittering intensify. Last time she'd been in this room, Elizabeth had talked for a few minutes, then slid into a restless, twisting nap, making occasional low, whimpering sounds that Piper could feel in the back of her own throat.

But when Piper reached the top of the stairs, she saw that Elizabeth's door was standing wide open. Music was playing. Elizabeth's bed was empty and so faultlessly made that it looked like a bed in a showroom, the satin and velvet throw pillows gorgeously heaped. Elizabeth had always had a soft spot for sumptuous bedding and a knack for unstudied elegance. Even now, Piper felt a stab of envy. When it came to home décor, Elizabeth was like those Frenchwomen who casually pinned up their hair and wound scarves around their necks in a manner that said, "Yes, this is perfect, and, no, you will never learn to do it."

Piper shook off this thought and took a step into the room. All the window shades were fully raised and the air danced with dust motes. She stood for a moment, confused, dazzled, staring at the empty bed, sunlight and James Taylor washing over her.

"Don't look so shocked. It's one of the privileges of having cancer: you get to stop pretending to be cool." Elizabeth's voice, followed by Elizabeth's laugh, a real laugh, ordinary and miraculous. Piper's startled heart seemed to bump against her ribs and she pressed both hands to her chest.

"What?" she gasped, turning toward the sound.

Elizabeth sat in a corner of the love seat, her feet

tucked under her, her hair still damp from showering. Piper saw that there wasn't a lot of color in her face, but her eyes looked more like her eyes than they had in a long time. Elizabeth wore the Juicy Couture sweat suit she'd bought herself as a joke for her last birthday, a bright pink velour talisman to ward off growing old.

"Hey, you," said Piper, plopping herself down in the armchair.

Elizabeth flashed a smile and shimmied her shoulders a little to the music.

"'Stop pretending to be cool.' Oh, you mean James Taylor?" Piper rolled her eyes. "I don't think even cancer gets you off the hook for that."

"Oh, come on," said Elizabeth, "listen." She tilted back her chin and closed her eyes, like a person letting rain fall on her face.

Piper closed her eyes, too. She listened. The headache began to waver and dim.

"Admit it. It's beautiful."

"Shhh," said Piper.

Because it was. It was beautiful. The guitar and the man's voice, both, were plainly beautiful, as austere and clear as the morning itself, as sitting in the room with Elizabeth, the two of them given over to listening. He was singing about going to Carolina, and it struck Piper as the purest, most unsentimental song she'd ever heard; even the sadness felt simple, scrubbed clean.

Because Piper wanted the song to never end, she spoke before it did.

"Yep," she agreed quietly, "it's a good song."

"Yep," echoed Elizabeth. And then, "My mom used to listen to James Taylor all the time. James Taylor, John Denver, Carly Simon, and what's her name with the hair. Boy, that stuff was contagious. Mom-music. My sisters and I still call it that. I remember catching my dad singing 'Annie's Song' while he changed the oil in the car."

"My mom," began Piper, then she stopped.

Elizabeth waited. Then she snapped her fingers. "Carole King. She's the one with the hair."

Piper thought about how her own mother had really been two mothers, the one before Marybeth Pringle had moved in next door and the one after. If the pre-Marybeth mother had listened to music, Piper couldn't remember a single song. In fact, whenever Piper recalled that mother, and she didn't do it often, she thought of her as steeped in silence, a wooden, distant woman with an unsmiling face.

The post-Marybeth mother, the one who grew her hair long, wore jangling jewelry, neglected her housework, and let Piper's older brother George and his friends smoke pot in the rec room, had listened to music all the time. Piper remembered her swaying around the kitchen or lying on lounge chairs in the backyard with Marybeth, both of them ridiculous in bikinis. Music had played then, loud and constant, but Piper couldn't remember anything about it. While Piper had not liked the pre-Marybeth mother much either (had craved her approval, had stored up every act or word of affection like treasure, but had never really liked her), the post-Marybeth mother had been worse because she was the mother who left. Because everything about her mother after Marybeth came had been weird and stupid and wrong, Piper knew the music had been, too.

"Anyway," said Piper, "music doesn't make a person cool or not cool."

"Oh, *please*!" Elizabeth almost shrieked. "What about high school? What about *college*? Piper, you are so wrong."

"I am so not wrong."

Elizabeth thought for a second. "Okay, if you were blond, beautiful, and queen of the world, maybe, *maybe* the music you liked didn't matter, but for the rest of us, trust me. It mattered."

"You were beautiful. I've seen the pictures."

"I was cute."

Piper shrugged, as if there were no difference between beautiful and cute, when of course there was. Looking at Elizabeth's face now, though, Piper could see that all the cute was gone, that a dry, pale angularity had taken over. Piper felt sadness rise around her. *Fine,* she thought.

"You know what, though," said Piper, "I was popular—there's no two ways about *that*—but I was never really cool. Not like the Talking Heads girls. You remember the Talking Heads girls?" Piper and Elizabeth had not gone to the same college, but it didn't matter. Everyone knew the Talking Heads girls.

"Oh, yeah. With their little lopsided haircuts. And those black leggings under skirts. Boys loved those girls."

The two sat without speaking, remembering and listening to James Taylor sing about Mexico. Then Piper said, "I went to see Teo Sandoval yesterday, like I told you I was going to. I took him your chart."

Elizabeth's expression of mild thoughtfulness didn't even shift. "Don't tell me," she said. Her voice was soft, but it was a command. "I mean, it's fine that you went. But don't tell me what he said."

"But—"

"I stopped. Almost a week ago. I wanted to stop, so I stopped."

Upon hearing this, in spite of everything she knew, in spite of what she'd waited hours and hours to tell Elizabeth, Piper's first thought was to say, "No, you can't stop. You cannot. You have to keep fighting this."

Piper didn't say this. Instead, she dropped her head and looked down at her lap. "I'm so sorry. I'm sorry for pressuring you into—" Elizabeth cut her off again.

"Piper," she said. She waited for Piper to meet her eyes. "I know you think you and Tom talked me into it. But you didn't. Or maybe you did. But not in the way you think. I wanted to do it. The thing is . . ." Elizabeth paused and Piper held her breath. The whole room seemed to hold its breath.

Elizabeth smiled. "The thing is, it's okay to do something just because the people you love want you to. Sometimes that's a good enough reason."

Piper stared at her.

"You hear me?" asked Elizabeth.

Piper nodded, her eyes stinging. How could she ever be without this person?

"Listen, Betts," she said, finally, "I hate to break this to you, but I think that girl Graciela hired to help her clean your house?"

"Mindy?"

"I think Mindy's been using 409 on your stainless appliances. In fact, I'm almost positive."

Elizabeth's laugh was the best, most alive sound in the world. When she could speak, she said, still laughing, "Now, *that* is the worst news I've heard all year."

Piper cleaned the appliances, of course, rubbed the silken cleaner over every inch, then polished with small circular motions until her wrist began to ache. Afterward, after she'd picked up Carter and Elizabeth's daughter, Emma, from school, stopping on the way to buy paper towels and two bunches of remarkable, nearly red lilies, one for the kitchen table, one for Elizabeth's room, and after she'd trimmed the stems and put the flowers in water, after she'd fed the children apple slices and peanut butter at Elizabeth's kitchen table, Piper baked the chicken, filling the rooms of Elizabeth's house with its gold-tinged aroma.

As she performed these tasks, Piper had a sense that they were more than tasks, that they were the edge of something large that would unfold, pushing its way into the future. As Piper tidied Emma's ponytails, wiped peanut butter off Peter's chin, assembled potatoes and wedges of onion around the chicken, she understood that she would go on to fill days and weeks with helping, would wake up mornings feeling the day's emptiness, how it stood waiting to be filled with duties the way you'd fill a jar with coins.

But what also began that day, without Piper deciding or even knowing, was a kind of campaign, a gathering of forces. Against—what?—cancer? Maybe death itself, although Piper would have recoiled in disgust at the melodrama of waging a campaign against either one, would likely have recoiled at the whole idea of waging a campaign at all. "Oh, please," she would have sneered, "get over yourself."

Still, there were moments over the next few weeks when what could only be called defiance ran into and through her body like a current.

One gray morning, Piper opened the door to two young men delivering a hospital bed. She'd been expecting them. The men were nice, polite, and they didn't just drop off the bed, but placed it in the space Tom and Piper had made for it in the dining room the night before, angling the bed per Piper's instructions, in such a way that Elizabeth would receive the morning sun.

But even though the men were nice, Piper hated them. She hated their big hands and their baseball caps. Their leather work boots—laced halfway up and the exact color of a Twinkie—made her want to scream. Mostly, she hated that they were strangers, strangers bearing witness to the private, shattering truth that a person in the house could no longer climb stairs and to the deeper, more private truth that the sick person desired to be downstairs in the heart of her home, among the people she loved.

While testing the workings of the bed, one of the men had said, admiringly, "It's fully motorized. Top of the line," and Piper had wanted to wring his neck, clobber him with his own clipboard. "Top of the line," as though the family were lucky to have such a bed in their house, as though Elizabeth should count her lucky stars.

After the men left, Piper went into the kitchen and made a Bundt cake, buttery and full of apples, redolent of cinnamon. Elizabeth's favorite. As she cracked the eggs, she whispered between clenched teeth, addressing no one and nothing she could name, "Fine. Fine. You did that. It's done. Elizabeth will sleep in the goddamn dining room. But this?" Piper almost threw the cupful of sugar into the bowl. "This you can't do a thing about."

She meant the cake. She meant the act of making it and the way it would turn out to be exactly right, a small, tangible victory. Piper stirred and stirred and stirred, saying with her whole body, "There is a limit. There is a limit to what can be taken away."

* * *

What truly surprised Piper, what she would look back on years later with wonder, wasn't the fury or the defiance. Instead, it was the peace.

It seemed impossible that you could stand in a kitchen making hot chocolate and grilled-cheese sandwiches with your best friend dying in the next room, the voices of her children tangled up with the voices of your own, that you could butter bread and watch, through the window, the trees relinquishing their leaves and hear the silvery tumble of water into a kettle, and be suddenly aware that what resided at the heart of every shape and sound was peace. A rightness hovering above all that was wrong, shimmering, like heat rising from a street in summer.

It seemed impossible, but it wasn't. Piper stood inside those moments and understood, as deeply as she'd ever understood anything, that living with Elizabeth's dying was the truest thing to ever happen to her. "Right here, right now." She thought again and again, "Right here, right now."

As with all things involving the care, feeding, and sleep times of small children, the period of Elizabeth's dying quickly fell into something close to a regular schedule. The most regular element in the schedule, its anchor, was that on weekday mornings, Tom and Piper woke their respective children early, got them dressed, and Tom dropped Emma and Peter off at Piper's house for breakfast. After that, the rhythm of a particular day shifted according to Elizabeth's needs, her levels of fatigue and pain.

For instance, on Mondays, Wednesdays, and Fridays, Piper took all four children to school, then shopped, ran errands, or squeezed in a kickboxing class before picking up the little ones at their preschool, phoning the Donahues' house on the drive back to see if Elizabeth were up to having the children at her house. When she was, Piper would take them there, feed them lunch, and await the twelve-thirty arrival of Ginny Phipps. When Elizabeth needed quiet, Piper would take Peter and Meredith to her own house, and Ginny would arrive and play with them there, while Piper left to pick up Carter and Emma at Tallyrand.

On these days, the children might stay at Piper's house all day, making mobiles out of sticks, fishing line, and autumn leaves or baking sugar cookies with Ginny, running around the yard, heaped like puppies on the family room floor watching the Wiggles, singing along at the tops of their lungs. Sometimes, Peter, who still napped, would fall asleep amid the noise, and Piper would carry him to Meredith's crib, pausing in the gray, feathery-edged dimness of the room to touch his hair or the creases the carpet had left on his cheek.

But often Elizabeth wanted them at her house, wanted them all, hungry for voices, bodies, and motion. Tom mounted a television in one corner of the dining room, up high so that Elizabeth could see it, and the children would array themselves around her, curled or sprawled on the bed or floor, tangled up in the big armchair, both confused and enchanted by the oddity of television in the dining room. Elizabeth would watch the children watching TV and Piper would watch her watch them.

What mystified Piper was that, most of the time, Elizabeth even seemed to welcome the presence of the strangers, to drink them in, too. Because her house was trafficked through by strangers now, daily: a shockingly young doctor, home health aides, nurses. When Piper or

Tom wasn't with Elizabeth, and sometimes even when one of them was, a stranger was present. Some of the strangers were quiet, some spoke almost constantly. One made Elizabeth laugh by talking back to the guests on *Oprah* or *The Today Show* the way Elizabeth and Piper always did: "Oh, get off your high horse, mister!" or "Newsflash: that red turtleneck makes you look straight-up fat."

No matter what their hands were busy doing, if Elizabeth was awake, the hospice workers kept as much eye contact with her as possible, as though to affirm, "You are here. You are not just a body damaged by illness. You are Elizabeth," which made Piper want to weep with gratitude. In fact, Piper alternated between wanting to embrace the hospice workers (an impulse on which she never acted) and wanting them to disappear from the face of the earth.

"Hospice," a strangely delicate, weightless word, Piper noticed, one that could be either whisper or hiss.

One night after Carter and Meredith were in bed, Piper sat at her kitchen table with Kyle's laptop open before her. Because many of Elizabeth's friends had asked Piper what they could do to help, Piper had decided to create a system of dinner drop-offs. While it would have been easy enough to ask people to cook main dishes that would freeze well and to bring them whenever they chose, Piper thought that freshly prepared, still-warm dishes would taste better, and she believed emphatically that each main dish should be accompanied by a healthy, vegetable-based side dish. Additionally, she wanted to build variety into the system, to avoid the potentially demoralizing effects of, say, evening upon evening of pasta.

Consequently, the schedule of dinners had become a three-part package: a cover letter describing the system and including the particular culinary likes and dislikes of the Donahue family members (no pimiento, no sesame oil, no smoked fish, et cetera); a schedule of who would bring dinner, one to two hours prior to the six P.M. dinner hour, on which days; and a phone-number list so that the dinner providers could consult previous dinner providers as to what they'd brought so as not to duplicate recent menus.

When Piper had been working at this for about half an hour, Kyle pulled out the chair next to hers and sat down. Glancing quickly sideways, Piper saw Kyle's hands clasped on the table in a formal manner. *Oh, for God's sake,* she thought, *whatever it is, not now.*

"Piper," he said, quietly.

"Two secs," said Piper, although she knew it would be much longer.

"Piper," Kyle said, "we need to talk."

Piper heard the intensely serious note in his voice. The intensely serious note irritated her. The nights that followed the days of caring for Elizabeth's home and family in addition to her own fell into two categories: wired, almost feverish nights when the energy refused to leave Piper's body, or hollowed-out nights. This was a hollowed-out night.

"Hey, Kyle," said Piper, knitting her brows at the computer screen, "can you show me how to do that program again? You know. Whatsit. The table thing. Um, the, oh gosh . . ."

"Spreadsheet," Kyle supplied, enunciating the word with a precision that managed to convey patience and impatience at the same time. Then he reached over and closed the laptop.

"Why." She leveled a deliberately expressionless stare at him. "Did you do that?"

"Piper," he began again, his voice softening, "we have to talk. You know we do."

This surprised Piper, the assumption that she knew what was coming. She had no idea. She merely looked at him, waiting.

"Look, Piper, I've been wanting to talk to you for a long time, but you're never—"

"Don't say it," she said, cutting him off. "Don't say I'm never here. *You* are never here."

Kyle sighed and looked down at his laced fingers, nodding. "You know, that's true. I haven't been spending a lot of time here lately." He looked up at her. "Don't you ever wonder why?"

Suddenly, Piper felt rocked by exhaustion, by the need for sleep. Her head felt heavy on her neck. "I don't know," she said, searching for the answer he wanted, the one that would end the conversation and allow her to go to bed. "Maybe? Maybe I wonder?"

Kyle made a huffing, exasperated sound and squeezed his eyes shut, shaking his head as though in disbelief, then popping his eyes open. Like something out of Looney Tunes, Piper thought. She cringed away from him, pressing her shoulder blades hard against her chair back.

"Maybe? Maybe?" Kyle shouted the words.

"Can we do this another time, Kyle?" Piper's voice was small. "Please."

Kyle unclasped his hands and dropped them onto the table, fingers splayed. He sat that way for so long that Piper began to think he was finished, but as soon as she started to rise from her chair, he said, "I'm not happy, Piper. I am just not—happy."

Kyle wasn't happy. He was just not happy. The words

echoed around the hollow places inside Piper—*happy, happy*—and then, she wasn't tired anymore, and the hollow places weren't empty anymore; they were flash-flooded with fury. She didn't know if she wanted to slap her husband or throw her head back and laugh. *Kyle* wasn't happy. Kyle wasn't *happy.*

Scraping together what self-control she could find, Piper drew in a breath and met Kyle's eyes. "Today." She took another breath. "Today Emma climbed into my lap so that she could whisper in my ear. She said, 'I'm glad Mommy is in bed all the time now because I was worried about whether she would fall forward or backward when she died. I didn't want her to get hurt.'"

For a moment, Piper wondered if she really had slapped Kyle. He looked like a man who'd been slapped. Then his whole body, beginning with his shoulders, seemed to deflate. He stood up and turned to leave. Without turning back to Piper, he said in a flat voice, "Sometimes I think you love Elizabeth more than you love any of us."

Piper watched his back as he left the room, his white shirt. Then she watched the spot where the shirt had been, stunned into trembling by what she was thinking. The thought had all the force of fact: *Not more than any of you. Not more than Carter and Meredith. But more than you. I love her more than I love you.*

SEVEN

Cornelia

*A*n e-mail from my sister, Ollie:

> **This falls outside the purview of my expertise,
> but as I see it, the problem with you, Cornelia, is
> that, in managing the stressors in your new envi-
> ronment, you're relying on the "fight-or-flight"
> response, a biobehavioral pattern that was long
> assumed to apply to both men and women. The
> new and well-supported thinking on this subject
> suggests that, in fact, women more readily and
> effectively cope with stress through "tend-and-
> befriend" behavior, which, like most behaviors, is
> undoubtedly the result of evolutionary pressures.**

This was just the teaser, the catchy little prelude to a
three-page, single-spaced missive the upshot of which
seemed to be that, in moments of stress, rather than
growing combative or withdrawing, the fittest women
have survived by employing a coping strategy that in-

volves caring for their young; creating supportive relationships with other women; or both.

Tend-and-befriend. Get it?

If you can, put aside the fact that anyone who begins a letter of sisterly concern with the words "This falls outside the purview of my expertise . . . ," continues with the words ". . . the problem with you, Cornelia . . . ," and ends with a bibliography and a list titled "Suggestions for Further Reading" has bigger problems than I could ever dream of having.

Put aside the rampant use of the passive voice, of which "a biobehavioral pattern that was long assumed" is just the first of many examples. *Who* assumed? You? Because I'll tell you right now, I assumed nothing of the sort.

Put aside the dubious wisdom of advising a woman whose chief complaint is being unable, for the first time in her life, to make a single female friend that the solution to her problem, since she has no offspring to tend (although I'll give Ollie this: if I had an offspring, you can bet your last dollar that tending her or him would have made me feel a hundred percent better, a *thousand* percent better), is to *make a female friend,* preferably many female friends, that her salvation lies in creating a tightly woven network of nurturing, sustaining female friends.

Put aside the fact that Ollie waited nearly a month to send this e-mail after getting mine, by which time her advice was verging on obsolete. (Although, to be fair, I should point out that a month in Ollie time is roughly equivalent to a week in regular human time, so that, while she was tardy no matter how you slice it, she really wasn't *obscenely* tardy.)

And finally, put aside the fact that I never solicited

her advice in the first place. In fact, I was careful to do anything *but* solicit her advice. A simple "I feel your pain, sister" would've suited me fine.

If you can find it in your heart to put aside all of the above—and I don't blame you if you can't since I, who, for reasons mysterious even to me (habit? DNA? evolutionary pressures?), love the woman and understand that despite all of the above, she loves me, too, barely managed it myself—what you'll get is an uncluttered view of an exasperating but inescapable truth: Ollie was right.

Lake invited me over for dinner. Actually, I invited her over for dinner, but before I quite had a handle on what was happening, she'd whisked the invitation out of my hands and flipped it neatly on its head, so that I suddenly found myself thanking her and asking her what I could bring and she found herself saying, "My pleasure," and "Not a thing," a "not a thing" that I assumed included Teo, since she knew he existed and didn't mention him. I also knew he existed and didn't mention him, both because she didn't and also because, though my love for Teo is boundless and eternal and so forth, women cannot live on husbands alone. I wanted a girls' night. I did, I did, I did.

And about five seconds after I stepped into Lake's house, just after I'd traded my armful of dahlias— shaggy, yam orange, and glorious—for a glassful of plummy Chilean cabernet, I felt my body begin to empty of stress. To empty of stress and to fill with what my sister, God love her, would doubtless identify as a rush of estrogen-enhanced oxytocin accompanied by shots of serotonin and dopamine, but what felt to my hopelessly right-brained brain an awful lot like well-being accompanied by ease.

Heavenly smells and an Ella and Louis duet wafted from the kitchen.

"Come in the kitchen and save me from myself," moaned Lake.

She was barefoot and had her hair twisted up into a fabulously untidy knot, a damp, fabulously untidy knot. Even pinned up, the hair seemed to be alive, damp curls making their escape, leaping and corkscrewing in improbable directions. In the crook of one arm she held the dahlias, in her other hand she held a gorgeous head of Boston Bibb, celadon green and as ruffled as an Elizabethan collar.

Looking at her, I had to smile because a hostess who greets her dinner guest with wet hair, a glass of wine, and a head of lettuce is my kind of hostess, and also because, standing there, the flowers flaming, Lake looked like something out of Greek mythology, a harvest goddess, maybe. A life force.

"I've got this slab of triple crème sitting on my countertop that's half the size it was an hour ago," she wailed.

The sense of well-being spread down to my fingertips, to the ends of my hair. I laughed.

"Sounds bad," I told her. "Sounds like I got here just in time."

Demeter.

The name came to me a couple of hours later. Demeter, Greek goddess of the harvest, although at the moment the name popped into my head, I wasn't thinking of Demeter the harvest goddess. I was thinking instead of Demeter the mother, the one who stalked the world, wild-eyed, searching for her lost child, a blazing torch in her hand, her fury loosing famine on the world.

* * *

Because Lake had a child. Lake had a son. Dev.

I was thunderstruck.

He ate dinner with us, Dev did, and even as he sat before me, a flesh-and-blood boy picking the olives from a gargantuan mound of chicken tagine before devouring it with a thirteen-year-old boy's passionless efficiency, the thunderstruck feeling never left. If anything, it became more striking, more thunderous.

I wasn't surprised that Lake had a son. I'd been expecting a son. "Come to dinner at my house," Lake had said. "You can meet my son, Dev."

I *was* surprised that Dev was thirteen, but even if Lake had told me ahead of time, I would have been no better prepared for Dev, because calling Dev a "thirteen-year-old boy" was kind of like calling Emily Dickinson "a brunette" or Ben Franklin "the inventor of the swim fin."

He *looked* like a thirteen-year-old boy. His features seemed to be less mismatched and more fully baked than my two younger brothers' had at that age, although, when I think about it, the early teen years may have been particularly unkind to Cam and Toby. They're fine now, but Toby, for instance, walked around with what was manifestly someone else's chin and nose until well into his fifteenth year. Dev wasn't pretty, but his face, grounded by his mother's square jaw, made a kind of sense, and his smile, when I finally saw it, turned out to be startlingly lovely, like a flock of white birds suddenly landing in your front yard. But he walked like a thirteen-year-old boy, loping and jointless, and when he sat, he sat like one.

We talked about poetry.

It began with Lake asking Dev the classic dinner-table question, "Anything good happen in school today?" And because Cam's and Toby's answers to this question had almost invariably included descriptions—gleeful and in Technicolor—of some poor kid's vomiting in a hallway, I put down my glass of wine and braced myself.

Lucky I did, too, because the next thing Dev did was think for a second and then say, "Well, actually, we had this pretty cool discussion about sonnets in Ms. Enright's class."

I have some experience with thirteen-year-old boys and sonnets. Actually, I had one experience with one thirteen-year-old boy and one sonnet over twenty years ago. He was John Spencer Cropp, the only kid in the eighth grade who was shorter than I was, which likely means he was the shortest eighth-grader in school, possibly state, history. And even though I couldn't bring myself to so much as hold John Spencer's hand, which was much smaller than mine, sawed-off-looking really, and sweaty, he was the closest thing to a boyfriend I had before I hit the age of sixteen and dated an exchange student from France with cigarette breath and a girl's name.

John Spencer wrote me a sonnet, and rather than simply slipping it into my backpack or passing it to me in class, he mailed it to me, mailed it in a nine-by-twelve-inch envelope so that it came to me flat and, as his enclosed note indicated, suitable for framing.

The sonnet, "I Love You, Cornelia," began: "Love is not all: it is not meat nor drink," and ended "I might be driven to sell your love for peace, / Or trade the memory of this night for food / It well may be. I do not think I would," and I still regard it as one of the loveliest love poems in existence, for which I've always wanted to thank John Spencer Cropp, who grew up to become one of the youngest and smallest state senators in Virginia history. Of course, I'd like to thank Edna St. Vincent Millay as well, since she was nice enough to write it.

Before I knew about Edna, right after I'd received the poem, I showed it to my sister, Ollie, who honked out a derisive laugh and said, "John Spencer Cropp wears socks with flip-flops. Don't be a dipshit, Cornelia," and I had to admit that a similar, though more gently worded, thought had been niggling around in the back of my brain, too. Sadly, these doubts were confirmed later that day when John Spencer quoted the poem to me dramatically over the phone and pronounced "food" so that it rhymed with "would" and then followed up by saying, "This poem's in a special form you inspired me to make up. It's called a sonnay."

Here's what Dev said:

"So, I guess that the word 'sonnet' comes from *sonnetto,* which means 'little song' in Italian? But I don't think a sonnet's that much like a song. It's so short, and it just doesn't feel like a song. You can usually *get* songs just by listening once because they're, like, all airy, and there's just no air between the lines of a sonnet, you know?"

I did know. I knew because I had been reading sonnets for twenty-plus years, held a B.A. in English from a prestigious (although not superprestigious) university, and had even gone so far as to attend a Ph.D. program in literature, if only for a single semester. How *Dev* knew I couldn't imagine, but if my fellow students, if my *professors* in grad school had brought half of Dev's keenness and wonder to the task of examining literature, if their faces had looked like Christmas morning as they'd talked about sonnets, who knows? I might have stayed for the whole shebang.

"So what do you think a better name would be?" I asked him, which I thought was an original, evocative question, but the casual manner with which Dev grabbed it and took off running told me it wasn't that original after all. A glance at Lake, though, the expression on her face as she looked back at me, told me that with the question, I'd passed some kind of test.

"I've been thinking 'little box,' which probably sounds weird, but I noticed that sonnets are usually about something big. A big feeling or a big idea. Like, we read this one called 'Design' by Robert Frost? And he starts by describing three things clustered together: a white spider, on top of a white flower, holding a dead white moth. And he thinks the combination of these things is really creepy because they all make him think about death."

"'Assorted characters of death and blight,'" I quoted, and as soon as I said this, Dev's glowing face glowed harder, brighter, eyes starry and a crimson stain running down the centers of his cheeks, and I felt as proud as if I'd written the words myself.

"Right, right, so you know it! Awesome! And then the poem starts to wonder how these three things that aren't usually white—because that kind of flower is always blue—ended up together, and at the end, the poem can't decide what's worse: the idea of malevolent forces out there, um, 'a design of darkness' or the idea that it's just an ugly coincidence, like there's no plan out there at all. There's just randomness."

He paused, new thoughts flickering over his face and being born inside his dark blue eyes, then took a bite of couscous, chewing and swallowing it carefully. If Dev could rush along full tilt, his ideas zipping ahead, it seemed he could also slow down and allow a thought to form. I could almost see it forming, folding and pleating itself, like origami paper, into something intricate and surprising.

"So all that's a big idea," he continued finally. "But you know what? Maybe it's not just a poem about an idea. I think it's a poem about a person, too. One individual, human guy."

"You do?" I asked, truly intrigued. In fact, I was as intrigued as I'd been in a long time, intrigued and comfortable, both. Ollie's tend-and-befriend theory didn't include a word about discussing poetry with a teenage boy, but it should have. I felt as entirely at home in that moment as I had anywhere outside my own house.

"Yeah," said Dev. "If I'd found those three white things together, I know I wouldn't have thought all that stuff. I wouldn't have thought it was dark or about death. I bet I would've thought it was cool. Something amazing. Especially how the genes of the flower carried some mutation that made it different from the others. Because without mutations, there's no evolution, right?"

I nodded, taking his word for it.

"But maybe seeing what he saw made Robert Frost sad or dark or whatever because he was already sad and dark to begin with."

Wow. Wow, right?

My first impulse was to cheer, to hoist Dev onto my shoulders and parade him through the streets, but I didn't want to embarrass him, so instead I said, "I always thought that about Frost. No matter what people think, he's as good at staring at the void as anyone.

Better. So you're thinking that a sonnet is a way of distilling a big idea or emotion until it fits in a tiny box."

"Right. Like with 'Design,' Frost is worried that there *is* no design, no shape to what happens, so he does what he knows how to do: he puts the worry into a poem that has a small, really definite shape. Fourteen lines. All that stuff." Dev looked up at me with his white and sudden smile. "Sorry if I'm not explaining this that well. I just thought of it."

"Oh, I'd say you're doing a pretty decent job." I smiled back at him. "Pretty decent. For just having thought of it and all."

Suddenly, Dev looked sheepish. "I've been talking a lot, right?" Dev swiveled his fork around his plate. He caught the fork tines on the edge of a lettuce leaf and flopped the leaf over so that it covered his pile of olives.

"A lot," agreed Lake, nodding emphatically, curls hopping and shimmying. "Talking a lot and treating your olives like nuclear waste. Why, may I ask?"

Dev rolled his eyes, made a horrific gagging face, and—just like that—he was all-boy, all thirteen-year-old.

"I told you *before*, Mom. Give me an olive and all I think is eyeball, eyeball, eyeball."

Lake told me a story about aspirin.

"It was Dev's third birthday," she began. "We'd had a party. A few other mothers, maybe five kids total, but somehow it turned into a circus. One kid started screaming about the cake being vanilla, and it was like a string of firecrackers going off. Boom boom boom. In two minutes, they were all completely out of their minds, including Dev."

Lake sat cross-legged at one end of her sofa, a throw pillow in her lap; I sat cross-legged at the other. We drank hot tea out of the kind of thick white mugs that are a joy to hold. Lake laughed.

"Especially Dev. So all the mothers left with these howling, convulsing wolverines dangling from their arms, and I put Dev down for a nap. He'd pretty much given up naps by then, but I tucked him in and told him I had a splitting headache, which was true, and was going to take a nap, too, in my room."

Lake paused. Her living room was brightly lit, but remembering worked like candlelight on Lake's face, softening its lines.

"So I'm lying there, almost asleep, and suddenly there's Dev, standing next to the bed, holding out his palm. And when I look at it, I see that he's handing me something, two tiny white somethings, and then it hits me that they're aspirin. And I sit up and grab them and grab his hand, and I'm shouting at him, 'Oh my God, how many did you eat, how many were in the bottle, was it a new bottle, I have to call 911.' He's so calm, standing there."

She paused again, gazing down at the pillow in her lap, one finger tracing the pattern of its fabric, and I could tell she was seeing his face, exactly as he'd looked that day. In spite of myself, I felt a longing so keen it was almost envy, and a partially healed-over hurt inside me began to ache.

"He said, patiently, 'I didn't take any. *I* don't have a headache. *You* have a headache.' I couldn't quite comprehend what he was saying. I said, 'You climbed up on the sink?' He nodded. I said, 'Are you sure you didn't take any?' even though for some reason I knew he was telling the truth. I was so relieved. I hugged him so hard that he said, 'Ow.' Then I thought about the bottle of aspirin, and I asked him, 'How did you get the pills out of the bottle?'"

Lake smiled and shook her head. "The look he gave me. Like that was such a ridiculous question. And he said, 'It was on the lid.' 'What was on the lid?' I asked him."

I was so busy being amazed that a child of three could be so thoughtful that I almost didn't understand what Lake was saying. Then, I understood.

"What did he say?" I asked.

She grinned. "He said, 'Push down and turn.'"

Lake told me a story about stealing library books.

"Two of them. One was a history of physics. The other was about sonar. He wrote in them, all over them, in the margins, on the inside of the back cover, taking notes. I remember he wrote, 'He saw his wife's bones! Cool!' next to a section on Röntgen. He was in fourth grade. Old enough to know better than to write in library books."

"What did you do when you found them?" I asked.

"I didn't find them," said Lake, "he brought them to me. He was crying. He'd gotten so excited that he forgot they were library books. I said, 'You forgot twice?' And he had. I could tell he had. He was a pretty rule-abiding kid. Still is. He was so upset when he realized what he'd done.

"That was one of our seriously broke periods. I let him keep the books and, when I got the notice from the library, I told the librarian I had no idea what they were talking about. I told her I'd definitely returned the books a week ago. I could tell she didn't quite believe me, but she knew a little bit about Dev. She cut me a break."

Lake sighed. "Sometimes I felt like his brain was this hungry, pacing animal, and I had to keep throwing it chunks of meat."

Lake told me a story about Dev's seventh-grade science teacher, and, suddenly, her voice was pure acid, burning, burning. Burning a hole in the moment and back through the tissue of time to that teacher standing in his classroom, pouring cruelty down on the person Lake loved the most.

I thought, *She'd kill that man, if she could.* And that's when it came to me: Demeter. Threatening, laying waste, making terrible bargains. Doing whatever it took to drag her child out of hell.

I told Lake about Clare.

Although as soon as I'd begun telling her, I wished I hadn't because up until that moment, our conversation had been the best possible kind of new-friend conversation. Do you know what I mean? We talked like two old friends, while still being happily conscious of the sparkle of newness shining on the surfaces of us and all we said.

But the moment I brought up Clare, it was as though someone had hit a switch, a spotlight had come on, and we sat there blinking at each other in the stark, arctic light, two strangers, our shadows thrown, looming and separate, onto the wall behind us. I'm not sure why that happened, but it happened.

"I have a thirteen-year-old in my life, too," I began, and boom: Lake's eyebrows flew up her forehead in an expression I could not name. Skepticism? Shock? Scorn? Ordinary friendly interest disguised as skepticism, shock, or scorn? I hoped for this last, but when

Lake spoke, her voice contained a note of something equally hard to pin down, but something that could not in a million years be mistaken for ordinary friendly interest.

"I didn't realize you and your husband had children," she said, and the words surprised me, like a slap. I'd told her earlier in the evening that my husband and I did *not* have children, and in Lake's mouth, the words "your husband" sounded like an accusation. Tension began zinging back and forth across the three feet of space that separated us. You could almost hear it.

"We don't," I said carefully, "not yet. I thought I'd told you that."

I waited, feeling the moment teetering on an edge. To my relief, Lake's face relaxed, her eyebrows settling down like blackbirds landing on a telephone line.

"I'm sorry," she said with a rueful smile. "Of course you did."

I kept waiting.

"I think sometimes," Lake sighed, "sometimes I feel a little sorry for myself. Or maybe I always feel a little sorry for myself and it just surfaces now and then. The struggling-single-mom-of-a-teenager thing. Like no one else in the world has ever gone through it. I'm sorry I snapped at you."

I softened then, because I could see that: loving your son ferociously but longing, now and then, for a different life, that longing popping out in short, bitter bursts. I thought about how Lake must see me: a woman her age, happily married, jobless (for now), childless (oh, childless), my life resting—however uneasily—on my green, regularly mown patch of the upper-middle class.

"I feel my own luck," I wanted to tell her, "I live in gratitude." Also, "I wasn't always the person you see now." And finally, "I have lost things I will never stop missing."

Instead I said, "Don't be sorry. You're right. I don't know what it's like to be a mother." I smiled. "And it's good for me to get snapped at now and then," which was—and is—the god's honest truth, although that didn't mean the snapping didn't sting. I felt it still, a tingling spot of pain.

"Tell me about your thirteen-year-old," said Lake.

I almost didn't. I liked Lake, I understood why she'd bristled at the idea of my knowing what it was like to be a mother, I wanted to be her friend. But I almost didn't tell her about Clare because Clare Hobbes is a subject I hold as close to my heart as any. That's not quite what I mean, "close to my heart." Clare and her mother live in Virginia, down the street from my parents, but Clare just as surely lives *in* my heart, and, I don't know about you, but I don't go around revealing what's in my heart to just anyone. I wasn't sure I trusted Lake. I was pretty sure, but not as sure as I'd been a few minutes earlier.

I thought about Dev, though, about Lake's love circling him like a ring of fire, about how she'd decided to let me in. And I hope you won't think I'm a hopeless nut job when I tell you that, sitting on Lake's couch, I also thought, fleetingly, of Søren Kierkegaard, about whom I know next to nothing but who pops unbidden into my head from time to time, looking, disconcertingly and inaccurately, like Hans Christian Andersen and saying something like this: rational thought is as holey as a moth-eaten sweater; at some point, girl, you need to take a leap of faith. He's talking about religion, but I'd say the same is true for friendship, the two having never been that far apart in my mind.

So I leaped. I told Lake about Clare. "I wanted to be her mother." That's part of what I said.

I met Clare two years ago when she was eleven and in trouble. In a short span of time, she'd lost her mother and her father, and while her mother came back, her father never did. Her mother, Viviana, was sick with bipolar disorder, and one bad day, she stopped her car and dropped Clare off by the side of the road, by the side of the road and into my life.

"And my life got bigger," I told Lake. "With Clare in it, my life got really, really big. Big and real and good."

"So you wanted her to stay in it." Lake nodded, with so much understanding on her face, I could've hugged her.

"During that stretch of time when Clare and I were—going it alone, I would've given anything, done anything to bring her mother back. And then she came back . . ." I broke off. When it comes to Clare, sometimes, the past isn't past. The past can get as present as any present ever was, so near that I feel its breath.

"But you're still close?" asked Lake.

"We are." I brightened. "In fact, she's coming for Thanksgiving." I brightened more. "And here's an idea: you and Dev join us."

Lake opened her mouth, then shut it, then smiled a small smile. She did not speak.

"Teo would love to have you. He's a more-the-merrier guy from way back. And Clare and Dev would get along like gangbusters, I can almost guarantee it."

Lake still didn't speak.

"Whatever gangbusters are," I added, as a way of giving her a bit more time to reply.

Lake didn't reply, not even to speculate as to the origins of the term "gangbusters." Instead, she sat there, smiling

that small, small inscrutable smile, like Mona Lisa herself, although I must say that until that moment, I'd never
found Mona Lisa's smile particularly interesting or even
particularly a smile. Looking at Lake, I understood what
probably everyone else already knows about the woman
in that painting: we are drawn to her not because of what
the smile gives us but because it gives nothing. We are
waiting to get past the smile. We are waiting—we've
spent centuries waiting—for the woman to speak.

Even though I'm more comfortable with silence than
some people are, Lake seemed so poised to give Mona
a run for her money that a speech got busy assembling
itself in my head, a speech beginning with promises
of homemade cranberry sauce and oyster stuffing and
culminating in loving descriptions of my grandmother's butter-twist roll recipe. It was a decent speech (who
could resist any invitation involving the phrase "butter-
twist"?), but delivering it would have made me feel
more like a used-car salesman than I had in ages, so I
was thankful when Lake spoke up first.

"You're so nice to offer," she said, slowly. "But Dev
and I, it's been just the two of us for so many holidays that the whole family thing . . . The whole *other
people's* family thing. Well." She paused, a pause I
feared would grow into another enigmatic and potentially multicentury silence but did not.

"Can I talk to Dev and let you know?"

Of course I said, "Of course."

I breathed an inaudible sigh of relief that Lake and I
had emerged from that moment intact, but I shouldn't
have. Because a few seconds later she sat there in front
of me and, with lightning speed and without moving a
muscle, flat-out disappeared.

Wait. That's not exactly what happened. It's important that I get this right.

Look, my first real conversation with Lake leaped and plunged and stalled and sneaked up on me as much as any first real conversation I've had in my conversational history, so I hope you'll see the sense in my zipping briefly into left field as I describe what happened next, the weird thing that happened to Lake's face, and will forgive whatever annoyance the zipping may cause. If you can't, well, you wouldn't be the first.

But, please, try this:

When my friend Linny decided to pursue photography with her whole, sweet, capacious, hard-beating heart rather than with half a heart, as her grandfather before her had done to his everlasting regret, this same grandfather, Poppy Phil, gave her a camera.

The camera was a stunner. I have loved many an inanimate object. I have a long history of coveting soup ladles, cloche hats, black 1950s desk telephones, bentwood rocking chairs, Macintosh computers, and every single art nouveau sign I have ever seen. I once almost stole a silver-and-glass spaceship-shaped tabletop cigarette lighter from my neighbor's apartment even though I don't smoke, and I have never glimpsed an Airstream trailer without getting a lump in my throat.

But I've always been a sucker for externals alone: the shape, the shine, what the surface suggests to my palm. So mechanically disinclined it's verging on criminal, I never understood the beauty of an object's workings until Linny sat my reluctant self down one day and showed me her camera. Within fifteen minutes, I had fallen hard for the whole gadgety, eyelike nature of the thing: a tiny piece of glass slowing, bending, organizing light—*light*—into your grandmother, the Grand Canyon, the begonia on the windowsill, the film keeping the image like a secret. Grandmother, canyon, begonia tucked neatly into the sleek black box, like bugs in a jar. My mind boggled.

But the part of the camera that made my heart sing the loudest, the niftiest of the nifty was the iris: the mechanism behind the lens that swivels open and swivels closed, or almost closed, to control the amount of light. Part whirlpool, part metal-petaled flower, blossoming, unblossoming.

After I said "Of course" to Lake, I said this: "Since you don't have family nearby, what made you decide to move here, if you don't mind my asking?" And like most people who end a question that way, I assumed Lake would *not* mind my asking. It seemed a natural question, after all.

Lake didn't shift her gaze or twitch a lip, and her eyebrows floated serenely above her eyes. Truly, her face changed in no nameable way, but—and I'm describing this as best I can—before the word "asking" was out of my mouth, Lake's mechanical iris whirled shut with a nearly audible *shoop,* leaving an aperture so narrow, nothing, not even light, could get through. She didn't shut down. She just shut. It was plain spooky.

When she answered my question, she was a woman speaking from behind a wall, and I knew as well as I knew anything that her answer was a lie.

"Steffi Levy, the principal at Dev's elementary school, a good friend to both of us, knew someone on the board of the charter school here, where Dev goes now. She helped him get in."

The lie came out whole but awkward, like a new shirt you wear without bothering to launder it first (Teo Sandoval has been known to do this), stiff and creased in all the wrong places. A rehearsed lie making its first public debut.

I can't stand lies. Probably no one can. Probably everyone is, to varying degrees, allergic to them, both spiritually and physically. Lies make me feel low and ignoble, and also itchy, like there's sand under my skin. The only thing that feels worse than hearing a lie is telling one. For a few seconds, I was too uncomfortable in my own skin to speak. I just sat there. Then Lake the shape-shifting woman shifted again.

"What about you, city girl?" she asked, affectionately, crinkling the corners of her eyes. "What made you leave the city? How'd you end up in this one-horse, three-mall, no-spaghetti-puttanesca-serving town?"

There were two possible answers to this question: one for strangers, one for friends. Lake sat smiling at me and lifting the brown Betty teapot, offering me more, but I could still envision the blades of the iris flashing closed and I could still feel the lie prickling along my arms, so I placed my hand over the mouth of my mug and said, "No thanks, I've had enough."

Then I told Lake, "Teo took a job at a hospital in Philly, and I'm applying to some schools in the opposite direction, so we picked a midway point." I shrugged an insouciant, brows-lifted, Holly Golightly shrug. "And here we are."

My voice was crystal clear and carried in it the suggestion of a laugh. I met Lake's flame-blue gaze as easily, as steadily as you please. But despite my belief in leaps of faith and even though I knew it would make me feel like a traitor and a thief, I handed her the stranger's answer, the one so partial you could never call it truth.

Eight

$\mathcal{P}$iper was reading to the kids when Elizabeth called. "I'm reading to the kids," Piper told Elizabeth, and instantly cringed at what she heard in her own voice: the snag in rhythm, the pause before the phrase "the kids." Piper blinked her eyes hard in a brief prayer that Elizabeth hadn't heard it, too. The pause had been tiny, heartbeat size, and Piper was pretty sure it hadn't been noticeable. But Elizabeth had been Piper's best friend for years; she was fine-tuned to notice the unnoticeable.

Carter and Emma had been born two weeks apart, and they'd been their separate names for perhaps the first two months. "Carter and Emma," Piper, Elizabeth, Kyle, and Tom would say, "Carter and Emma love the ceiling fan." "Carter and Emma hate the BabyBjörn." Very quickly, however, Carter and Emma became "the babies."

"Come see the babies." Elizabeth and Piper must have said those words or words like them to each other hundreds of times, so often that the moments blurred and were lost the way the ordinary always blurs and is lost. But recently Piper found herself recalling individual instances, holding each one vivid and sharp inside her head.

"You've gotta come see the babies." They were at Piper's house. The babies must have been about three months old. Piper remembered Elizabeth in a loose blue shirt, running in from the living room, her face dewy (the nursing months were particularly kind to Elizabeth's skin, both times) and awestruck, and she remembered how they'd knelt eagerly on the floor to look at the babies, who had fallen asleep, side by side under the arches of the baby gym.

Piper and Elizabeth looked at the babies' crescent eyes and newborn otherworldliness, smiles and frowns skimming over their sleeping features like the shadows of birds over the surface of a pond. Then they looked at each other and smiled, and Elizabeth said, "Can you believe how lucky we are?" And what Piper understood only in retrospect was that the luck they felt wasn't just at having such perfect children, but at having each other. It was one of the biggest things between them, to have been mothers together back when every little thing was a miracle.

Later, the babies became the kids and Meredith and Peter became the babies. Now, all four were "the kids," an umbrella of a phrase with the children tucked safely underneath it, and this was luck, too. "You are loved by your two parents," the phrase said, "And by two adults who are not your parents," and also, "You have each other." When Piper said, "I'm reading to the kids," Elizabeth knew, they all knew, that she didn't just mean Carter and Meredith.

But now the phrase wasn't natural. It was deliberate, a decision. Elizabeth would die soon, so the children weren't under one umbrella anymore; they didn't share the same luck. When Piper watched Emma and Peter playing—Emma lining up stuffed animals and dolls, making an audience, or Peter playing trucks in the cold yard, with his red cheeks and tiny fog of breath—for the first time ever, they looked lonely, set apart by everything they were about to lose.

"Can you get someone to watch them for a sec?" said Elizabeth. "I need to talk to you." The urgency charging her voice frightened Piper. Was this *it*? Would Elizabeth know if this was it?

As she had several times over the last few weeks, Piper thought about her friend Kate, who got blinding, nightmarish migraines, each of which was preceded by what Kate called an "aura." For five or ten minutes before the headache engulfed her, Kate was beset by feelings of panic and dizziness, colors got dimmer, silver zigzags like lightning bolts danced in her peripheral vision. Naturally Piper couldn't even think the word "aura" without wincing, but she wondered if death had an aura. Would Elizabeth get a warning? Would she feel death rolling toward her like a train or a storm?

"What's up?" Piper kept her voice steady, but fear knotted inside her chest, crowding out her lungs. She stood up and walked out of the room, away from the children. She stood at her front window, looking out, distracting herself, trying to place some distance between herself and whatever Elizabeth was about to say. Cornelia and Teo were in their front yard raking leaves, Teo with long, easy strokes, Cornelia with intensity and precision. *Short people always try too hard,* thought Piper.

"I sent Tom out on some errands," said Elizabeth. "I want to talk to you alone. Call Mrs. Finney to watch the kids."

Piper watched Cornelia shake her rake, frown, and

then carefully pick the remaining speared, intractable leaves off the tines and place them on the pile.

"Mrs. Finney's in Florida," Piper said, nervously. "Or New Mexico. I can't remember. Wherever her son Aaron lives now. Aaron, right? Or is it Adam? Phoenix, maybe. One of those hot, dry—"

"Piper!" Elizabeth's impatience made Piper's heart beat so fast she couldn't think. Her mouth formed the words "fine, fine, fine, fine."

"Betts," she whispered, "are you okay?"

Elizabeth groaned, a theatrical, exasperated groan, and Piper drew in a long, deep breath. A person wouldn't groan like that if she were about to die.

"I'm not dying, if that's what you're asking. Not right this second. But it's not like I have a lot of time to fool around."

"Okay, I'll call someone to watch the kids."

"Someone close."

"Cancer is making you bossy." Piper breathed and breathed. The breathing felt so good, she almost laughed out loud. "As your friend, I feel I should tell you that. I'll call Carrie."

"Who*ever,* Pipe. Tom won't *live* at the grocery store."

Piper hung up and leaned against the wall for a few seconds with her eyes closed, empty-headed, drinking in air. Then she called Carrie Lucas, who lived down the street. The answering machine came on, and Carrie's cheerful voice telling her exactly how to leave a message made Piper want to scream. *After the beep.* Really, Carrie? *After* the beep? Are you *sure*? With her thumb, Piper viciously mashed down the button on the phone without leaving a message, her whole body longing to slam a receiver. She seethed. "Why is every damn phone in this house *portable*?"

She glanced out the window again at Cornelia and Teo.

"Kids," she shouted, "I'm running across the street for two secs. I'll be right back."

Piper found Elizabeth in the kitchen. She was sitting in the armchair that Tom sometimes carried in from the dining room because the wooden kitchen chairs hurt Elizabeth's back. Piper searched Elizabeth's face and was relieved to find it free of the hard-etched lines and tightness that meant real pain. The anti-inflammatory drugs were working, then, all by themselves. They might not work forever. The doctor said Elizabeth would probably need opiates before long, but these were working for now, and, as Elizabeth said, "for now" was good enough for her. These days, it was even good enough for Piper.

In fact, Elizabeth looked better than pain free. Elizabeth looked like Elizabeth. All that urgency, and here she sat, inhabiting her body with certainty and calm.

"Do you remember when Tom and I trained for that half marathon? Back before Emma was born?"

Piper did remember. For six months, Elizabeth had lived in a world fitted out with PowerBars, designer water, wicking fabrics, neon running shoes, plastic watches, and its own peculiar vocabulary. Piper imagined that she felt like a person must feel whose best friend joins a cult or develops a recreational drug habit. You couldn't have paid Piper to become a runner, and she found most of the accoutrements highly distasteful (*plastic watches?*), but she felt left out all the same. Piper recalled a beach trip with Elizabeth, watching her sit in her beach chair with her smug brown calves and her *Runner's World* magazine and having a mad urge to yank the magazine away and pitch it into the sea.

Could Elizabeth have known how Piper felt? Was that what this conversation was about?

Piper nodded. "I remember how great your legs looked."

"Wrong," snapped Elizabeth, pointing at Piper. "You are so wrong. My legs looked *awesome*!"

"Okay," shrugged Piper, "I'll give you awesome."

Elizabeth grinned, a grin that slowly shifted into a smile with distance in it and something besides happiness. Not sadness, thought Piper, and she searched her mind for the word.

"Tom and I would stretch together and plan out our route, talk about whether we were up for hills that day or whatever."

Wistful, thought Piper, surprising herself. Now, where did that come from? Piper knew for a fact that she had never spoken the word "wistful" in her life. But there it was: Elizabeth's smile was wistful.

"And sometimes, while we were running, Tom would drop back to watch me and then catch up and say something like, 'I thought your stride was looking a little short. Your hamstrings tight?' I loved that."

"You did?" asked Piper.

"Yes. I did. It's hard to explain why." She paused. "The running just *belonged* to us. We were in it together. And we were equals."

"Oh," said Piper, and Elizabeth must have heard the boredom in her voice because she darted her a look.

"No, not like that. I'm not talking about *feminism,* Piper. We were just . . ." She hooked her forefingers together emphatically.

"We were closer than we'd ever been." She paused. "And I knew it. I didn't just realize it afterward. I got to know it while it was happening, which doesn't always happen."

"Well, great," said Piper brightly, "that's super."

Elizabeth continued, "What I didn't know was that it was the closest we would ever be."

"What?" There was nothing wrong with Elizabeth's marriage. It was as solid a marriage as anyone's, for God's sake, as solid as Piper's own.

"That's crazy, Betts. You and Tom are fine. You have two beautiful children and a beautiful home. You and Tom are happy!" Piper heard the anger in her own voice.

Elizabeth sat up in the armchair and, with her hands on her knees, leaned toward Piper. "Here's what I need to tell you: two weeks before I got diagnosed, I asked Tom to move out."

Almost before Elizabeth had gotten those words out, Piper was saying, flatly, "I do not believe that."

"I wasn't in love with him anymore."

"Oh, give me a break, Elizabeth. People say that all the time. In love. Not in love. We're not teenagers, in case you haven't noticed. We have *lives*."

"We used to be in love," Elizabeth insisted. "When we were training for that race, we'd come home from a run totally exhausted, but we were pulling off each other's clothes before we were even through the door."

In a flash, Piper had a sense memory: yanking a shirt over someone's head, sticky skin, the taste of salt. "Oh, that's what you're talking about. That's not love," Piper pointed out, coolly. "We've all done that, but that is not love."

In fact, Piper and Kyle had never pulled off each other's clothes before they'd gotten through the door. She thought about Kyle's hand on her lower back, under her shirt, the way he'd slip his fingers just a few inches inside the waistband of her pants. Or the way she'd come up behind him and rub his shoulders. Although they hadn't used them lately, Kyle and Piper had signals, which was just the way they liked it. Piper believed signals were civilized and a sign of mutual respect.

Elizabeth sighed. "Piper, I'm trying to tell you something about me and Tom. I need you to listen."

"Okay."

But Elizabeth didn't speak for what felt like a long time. Then she said, "I never ran that race. Remember? I found out I was pregnant with Emma, and we decided it wasn't good for the baby. And then we had Emma, and nothing was the same."

"Children don't ruin marriages," Piper pointed out, firmly. Elizabeth did not seem to hear her.

"We fell into these roles, Tom and I. He went to work. I took care of the baby. We became—a household. Do you know what I mean?"

Piper just nodded. Of course she knew what Elizabeth meant. What she didn't understand was why that was anything to be unhappy about. Roles were natural in a family, essential. There was nothing wrong with a household. Wrong? When done right—a well-constructed schedule, flowers on the table, fun built into every day, the proper division of labor—a household was like that domed thing in Arizona. A biosphere. A small and perfect world.

"Which I guess could have been okay, except that I was mad at him about it." And then Elizabeth began to list the reasons she was mad, and Piper didn't exactly tune out, but she didn't need to be fully tuned in either because the list was the same as everyone's list. Piper and every one of Piper's friends had the same complaints; their voices bristled with the same indignation. He never gets up in the middle of the night. He goes on a trip and brings the two-year-old a football and the four-year-old an Elmo. He can't pack a baby bag to save his life. He fails to pare and slice the children's apples. He fails to cut the itchy tags out of the children's clothes. Who hadn't had that conversation a hundred times? It was a real conversation every time, too, but nothing changed. Change wasn't the point. The point was to recite the litany and feel better afterward. Everyone knew that, including Elizabeth.

Suddenly Piper said, "You're not telling me the real reason you threw him out."

Elizabeth looked startled, then she blushed. *Uh-oh,* thought Piper.

"No. I'm not." She blushed more. Elizabeth was not usually a blusher; Piper had always envied this.

"I met someone," Elizabeth blurted out.

Piper recoiled, and before she could stop it, she was hearing her mother's voice, brassy and triumphant, her mother telling her father, "I met someone. Someone who makes me feel alive." Trite, stupid, selfish words. *Oh, no,* thought Piper, *not Elizabeth. Anyone else, but I need to keep Elizabeth.*

"Don't look like that," said Elizabeth, her face still dark pink. "I didn't sleep with him."

"Oh, thank God." Piper's eyes were stinging.

"I met him at yoga," said Elizabeth. "And we had coffee a couple times a week. First at this little funky, awful coffee place for art kids, and then at his house. He was divorced."

"You went to his house? When you were supposed to be at yoga?" *Yoga,* thought Piper. *What kind of man goes to yoga?*

"We kissed exactly four times," said Elizabeth, and in spite of all the blushing, the happiness in her voice was unmistakable. "He had this little wrought-iron table in his kitchen, and we held hands across it all the time."

Then she laughed. "But it was *hot* hand-holding."

"Elizabeth!" But Piper found that she was laughing, too. Four kisses and hand-holding. Piper wanted with her whole soul to hang on to Elizabeth until time ran out. She could laugh about four kisses and hand-holding.

When their laughter ended, Piper said, "So you were going to leave Tom for hand-holding man?"

"Mike," corrected Elizabeth.

"Mike?" The name was all wrong. Once Elizabeth had shown Piper some yoga poses. What business did a guy named Mike have doing downward dog in those loose black pants and, what? A tank top? Piper gave an involuntary shudder.

"I wasn't in love with Mike," sighed Elizabeth, "but Mike reminded me to want to be in love. He reminded me that passion is one of the necessities of life."

With difficulty, Piper repressed a snort of disgust. Passion. A word from a romance novel. Swarthy men. Corseted women with rivers of blond hair and high, heaving breasts, round and white like softballs. No one had breasts like that.

"I disagree," said Piper. "Of course, you're entitled to your opinion, but passion is sloppy and over the top and immature, and, anyway, it doesn't last. You don't build a life on it. Passion makes people lose their heads." Piper's own mother, for example, had lost her head and left her sweet, hardworking husband alone in his big house with his kids.

"But everyone deserves that! I wanted to lose my head at least a little every day." Elizabeth closed her eyes and hugged herself with her own arms. "I don't regret wanting that. But I regret how I did it. I didn't tell

Tom about Mike. I blamed him for everything. I told him he was selfish and a workaholic. I accused him of neglect. I remember screaming that word at him, and that's the worst thing anyone can say to Tom."

"What happened after that?"

"He got mad. Then he got sad. He begged me to go to counseling with him, but I said it was way too late for that. Maybe it wasn't, but it's like once I decided to divorce Tom, I got so energized by the idea of a new life that I forgot everything else."

"I can't imagine being divorced," said Piper, keeping her voice as nonjudgmental as possible. In truth, she wasn't feeling judgmental, not at that particular moment. It was a simple statement of fact. "Think about Jilly Keyes."

Three years ago, Jilly's husband, Chad, had taken her to Melt, the upscale fondue restaurant in town, in order to break the news that he'd been transferred to Switzerland, and that it was nothing personal, but he believed the transfer was a sign that their marriage was over. It was an opportunity, he'd reportedly told her, a challenge to start fresh in a new country, and he had to rise to that challenge. He owed it to himself.

Although Piper had received the story third- or fourth-hand, she knew precisely what his voice had sounded like when he'd dropped this bombshell: pompous, exuberant. *A challenge,* as though leaving his marriage made him Christopher Columbus or that rich guy who kept trying to circle the globe in a goddamn balloon. Chad Keyes was a grade-A ass. A fondue restaurant? A restaurant, any restaurant, was a hideous breakup venue. But *fondue*? Imagine life as you know it ending over a pot of liquid cheese.

Outraged, Piper and Elizabeth and their whole set

had rallied around Jilly and her three truculent children. They'd helped with carpooling, babysitting. Kate invited her to her annual holiday party; Piper treated her to a day at Paradise Found, the whole package minus the seaweed wrap, which they all agreed was a waste of money. But after the first few months, the flow of invitations began to dwindle and, in time, stopped altogether. Jilly became a kindergarten teacher at one of the local private schools (not, thank God, Tallyrand), a shocking decision of which no one approved. How awkward, to attend parent/teacher conferences with a woman you used to have dinner with, sitting across the low classroom table from Jilly, who'd begun wearing ethnic jewelry and purple wool-felt clogs.

The truth was that there was no room in Piper's world for a divorced mother. Parties, cookouts, dinner dates, trips to people's vacation homes in Stone Harbor or Rehoboth: to participate, you had to be married, preferably with children. One or two married couples without children hung on to the edge of the social circle by the skin of their teeth. But a divorced woman? Piper could imagine becoming a divorced woman about as much as she could imagine becoming a tightrope walker for Barnum & Bailey.

"That's just it," said Elizabeth. "I didn't think about Jilly. I only thought, 'I want out.'"

"And then?"

"And then I finally went in to have those symptoms checked out, and then I got diagnosed. It didn't seem like the time to divorce my husband." Elizabeth gave a bitter little laugh. "I thought I'd get better and then we'd do it later. But if I was going to be sick for a while, Emma and Peter needed a stable home with their dad in it."

A Christmas cactus sat in the center of Elizabeth's kitchen table, and Piper began to fiddle with it, pinching off spent blossoms, moving the cactus fronds around. *This Christmas cactus is blooming too early,* Piper thought, scornfully, *and a Christmas cactus is not a centerpiece plant.* Paperwhites, yes. Amaryllis, yes. Christmas cactus, no.

"I think Ginny put this plant here. It's the wrong place for it."

Elizabeth took one of Piper's hands, lifted it off the plant, and held it. "I didn't tell you because I thought you would try to talk me out of it," she said gently. "I'm sorry."

Piper didn't meet Elizabeth's eyes, but she nodded and squeezed her hand.

"But I'm telling you now because I'm afraid for Tom, and I'm afraid for the kids."

"Why?"

"He hasn't been doing well; you've probably noticed that. And today he broke down, just—broke. Fell apart. He said he couldn't stand it that he'd ruined my life by being such a terrible husband. He even said that maybe if he'd been better and I'd been happier, I would not have gotten sick."

"That's ridiculous," scoffed Piper. "Unhappiness doesn't cause cancer."

"No. And I don't think he really believes that. What's killing him is the idea that I will die unhappy, in a miserable marriage. He hates that my life isn't ending on a good note." Until Elizabeth covered her face with her hands, Piper had not noticed that she'd started to cry. "So I told him that he's a good man and was the love of my life, both of which are true. I tried to tell him all the things I hadn't told him before. How it was both our faults, how I'd taken over with the kids and not let the two of us be in that together. Mostly, I wanted him to understand the real reason I'd thought our marriage was over. It was over because we forgot to stay in love. Both of us."

Elizabeth leaned back, exhausted. When she spoke again, her voice was hollow and sad.

"I told him all that, but when I'm gone, I'm so afraid he's going to let guilt eat him up. It's bad enough now, but when I die . . . A man drowning in guilt and hating himself is not going to be a good father for Emma and Peter. They need to feel like they're allowed to be happy. I want him to set that example for them."

Elizabeth looked hard at Piper. "So keep it. That information about Mike. I didn't tell him that. But you keep it. And if you need to use it, even if you need to . . . embellish it, do it. Add sex. Add orgies. Whatever it takes to make him understand it was my fault, too. Promise."

"I promise," said Piper, so adamant she was almost severe, "I'll help him. You stop worrying about that, now, okay? I'll take care of everything."

No one said anything. Then Elizabeth smiled a smile that was like a plant opening in the sun. "Good." She snapped her fingers in the air. "Now, put on my James Taylor and get those children over here."

"I'll be right back."

"Wait," said Elizabeth, her eyes full of mischief. "Call Cornelia and Teo. Ask if they'll walk the kids over themselves."

"You're kidding, right?"

"I want to meet the new neighbors." She grinned. "And I want them to meet me. I don't want to be the mystery cancer victim down the road."

"Ha!" Piper eyed Elizabeth. "I know you, lady, and you want to flirt with that Dr. Sandoval."

"While I still can," sang out Elizabeth, and she laughed. "While I still have breath in my body!"

Ten minutes later, as she sat in Elizabeth's kitchen with her neighbors, hearing the children play in the sunroom and James Taylor sing a lullaby to himself, Piper discovered that she did not dislike Cornelia Brown. She knew that the feeling, or lack of feeling, might not last and half hoped that it wouldn't, but for the moment, there it was, a smoothness across her forehead, a loosening in the place where her lower jaw met her ear.

From the moment that Elizabeth had become more or less homebound, Piper had kept a mental list of all of Elizabeth's visitors, and before long, the mental list had grown into a kind of detailed catalog, an internal spreadsheet documenting the behavior of each visitor: what they brought, how frequently they came, how long they stayed, and, above all, how they behaved toward Elizabeth. Some of the information in the spreadsheet came from Elizabeth herself because Elizabeth had not morphed into a sugary, pure-souled cancer patient like the ones on television. She wasn't above dissecting and dishing about her visitors with Piper, a fact that made Piper want to fall down on her knees with gratitude.

For Elizabeth's part, the laughing, imitating, and eye rolling that accompanied this dishing was good natured. But Piper was on the job. She was eagle-eyed and keeping watch, and there was nothing amusing about the information she was storing up. There would be a day of reckoning. Piper had no sense of when the day would be or what would happen on it, and the phrase "day of reckoning" almost certainly did not exist in her personal lexicon, but she knew that there would be one, and you could see the knowledge enter her gaze and her posture whenever someone crossed the threshold of Elizabeth's house. The day of reckoning would come, and when it did, Piper would be ready.

There were many wrong and unforgivable ways to approach Elizabeth. Tentatively, as though she had a bomb strapped to her body. Loudly, with a pasted-on, cheek-splitting smile. Tearfully. Patronizingly. Megan had failed to make eye contact and had addressed all of her remarks to Piper. Liddy, who hardly knew Elizabeth, had immediately taken her hand and held it for the duration of the visit. Allie had stayed, literally, two minutes, shifting her weight from foot to foot, like a kid in the principal's office. Parvee had wept out loud. Tom's work colleague Roland had spent ten minutes recalling how good looking Elizabeth used to be, what a "slammin' bod" she'd had, and smiling a sharky smile that made Piper want to knee him in the groin.

A few visitors had been fine, relaxed and blessedly ordinary. And Kate, ditzy, dismissible Kate, was perfect every time. She'd waft in on a cloud of breezy goofiness, bearing wonderful gifts: the latest *Us* and *People,* a box of Hostess Twinkies, a manicure kit with the season's new OPI colors, or a rumor that the Hollanders and the Tifts had engaged in wife swapping the previous weekend ("Digital videos! They say there are digital videos! How hysterical is that? *Digital?*"). If it were up to Piper, and Piper believed it might be, Kate's place in heaven was a done deal.

So when Cornelia walked through Elizabeth's kitchen door, Piper sat serenely in her powder blue sweater and jeans, one toffee-colored loafer crossed over the other, but inside, she was all watchdog, ears pricked, nose in the air, a ridge of hair rising along her back.

Cornelia had Peter in her arms.

She walked over to Elizabeth, smiled an undeniably true smile at her, and said, "Emma laid down the law, I promise you that. She told me in no uncertain terms that never, under any circumstances, is Peter to be carried. Absolutely, positively not."

Elizabeth smiled back and said, "And yet."

"He climbed me like a tree frog and gave me this sweet, hopeful look."

"Oh, yes. I know that look."

"So you know my hands were tied."

Elizabeth laughed. Then she reached out and gave one of Peter's sneakers a tug. "Okay, tree frog of mine, give this poor, manipulated woman a break."

"First things first," said Cornelia to Peter, and she placed a kiss on his temple, then set him down. *That's a woman who wants a baby,* thought Piper. Cornelia turned to face Elizabeth again and held out her hand.

"Cornelia Brown."

"Elizabeth Donahue." Piper watched Elizabeth squeeze Cornelia's hand, then glance over Cornelia's shoulder. "And where is that famous husband of yours?"

Cornelia groaned. "The story of my life. The most camera-shy man on the planet and *he* gets to be the celebrity." She turned and squinted out the window. "Teo appears to have gotten no farther than your yard, where he is right this second turning Emma, Carter, and Meredith into wild beasts, I'm sorry to report. He has that effect on children." She walked to the window, rapped on it, then shook her finger at Teo.

"He seems to have had that effect on some of our female friends as well," said Elizabeth archly.

Piper eyed Cornelia. She knew Elizabeth was watching, too. They both made emphatic fun of the jealous wives they knew, so they were a little disappointed when Cornelia turned back to Elizabeth with twinkling eyes.

"Ooh, be sure to tell him that," she said, evilly. "He'll turn eleven shades of red and then die of embarrassment." Piper noted with grudging approval that Cornelia didn't flinch, the way some people did after saying the word "die" in front of Elizabeth. On her last (and, if Piper had her way, final) visit, Connie Abernathy had actually apologized for the phrase "drop-dead gorgeous."

Elizabeth narrowed her eyes at Cornelia and asked, "So tell me, what do you think of James Taylor?"

Cornelia winced, just a little, but before she could answer, Teo fell through the kitchen door, children all over him. He was flushed and there were leaves in his hair. Piper shot Elizabeth a glance, but Elizabeth was clapping her hands in the air like a flamenco dancer.

"Kids!" she shouted. "Begone! Playroom! Pronto!"

When Piper returned from settling the kids in front of a Dora the Explorer video, Cornelia and Teo were seated at the table. Teo was pouring San Pellegrino, and the green glass of the bottle in his hand made Piper notice his sea glass green eyes. She wondered if Elizabeth noticed, too. Then Piper saw the glass in Teo's hand. Granny Bebe's Waterford. Elizabeth didn't allow most people to *breathe* in the direction of Granny Bebe's Waterford. *You'd give a handsome man the shirt off your back,* thought Piper, and the thought made her giggle.

"What?" said Elizabeth, turning around. She widened her eyes at Piper for a split second, a signal that meant "He's amazing."

"Nothing."

"Okay, Cornelia," said Elizabeth, whacking the arm of her chair, "no weaseling out. What's your position on James Taylor?"

Cornelia bit her bottom lip. "Honestly?"

"Oh, yes," said Elizabeth. "Honesty is a must."

"Honestly, I'm not a fan."

"Did you hear that, Pipe? Cornelia's not a James fan!"

"Well, who is, Elizabeth?" And before Piper knew what she was doing, she smiled at Cornelia, a natural, guileless, unsardonic smile, and that's when it hit her that she didn't dislike her. *Well,* she thought, startled. *Well. It doesn't mean I like her, either.*

"Except," said Cornelia.

"Except what?" asked Elizabeth.

"There's one song. About North Carolina. I like it."

Elizabeth turned to Piper with a triumphant "Ha!"

"It's like 'The Lake Isle of Innisfree.' Or Wordsworth's field of daffodils. Or, oh, you know, Frost's birch trees. In the same family as those poems. 'I'd like to get away from earth awhile.' All that stuff."

Here we go, thought Piper with disgust. Wordsworth's daffodils? What the hell was she talking about? Then she saw Teo looking at her and she blushed, hoping her thoughts hadn't shown up on her face.

They must have, though, because suddenly Teo was grinning at Piper and saying, "She can't help it. It's like a mild form of Tourette's."

Amazingly, Cornelia didn't get angry or embarrassed. She laughed. "All right, all right. You know what I mean. It's a song about keeping a place in your mind that you can get away to."

"I do," said Elizabeth, quietly, "I know exactly what you mean."

In the stillness that followed this remark, Piper waited.

Cornelia looked straight at Elizabeth with frank compassion in her eyes. "I bet," she said, and her tone wasn't pitying or sentimental. It was a tone with which even Piper could not find fault. So maybe Cornelia could do that, then, strike the right note. Maybe she could fill a moment without making it spill over. Piper would not have thought so, but there it was: a good moment. Still, after a few seconds, Piper had to end it. It needed to end.

"Hey, Betts," she called out, "know what *I* bet? I bet Cornelia was a Talking Heads girl."

"Cornelia, were you a Talking Heads girl? In college?" demanded Elizabeth.

"Um," said Cornelia.

Teo laughed. "It's a band."

"I *know* it's a band!"

"My wife was not a Talking Heads girl," said Teo, talking to Piper and Elizabeth, but looking at Cornelia. A little shiver went through Piper. *There it is,* she thought. His eyes when he looked at his wife, his voice when he said "my wife." The thing Elizabeth wanted to leave Tom to go find. "My wife has been a walking anachronism for years. Decades. Since she could walk."

"The guy," Cornelia continued, "with the Laurence Olivier eyes!"

Elizabeth burst out laughing.

"Oh, yeah, that's him," said Teo, dryly. "Who were you listening to in college, Cornelia? Chet Baker, wasn't it?"

Piper hadn't seen Elizabeth laugh so freely in months.

"And the big suit!" cried Cornelia. "The *enormous* suit." With both hands, she traced the shoulders of the enormous suit in the air.

"No, wait, Chet Baker was high school. I remember the poster on your wall. College was . . . Who was college?"

"College was a lot of people, a lot of—bands. I liked Elvis Costello, remember that?"

"Yeah, yeah. You might have liked Elvis Costello. That sounds like you, sort of. All that wordplay and cleverness. But you *loved* . . ."

Cornelia dropped her hands in defeat and sighed, "I loved Hoagy Carmichael."

"Oh, that's impossible," gasped Elizabeth, mid-laugh. She reached over and squeezed Cornelia's hand. "Hoagy Carmichael," she exclaimed, happily. "I don't even know what that is!"

Here was Elizabeth, flirting with all of them, making new friends as if she had all the time in the world. Piper wasn't jealous. Faintly, from the playroom, she heard the kids shouting along with Dora, *"Y vámonos!"* Let's go. Piper touched her hand to her mouth. For the second time in twenty minutes, she caught herself smiling without meaning to smile.

The next morning, Monday morning, Piper woke up early to fry eggs and bacon for her husband, a task she performed infrequently even in the best of times. She hated the way grease lay like a mask on her face, the way her hair kept the odor of bacon for hours. As she'd known it would be, this morning's frying was more unpleasant than ever. Now the hissing and spitting, the white-and-yellow egg floating on top of the oil set her nerves on edge. But when she placed the plate of food in front of Kyle, she felt a little of her worry, a tiny corner of it, dissolve. There. She was doing it. She was paying attention to her husband. Before she walked away, she kissed the top of his head.

Later, after the kids were at school, Piper sat on the love seat in her living room with her book club's latest selection open on her lap. It was a book about a small town on the plains of Colorado. She hadn't attended a book club meeting in months and knew that she would not attend the next one, but she liked the book, even though it was not the sort of book she usually liked. When she read it, without knowing exactly why, she felt quiet and clean. It was a life she would never have and had never wanted: working all day under the sky with your muscles straining and the wind chapping your skin. Now, though, it seemed like something to regret, not living that life. Just then, Piper thought that life seemed like the right kind of loneliness.

Piper jumped at the sound of the doorbell, then closed the book and slid it under a cushion, embarrassed to be reading away the morning. She wriggled her feet back into her loafers, then went to open the door.

Cornelia stood on Piper's front porch with a sippy cup in her hand and outrageously bright running shoes on her feet. Other than the shoes, though, she looked fairly normal in her jeans and black Patagonia fleece. In fact, standing there in the sun with her big eyes and small, finely cut face, Cornelia was pretty. Piper could give her pretty. The hair was a disaster, of course, a train wreck, but if Cornelia grew it out, she might even verge on very pretty.

Cornelia smiled and held up the sippy cup. "My mother's rule is that if someone leaves a container, you must return it full. But I was pretty sure we didn't have the right kind of milk."

Cornelia's friendliness threw Piper off and she felt suddenly shy and stiff, unsure of how to behave, a feeling that she knew was familiar but couldn't place for a second. Then it came to her: she felt like she sometimes used to feel the morning after falling into bed with a stranger. Oh, God, what a stupid, ridiculous idea.

"Oh," she said briskly, taking the cup. "Well, you do whole before age one and then switch to two percent. After two, kids can get plaques."

"Really. On their teeth?"

"Arteries," said Piper.

"I see," said Cornelia, and she stared blankly at Piper for a moment, then said, "Okay, then. I'll see you later."

"Thanks for the cup," said Piper, and then, as Cornelia started to walk down the steps, she added, "My mother had that rule, too."

Cornelia turned around.

"I mean, she had it for a while, before she left my dad and ran off with a guy she met at the farmers' market."

Piper's whole body went rigid; she felt like she'd been struck by lightning. Had she really just said that? Out loud, to a woman she didn't even like?

"I'm . . . I." Piper cleared her throat. "What an inappropriate thing to say. Please forget I said it."

Cornelia looked puzzled, then she said, "Okay. Forgotten." She paused. "Do you want to go for a walk?"

It wasn't bad. It was easier than Piper thought it would be. They walked through the neighborhood and then a little way into the park across from the neighborhood. The sky was beautiful between the trees, like scraps of blue silk caught in the nearly bare branches, and Cornelia didn't mention Piper's mother and the farmers'-market man once. They made small talk, and Piper excelled at small talk. She felt at home talking small talk, and if she also felt a bit let down, she didn't think about it.

Then she said, "It seems like you enjoyed New York City. What brought you guys here?"

It was an easy enough question, and Cornelia answered it easily, almost automatically, "Teo took the job."

"In Philadelphia," finished Piper.

"Right," and then Cornelia didn't stop walking or slow down or stumble, but something shifted in her shoulders or the angle of her body, a tension entered her stride, and she said, "I wasn't getting pregnant."

"Oh, okay," said Piper, in a tone of voice that implied she knew exactly what Cornelia was talking about. And she did. She'd certainly had her share of friends who'd struggled with infertility. Then she had a thought. "But you were in New York. There must be good specialists in New York."

"There are." Cornelia kept walking, her eyes focused on the path in front of her. Then she stopped walking. "I wasn't getting pregnant because I kept going back on the pill."

She looked at Piper, wide-eyed, as though she'd been startled, then bent down to pick up a stick shaped like a divining rod. "I can't believe I just told you that," she said, quietly.

"I had a miscarriage," Cornelia continued. Her mouth turned down at the corners after she said this, and Piper looked at the ground, not ready to see this woman cry, but when Cornelia spoke again, her voice was steady. "In the fourteenth week."

"I'm sorry," said Piper. Motherhood was her territory. Her compassion was real, but Cornelia seemed not to have heard her.

"And then the day after that, the towers came down." Cornelia tossed the divining rod into the woods and started walking again.

"God," said Piper.

"It's not a terrible story," said Cornelia, quickly. "It's nothing compared to most of the stories. Teo worked uptown, on the Upper East Side, and we'd just found an apartment near there, but we still lived in Brooklyn. It's ridiculous to live in Brooklyn and work uptown, I know, but Teo's great-aunt left him the apartment when she died."

Piper tried and failed to picture a map of New York in her head. Brooklyn? The place with the brownstones. Was it down at the bottom of the map?

"Was Teo working?"

"He was giving a lecture at a hospital downtown."

"Oh, no."

"No, no, I knew he was okay. I don't watch a lot of TV, but a neighbor came by to tell me what was happening, and right after that the phone rang, and it was Teo. This isn't about my thinking I'd lost him. This isn't anywhere close to the category of tragedy. He was fine. He walked home. Like everybody else."

Cornelia slowed down. She turned her face to Piper and her eyes were frightened looking and her voice was small and hollow. "But his face. He didn't come inside right away. He leaned against the doorjamb, his whole body leaned. I've known him since I was four years old. But his face was so old and tired, it seemed to belong to someone else. My husband's face, with no light in it." She paused, then said, "We rallied, like everyone else. We moved to our new apartment, but the miscarriage and that awful day and his face that I couldn't get out of my head . . ."

Cornelia laughed a stinging laugh. "I've always been kind of a coward, if you want to know the truth. But I wasn't exactly scared. I just wanted to be someplace else, someplace—boring, I guess."

"Well, of course you did," said Piper, and she touched Cornelia's arm at the elbow, just took hold of her fleece for two seconds then let go, but suddenly everything felt like too much.

"Who could raise children in the city anyway?" Piper scoffed. "There should be a law against it."

Cornelia sighed and gave Piper a weary smile that Piper had seen on other faces, too, her mother's, Kyle's, even Elizabeth's, one that said "Just when I thought we were getting somewhere." The smile hurt. Piper cocked her head and frowned thoughtfully at Cornelia.

"Not to change the subject, but have you ever thought of growing your hair? Maybe a little bob?" After Piper said this, she felt much better.

NINE

> No, this trick won't work . . . How on earth are you
> ever going to explain in terms of chemistry and
> physics so important a biological phenomenon as
> first love?
>
> —ALBERT EINSTEIN

Generally speaking, Dev wasn't all that interested
in the notion of time travel. Sure, he'd watched reruns
of the PBS special, had read a little about wormholes,
Hawking's chronology-projection conjecture, the grandfather paradox, all that stuff, but, while it was interesting enough and even though he got the idea that it was
supposed to, it just didn't set Dev's brain on fire. Even
so, during that bad seventh-grade year at his old school,
Dev had definitely fantasized about time travel: zinging
Mr. Tripp right between the eyes with one last, devastat-
ing, mind-warping remark, then—wham—disappearing, zipping forward into a future where he discovers a
cure for Mr. Tripp's fatal disease just in time to save the
man's crummy little life.

But even as the fantasy played itself out in Dev's

head—Dev tall and solemn in a white coat, empty-
ing a syringe into Mr. Tripp's shriveled, almost-dead
arm, Mr. Tripp simultaneously thanking him and beg-
ging for forgiveness with tears pouring down his face,
Dev saying simply, quietly, "I'm just doing my job, Mr.
Tripp"—Dev had been 99.9 percent certain that it could
never happen. He didn't absolutely rule it out, but if
traveling forward in time meant moving faster than—
or even almost as fast as the speed of light and Dev
was pretty sure that it would have to mean this—then,
nope. No way—670,000,000 miles an hour? Nothing,
no *matter,* no matter what, could move that fast.

Sometimes, though, Dev got the weird, fantastic
feeling that he *had* leaped ahead. He'd sit in his ninth-
grade life in a new school, a new town, and feel a whole
country's worth of distance stretch out between himself and his old life, and suddenly seventh grade would
seem like ancient, ancient history, a hazy splotch on
another coast, in another time zone, and he'd imagine
eighth grade, the year that had never happened—and
it would've been a crap year, he knew that—slipping
through a hole in time, spinning downward, vanishing.

No way would he go back. Einstein himself could time-
travel into Dev's room and offer him a million bucks and
the Nobel Prize to wiggle through a wormhole with him
back to Dev's seventh-grade year, and Dev would say
(very, very respectfully), "Thanks, but no thanks."

Still, with three months of his new life under his belt
(and those three months had gone by at least twice as
fast as they would have if he'd stayed in California: relativity in action), Dev could see that there had been one
advantage to the old life: invisibility. Once the other
kids had stopped buzzing about his confrontation with
Mr. Tripp, once Dev had clamped his mouth firmly

shut, it was like the atoms of his body had transformed into a substance that failed to reflect light in the visible spectrum. Like light waves traveled right through him. He'd become invisible, a nobody.

Dev was somebody at Liberty Charter. He wasn't a somebody with a capital *S* like Aidan, but he was a kid people knew, a kid people greeted with grins and fist bumps, or said "Sorry, man" or "My bad" to when they jostled him accidentally in the hallway. People laughed at his jokes, listened to him when he talked, asked him what he'd gotten on tests (then usually groaned or said something like "You *suck*" in a friendly way once he'd told them).

And Dev liked it. He liked being visible. For the most part, visibility beat invisibility, *crushed* invisibility any day of the week. What Dev figured out before long, though, was that when you were visible, people didn't just talk to you, they also talked *about* you, and this was the downside, the part Dev could definitely do without. Even though no one said anything truly bad about Dev, he disliked being gossiped about. It embarrassed him.

Far worse than the embarrassment, though, was the inaccuracy. In ninth grade at Liberty Charter, Dev discovered that once a story got told enough, the story became the truth no matter how much you tried to set the record straight, and this made Dev crazy. For Dev, records needed to be straight. Facts needed to be provable. Truth needed to be true.

And the true truth was that Lyssa Sorenson was *not* his girlfriend. She couldn't even accurately be called his friend. But Dev could have shouted himself hoarse pointing this out to people and no one would have believed him, no one but Aidan. In fact, as far as the kids

at Charter were concerned, the more Dev told them that
Lyssa wasn't his girlfriend, the more they were certain
that she was, and what kind of sense did that make?

She sat next to him in advanced biology. At first she
sat there because Dr. Kimani had seated them alpha-
betically for a few weeks in order to learn their names.
After that, she stayed there for reasons Dev could only
guess at but that he thought had almost nothing to do
with Lyssa's liking him—it wasn't clear that she did
like him—and everything to do with her trusting him.
Or at least with her not trusting anyone else in the class.
Lyssa had a secret, Dev knew the secret, Lyssa knew
he knew, and she was counting on him to keep it to
himself. She had no guarantee that he would, of course,
because she'd never talked to him about the secret, not
even once, not even to laugh it off or explain it away,
and people leaked other people's secrets all the time,
but in this case, Lyssa got lucky. She got seated next to
the right boy.

They didn't sit at desks, but at short tables, just long
enough for two people, barely long enough, in fact. Despite being so close, it took Dev a full week to notice,
even though he was a noticing kind of guy. Lyssa was
that deft, that quick and subtle.

There were three rituals. Dev assumed that there
were probably a lot more, outside in the world, and this
thought made him feel heavy, waterlogged with compassion, so he tried not to think it. But inside the classroom, there were three: one for sitting down, one for
getting up to go someplace else in the room, one for
getting up to leave. Each ritual began with Lyssa stack-
ing her book, binder, and spiral notebook precisely in
front of her, the edges of the books parallel to the edge
of the desk. Then she'd perform whatever combination

of finger taps, nose touches, tiny shrugs, and sounds the situation required. The getting-up-to-go-someplace-else-in-the-room ritual was the shortest, the getting-up-to-leave ritual the longest and most complex.

Once Dev began noticing what she was doing, he would take enormous care not to watch her. He'd read or study his notes or talk to Eli Tran, who sat at the table next to theirs. But one day, while he was writing, his pencil broke, just snapped in half, which didn't happen every day, and, without thinking, he turned to ask Lyssa if she'd ever seen a pencil break like that, right in the middle of ordinary pencil usage, and there she was, her index finger touching her nose, and even when their eyes met, she didn't stop, didn't miss a beat: two lifts of her thin shoulders followed by four book taps followed by a whisper-soft clearing of her throat.

What was strange was that even though Dev's automatic response was to whip around, look anywhere else, he didn't. His brain was screeching, "Look away, you moron," but his eyes couldn't obey. He was like a deer in headlights, frozen by her gaze, although that wasn't quite right because she was the one who looked scared, terrified even, but he also understood that she wanted him to see her. He had no idea why she'd want that, but whatever she was afraid of, Dev knew it wasn't him.

So when they were finally allowed to sit wherever they chose, Dev and Lyssa stayed where they were. And when it was time to pick a lab partner, all she had to do was glance at Dev, and before anyone else could speak (because there was always the chance someone else would pick him, since he was pretty excellent at biology), he shot up his hand and said, "I pick Lyssa."

After all that, it probably should not have surprised

Dev when people began teasing him about Lyssa being his girlfriend, but it did surprise him. It bugged him, too.

"I never even thought about her like that," he'd protested to Aidan, "not for one nanosecond."

"That's good," said Aidan, "because that girl is ten kinds of crazy."

Dev had shot Aidan a look. "What do you mean?"

"I mean that you can see every bone in her body *through* her clothes, and she's got fuzz growing all over her, like a freaking peach, and no girl is that skinny without being crazy." Then he added, "Plus, she's a ballet dancer. Does it every single day after school is what I heard. And ballet dancers are all psycho."

"What do you know about ballet dancers?" scoffed Dev.

"It's a well-known fact. All women are clinically insane, but especially ballet dancers. Psycho. Extremely psycho. Trust me."

Given Dev's inside information about Lyssa, he wasn't exactly in a position to argue this point. No one could call Lyssa's rituals a sign of good mental health. Sometimes, she would start a ritual over two or three times, making herself get the sequence exactly right before she allowed herself to open her book or get up or whatever. And once, when they were working at a lab table and the fire alarm had sounded and Dr. Kimani had started herding them straight toward the door, calling out, "Don't stop to get your books, people; just go," the stricken expression on Lyssa's face was like nothing Dev had ever seen, and the girl went rigid, stood rooted to the spot like some stiff, skinny tree. Gently, even though he knew people would talk about it later, he'd taken hold of one painfully thin arm and steered her out of the room and through the hallways, her body trembling fast, almost imperceptibly, like a tuning fork, and he'd wanted to ask her, "What do you think will happen? What do you think you're controlling with all that weird stuff?"

She was crazy, no doubt about it, but privately, Dev realized it was a kind of crazy he could understand, at least a little. The laws of physics, Fibonacci numbers, that πr^2 would give you the area of a circle every single time, always and forever: these things reassured Dev. He loved the consistency of the multiplication table, the moment when two sides of an equation balanced. And he believed a lot of people felt that way. Even those chaos-theory guys were actually trying to show that if you took a step back, or two, or a billion and looked at the big picture, chaos wasn't chaos at all.

Dev thought that probably he and most of the people on the planet wanted the world to make sense and hold together as much as Lyssa did. Maybe the difference was that, deep down, he and most of the rest of the people on the planet believed that it would.

If Aidan were right about Lyssa and right about ballet dancers (although Dev wasn't ready to accept the psycho-ballet-dancer theory as fact, not without a lot more evidence), Dev wondered if he was also right about women. Probably not. It seemed unlikely that roughly one-half of the human population could be clinically insane (where did Aidan *get* phrases like "clinically insane"?), but given Dev's recent experiences with his mother and with Lyssa, he couldn't be sure.

Because if order, pattern, predictability were part of Lake's job description as a mother—and Dev strongly believed that they were—Lake was falling down on the job. To put it mildly. Lately, Lake made no sense whatsoever. If somehow Lyssa Sorenson woke up to find that her own mother had transmogrified into Lake, within forty-eight hours, the girl's head would explode, no doubt about it.

Take Cornelia. Dev could tell that his mother liked Cornelia. *Dev* liked Cornelia. Cornelia was cool, and not only because she could quote Robert Frost and talk to Dev without making him feel like a freak show or a lab rat but also because she'd made his mom relax. He even thought she had made his mom happy, that night she'd come to dinner. After he'd gone to bed, he'd heard them talking in the living room, just a distant, indistinct murmur, no words, but he didn't need to hear words. Without meaning to, Dev seemed to have become a kind of seismograph when it came to his mother's moods, and from the peaks and valleys of that murmuring, at least what he overheard before he fell asleep, he knew the conversation had been a good one.

But then, a couple of days later, he'd heard his mother on the phone turning down Cornelia's invitation to Thanksgiving dinner, using the excuse that Dev really looked forward to spending the holiday at home, with just the two of them present. Beyond the fact that this made Dev sound like the world's whiniest mama's boy, it was a flat-out lie. Back in California, holiday dinners tended to be pretty informal, but usually there was a crowd: Lake's restaurant friends; Principal Levy and her husband, Brewster; wayward neighbors; some guy Lake was dating; even people like their mail carrier or the oral hygienist who cleaned Dev's teeth. Anyone who didn't have a lot of family nearby or any family at all (and when Dev looked back, he realized how many people they knew fell into these categories) would show up with a big dish of something or a bottle of wine and sit around eating, talking, and yelling at foot-ball games.

When Dev confronted Lake with these facts, she didn't get mad or try to say that Dev had misheard. Instead, she said, "You're right. The thing is, I think I miss you. *I* wanted it to be just us. I don't know why I didn't just tell her that," with such a sweet, rueful look on her face that Dev didn't have the heart to stay mad. "Anyway," Lake had continued, "Cornelia invited us for dinner the night before, and I told her we'd go to that."

But *then,* when the day before Thanksgiving rolled around, an hour or so before they were supposed to leave for Cornelia's, Lake began to press her fingers to her eyes and her temples and say that she'd been trying to evade it all day, but here it was: one of her headaches, a bad one, like a siren blaring in her head except without the sound, a comparison that would have interested Dev if he hadn't been totally thrown for a loop by the next words out of her mouth.

"I don't want to let Cornelia down, Devvy. So you're going alone. Ride your bike."

"Alone," said Dev, incredulously. "Yeah, right. Are you clinically insane?"

"I'll thank you to get the sarcasm out of your voice."

Dev dropped his eyes and mumbled, "I wasn't being sarcastic," but as irritated with her as he was, with this last comeback, Dev had crossed his own rudeness line, not just Lake's, so he followed up by saying, before his mother could say a word, "Sorry, Mom. But I'm not going. You don't even like me to ride my bike in the dark."

"You'll be on easy roads the whole way, and you'll wear your reflective vest. And you're going."

He'd gone, of course. With the reflective vest over his jacket even though the sun was still up, Lake's cell phone clipped to his waistband, and a bottle of wine stuffed into one of his panniers, which, he'd pointed out coldly to his mother, could possibly get both of them arrested, since he was thirteen years old, a fact that had apparently slipped her mind in recent days. But she'd just smiled with one hand pressed to her temple, as though she could push the headache back to wherever it had come from, and shooed him on his way.

Dev had ridden the almost three miles to Cornelia's house comforting himself with a detailed scenario in which he was run off the road by a crazed ice-cream-truck driver and plunged into a three-week coma: his head swathed in bandages like a Civil War soldier's, Lake sitting by his hospital bed, eaten up with guilt, "Can you ever forgive me?" the first words out of her mouth.

"Aidan was right," Dev muttered through gritted teeth, "females are all clinically insane."

But even if Dev had honestly believed this as he said it, the belief would've had one of the shorter life spans in belief history because approximately four and a half minutes later, Dev met Clare, and even the most exasperated, most fed-up kid in the world couldn't help but notice that Clare Hobbes was both unmistakably female and unmistakably sane.

She was playing catch with a man in Cornelia's front yard.

Even though Dev saw Clare before he saw the number on the house and even though he'd never been there before or met her before and had even forgotten that a girl his age would be there at all, he turned into the driveway without hesitating, his cheeks burning at the image of himself in his stupid reflective vest, but still feeling positive, 100 percent sure that he was in the right place.

He leaned his bike against the side of the house, then got out of his helmet and vest as fast as he could, and stood there, absently trying to ruffle his hair back to its normal shape, thinking about the bottle of wine inside the pannier. Forget it, he decided. He'd get it later. How idiotic would it be to walk up holding a bottle of wine like some cravat-wearing yacht guy? Just then, with horror, he realized what he was doing to his hair. "You bonehead," he growled at himself inside his head. "She's just some girl."

Then, suddenly, she was three feet away from him, her hands on her hips, her smile cutting through the early-evening dimness.

"Nice bike," she said, but she wasn't looking at the bike. With big dark sparkling eyes, the best eyes he'd ever seen, Clare was looking straight at him.

"Thanks," he said. "You're Clare, right?"

A voice yelled, cheerfully, "Heads up!" and a football came flying from out of nowhere, and in what had to be one of the most glorious moments in human history, without thinking, Dev jumped up and caught it, just snagged it out of the air. For a second, he and Clare stared at the ball in his hands. Then Clare started to laugh a startled, happy, jingly laugh.

"That's right," said Clare, her laughter filling the crisp air like sleigh bells, "I'm Clare."

Whenever Dev remembered that night, and he'd remember it for a very long time, what never stopped amazing him was how normal it felt. Not everyday, no-big-deal normal. More like extragalactic, superradiant, night-in-a-million normal. Normal turned up a couple of thousand notches, but normal nonetheless because, against all odds, with so many reasons to feel nervous, shy, and out of place, Dev spent the entire evening feeling precisely and absolutely like himself.

They were all nice: Clare; Cornelia; her husband, Teo; her brother Toby, who'd thrown the football and who was also a visitor, stopping in for a couple of days on the way to move in with his girlfriend in Philadelphia. Their dinner-table conversation was like a good-natured, five-way Ping-Pong game, with Dev himself getting in an excellent shot now and then, if he did say so himself. Later that night, Dev would lie in bed letting individual, small, clear-cut memories rise to the surface of that whole great stretch of remembered evening, and the word that kept coming to him—and maybe Clare's jingle-bell laugh had something to do with this—was merry. They were a happy group, funny, kind, vivacious, vibrant. Merry.

Toby was the loudest, calling Cornelia corndog, Teo uglyman, and all through dinner, shooting no-look passes Dev's way—a carved wooden napkin ring, a Peking duck pancake (they were having Chinese takeout), a fortune cookie—all of which Dev caught, provoking Toby to high-five him and shout things like "Little brother's got the hot hands!"

Cornelia was the funniest, telling stories from when she, Toby, and Teo were kids together: Teo's crush on someone called the Bionic Woman. (Teo to Dev: "If you'd seen the episode where she goes undercover as Savage Sommers, professional lady wrestler, I think you'd understand"); Toby eating insects for money. (Dev to Toby: "Worms?" Toby to Dev: "Japanese beetles." Cornelia to Dev: "*Cooked* Japanese beetles." Dev to Cornelia: "In the microwave?" Cornelia (dryly) and Toby (proudly) to Dev: "Air popper.")

Teo was the quietest, and although he did almost as much teasing as the others and although they were all really friendly, Teo was the most considerate, making sure Dev felt part of things, catching his eye, drawing him in, asking him questions about himself in a truly interested, not-CIA-operative kind of way. They talked about music, and it turned out they liked the same kind: punky but melodic and un-mean, music that made you want to jump up and down hard, but that didn't make you want to smash things. As Dev was walking out the door, Teo slipped him CDs by Social Distortion ("Social D circa 1990, their kinder, gentler, less-addicted period"), the Clash, and a band from Texas called Bowling for Soup.

But even while all this went on, all the talking and laughing (once Toby even sang, if you could call it singing), Dev never stopped noticing Clare. She didn't distract him, exactly. It was what happened with math problems sometimes or hard concepts, or, recently, with poems. He could be giving his attention to other things—really focusing—while part of his brain privately worked on Schrödinger's cat or the Koch snowflake or "The Man with the Blue Guitar" or whatever other nut he might be trying to crack, like those supercomputers that keep constantly, silently solving problems (how to predict tsunamis or figure out protein structure) while the rest of the world sleeps or goes about its daily business. Not that Dev's brain or any part of it was a supercomputer and not that Clare was a problem to solve. There was just a lot to notice about her. Dev believed there was more to notice about Clare than about any girl he'd ever met.

For starters, she used adverbs more than most people did, a lot more. She ate the twice-cooked pork—so loaded with peppers that one minuscule bite made Dev want to scream and run around in circles until he fell down—like it was potato salad. Her eyebrows were long, straight, symmetrical lines. She had a delicate, now-you-see-it-now-you-don't cleft in her chin (since cleft chins were far more common in males, Dev made a mental note to look up exactly what genetic odds Clare had beaten to end up with this trait). Her glossy ponytail curved at the end like a comma.

Dev spent at least fifteen minutes trying to put his finger on what about her reminded him of Aidan before he realized that it was her gaze: direct and true. In Dev's admittedly limited experience, most girls his age didn't look at boys this way. Come to think of it, most *kids* his age didn't look at anyone this way. They'd look at challenging, knowing, sarcastic, flirtatious, wary, many, many gradations of bored, attitude that slid across their eyes like those transparent membranes lizards and sharks have, and the trick was to figure out what was underneath. It was like a guessing game, and even though Dev believed he was better at playing it than he used to be (because he used to suck), he knew he wasn't great. When her eyes weren't flashing naked panic or fear, even Lyssa gave Dev shrugging, sideways glances he found about as easy to read as quantum theory.

They played chess.

It was Clare's idea. She told Dev that since she'd learned the game two years ago, she'd had a rivalry going with Cornelia's father, Dr. B., who lived in her neighborhood.

Clare grinned at Dev. "Cornelia says you're smart.

Maybe I can steal some strategies." She led him into a book-lined room with a big desk at one end and a fireplace, but no fire, at the other. In front of the fireplace stood a tiny chess table with curving, gold-tipped legs and a leather chair on either side of it. "Besides, Cornelia's chess table is too pretty to leave in here all by itself. She rescued it from some junk shop and refinished it, and Teo surprised her with these carved rosewood pieces from Germany." She lifted the white knight, a horse with two heads pointed in opposite directions and cupped it in her palm for a few seconds, then handed it to Dev. It was heavy, smooth, and warm from her hand.

"But you know what's funny? They don't play. Cornelia doesn't even really know how. They just think this stuff is beautiful." She smiled at the knight Dev held. When Clare talked about Cornelia and Teo, the love was obvious. They were people who belonged to her. Dev caught himself wishing that she'd talk about him like that, and then gave himself an imaginary "Get real, moron" punch in the arm.

Dev didn't make a habit of playing games like chess with people he'd just met. Basketball, yes. Chess, no. He wasn't any Bobby Fischer guy who could make one move and see the next twenty moves light up like a constellation in his head, but he had studied the game a little, which was more than most people had done, and he had a kind of knack for it to begin with, so consequently he could usually win. And even though Dev wasn't generally one to dumb himself down for public consumption, mainly because when it came to subjects that interested him, he'd get too caught up to put on an act (the Mr. Tripp incident being a case in point), he wasn't a show-off either, and whenever he played chess, he sort of felt like one. He knew Aidan well enough now to not mind stomping him now and then (although Aidan could give him a run for his money), but he had just met Clare.

As soon as they started, though, Dev knew everything was fine. For one thing, Clare could play, no doubt about it. But as Dev watched her, her straight back, her hand hovering over but not touching a piece until she was ready, the way her eyes flickered over the board, he understood that she wouldn't mind losing. She wouldn't love it, but losing wouldn't shake her up or make her mad. The Berkeley psychologist had called Dev "self-possessed" and, at the time, he hadn't been exactly sure what that meant, but as he played chess with Clare, the word suddenly made perfect sense. The same way Teo and Cornelia belonged to Clare, Clare belonged to herself. Clare liked being Clare, the same way that Dev had always (even when he was friendless and invisible) liked being Dev.

"So at dinner you said something about your mom being in Antigua?" said Dev. "Is that why you're spending Thanksgiving here?"

"No. Not exactly," said Clare, shaking her head. "More like she's in Antigua because I'm spending Thanksgiving here."

"Oh," said Dev, vaguely, "got it."

Clare smiled. "Not biologically, but in every other respect, Cornelia and Teo are part of my family. I mean, my mom's my mom. I love my mom. But Cornelia and Teo and I need time together every few months. We all know that. Even my mom. Maybe even *especially* my mom."

Clare looked down at the board. Dev saw a risky but potentially great move she could make, and when

Clare's eyes stopped zigzagging across the board, imagining moves, and paused on a single chess piece, he saw that she saw it, too. He waited, liking that she didn't hunch over the board in concentration but just dipped her chin down a little with her hands in her lap and lowered her eyes, her long, feathery eyelashes tilting like tiny awnings. She made the move, then shifted her clear, root beer–colored gaze back to Dev.

"My mom's bipolar." She said it matter-of-factly. "Actually, she says manic-depressive's a better term for it. Less cold, more accurate. What do you think?"

Dev thought for a second. "The chef at this restaurant where my mom used to work would tell people he got his stomach stapled. He said gastric bypass sounded like traffic and bariatric sounded like weather. Bipolar sounds like geography."

"Precisely. And don't things with poles always have two of them?" She held up her hand. "Wait, don't answer that."

"Why?"

She laughed. "Because I can tell you're about to give me a really complicated math answer, and I bet I wouldn't get it."

"*I* don't get it," said Dev sheepishly, "but I think I remember reading the word 'tripolar' somewhere."

"Anyway, my mom didn't show any symptoms until a couple of years ago, but neither one of us knew that they *were* symptoms. My dad was out of the picture, so it was just the two of us, and I knew something was wrong, but I didn't know what. Eventually, my mom had a breakdown—she calls it a breakdown—an incredibly awful one, and she took off in her car. Just left because she was so confused and didn't know what she was doing."

"Wow," said Dev quietly.

"Cornelia and Teo swooped in and took care of me. They didn't even know me, but they did it anyway, like it was the most normal thing in the world. We got to know each other really, really well." She raised her eyebrows and grinned. "You want to know what I think?"

"Yeah," said Dev, unable to think of one thing he wanted more.

"I think there are certain people who change the way time moves. Cornelia and Teo are people like that. I've only known them for two years, but really, in reality, I've known them for a long, long time." Clare paused. "What do you think?"

"I think Einstein couldn't have said it better himself." Dev took a breath. "But you might want to consider another possibility."

"Did I say you could poke holes in my theory?" Clare folded her arms. "Okay, what? What's the other possibility?"

"Maybe it isn't Teo and Cornelia who change the way time moves." Dev bought himself a couple of seconds by squinting down at the chessboard, pretending to consider his next move. Then he looked up into Clare's expectant face and shrugged. "Maybe it's you."

He ended up telling her everything. All of it: Mr. Tripp, the Berkeley psychologist, their sudden cross-country journey and seemingly random relocation, the genius-kid school applications, his mother's current craziness (although he took care not to use the words "crazy" or "clinically insane"), and finally, most importantly, most surprisingly, his theory about his father.

Except that Dev wasn't really surprised, even though he'd absolutely decided to keep that theory a secret and even though, under ordinary circumstances, Dev was an ace secret keeper. It hadn't just slipped out, the theory; he had set his sights on it from the second he started to tell Clare about himself and then had talked deliberately toward it, and when he said the words "I think my dad's here. Someplace nearby. I think he's why we came," Dev didn't follow up with so much as an "oops," not even a silent one.

Later, as he tried to put into words how this had happened, the phrase that popped into Dev's head first was "truth serum." Being with Clare was like drinking truth serum. But as soon as he thought this, he recalled that all the truth serums he'd ever heard of, maybe even including the Harry Potter potion Veritaserum, were sedatives. They depressed the central nervous system and interfered with judgment. As Dev talked to Clare, he felt the total opposite of depressed (he didn't feel all that sedate either), and, if a person could be a fair and objective judge of his own judgment (which Dev had to admit was a biggish "if"), he believed his judgment had been just fine. In any case, he'd stand by it until hell froze over.

So then the next word that came to Dev was "trust." Probably trust serum did not exist, but if it did, Dev knew that it wouldn't depress your central nervous system or anything else. A single sip of trust serum would zip around your brain flipping switches (maybe in your cerebral cortex? your limbic system? Dev was a little fuzzy on neuroscience) until you felt so flooded with lucidity and certainty that you would happily roll your most carefully guarded secrets into a ball small enough to place in someone's palm, and then you'd do it: you'd give it away.

Telling Clare was right. It just was.

Three seconds after he finished telling her, though, Cornelia walked into the room and said, "Your mom called, Dev, to say it was time to come home. I'll only agree to release you, though, if you solemnly vow to come back soon."

"How soon?" demanded Clare. "Tomorrow soon?"

Dev looked at the floor and smiled. "Tomorrow's Thanksgiving."

"Right," said Cornelia. "And Dev and Lake have dinner plans."

"Do they have dessert plans?" asked Clare.

Cornelia looked carefully from Clare to Dev, then said, smiling, "I most sincerely hope not."

For a second, no one said anything, and then Cornelia said to Dev, "Toby'll take you. He's outside right now popping your front wheel off." At Dev's look of alarm, she added, "Which is one of the few things the boy knows how to do. When it comes to bikes, snowboards, skis, surfboards, my baby brother's your man. That's about it, though. So, do we have your solemn vow? You'll come back soon?"

Dev raised his right hand and slapped his left onto an invisible stack of Bibles.

After Cornelia left, Clare turned to Dev, took hold of his forearm, and whispered, "I bet your theory about your dad is right. But you need to come back so we can figure it out."

Dev focused on the sensation of her hand on his arm, memorizing the pressure of each finger individually. "I'll come back. But what do we need to figure out? I mean, as a theory, it's pretty figured out, right?"

Clare gave her head a small, impatient toss. "Not the theory. The theory's solid. Your dad's here, somewhere." She squeezed his arm. Her face was inches from his and so smooth it looked like someone had polished it. "The question is: what are we going to do about it?"

"Yeah," Dev nodded, "I'll come back." Dev was nodding, he was answering her, but all the while, Clare's last sentence was bouncing around the inside of his head and his heart was pounding in his chest and he was thinking how weird it was—good weird, miracle weird, even—that one word, one puny pronoun could be the single best sound he'd ever heard in his life.

If it hadn't been for Clare's phone call, Thanksgiving would have been a complete bust. Thanksgiving and the day after that and the day after that, a line of busted days stretching who knows how far into Dev's future. Because Lake said no. What was more infuriating was that she didn't just say no, that they couldn't go to Cornelia's for dessert on Thanksgiving Day, she said they couldn't go because she'd *invited* someone to have dessert with *them*. Mr. Pleat from next door, a regular-looking man who'd said hi to Dev a few times, talked to him about stuff like his bike, the weather. After Lake's headache had faded, she'd ended up having a long conversation with Mr. Pleat over the low rail that separated their back deck from his. He'd always struck Dev as a nice enough man, but suddenly Dev and every atom of Dev's being wished he'd spontaneously combust. His name was Rafferty.

"Rafferty Pleat?" Dev had practically spat. "That name's totally fake. The guy's probably in witness protection."

"If he is, he didn't mention it," replied Lake, coolly. "He's a contractor. He rehabs old houses, and his wife threw him out six months ago and they're currently em-broiled in a hideous legal battle because she wants to move to Florida with their four-year-old daughter, so you might consider directing a little compassion his way."

Man, his mom could fast-talk when she wanted to.

"Besides," she added, "some would say that a person named Deveroux Tremain doesn't have a leg to stand on when it comes to calling other people's names out-landish."

Dev could have pointed out that (a) he hadn't exactly named himself, and (b) at no time had he ever used the word "outlandish," but instead he said, in his most self-satisfied voice, even though he wasn't feeling satisfied at all, "So now you have to explain to Cornelia that you can't come to her house for dessert because you're inviting someone else for dessert when you already told her that you wanted the two of us to spend Thanksgiv-ing alone. Have you thought about that, Mom?"

Apparently, Lake had thought about it because the next thing she did was dial Cornelia's number and tell her precisely that in a warm, friendly voice and with a heavy emphasis on Mr. Fake-Name's sad aloneness that made Dev want to throw up.

If five minutes after Lake had hung up with Corne-lia, the phone hadn't rung, Thanksgiving would have sucked. If Dev had come out of his room to eat dinner at all (and he probably would have, since the image of his mother eating turkey and stuffing all by herself would have been impossible for him to swallow, no matter how furious he was at her), the relentless grim-ness of the meal would have been eclipsed only by the relentless grimness of dessert with Rafferty Pleat. But the phone did ring, and while no phone call could have erased the Molotov cocktail of maternal craziness and outrageous injustice Lake had thrown at Dev, this one came pretty freaking close. It was Clare.

She said, "Two questions. First, can you come over Saturday?"

"Yes," Dev said without hesitation. Lake and ten herds of wild horses could not stop him from going. He waited for the second question, thinking please please please let her say something like, "Have you been thinking about me as much as I've been thinking about you?" which would have embarrassed the hell out of Dev, but in the best possible way.

"Second, do you know how the buses work around here?"

"Uh, no," admitted Dev. "But I can find out. Why?"

"I looked in the phone book," said Clare, "and I have two words for you."

"What are they?"

Her voice rose and rippled with excitement. "Dev, I really think this could be it!"

"You do?"

"I do. I truly, truly do."

"Tell me." In the short silence that followed, Dev held his breath, wanting to hear her breathe or cough, not wanting to miss anything.

Then, slowly, with a pause between the words, Clare told him: "Tremain Cycles."

"What will you do if it's him?"

The bus was smotheringly hot, and the driver had obviously skipped the day they'd covered gradual stops and starts in driving school, but Dev didn't mind. If he and Clare had been racing over the plains in a covered wagon, pursued by ravenous wolves, he wouldn't have minded either. But the bus was nice, sun falling across them, the world outside a long blur of brown, green, and blue. Clare sat next to him, so close that a piece of her hair, like a shining ribbon, rested on his shoulder, and Dev held as still as he could, as though the hair were a dragonfly, some small, light thing he didn't want to startle away.

Her question caught him off guard, and he realized he'd almost forgotten where they were going.

"I mean," she continued, "I was wondering what you want to happen. Or if you want anything to happen." Her voice sounded worried, so Dev turned and looked at her. She was fiddling with the zipper of her jacket.

"I guess I'm not sure what I want," he said.

When her eyes met his, they were worried, too. "But you want to be here, right?"

"Right." He smiled, but she didn't smile back.

"I mean, you want to do this, don't you? Because that bike shop, it was right there in the phone book, in the business white pages, and you didn't find it. After I got off the phone with you on Thursday, I thought about that, how if you didn't find it, it could only have been because you didn't look for it."

"Oh," said Dev, "I see what you mean." He saw what she meant, and what he wondered was why he hadn't thought about that before. For days and days, he'd walked around with his theory, not doing anything, but as soon as Clare had told him about the bike store, he'd wanted to go. He'd wanted to look for his father.

"I started to worry that"—Clare broke off, blushing—"that maybe you only came because you wanted to see, or you wanted to be with . . ." She stopped talking.

"With you." Dev just said it. He knew it would change everything, but he said it anyway.

"Because we could have done something else," Clare said, quickly. "We still could."

Dev considered this for a while. Then he said, "Here's what I think."

"What?"

"I think I always wanted to look for him, and maybe if I hadn't met you, I would have told Aidan everything. I thought about telling him, but I never did. Maybe I would have, though, whenever it felt like the right time, and he would have gone with me. I don't know." Dev ran his hand through his hair impatiently. *Just talk,* he thought, *just say what you have to say.*

"I wanted to find him," Dev said, slowly and quietly, "I just didn't want to do it by myself."

Suddenly, Clare smiled and said, teasingly, "Maybe you were waiting for me to show up."

Dev found himself looking down, then, and there was Clare's hand, her long fingers and short nails. First he was looking at it, then he was holding it, such a natural transition that a full four seconds passed before he comprehended what he'd done, but then his heart started ticking like a time bomb, and a giant black wrecking ball of panic came swinging toward him fast. He felt like the kid in the museum who doesn't even realize he's reached out and touched the painting until he hears the alarm and feels the guard's big hands on his shoulders.

But before he could pull his hand away and go shooting down a bottomless pit of apologies and humiliation, Clare's hand was shifting inside his, and then their palms were pressed together, their fingers interlocked—Clare, Dev, Clare, Dev, Clare, Dev, et cetera—and nothing, not one thing was wrong with that.

Out of the corner of his eye, Dev saw that Clare was looking straight ahead with a small, thoughtful smile on her face. He didn't turn to her. He didn't speak. For the rest of the ride, Dev sat there holding Clare's hand and thinking, *Clare's hand is connected to the rest of Clare,* which felt like a revelation, like the best news he'd ever heard.

The bike was a beauty. Fifteen pounds of aerodynamics and carbon fiber, a composite so unimaginably light and strong that they made satellites out of it. Dev traced the lean, seamless silver tubing with his eyes, thinking of all the science, all the work and imagination that had gone into making this single perfect object. Dev didn't want to own the bike; he had no use for it, but as he looked at it, he felt a piercing, nameless longing filling him, and suddenly he thought about Plato, whom Ms. Enright had just had them read. Maybe Dev's soul remembered this bike from the realm of pure forms; maybe this bike made his soul homesick. *Oh, shut up,* Dev told himself. *Could you be normal for, like, two seconds?* But the longing didn't go away.

With effort, Dev shifted his gaze off the bike and swept it slowly over the bike shop. Bikes stood in rows and hung gleaming from the walls and ceiling. It was hard to tell the employees from the customers, but eventually, Dev figured out that the guys wearing oversized, long-sleeved white polo shirts were salespeople. Saleskids.

"Let's go," he whispered to Clare, "they're all about eleven years old."

Clare drew in her breath and nodded toward the back of the store. A tall, brown-haired man was lifting bikes onto one of the wall racks. He wore a white shirt, too, but he was older, maybe forty, and he moved like a person in charge.

"He looks like he owns the place," said Clare softly.

Suddenly Dev felt too tired to move. He looked back at the silver bike. *If only,* he thought, and the homesick feeling swamped him. If only I were eleven years old. Or eight. If only we were here to see this bike.

He looked at Clare. Her eyes were almost level with his own.

"You're tall," he said.

"I know," she said.

They were still holding hands, but it felt different from the way it had on the bus. Now, they were like two kids lost in the woods. Hansel and Gretel, scared and small, comforting each other. That wasn't how Dev wanted holding hands with Clare to feel, so deliberately, gently, he let go and walked toward the back of the store.

The man's back was to them. Dev noticed that his hair was thick and grew in a counterclockwise swirl around a single crown. Dev touched the back of his own head, but dropped his hand as the man turned and saw them. The man's jaw was square and his eyes were interesting, a blue so pale it was almost white. He smiled.

"Hey, guys," he said. "What can I help you with today?"

That's when Dev noticed his name tag. ED. Exactly what a guy named Teddy would get called when he got older. Ed Tremain. He heard Clare say, "Oh!" She laid a hand on Dev's back. Clare had seen the name tag, too.

"Uh, well, actually," said Dev. His voice came out hoarse and softer than he wanted it to be. He cleared his throat. "I was wondering about the name."

Puzzled, the man frowned slightly, two deep lines like quotation marks appearing between his eyebrows. He looked down at the bike he'd been about to lift and his face relaxed.

"Gary Fisher," he said, nodding. Dev saw that the name ran in slashy-looking letters along the bike's down tube. "A lot of people call Gary the inventor of the mountain bike, which I wouldn't necessarily agree with. An awful lot of people were modifying bikes on their own back then, in their garages, probably coming up with all the same changes independent of each other."

Then Ed said a surprising thing. "Like hedgehogs and porcupines. Different times, different places, different—what do you call it—species, but they both ended up with spines. There's a word for that in science." He scratched his head, thinking.

"Convergent evolution," said Dev, solemnly. It was him. It had to be.

"Bingo!" Ed grinned and pointed a finger at Dev. "Anyway, Gary Fisher makes a nice bike, that's for sure."

"I bet," said Dev. "So do you own this store?" Even though Dev already knew the answer, he asked. He had to ask.

"Sure do," said the man.

Dev looked at Clare, looked back at the man, took a deep breath and said, "I'm Dev," and then, because Ed's face didn't change, he added, "Tremain."

Dev watched understanding dawn on Ed's face, but then, to his surprise, the man laughed.

"I get it," he said. "Here I'm going on about Gary Fisher and evolution, and *that's* the name you meant. Yeah, I bought the place from Bob Tremain a year ago last December."

Dev stared at Ed in confusion.

Clare spoke up. "Was he a relative of yours? Are you a Tremain, too?"

"No," said Ed, "the guy was *old* enough to be my dad, but nope. I'm Ed Buchman." He put out his hand, and Clare and Dev took turns shaking it. "How about you? You related to old Bob?"

Dev hesitated. "Maybe," he said finally, lamely. "I think I might be."

"Is he from around here, do you know?" asked Clare.

"No," said Ed. "He'd lived here a little while, but Bob's from somewhere out in the Midwest. Ohio. Michigan. Something like that."

"Iowa?" suggested Dev.

"Could've been." Ed nodded. "He and June retired to Florida, but they've got a couple of kids settled not too far from here. A son in Philly, I think. And a daughter in Baltimore."

When Dev just stood there, fuzzy brained and tired, not saying anything, Clare finally said, "Well, thanks, Mr. Buchman."

Dev wanted out of that store, then, about as much as he'd ever wanted out of anywhere, but he was rooted to the spot. Like Lyssa, he thought with irritation, Lyssa at the fire drill. *You lived without knowing your stupid father for almost fourteen years,* he berated himself. *Why does everything have to be such a big deal now?* He pulled himself together before Clare had to take his arm and shuffle him out of the store.

"Yeah, thanks," he said.

Outside, he took off his jacket and breathed. The bike store was in a strip mall, but with the air in his lungs and on his skin and with the intense blue sky over his head, Dev could have been in Oregon or Montana, some vivid, elemental, rinsed-clean place with mountains towering over him instead of Super Fresh and Office-Max. He was that glad to be out of the store, and he felt light, as though he'd lifted the tangle of hope, dread, disappointment, and relief out of his chest and left it there, dropped it between the bikes on his way out.

After a moment, Clare touched his shoulder. "Hey, you," she said. Her eyes searched his face the way, a couple of nights ago, they'd searched the chessboard for the right move. Then she began, carefully, "The son in Philly . . ."

"I know," said Dev. "Maybe I'll try again." He paused. "I don't know if I want to, though." He knew he might feel differently later, but for now, it felt good to be fatherless, to be the same old Dev he'd always been.

He and Clare started walking toward the bus stop, their shadows stretching out ahead of them. Dev watched the girl shadow take the boy shadow's hand, and he realized that the homesick feeling had disappeared. In its place was a new feeling, too new to have a name.

"How cool would that have been, though?" He shot Clare a sidelong, happy grin. "A dad with a bike shop?"

Clare laughed her jingle-bell laugh, and Dev realized that what he felt was young. He'd been young all his life, of course he had. But now he was aware of it. Every cell, every *electron* of his body felt young: unencumbered, uncluttered, as clean as the clear blue sky.

TEN

❦

Cornelia

It's highly unlikely that my brother Toby will ever have a George Bailey moment: suicidal on a bridge above roiling water; snow swirling like chaos; his fat, sweet guardian angel teetering on heaven's edge, set to jump in and save the day. It's unlikely for all the reasons that would make it unlikely for anyone: one being the dearth of credible evidence supporting the existence of guardian angels; another being the fact that, as I too often have to remind myself, life is life and movies— even classic Capra/Stewart collaborations—are only movies. But Toby caught in a wild-eyed, rock-bottom, George Bailey moment is unlikely for other reasons, as well, reasons that have to do with Toby being Toby.

The boy is just plain buoyant. Hardwired for lightness. Ollie would probably have some impenetrable scientific explanation for this, but even I can tell you that if she stuck Toby's DNA under some ultra-whizbang, crazy-high-powered microscope (and if such microscopes exist, you can bet Ollie's got one), she'd find the genetic equivalent of "Life's a Beach" or maybe "Life's an Awesome Mountain to Slide Down" stamped on every last gene. And even I can see that being Toby brings with it some distinct evolutionary advantages. Men like my little brother don't brood or introspect or even sit still much. If they ever do hit rock bottom, it's only to bounce off it and head skyward.

But *if* Toby's guardian angel ever did have cause to swoop down and show him what life would be like if he'd never been born, there's a huge chance that they would find his sister Cornelia in a sorry state. I've imagined various possible incarnations of this state, visualized the dreary particulars of each possibility, and all of them are far too dreary to regale you with. But trust me when I say that each imagined incarnation was truly, deeply, and stunningly *sorry*.

Toby is my litmus test. He was probably my litmus test for a very long time, but it wasn't until one miserable evening at the end of my first and last semester of graduate school that I was fully, blessedly conscious of this. In fact, if I have anything to say about it (and really, who else would?) the Toby Brown version of *It's a Wonderful Life* would prominently feature a flashback to that very evening.

I was there—on a hilltop surrounded by the plunging gorges, streams, and maple trees of central New York State—to get a Ph.D. in English literature. That's not true. I was there to read a lot of books and to discuss them with bright, insightful, book-loving people, an expectation that I pretty quickly learned was about as silly as it could be.

Certainly there were other people there who loved books, I'm sure there were, but whoever had notified them ahead of time that loving books was not the point, was, in fact, a hopelessly counterproductive and naive approach to the study of literature, neglected to notify me. It turned out that the point was to dissect a book like a fetal pig in biology class or to break its back with a single sentence or to bust it open like a milkweed pod and say, "See? All along it was only fluff," and then scatter it into oblivion with one tiny breath.

I'm getting worked up and metaphorical on you. I know I am. But it was a rough time. Nowadays, I want to be smart, but back then, I'm afraid I wanted to *seem* smart, too. I wanted to make a smart impression, so I'd do what everyone else did, no matter how wrong it felt. But one afternoon, after a British literature seminar, I sat alone in the room staring down at my copy of *Howard's End,* feeling like I'd just stripped the clothes off my grandmother and sent her out wandering in the snow.

After that I stopped talking in class and started dating Jay West, the undisputed star of the program. I dated him because he was the undisputed star of the program, a fact of which I am properly ashamed, and he dated me for reasons that still remain cloudy, although I suspect they had something to do with my resemblance (which existed only in his imagination but which he related in breathy tones to me on more than one occasion) to the actress Winona Ryder.

He wasn't unattractive. He was handsome in a gaunt, beaky, dark-browed, mop-topped way. In fact, now that I think about it, Jay had precisely the kind of looks that would play beautifully in a black-and-white film.

Imagine the scene. Early December, final exams and papers only just laid to rest. The interior of a noisy, cozy pub with long wooden tables and a stone fireplace; firelight dancing inside wineglasses and throwing shadows around the room. Six graduate students around a table, one particularly slumped, taciturn, and anemic looking (me), and my brother Toby, newly nineteen, fresh out of his first semester of college in Colorado, in town to do some hiking and then drive his nondriving sister (I know how; I just don't like to) home for Christmas break. And, of course, in the center of everything: Jay, talking, *expounding* on Sylvia Plath and psychopharmacology with the part-genius-prophet, part-Nosferatu fire in his eyes that always accompanied his expounding and that sent English Department women (minus his girlfriend) and some men into varying states of swoon.

"Fuck Prozac. Fuck lithium. Fuck Haldol and clozapine and TCAs and MAOIs. Fuck selective fucking serotonin fucking reuptake inhibitors. Thank *God* Plath was born when she was. If she were around today, we'd pump her full of all manner of shit to keep her 'happy' and 'functional.' For what? So her kids would grow up with a mommy? That wouldn't be medicine. It would be barbarism. Because we need *Ariel,* and only a frenzied poet on the brink of suicide could write *Ariel.* We need Plath's suicide. We need her to stick her head in the oven while her kids sleep upstairs. We need *Ariel.* We *deserve Ariel* more than those kids, more than *any* kid ever deserved a mother."

I'm not kidding. This is how he talked. Like he was auditioning for the role of Moses in some cheesy, profanity-laced remake of *The Ten Commandments.* Like no one in the whole history of the world had ever considered the positive impact of mental illness on creativity.

"You don't even like *Ariel.*" I said this. Why I bothered, I have no idea.

"What?"

"You called it thin. And obvious."

Jay looked as if he'd just found gum on his shoe. Fresh gum.

"I don't have to *like Ariel. Liking* is irrelevant. What's relevant is the splash and the outward rippling concentric circles of water. *Ariel* may be thin, by my standards. It may be obvious. But it made a splash. I don't *like* the New Testament particularly. I'm not a believer. But I happen to find it tragic that if Jesus Christ were alive today in the United States of America, he'd end up with a pretty wife, 2.5 kids, and a split-level home in the burbs. He'd be a shoe salesman because we, in all our barbarism, would have *tamed* him with antipsychotics and lithium and who the fuck knows what else."

Silence. Then my brother Toby said, "Yeah. But probably we wouldn't have, like, crucified him." He grinned and took a big slug of beer.

Jay didn't laugh good-naturedly. No one did. He didn't even look at Toby. Instead he looked at me, ruefully, shook his head, and said, "My poor girl."

I didn't stop to analyze this inscrutable comment, because first, I was smiling. Then I was laughing, not because Jay was a pompous, ridiculous idiot, not even because what Toby said was really quite funny (quite insightful, too), but out of pure joy. Because right at that moment, I knew I would leave. It would be hard. I wouldn't do it right away. I would come back from break and tough it out for two more pointless weeks. But there in the bar, I understood with absolute clarity that someday soon I would pack my bags, give up my fellowship, and head for home.

If Toby hadn't come along, I might have stayed. I had always been an excellent student. In all my life, I had never quit anything nearly as important as graduate school, and when I quit, I fell into a pit—a fairly shallow pit, but a pit nonetheless—of self-recrimination and embarrassment. But eventually, I climbed out and walked away with my soul intact and with a secret weapon in my arsenal, my litmus test: Toby could be—and usually was—exasperating and boneheaded, but he was also exuberant and bighearted, and anyone who could not like him was gone, gone, gone.

Toby was in love.

He sat with his feet and a sweating glass of Gatorade on my new coffee table and described it to me thus: "I was just going along, minding my own business, and the girl blindsided me. A total body slam. I was like, 'Dude, you've *gotta* be kidding me!'"

Lest that flight of rhapsody cause you to pigeonhole Toby a hopeless romantic, let me assure you that while he was—and is—certainly hopeless in numberless ways, he had never been, not in all of his twenty-nine years, in love. Not even a little. Not even in *high school,* if he could be believed, and I'm pretty sure he could.

He'd always dated a lot. A lot-a lot. I have no hard numbers, but my mother's theory is that when it comes to counting Toby's girlfriends, it's best to apply the same method scientists use in estimating populations of okapis or pygmy marmosets or whales: for every one you meet, assume there are three hiding somewhere nearby. (Actually, my mother may be wrong about scientists using this method. It sounds sort of unscientific, but it also sounds sort of right, doesn't it?) And I've met plenty. While there have been a wide variety of types—preppy, crunchy, outdoorsy, athletic, even, occasionally, tattooed and pierced (although not excessively, nothing they couldn't cover up for a visit from

Grandma)—there's also been a certain uniformity: all were sweet and upbeat, all worshipped the Dave Matthews Band, all were what Toby describes—with profound admiration—as "fun girls."

Until Miranda.

"Miranda's a lot like you," said Toby, throwing a throw pillow at me for emphasis, "except taller. And younger." He grinned. "And, you know, curvier."

"I do *not* know," I said coolly, slipping a coaster underneath the glass of Gatorade. "And I'm fun."

"You are," agreed Toby, nodding, "you're fairly fun. Fun's just not the point of you."

As I considered the implications of this, Toby began, "I like to be around Miranda—"

"You love to be around Miranda," I corrected, gloating.

"Watch it, corndog," he warned. "But yeah. I love to be around Miranda, it's *fun* to be around Miranda, but not because she's fun. Just because she's . . ."

"Miranda?" I suggested.

"She's smart. She's—what's the word—*contemplative*. She has these great, chocolate brown, serious eyes, and you can just tell that she's, like, studying the world, not just cruising around it like a, a . . ."

"Dune buggy?"

Toby has Windex blue eyes. He rolled them at me now.

"You can take the girl out of Barbie's Bungalow Beach House but you can't take Barbie's Bungalow Beach House out of the girl," he said, which didn't quite make sense, but was clever all the same. Fairly clever.

"You were two when I stopped playing with Barbies," I said. "They must have made quite an impression."

He ignored this. "And she reads everything. And

has excellent taste in, like, everything. Wine, movies, clothes."

"You're right," I said, seriously, "she is a lot like me."

"Yeah, she even loves those flowers you love. Your favorite. Those big fluffy ones."

"Miranda loves peonies?" I was touched that my little brother remembered my favorite flower, even if he didn't, quite. He remembered I *have* a favorite flower. Truth be told, I was touched by the whole conversation. I got up from my chair and walked around the new coffee table in order to kiss Toby on the cheek.

"Peonies. Yeah." He laughed and pretended to wipe off my kiss. I settled myself down on the sofa next to him.

"Tell me more," I told him.

So he did. He told me that her name was Miranda Bloom, no middle name. He told me she was Jewish. He told me that she had an older brother named Philip who played the oboe for the Boston Symphony. He told me that she would turn twenty-three the day after Christmas, although he was quick to add that she didn't celebrate Christmas, which was not terribly surprising to me. He told me that she was studying to be an occupational therapist. He told me that she had grown up in Detroit and, of her own volition, had practiced vegetarianism from the age of six to the age of seventeen and had double-majored in psychology and art history and wore scarves and kept her shoes in the boxes they came in and laughed her brains out at Looney Tunes and looked amazing in a sweater and loved French and Vietnamese food, stinky cheese, chocolate cupcakes, Sancerre, all sushi with the exception of sea urchin, and Eagle Brand sweetened condensed milk straight out of the can.

"And you," I added, "she loves you."

Toby gave me the faux-suave look he'd been using since he was eleven years old, pretended to twirl his mustachio, and said in horrifyingly accented French, *"Mais oui, ma soeur foufou! Naturellement!"* But I'd seen something skitter across his face right before he said it. Anxiety maybe. Or self-doubt. Either of which would have alarmed me because neither had ever, to my knowledge, skittered across his face before. Somewhere in all this love I'd been hearing about there was a hitch.

"So you and Miranda have been together for how long?"

"For the best seven months of the girl's life."

"Seven months," I said, in what I'm positive was a neutral tone, although I admit that the neutral tone may have been somewhat undermined by my adding, "And you're moving in."

"Whoa, sister," said Toby, pulling in invisible reins. "Aren't you the girl who took, like, thirty years to figure out you were in love with a guy who's obviously (a) the greatest and (b) the best-looking human being in the *en*tire history of the world? The girl who didn't even think he was *attractive* for thirty years? And then married him, like, two days later?"

"Twenty-seven years," I corrected. "And four months later. And, yes, I am that girl."

It was true. As I've mentioned, I've known Mateo Sandoval since I was four years old. I've *loved* Mateo Sandoval since I was four years old, but until my relatively recent headlong, irrevocable, and utterly unforeseen plunge into being *in* love with him, I had spent years and years nearly oblivious to his charms. I say nearly oblivious because I knew like I knew my own name that he was kind and funny and smart, and I suppose I knew he was handsome—I have eyes, after all—but while these facts existed in my consciousness, they never weaseled their way into my unconscious or under my skin or into my soul or wherever those kinds of facts weasel in order to make your heart race and your breath shorten. Before he became my sun, moon, and stars, Teo was just Teo.

"Your point being?" I asked.

"Maybe you're not such an expert on timing? Maybe your own sense of timing is a little—what's the word?"

"Off?"

"Askew." Toby was teasing me, but I could still see faint footprints of the skittery doubt and worry all over his grinning face, so it didn't surprise me when he dropped the teasing voice and the grin and said, dolefully, "Anyway."

"Anyway what?"

He took a breath, gearing up, but then let it out and shrugged. "Anyway, seven months is a looooong time. Could be a record."

I looked him in the eye for a few seconds, then said, "That wasn't what you were going to say. Was it?"

Toby looked back at me. "Nope."

After a gulp of Gatorade, Toby leaned his curly-haired head to one side, then the other, as though whatever he had to impart required a thoroughly limber neck. He turned to me with a toothy, half-rueful, half-mischievous smile. "She doesn't exactly know I'm coming."

The hitch. Not a small hitch either, in my opinion, although you wouldn't have known it to look at Toby. He laughed.

"Relax, Cornelia. It's not a big deal." He rolled his eyes. "You know how women are."

"No. How are they?"

"When Miranda left for graduate school, she came down with a mild case of 'I love you, buts.' It happens."

I stared at Toby in confusion for several seconds, then said, "Miranda's pet name for you is Butts?"

Toby is prone to immoderate, explosive laughs. I was only thankful that the question hadn't hit him midsip or my sofa would have suffered under a deluge of anti-freeze-colored sports drink.

"Butts!" spluttered Toby, his face purpling. "Butts! Now that would explain a lot, wouldn't it?"

He kept laughing. I sighed and looked at my watch.

When the guffawing petered out at last, Toby explained. "'I love you, *but* I'm only twenty-two.' 'I love you, *but* I need some space.' 'I love you, *but* I'm not sure I can see a future with you.' 'I love you, *but* I need to forage a life for myself first.' Like that."

"Forge," I said, distractedly. If Miranda was saying she wasn't sure she could see a future with Toby, it didn't sound like she had a *mild* case of anything. In fact, all those "I love you, buts" seemed to add up to one very large "I don't love you enough."

"Sic," said Toby.

"What?"

"You know, 'forage [sic].'" He made brackets with his hands. "As in she didn't really say that. My mistake."

Part of my brain marveled at the fact that Toby had a working knowledge of "[sic]," but most of it was too busy worrying about his impending heartbreak to notice.

"Butts," he chuckled, softly, shaking his head in wonder.

I sighed. Miranda Bloom was about to blindside and

body-slam this sweet blue-eyed boy again, so hard his teeth would rattle, and he had no idea.

"Toby," I began, carefully. Then a thought hit me. "Toby, there's an SUV chockful of your personal belongings sitting in my driveway. You were just planning to show up at her new apartment tonight with all of your . . . crap?"

Toby winced, ducked his head, then swiveled his eyes up at me with a look I'd seen him use before, a winsome hybrid of sheepish and beseeching. Unlike the rest of the kids in our family, who learned early on how to verbalize our myriad desires (legend has it that my first full sentence was this request for buttered toast: "I want a grilled cheese sandwich with no cheese," which various family members flaunt as early and damning evidence of my roundabout linguistic style), Toby spoke not more than two intelligible words until he was all of two and a half. Instead, he developed a full-bodied, wordless eloquence, and toddled around emoting like a tiny male Mary Pickford, a talent that remained even after the onset of speech.

Now with a single look he managed to convey something along the lines of "You are—no joke—the world's coolest sister. I mean, seriously, your generosity and kindness are beyond colossal, and even though in a classic Toby dumb-shit move, I totally neglected to run this by you beforehand, and even though you and Teo just moved into this awesome house and were probably into the idea of some alone time, I sincerely hope that you'll let me hang out for a while in this my hour of need. Because you rock."

"Oh, Toby," I groaned.

"You'll hardly know I'm here."

I raised an eyebrow.

"Mostly I'll be, you know, elsewhere, waging my campaign to get Miranda to let me move in. Like a siege. This'll just be my base camp."

"What a lovely metaphor."

"Love is war, right? Oh, and I have a lead on a job in Philly, so consider me a renter." Toby smiled a smile calculated to melt my heart. I glared, first at his cheeky expression, then at his sweaty Gatorade. *No,* I thought, *no way, not this time, buddy boy.*

"No," I said, shaking my head, "no, no, no, no, no."

He kept smiling.

"I said no."

"And this is a no-means-no situation?"

"Yes," I said vehemently, but of course it wasn't. When I began to whack the heel of my hand repeatedly against my forehead, Toby tackled me in a bone-crushing hug, crowing, "I knew you'd let me stay, I knew it, I knew it, I knew it . . ."

"Get off me, you Saint Bernard."

I pushed him away, and said, "And I'm not letting you stay. I'm only saying I'll discuss it with Teo."

"No need," he said, cheekier than ever, "I caught him on his way out to drive Clare back this morning. He gave an enthusiastic thumbs-up."

Just as I was commencing to stew and mutter about this, the doorbell rang.

Toby scrambled to his feet, and said quickly, "Uh, and I have, like, one other piece of news? But it can wait."

At the expression on my face, Toby said, "No, no, it's good. It's amazing, actually. You'll love it. I love it. Right now, though, gotta get the door."

I stood up and stamped my foot. "Toby, just tell me. Now. This minute," I commanded.

Toby did not do as he was told. Instead, he bounded over to the door and flung it open. Lake stood there in a purple felt cloche hat, holding a chocolate cake.

"Cool," exclaimed Toby, wide eyed. "How'd you know it was my birthday?"

"Ah. You must be Toby," she said dryly, but the way her mouth was twitching at the corners told me that Lake would pass the Toby litmus test with flying colors. "I'm Lake. I think you met my son, Dev."

"Yeah, right. Dev's a nice kid. A dim bulb and all, not a lot going on upstairs, but nice." Toby grinned and held out his arms. "So, Lake, may I take the cake?"

"Oh, please," I growled at Toby, with a look that said *I am not finished with you by a long shot,* "when in your life have you ever done anything else?"

I was happy to see her. It was a complicated, wary happiness, since the last time I'd set eyes on Lake, her face had swiveled shut and told me lies, but it was happiness all the same. And there was something else, too, some feeling I hadn't felt toward her before. Not pity, exactly. Call it tenderness. Despite not having known her for long, I'd seen a surprising number of Lakes, and the Lake who stood newly cakeless in my foyer, purple hat in hand, was not one I'd ever seen before.

She seemed to have bigger eyes and to take up less space. Even her hair seemed tamer. And she stood differently. She didn't stand on the earth as though she owned it, absolutely sturdy, as though a different, better gravity worked on her than on the rest of us. Mostly, though, it was the look in her eyes that had changed. The arch blue burning was gone. Lake looked at me and around my house with this odd combination of worry and eagerness, as though she'd lost something and needed it back, as though she were hoping she might find it there, but was so afraid she wouldn't that she wasn't sure she even wanted to look.

It hit me then: Lake needed a friend, probably more than I ever did. She wasn't desperate (I thought that in her own way, Lake must be as immune to quiet desperation as Toby), but she needed a friend, and her need made her fragile as I'd never imagined she could be. So, with the sudden tenderness tugging on me like a gentle current and because I've required enough second chances myself to be a true believer in them, I took three big steps toward Lake, hugged her, sat her down, and made her talk.

It didn't take much. The story was right there, ready to be given away. Sad and full of loss, but also a love story if I've ever heard one.

The story started before Dev was born, with the pre-Dev Lake, a smart, utterly lonely Midwestern girl who'd found herself in the center of a Cinderella tale. "I wasn't that exceptional. But I grew up in a town where nothing was exceptional. I was it, the point-to girl. As corny as it sounds, I was hope."

When she was named a National Merit finalist, the local paper did a long, glowing article, with photos of her with her beaming parents—"My SAT scores made the front page, literally"—and followed up with a series of articles tracking Lake through her senior year of high school.

"My father had always been a silent, angry guy. Still waters run deep and shark infested. They'd pop up now and then and bite. But whenever the reporters showed up at our house, the guy became a charmer, the proudest papa you ever saw."

"What about your mom?"

"She wanted so badly for me to get out, to go somewhere and shine. I think she'd wanted that for me since the day I was born."

The Sunday before Lake left for Brown, her family's church had thrown a party for her. "It was supposed to be for all the graduates who were going on to college. There were four of us. Two were going to the community college down the road. The other one, a girl named Beth Wolter, had deferred her acceptance to the state university because she was pregnant. So the party was really for me. Pretty much the whole town came. I hated it and loved it, and I hated that I loved it."

She'd gotten pregnant with Dev at the end of her sophomore year, except, of course, back then she didn't know that it was with Dev.

"My boyfriend from home drove all the way out to pick me up. I didn't tell anyone I was coming. I remember sneaking around the house to the back door like a burglar and seeing my mother's face through the kitchen window. She was peeling potatoes at the sink, and I just stood there thinking, 'She doesn't know. This is the last time I'll see her when she doesn't know what I've done.'"

When Lake told me the next part, her voice hardened. "It was like a fucking tidal wave had hit our house. I knew it would be bad, but it was so much worse than I'd thought it would be. My dad was a lunatic, of course. I'd expected that. But my mother was a thousand times worse. And what's so strange is that even while she was saying awful things to me, I understood that she wasn't disappointed *in* me, like my dad was. She wasn't thinking about what the neighbors would say. She was disappointed *for* me. God, it was insane: these two conservative, churchgoing people screaming at their upstart liberal daughter to have an abortion."

After a tiny hesitation, I said, "Can I ask you a question?"

Lake gave a wry smile and said, "The million-dollar question." She sighed. "I've been pro-choice since the day I learned there was such a thing as pro-choice. Way before I went to Brown. And two years before I got pregnant, I was calling Beth Wolter a fool for not having an abortion."

She took a sip of coffee. "I've thought about it a lot over the years. Why I did what I did. And what I think is that growing up, I was always alone. I never felt like I fit in with anyone. My mother told me it was because I was special." Lake laughed a short, bitter laugh. "The way she described it, it was almost biblical, like I'd slid down a beam of light straight from heaven into this dark, depressed town. I know I was smart. Not as smart as Dev. I never had the fun with it that Dev has, puzzling things out all the time.

"Anyway, I kept waiting for the day I could leave and find *my* place, my people. But when I got to college, it was all rich, beautiful kids. I know it's not possible, but at the time I could've sworn they all knew each other. From summer camp or boarding school or some island where their families all hung out together laughing, with tinkling drinks and white shirts and blond dogs running around."

"Wasn't there anyone who you felt at home with?"

Lake looked at me for several long seconds. "There were one or two people who were important to me. Or

who I could've let become important to me. But it just
didn't happen."

"Maybe you wanted a reason to leave."

Lake nodded. "Maybe. It was more than that, though.
When I found out I was pregnant, my first thought was
'Now there will be another person like me.' That probably isn't a very 'healthy' reason to have a baby." She
shrugged.

Lake had left and never gone back, left with Dev's
father, Teddy, a restless twenty-one-year-old, a nice boy.

"He thought it was an adventure. Get the hell out of
Dodge, you know? But after Dev was born, I could tell
Teddy was in over his head, and he was the kind of
person who would've done the right thing until it killed
him. But his heart wasn't in it. So I took Dev and left."

"Has Dev ever met him?"

Lake shook her head. "I call my mother now and
then. Not often. But Dev and I haven't seen anyone
from back home. It just seems easier."

I tried to imagine not seeing my parents for fourteen
years, how not seeing them could possibly be easier
than seeing them. I failed. But Lake's parents aren't my
parents. I am not Lake.

Lake looked down at her coffee. When she looked
up, the fierceness was back in her eyes. "I just wanted
him. I never wanted anything so much in my life."

I understood this kind of wanting, and because my
eyes were suddenly full of stinging tears, I got up from
the table and went into the kitchen. When I got back,
Lake was in the living room, holding the double-photo
frame that sat on our mantel. In both photos, Teo and I
are side by side, grinning like demons. One was taken
on our wedding day, the other some twenty-five years
before.

"The dynamic duo," I said, smiling.

Lake set the picture down quickly, looking confused. "You two, you've been together since you were kids?"

I laughed, "Well, not together-together. We grew up a few houses down from each other. Our parents are best friends, and all of us—Ollie, Toby, Cam, Teo's sister, Estrella, Teo, and I—we were like one, big, loopy family. But Teo and I took our time falling in love."

"How much time?"

"It's just been a few years." I felt embarrassed by how cozy and sweet this must sound to Lake, how easy. But Lake smiled at me and plopped herself down on my couch.

"It must be—comfortable, being married to someone you've known for so long. I bet it feels homey," she said, "familiar."

I considered telling her the whole truth, that, yes, it was comfortable; it did feel like the best kind of home. But also how loving Teo could feel anything but familiar, how it could mean walking a fine silver edge between exhilaration and ache, and how there were long moments—entire mornings even—when focusing on just one aspect of him—the back of his hand, the colors in his face, his voice—was all I could manage because the whole of him might overwhelm me. Or how I'd lie in his arms in bed after making love, luminous with gratitude and thinking the words: *I am poured out like water, I am poured, I am poured out, I am poured out like water.*

Even our shared childhood, the parts of Teo's story I'd carried around with me as casually as I'd carried anything and for as long, could become almost unbearably present and precious to me: that the man on the edge of the bed, putting on his blue shirt in the dark, was once the boy who slept in a tent in his backyard for the week following the death of his grandfather would hit me with all the force of past and present both and make me want to weep.

Or this: As Teo knelt before me with his head in my lap, grieving for our lost pregnancy, time became a telescope closing, and the eleven-year-old kid he'd once been was suddenly right there in the room with us, the boy who'd dragged me out of my warm house and up to the roof to watch the Leonid, his face exultant, counting streaks of light under the miraculous sky.

Could I tell Lake any of this? Would she want to hear it?

I said, "Sometimes it is, and sometimes it isn't."

"And your parents," she said, "all four of them. I bet they're clamoring for grandchildren."

"Oh, well, you know," I said, shrugging.

"So what about it?" she asked. "What's your timeline?"

I should have told her then. Everything pointed to it. Lake had just told me the story of her life, and I felt closer to her than I ever had. Surely she deserved to hear what I was desperate to tell: the miscarriage at fourteen weeks, *fourteen*, just as we'd gotten the first, risky trimester behind us; blood on the white floor; me doubled over with my arms around myself, trying to hold it in, keep it safe, saying, "It's okay. I promise. I promise." I was still bleeding when the towers fell, and I spent weeks afterward torn between consolation and despair: between finding my own loss so small, so feather light and bearable compared to the huge, shattering, manifold losses of that day and feeling— selfishly, I know—that the devastation on television mirrored my own.

Entirely by accident, for reasons I still don't understand, but that perhaps had something to do with the
pure, feral grieving I'd heard on the other side of Piper's
door that afternoon and with her eyes when she looked
at Elizabeth, I had turned this story over to Piper.
Piper, who didn't even like me. I'd trusted Piper, and
even though she'd shaken off the moment of my trusting her with one toss of her blond head, I found—and I
understand this even less—that I didn't quite regret it.

If I could tell Piper, I could tell Lake.

But I took a deep breath and said, "I don't know
that we have a timeline. Whenever it happens, we'll be
glad."

We were.

Two days later: pink lines in a plastic window.

All those Annunciation paintings had it right: the
descending angel, white lily, cascading light, the
woman's face bespeaking humility, fear, elation, or
all three at once. It should be momentous, an announcement accompanied by singing choirs, auroras
of gold.

Even a blood test, a doctor striding forth in a lab coat
bearing tidings of great joy would feel more fitting.

But however I got the news, I got it.

When Teo got home, I was sitting on the sofa, waiting for him. He sat down next to me, and he must have
seen something in my face because he didn't say anything, just picked up my hand and pressed it against his
mouth.

"I'm five feet tall," I told him. "Will you love me
when I'm spherical?"

And there it was, around his face for maybe half a
second, an aurora of gold. "Cor," he said. Latin for

heart. A nickname he almost never uses, one so private, it's almost a secret from us, too. "I've been waiting my whole life to love you when you're spherical."

He kissed me. I kissed him back.

"So," I ventured finally, "are we opting for cautious optimism?"

Teo smiled his beautiful smile. "No way. Full speed ahead."

"Are you sure?"

"Not even optimism. Are you kidding? Jubilation. Incautious jubilation."

This is why I love my husband.

"Okay, then." I pressed Teo's hand to my belly and looked down at it. "You hear that in there? Your father says incautious jubilation, so incautious jubilation it is!"

And it was.

ELEVEN

𝒥n the last weeks of Elizabeth's illness, when she had the presence of mind to want on her own behalf, Piper wanted to remember everything, wanted to store every image, word, and hour, even the bad ones. But time moved so erratically—screeching by; slamming to a whiplashing halt; limping with excruciating slowness, like an injured animal—and there was so little left for sorting or reflection that a lot got lost. Even so, Piper could pinpoint the precise moment at which she and Tom had become allies, a single force: exactly two weeks before Christmas, a pocket of stillness, no words exchanged, two sets of blue eyes locked together over the heads of children.

It had been lullaby time at Elizabeth's house. Wednesday evening. Kyle had finished work at a reasonable hour, for a change, and was at home putting Carter and Meredith to bed, and Tom was on his way back from taking Elizabeth's mother, Astrid, to the airport. Over the months, Astrid had come and gone, come and gone, politely, obdurately refusing Tom's offers to move into the guest room for an "extended stay" (there were no

right phrases; "for as long as it takes," "for the duration," "until the end," all wrong). Each visit, Astrid
would walk into the house, lightfooted and smiling, be
with Elizabeth for hours every day, helping to bathe her
on days when she didn't want to get up, coaxing her to
eat, talking and talking, and then after a week or so,
would leave looking flat, slack faced, and confused, as
though sadness were a drug.

Astrid would be back in a few days, having detoxi-
fied among her cats, her friends, her houseplants. Tom
would be back any minute. But for the moment, Piper
was alone, outside the entryway to what used to be
Elizabeth's dining room, listening to Elizabeth sing to
Emma and Peter. Lullaby time was the last ritual, the
one Elizabeth clung to with what Piper knew had to
be every ounce of stubbornness she had left after the
others (afternoon Popsicles, reading aloud, tickle time)
had become occasional, then sporadic, then had fallen
off altogether. Her voice, as diminished as the rest of
her, came out papery, almost tuneless, but Piper didn't
need to hear her to know the song because the song was
always the same—"Bridge over Troubled Water"—and
so familiar that Piper couldn't believe all the years
she'd spent not realizing that it was about motherhood.

Elizabeth was singing to her children, making promises about laying herself down, and Piper thought, *Of
course you would. Don't you think they know that?*
But tangled up with this thought in Piper's head was
another thought: Emma, worrying about whether her
mother would fall forward or backward when she died.
A sob caught in Piper's throat.

"I know. That song. It's rough, isn't it?"

Piper opened her eyes. Tom stood there in his coat
and gloves, concern in his eyes. Ever since Elizabeth

had stopped treatment, Tom had changed, thank God. Or changed back. He'd dropped the walking-wounded routine and that awful hangdog helplessness. He'd even gained a little weight. "And a good thing, too," Piper had told him one morning, giving him a poke to the sternum, "or eventually, I would have had to beat the crap out of you." They'd laughed, even though they'd both understood that she wasn't really joking.

"Yeah," Piper agreed, but she straightened and swiped a forefinger under each eye in a businesslike manner. "Sorry."

"For what?" asked Tom, quietly. "What could you possibly be apologizing for?" Months ago, Piper had made him agree to stop telling her "Thank you," and he'd stuck to it. But there were still plenty of times, like right then, when Tom was thinking the words so hard in her direction that he might as well have been shouting them, so she turned abruptly and peeked around the corner at Elizabeth and the kids.

"Looks like they're finished," whispered Piper, and she and Tom had walked into the room. But Piper had been wrong. They weren't finished, not quite.

The children lay pressed against either side of Elizabeth. Her eyes were closed and her face looked not just tired, but extinguished, as it did every night after lullaby time. The ritual exhausted her so much that Piper half wished she'd give it up, just let it go, but she understood why Elizabeth had hung on to it for so long. No matter where Piper was—an airplane, a grocery store—she didn't even have to close her eyes to conjure up the feeling, a full five-senses memory, of her children in impossibly soft pajamas, fragrant and damp from the bath, radiating heat, their little chugging breaths growing slower and slower the closer they got to sleep.

Emma wasn't asleep. When Tom and Piper got to the bed, she uncurled herself from around Elizabeth and sat up, her shoulders high and tense, locks of still-damp hair sticking to her cheek. Like blades of grass, thought Piper, smoothing the hair away with her hand. It was an absent, loving gesture, the kind any mother would make, and as she had many times over the months, Piper felt a pang of self-consciousness, touching Elizabeth's child as though she were Piper's own, even though Piper and Elizabeth had touched each other's children this way always, from the very first day of each child's life.

"What's up, Em?" asked Tom, smiling at her.

"It's two weeks until Christmas," Emma said. Her eyes were round and frightened, and as Piper watched, Emma shivered hard, her arms suddenly covered with goose bumps. Piper felt a rush of compassion. She recognized panic when she saw it. Panic was coursing through this child like electricity.

"That's right," said Tom, gently, "it'll be here before you know it."

Emma shook her head, adamantly. "No! It's too long." She looked at Elizabeth's face, then looked back, shifting her gaze between Piper and Tom. "I want . . . I want . . ." She broke off, but Piper knew what she wanted. Not eternity, not even a year. Two weeks. It was such a small thing for a five-year-old to want, so reasonable and limited. The smallness of Emma's wish made Piper want to cry.

Piper had looked at Tom, then; their eyes had met and held, and there it was: a resolution, a pact like the ones people seal with blood. Elizabeth was slipping away so quickly—sleeping a lot, knocked out by pain-killers or simple exhaustion, not eating much, rarely asking to get out of bed—but she would spend one last Christmas with her family, whatever it took. Tom and Piper would see to it. They would *will* it. Come hell or high water, thought Piper, furiously. Bring it on.

Tom had reached over and lifted Emma into his arms.

"No, it's not, Em-girl. It's not too long." He was talking to his daughter, but looking at Piper, and Piper nodded.

Seinfeld reruns. Mango sorbet. Carole King's *Really Rosie*. Bruce Springsteen's "Born to Run." Hugh Grant. Dim lights. Bright lights. Beethoven's *Moonlight Sonata*. Bing Crosby's "White Christmas." The J.Crew catalog. Curtains open. Curtains halfway open. Curtains closed. Chicken broth. *The Grinch Who Stole Christmas*. Bananas. Pink roses. Tom in his brown suede jacket. Emma singing "Jingle Bells." A cashmere wrap. Candy canes. The smell of frying bacon. The smell of baking sugar cookies. *SpongeBob SquarePants*. Cornelia's pumpkin bread. Kate's homemade applesauce. *Law & Order* reruns. Piper reading *Little Women* aloud. Astrid reading *Emma* aloud. Tom doing the crossword puzzle aloud. Evergreen-scented candles. Peppermint tea. Peter in his earflap hat.

Whatever made her smile, seem about to smile, laugh, seem about to laugh, lift her eyebrows, stop crying, sit up, wake up fully, fall asleep quietly, take an interest, tell a story, make a joke, put on lipstick, forget to be angry, feel like talking, feel like eating, feel like drinking, feel like getting out of bed. Piper and Tom would do all of these things, would give her every one over and over. Whatever satisfied her. Whatever made her ask for more.

This was their logic: if it worked once—Piper putting the cashmere wrap around her shoulders, Elizabeth rubbing the softness against her cheek, smiling and saying, "Heaven!"—it could work again. Or: if these things worked individually, they would work even better in combination. Cookies baking in the kitchen, *SpongeBob* on the television, a mug of peppermint tea steaming on the table beside her. Piper reading *Little Women, Moonlight Sonata* in the background, an evergreen-scented candle burning on the windowsill.

It sounded logical. It *was* logical. Piper told herself this, and she defied, *dared* anyone to argue. The hitch was that it wasn't really true, and, in her deepest places, Piper knew it. In her deepest places, Piper knew that like countless desperate people before her, she—she and Tom together—had begun to practice witchcraft. Piper remembered having done this as a child: if I wear the yellow shirt, it won't rain on Field Day; if I sleep with my stuffed cat on my left and my teddy bear on my right, I won't have bad dreams; if I set the table silverware first, plates second, my mother will act like a normal mother. If we watch for what makes Elizabeth feel alive, if we keep careful track, miss nothing, and give her these things again and again, she will not die.

Piper knew that the trick was to stay focused, to never let the goal of keeping Elizabeth alive until Christmas slip—even for an hour—from the forefront of her concentration. To accomplish this, Piper had systematically pulled the distractions from her life like weeds from a garden: volunteer activities, lunches with the girls, playdates, dinners, shopping, and because it was the season for them, holiday parties.

She and Kyle had fought about the parties. Actually, they would have fought about the parties, would have had six separate fights, no doubt, if Kyle had known

about all the invitations Piper had declined, but since
Piper was careful to dispose of the invitations quickly
and quietly, they fought about one party: Kate's, an
annual black-tie, champagne-flooded, no-holds-barred
sit-down dinner that felt as close to the kind of party
Truman Capote might have attended in his heyday as
any party in a fairly distant suburb of a fairly small city
anywhere in the country could feel.

Kyle had found the RSVP card with the regrets box
checked before Piper had gotten a chance to tuck a personal note into the tiny, engraved, silver-bell-embossed
envelope and send it winging its elegant way back to
Kate, who might not have been the brightest bulb in the
marquee, but who would've understood perfectly and
instantly why Piper and Kyle could not make it to her
Christmas party this particular year.

But Kyle had gotten to the RSVP card first. He'd
dropped it dramatically onto Piper's empty plate one
morning, while she was waiting for her toast to pop up
(somehow, without meaning to, Piper had begun to eat
carbohydrates again), and he'd launched into the most
infuriating kind of tirade regarding what he perceived
as Piper's skewed priorities and twisted sense of obligation. The tirade was delivered in measured, quiet
tones, but it was a tirade nonetheless, and what made it
worse was the way Kyle tried to disguise it, to coat his
anger with a fuzzy, blurring concern—like that awful
dandelion-fuzz mold that Piper kept finding on food in
her refrigerator lately—concern for Piper's well-being
that was so utterly phony it made her want to throw the
toaster at him.

She tried to block a lot of what he said, but some of it
got through, and Piper's mind seethed with comebacks.

"Kate's a terrific person and your best friend." (With

regularity, you call Kate "the brain-dead boob job."
Elizabeth is my best friend.)

"The kids miss you. I miss you." (How dare you suggest that I'm neglecting the kids? The kids are with me
all the time, you stupid shit, which you would know
if you were ever home, which you are not, but that's a
whole other conversation. And you don't miss me; if
you missed me, you'd bother to come home from work
before nine P.M. once in a while, which you don't, and
you'd stop finding reasons to go into the office on the
weekends. Furthermore, you probably think that I've
been too busy to notice these things, but I've noticed.
I've just been too tired to talk to you about them, so
you should be glad I'm spending so much time helping
Elizabeth and her family because it gets you off the
hook, and come to think of it, I'm sure you *are* glad.
Lucky you.)

"At some point, your altruism became selfishness,
Piper. Yes, that's what I said, your altruism crossed a
line and became selfishness." (Despite the fact that the
thought you just voiced is entirely meaningless, you're
so proud of yourself for having thought it and said it
and having included that big word in saying it, that you
had to repeat it for emphasis.)

"Your identity is so caught up in all of this that I
wonder who you'll be after Elizabeth is gone." (I am
being a friend. I am doing what a friend does. If you had
any real friends, you might understand that. Oh, God, I
don't know who I'll be either. I have no idea at all.)

"Superwoman Piper saving the day. I hate to say it,
but sometimes I think you're actually enjoying this."
(I am not saving anything. I am taking care of children. I am cooking. I am talking and reading books
and watching television with Elizabeth. I am doing one

job and then another. Don't say you hate to say it. You
don't hate to say it. Enjoying this? *Enjoying this?* Fuck
you fuck you fuck you.)

"This isn't normal. This isn't friendship, whatever
you think. This isn't love." (You wouldn't know love if
it walked up and slapped you in the face, Kyle.)

Piper didn't say any of this. She didn't say anything
at all. As Kyle talked, she moved the RSVP card off
of her plate, removed her toast from the toaster, spread
it with strawberry fruit spread, poured herself coffee,
took the plate and coffee to the table, and sat down.
When he stopped talking, Piper was holding her coffee
cup with both hands because her hands were suddenly
cold. All of her was cold. She was chilled and frightened, not by what Kyle had said, but by what she hadn't
said. Her own thoughts sounded very much like the
thoughts of a woman who did not love her husband, and
this was not the kind of woman Piper could be. We are
going through a rough time, she told herself. It happens
to everyone. She wanted to say this out loud, but she
couldn't. If she opened her mouth, she might shriek,
she might cry. At the very least, her teeth would chat-
ter. After a few seconds, Kyle made a disgusted sound
and left the room.

They went to the party, not because of anything Kyle
had said, but because the next day Elizabeth told her to
go. She insisted.

When Piper had arrived that morning, Elizabeth was
with Lena, her favorite of the hospice workers, and
she smiled at Piper over the powder blue photo album
Lena held open before her and said, "Peter." Peter's
baby album. As Lena turned the pages of the heavy
book, Elizabeth pointed out Peter having his first bath.

Peter in his super saucer, his bouncy chair, his swing, sleeping in the Björn on Tom's chest with his bald head flopped to one side. Peter had been a sweet baby, chirpy and rosy and heavily eyelashed, the kind you might see curled inside a flower in one of those Anne Geddes photographs.

When Piper walked Lena to the door, Lena said, "Elizabeth was a little restless last night, called out in her sleep a couple of times."

Piper felt a pulse of gratitude for the way Lena so often called Elizabeth by name when speaking about her. With others, sometimes even with Tom and Piper, Elizabeth was an omnipresent, inevitable "she." Lena smiled wryly, reached out and squeezed Piper's hand. Habitually physically aloof except with her closest friends, Piper was learning a language of small touches: a squeeze of the fingers, a hand placed on a shoulder or a cheek. Lena's squeeze said, "It was a harder night than I'm telling you it was, but she made it."

"But she's good this morning," Lena went on, nodding, "it's a good morning."

"When I see her sitting in a chair, smiling, I know it's a good morning. Thank you."

But when Piper reentered the room, she saw that the good morning had ended. The baby album was lying facedown and open on the floor, and Elizabeth's face was a mask of white-lipped, smoldering rage. Piper had seen Elizabeth like this before, but not often. Usually, the anger spattered out like grease from a pan and could be directed toward anyone: Piper for making the soup too hot, Astrid for hurting her head with the hairbrush, Ginny for not keeping the children quiet, Tom for buying the wrong fruit (tangerines instead of clementines), the wrong sheets (carded percale instead of mercerized sateen), the wrong small bottled waters (plain instead of fluoridated). She never let the children see her angry; possibly she didn't feel angry in their presence. Only rarely did they see her cry.

Everyone who knew Elizabeth admired her general demeanor of good-humored forbearance; they took it as courage, and Piper could understand that. It was courage. But Piper treasured the angry Elizabeth, the one who lashed out indiscriminately, ignoring considerations of fairness or proportion. Failing to rise above, Elizabeth seemed more earthbound, lashed to this life with ordinary human weakness and emotion. *Go for it!* Piper would think at those moments. *This whole thing is a fucking travesty. Take it out on everyone you know!*

But moments like this one frightened Piper, when the anger wasn't a short burst but a devouring fury that gripped Elizabeth with the force of a seizure. Invariably, this kind of anger left Elizabeth weepy and spent; it seemed to visibly suck life out of her. Now, from where she stood, Piper could see Elizabeth seem to catch her breath and then her chest began heaving too hard and too quickly, and Piper was running across the room, the phrase "irregular breathing" whipping around inside her head. Irregular breathing: like cool extremities, confusion, purplish mottling on the legs, irregular breathing was a sign of active dying.

Piper knelt beside Elizabeth's chair and took hold of her hands. They were warm. Impatiently, Elizabeth shook off Piper's touch, slapped her hands away.

"Betts," gasped Piper, "Betts, it's okay." Elizabeth glared at Piper with so much hatred that Piper fell back on her heels.

"It. Is. Not. Okay." Elizabeth shoved out the words

through gritted teeth, and then, someplace deep inside her body, a sound began forming, forming and rising, forming and rising, until it came out as an unearthly shriek. In a flash, Piper remembered a wedding she'd attended years ago at a former plantation house: the peacocks and their unbearable screaming.

"It's not fair!" screamed Elizabeth. "It's not fucking fair!"

For a full five minutes, she shrieked and ranted, her body racked with the effort. Finally, she picked up her glass of water and tried to fling it against the wall. Water arced upward, but the glass fell short and rolled to a stop on the silk Kashmir rug she and Tom had bought themselves for their tenth wedding anniversary.

With Elizabeth's wailing in her ears and with one fluid motion, Piper grabbed the glass and threw it as hard as she could. It went high, hit the crown molding, and shattered spectacularly, shards of glass raining down. The wailing stopped—for a second, Piper thought maybe time itself had stopped—and then Elizabeth began to laugh, not a hysterical laugh, as Piper might have expected, but a lovely, bubbly sound that seemed to fall around the room like confetti or snow.

The laughter didn't fix everything. What could? After it stopped, Elizabeth was wrung out and still deeply sad, but the laughter cleared a space where Elizabeth could talk and Piper could listen. In a parched almost-whisper, Elizabeth talked about her children and how she could not bear to leave them, could not bear the thought of all she would miss.

"The story," she said, sobbing, "I'll miss the whole story. Dating, college, jobs, weddings. I don't get to know how anything turns out, and I wanted to. I wanted to be there for all of it."

Later, she said, "Wow. I've been talking about myself for hours. Clearly, I need something new to think about."

Elizabeth gave a short laugh, smoothed her hair, and her smile held a trace of her old jauntiness. She said, "Okay. I didn't want to say anything before, but here it is: I need gossip, Pipe. And you are seriously falling down on the job. I know Kate's party is coming up because she sent us an invitation, and I get that you might not feel like going, but you have to. That's just the way it is. You go to that party and *get me some gossip*."

The party was not the ordeal Piper had imagined, but that was perhaps due to the fact that she never felt as though she were really there. When Kate opened the door to find Piper and Kyle, she did what Piper would consider, for the rest of her life, a beautiful thing: instead of ushering them in, she stepped down onto the porch, shut the door behind her, and enfolded Piper in a strong, true hug. "Are you sure?" she whispered in Piper's ear.

When Piper nodded, Kate turned, opened the door, Piper and Kyle followed her inside, and the change happened. Piper was present for the hug, but as soon as she stepped over the threshold of Kate's house, steeling herself for the onslaught of voices, music, and lights, a strange sensation overtook her. She felt weightless, flickering, transparent, and like she was watching everything through gauze. When people spoke to her, their voices seemed to come from a great distance.

So when Parvee Patel exclaimed, "You're so thin! What's your secret?" Piper did not feel like yanking out a fistful of Parvee's hair and saying, "A dying friend. You should get one," as she would have felt like doing under normal circumstances. She just smiled. (It was true, Piper had noticed it when she put on her black dress and found it loose. For the first time in her life, she had lost weight without knowing it, and, also for the first time, she had *discovered* she'd lost weight without caring.)

Dutifully, she collected gossip. Megan was pregnant at forty and was having neither CVS nor amnio. Jilly Keyes had reconnected online with her high school boyfriend, an attorney-to-the-B-list-stars, and had moved to L.A. to marry him. The Lowerys had stunned everyone by scrapping their plans to remodel their kitchen. Thad Ramsey's oldest son from his first marriage had gotten thrown out of college for cheating. Joshy Bray had almost gotten thrown out of kindergarten for cutting off a classmate's ponytail, but his father had won him an eleventh-hour reprieve with a large and well-timed donation to Tallyrand's annual fund. The Howards' country-house roof had leaked in the last big rain and while their antique four-poster had suffered damage, their (small, minor, but *still*) N. C. Wyeth had not. Margot Cleary had new lips; Amory Weiss had new breasts; Sydney Overton was spider vein free and loving it.

Through all of these conversations, the floating, absent sensation never left Piper. Several times, she thought bemusedly, *Who are these people?* and found it astonishing that not long ago they had been hers, a tribe the female half of which she had—there was no getting around it—presided over. She felt like a ghost, as though people might walk right through her, as though she were the one who had died. (Although no one has died, she reminded herself.) While she didn't miss this world, she saw from the way people looked at her—her dress, her hair, the newly visible butterfly of bones below her clavicle—and from the way they listened to her speak that she could still, at any time, step back into it, regain her old position, and the thought was comforting.

All evening, she felt Kyle's approval, and that was comforting, too. While they spent most of the party in separate conversations and were not seated together at dinner, she was constantly aware of his presence in the room, just as she was always aware of her children when they were in a public space. Now and then, as they always had, she and Kyle would catch each other's eyes and smile carefully calibrated smiles, ones that said things like "I'm fine," "Wait till you hear this," or "Rescue me." Earlier, they'd gotten dressed in silence, and he had neglected to tell her that she looked beautiful, but she saw that everything was all right now or almost all right. Nothing had been lost that couldn't be regained.

So the party was not a disaster. But as soon as the sole of Piper's Stuart Weitzman satin sandal touched Kate's front porch, the floating sensation vanished, Piper slid back into her body with a thud, and she nearly ran to the car, where, at Kyle's request, she had left her cell phone. There were three messages from Tom, one for each hour of the party, as he'd promised, the third of which had come in just ten minutes before. Elizabeth had eaten some of the egg strata her mother had made at her request (it had been a Sunday brunch staple all through Elizabeth's childhood), and had watched *The Grinch* with the kids, had done lullaby time, and had fallen asleep afterward.

In the most recent message, Tom said, "Elizabeth's

sleeping fine. No agitation or yelling out. Before she fell asleep, she asked me if you carried your satin Kate Spade something bag with the something feathers to the party tonight. So if you could report on that tomorrow, we'd all appreciate it."

Tomorrow. Piper closed her eyes and repeated the word inside her head, letting it unfold slowly, heavily, like a prayer: *to-mor-row*.

"Well?" asked Kyle, as she flipped the phone shut.

"She's alive," said Piper.

She died, of course. Not before Christmas. And not the day after Christmas, although Piper had woken in a panic at four A.M. on the twenty-sixth, certain that she'd somehow blown it, that all her bargaining for Christmas, Christmas, Christmas had been misunderstood by whomever or whatever she'd been bargaining with; "Christmas *at least*" is what she should have said. "Christmas for starters."

But Elizabeth lived through December and into the New Year, and for two days in late January, she appeared to be ready to live forever.

Cornelia and Teo dropped by on the first day. They'd come, separately and together, several times since that first visit, and once Cornelia and Elizabeth had watched a black-and-white movie that featured a man, a woman, a leopard, a dinosaur bone, and a lot of falling down. Piper had never liked black-and-white movies, but while she watched almost none of it and did not even know what it was called, she loved the movie because it had made Elizabeth behave like Elizabeth, laughing and calling out advice, warnings, fashion tips to the people on the screen.

Today, Cornelia and Teo brought a fat, gorgeous-smelling braid of homemade bread, still warm from the oven, and a ramekin of whipped honey butter.

That morning, Elizabeth had showered and dressed in the downstairs bathroom before Tom had even come down. She had told Tom that she had considered going upstairs, she'd felt that strong, but she hadn't wanted to wake up the kids. When Tom told Piper this in one of their quick update conversations on the back steps, she'd given an involuntary shudder and he'd nodded his understanding. Despite the drugs Elizabeth took to strengthen her bones, they were still frighteningly fragile, porous from the secondary bone cancer. A fall could be disastrous.

Tom had taken the kids to a birthday party. He hadn't wanted to go or to take the children away from Elizabeth when she was feeling so well, but she'd told him to go, go.

"She told me, 'I'll be here when you get back.' She was laughing, and I realized that that's what she wants from us, to act like this will last. But I'll be back in two hours max." He took off the glasses that until recently Piper hadn't even known he owned ("Kept falling asleep with my contacts in during my nights with Elizabeth," he'd explained, "I'd wake up with the things glued to my eyes"), and rubbed his eyes.

"You're not sleeping much at all, are you?" asked Piper.

"I'm fine. I lay down for a couple of hours last night," he said, then he shook his head. "But now I keep thinking, 'Man, what if she'd fallen in the shower?' And I can just see it, see her falling. I shouldn't have left her. I should have stayed downstairs."

But sitting at the kitchen table in black yoga pants

and the dark red cashmere sweater Tom had given her for Christmas, Elizabeth appeared less breakable than she had in months. Her eyes and skin were brighter, as though a light inside her body had been relit, and when she lifted her glass, pushed back her hair, her movements were suffused with a grace that Piper recognized as the simple absence of exhaustion. When Cornelia and Teo walked through the back door and saw her, Piper watched their faces register surprise, then delight, and for a moment, she felt glad that they didn't know what she herself knew: that this is the way it happened sometimes, a day or two of wellness right before the end, like a mirage in the desert.

Elizabeth saw their faces, too, spread her arms out and tilted her head, in a silent "Ta-da!"

"Wow," exclaimed Cornelia. "How gorgeous are *you*?"

Teo bent down, kissed Elizabeth's cheek, smiled, and said, "You're beautiful," as though he were just stating a fact. Piper remembered, then, what Teo did for a living. It was easy to forget because he never came to visit as a doctor, only as a neighbor. But he must know about the illusion of wellness and what it meant. Of course he did. When Piper took the bread out of Cornelia's hands, Cornelia touched Piper's forearm and said softly, "You okay?" and something somber in her eyes told Piper that Cornelia knew, too.

Piper put the bread on the ginkgo-leaf-shaped breadboard Elizabeth had bought during a trip that she, Tom, Kyle, and Piper had made to Vermont before the kids were born. She remembered how Elizabeth had collected leaves. All those hillsides burning with orange and red, so dazzling it wore you out, and there was Elizabeth preferring the shape, the gradations in color of a single leaf. Piper remembered her sorting the leaves afterward in her hotel room, turning them over and back, carefully placing them on the table before her like a gypsy with tarot cards.

When Elizabeth saw the bread, she grinned and said, "No bread knife, Piper. We're pulling this sucker apart with our hands."

The bread was good, which surprised Piper. Cornelia's pumpkin bread had been good, too, but Piper still had trouble picturing it: this arty, city-type woman with her haircut, scarves, and funky shoes measuring out flour and sugar, brushing on egg yolk.

After a few minutes, Elizabeth measured the bread with her hands and said, "Okay, I'm just eyeballing here, but I believe I've eaten six and a half inches of this loaf of bread."

"For those of you keeping score at home," said Teo, and he smiled at Piper. The man had a great smile. He wasn't Piper's type. His Princeton sweatshirt could have been a thousand years old, and in Piper's opinion, he desperately needed a haircut, but his smile was out of this world.

"So, Teo," said Elizabeth, giving him a grin that was evil and flirtatious at the same time.

"Uh-oh," said Teo.

"Our friend Kate happened to mention that she saw you playing basketball at the Y on Thursday with some of the guys."

"Since when does Kate work out at the Y?" asked Piper skeptically.

"Since never," said Elizabeth. "She was at some fund-raising meeting."

"Yeah, I was there," said Teo. "Glen Cheever talked me into joining the over-thirty league."

"The Doc Jocks," said Cornelia with a delicate wince.

"A bunch of lawyers mopped the floor with us," said Teo. "Lawyers get more sleep than doctors."

"Also," Cornelia reminded him, "your team. It sucks, I believe."

"Oh, yeah," agreed Teo, cheerfully, "it does."

"Kate didn't mention that." Elizabeth went on, coyly. "She did mention a certain absence of shirts."

"Not Teo," said Cornelia, "he's not a bare-the-bod kind of guy. More a hide-your-light-under-a-bushel guy." She mouthed the word "Shy."

"That's not what I heard," sang Elizabeth.

Cornelia looked at Teo with exaggerated shock.

"Cornelia, it was a basketball game. Shirts versus skins. Someone forgot the pinnies."

"Pinnies?" asked Cornelia. "You wear pinnies?"

"Forget it," said Teo.

"What *I* heard is that most of those guys had no business being shirtless in public," said Elizabeth.

"I bet," snorted Piper.

"What *I* heard is that the only one who really did," Elizabeth said, smiling sweetly at Teo, "was you."

Some men look good when they blush, thought Piper, and Teo was one of those men.

"And I don't know if you know this, Teo," Elizabeth went on, "but I was originally supposed to be on that fund-raising committee."

"You were not," said Piper.

"I think I see where this is going," said Cornelia with dancing eyes. "He'll never do it."

"I *was* supposed to be on that committee," Elizabeth lied serenely, "and if I hadn't gotten sick, I'm sure I would have been with Kate when she happened to walk past the open door of the basketball court."

"It's a lost cause, Elizabeth," said Cornelia.

But then, without saying a word, Teo ducked out of his sweatshirt, strode to the center of the kitchen, and put his arms out. "Pass it," he said to Elizabeth, and she passed him an invisible ball, which he dribbled a few times in a fancy way, then shot.

Piper watched Elizabeth toss back her head, hoot, and clap her hands, and she knew she should feel shocked. It was so inappropriate. A married man performing shirtless in a room, with two married women and his own wife watching and cheering as if they were at some ridiculous bachelorette party. Totally and absurdly, *embarrassingly* inappropriate.

Except that it didn't feel that way, not even—to Piper's surprise—to Piper, and looking around, she saw that no one, not even Teo, seemed embarrassed. She would not have believed it six months ago, but maybe there were times when the inappropriate wasn't inappropriate at all, when it was light and funny and exactly right. When it even held an indescribable loveliness. There's nothing wrong with this picture, thought Piper. And then she amended the thought: except cancer. The only inappropriate thing in this room is that Elizabeth is sick.

This was the first day of wellness.

On the second day of wellness, Elizabeth held her children all day long, read to them, sang to them, built Lego towers with them, touched their hair and their faces, spread their fingers open and looked at their hands. She told them over and over that they were perfect, that they made her life perfect. She told them that she would love them forever, that she would stay with them, would be invisible but with them, like air. They could talk to her, she told them, and she would listen.

Tom told Piper this afterward, because, for most of

that day, Piper stayed at her own house. For reasons she could not fully explain, she kept her children home from school. She had been careful all along to give each one time alone with her every day, but even so, she knew she hadn't been paying the attention she should. There were days when she would stare at herself in the mirror, and say, "Won't be winning mother of the year this year, Pipe."

Mostly she believed that everything would be all right. How could everything not be all right when she loved them so much? But sometimes, especially at night, she worried that she was marking them, changing them, that her concentration on Elizabeth, on Emma and Peter, was opening a loneliness in Carter and Meredith that they would carry around forever. While reading a book to Carter, she pointed to the letter *C,* and said, "Remember this letter that looks like a sideways smile? What do you think that one is?" Then Carter said, "Mommy, I *know*! *C* says *kuh*. *B* says *buh*. *D* says *duh*. You know I know all them!" And Piper felt a rush of panic because she hadn't known. If I missed this, she thought, what else have I missed?

At about eight that evening, after Carter and Meredith were asleep, Elizabeth called. "I want you, Pipe. Just for a few minutes? Can I send Ginny over?"

She wanted what she'd wanted many times before, the old promises: that Piper help Tom and the children to be happy, that Piper help Emma and Peter to remember her.

She said two other things, new things.

This: "I love you, and I know you, and you're a different person than you think you are. Bigger and wilder and nicer. Your heart is the best heart in town. Can you please remember that?"

And this: "I know some people want to be alone. But I want everyone there. I want everyone in the house when it happens. Tom, you, Kyle, Ginny, all the kids, my mom, Lena, if she can. I'll know you're all there. Even if I don't seem to know, I'll know."

As January began its gray, downward slide into February, Elizabeth began to die in earnest. It lasted three days. As she had wanted, they were all there. Even Kyle came every day after work and spent every night. Not for one second was Elizabeth alone.

What Piper would remember, for the rest of her life, about those three days was the talking, a gold wire of hum running through the house, day and night. They talked to Elizabeth. They took turns. They read to her and sang to her. Tom lay down next to her and whispered the story of the births of both children. They wet her mouth with a damp sponge and touched her hair, her hands, her face. They comforted her. They coaxed her. Astrid sang her lullabies, hymns, and songs by Carly Simon, Roberta Flack, James Taylor. They assured her. They gave her permission to go. Peter threw himself down on the kitchen floor, kicked, and refused to see her, saying, "I don't like her like that." But later, when Piper came into the room to give Tom a break, she found Peter curled up like a cat at Elizabeth's feet, his arms around both her ankles, as Tom told the story of the day he found out he was having a son.

When Piper was entirely alone with Elizabeth, she gave her her secrets. The secret men, the lovers, all through college and until she'd met Kyle. She tried to articulate what she had never articulated before, even to herself: how it wasn't about power, exactly, not having power over someone, anyway; how, despite what people said about girls who slept with a lot of men, she was sure it wasn't pathological, a search for a lost father (her father was never truly lost, not even after his wife left him; he merely shrank) or a crazy need for attention (she'd always gotten plenty of attention). She had neither loathed nor disrespected herself. In all those years, she had never felt desperate, never, and even now, she didn't feel ashamed.

She'd liked it. She'd more than liked it. Each time, she'd felt in possession of a fierce, elemental beauty, lifted, intoxicated by tenderness, free. At the time she'd believed in a distinct difference between herself and the whole category of sluts, tramps, floozies whom she scorned openly and without mercy. Now, just now, as she spoke to Elizabeth, she began to doubt that difference. Not that she considered herself, retrospectively, a slut, but it occurred to her that maybe the others weren't sluts either. Maybe they'd all had their reasons.

"I'm sorry," she told Elizabeth, "I don't know why I never told you before."

Piper was not with Elizabeth when she died. Although it was midafternoon, she was sleeping in the overstuffed chair in the sunroom, dozing, but about to tumble headlong into real sleep when she heard Astrid call out, "Oh, God, she's gone. Tom! Piper! She can't be gone."

As Piper ran to the dining room, she felt an eerie blend of dread and excitement, like she'd felt when she was a kid about to go off the high dive at the pool. And when she saw Elizabeth, it was like going off the high dive again, except that she didn't step off into nothing; something broke under her, gave way, and she was falling. She was standing upright, looking at her dead friend, but she was dropping, dropping, dropping.

Because Astrid was right, Elizabeth couldn't be gone. They had known she would go for so long, they had prepared themselves, but what it came to was this: her death was impossible.

Piper had wanted to behave calmly and with dignity, but her heart was like a door slamming repeatedly inside her chest. She cried out, frantically, "Tom!" But when she turned around to find him, there was Kyle, his soft shirt. He pulled her into him, and, helpless, like a child, she went.

What followed, after Elizabeth was gone, when the days were full of tasks, phone calls, and comforting, was a kind of cleanness. After having felt cluttered, clenched, and panicked for so long, Piper felt clean. Not refreshed, but bare and stinging, as though she'd been scoured inside and out. There was so much to do, but every task was finite. There were lists full of things Piper could accomplish and cross off. "There," she would say, "that's done." Occasionally, especially when she held one of the children, she'd feel the unbearable encroaching, and quickly she'd shift her thoughts or set her hands to something else, whatever needed doing, the next thing.

So the day before the funeral, when Kyle came to her as she was preparing for the day ahead and told her he was leaving her, she turned patiently toward him and said, "Not now. I don't have time."

"It's never the right time. I've needed to do this for so long, Piper, a really, really long time, and I keep waiting for a space to open up, but you're always going, going, going."

Really, really. Going, going, going. Piper looked at him.

"Elizabeth has been dead for three days," she said.

She turned to the mirror and began to brush blush onto her cheeks.

"I know that. And before that she was dying and before that she was sick, and after the funeral, you'll be dealing with her kids, our kids, Tom, Astrid, your grief." He ticked the items of this list off on his fingers.

Piper turned and stopped him. "My grief? Don't talk about my grief. You don't know the first thing about it." Even now, she wasn't angry.

Kyle threw up his hands. "You're right. I don't know the first thing about you. How would I?"

"We'll talk about this later."

"I'm leaving the day after the funeral."

"No, you are not," said Piper, calmly.

"Piper, I'm in love with someone else."

"That doesn't matter." It was true. She could imagine a time when it would matter, but now the information was nothing. Relative to everything else Piper had felt, learned, and done and to everything she still needed to do, the information that her husband was in love with someone else and wanted to leave her was immaterial, bodiless. In the balance of Piper's life just then, this moment weighed nothing at all.

Well, look at that, thought Piper as the moment ended, *that's done.* She snapped her compact shut, turned, and walked out of the room.

Twelve

Never again would birds' song be the same.
And to do that to birds was why she came.
—ROBERT FROST

As the back end of the noxious-fume-spewing, banana-hauling eighteen-wheeler came bearing down on Lyssa's minivan with greater and greater speed, its dingy white rectangle looming dizzyingly larger and larger, Dev's brain did not automatically correct these impressions ("the minivan is actually the accelerating body"; "the truck isn't changing size, we're just getting closer") as it ordinarily would have done and certainly it didn't wander off on a tangent regarding the Doppler effect, radial velocity, and redshifts as it ordinarily *might* have done. Dev's brain had other fish to fry. As he sat in the passenger seat with Lyssa behind the wheel and with Aidan in the backseat turning as green as it is possible for a kid with brown skin to turn and, over the kind of dance-club music that you feel with your sternum as much as hear with your ears, hollering, with uncharacteristic profanity, "Slow the fuck down, Lyssa," part of

Dev's mind was busy choking out the prayer, "Please don't let this crazy girl kill us. Please let us get to Philadelphia in one piece." Another part, a quiet, eye-of-the-hurricane part, was thinking how later that night, in an e-mail, he would describe the moment on the highway to Clare.

Ever since the weekend following Thanksgiving, Dev had been leading a Clare-infused life. "You're obsessed," Aidan had teased him, but it wasn't obsession. It wasn't that thoughts of Clare drove out other thoughts. Okay, so this happened from time to time, once or twice a day, but mostly it was that Dev went about his normal life, except that everything he did or said or thought or read or saw or heard had just a little Clare in it, a tint, a touch, an inflection. She didn't take over, but she was never absent.

They e-mailed each other every day. They both liked regular, old-school, time-to-get-it-exactly-right e-mail best. But they would have one IM exchange, a short one, at nine o'clock every night. Last night Clare had written, "Right after you read this, go look at the moon, and I will, too." The moon had been in Dev's favorite phase, the earliest waxing crescent, a lucent shaving so fragile it looked like if you breathed on it, it would melt, so Dev held his breath, thinking, "Clare is looking at the same moon," and then, "Even the sky's different because of Clare," and then, "Get real, moron; of course the sky's not different."

But these days, Dev was figuring out the gap between empirical and experiential knowledge and learning to appreciate both. Empirical: the earth revolves around the sun. Experiential: the sun rises in the east and sets in the west. Empirical: The universe is composed of celestial bodies, hydrogen, radiation, matter that re-

flects or emits light, matter that does not reflect or emit
light, and so forth. Experiential (as far as Dev was concerned, and he knew better than to mention it to anyone
else): the night sky had changed; Clare was there, in
the moon, in the planets, in the stars, and in the dark
matter—invisible, mysterious—between the stars.

Sometimes, though, he went too far. Like recently,
he'd been thinking even more than he usually did about
quantum nonlocality, the way once two electrons were
entangled, you could separate them, shoot them hundreds of thousands of miles in opposite directions, and
they'd stay linked: if you set one of them spinning, the
other would instantly spin at the same speed in the opposite direction. They weren't talking to each other; com-
munication was not whizzing back and forth faster than
the speed of light. The two particles just existed outside
regular reality, outside of spacetime, in a state where
distance was meaningless, where distance *wasn't*. All of
which was so cool and hard and bizarre that Dev didn't
blame himself for thinking about it. He didn't know how
anyone who'd heard about it could *not* think about it
pretty regularly, like at least once every couple of weeks.

But a few days ago, Dev had gone one step further.
Or more like one step backward, one humiliating,
mammoth-sized *leap* backward. Tentatively, he'd tried
out the thought: *Clare and I are like that. Entangled.
In a state where "apart" doesn't matter,* and suddenly,
he was the guy on the edge of a cliff, one foot dangling, a guy in serious need of being yanked back from
the void and whacked on the side of the head, which is
exactly what, just in the nick of time, Dev did to himself. Once you started making physics metaphorical,
applying it to human feelings, you were doomed. You
might as well pack it up and head off to the land of the

unscientific and hopelessly sappy. Besides, there were moments when "apart" did matter, when the miles between him and Clare took the wind out of Dev like a punch to the solar plexus.

In any case, right then, Clare was lucky that she and Dev lived safely inside the classical, macroscopic physical reality of Newton and Einstein where distance was distance, because the passenger seat of a minivan about to slam smack into the back of a forty-ton banana truck and get crushed like a soda can was, in Dev's opinion, a very bad place to be.

At the last second, Lyssa braked, swerved to the left, sent the minivan careening and squealing into what was by some miracle an empty lane, and abruptly slowed to thirty-five miles an hour. She glanced witheringly at Dev, turned down the music, then rolled her eyes at Aidan in the rearview mirror.

"God, you guys are totally jumpy," she said with disdain.

"Uh, yeah," snorted Aidan, "watching your life pass before your eyes and under the wheels of a tractor-trailer'll do that. Ever notice those cute white signs on the side of the highway with the cute black numbers on them?"

"My dad says that no one really expects you to go the speed limit. Not even the cops. It's, like, not even safe?" Lyssa took both hands off the wheel in order to tighten her ponytail, despite the fact that it was already pulling the corners of her eyes oddly upward and appeared to be seriously testing the elasticity of the skin over her temples.

"Jeez," breathed Dev as the minivan slid over into the next lane of its own accord.

"My dad says even the cops recommend that you

drive at an average speed of seventy miles per hour on the highway."

"I never heard that," said Aidan, "but you keep driving like that, I'm sure we'll see a cop soon, and you can ask him."

"What do you think, Dev?" demanded Lyssa.

"I think your dad probably wasn't recommending that you achieve the seventy-mile-an-hour average by jumping between one twenty and twenty."

Lyssa rolled her eyes again. "Stop it already. Are you, like, doing calculus in your head twenty-four seven?"

"You," said Aidan to Lyssa, "are a crazy person."

Dev glanced nervously at Lyssa, who was most certainly a crazy person. "Nah. She's just kind of—distracted."

"She is clinically insane."

Lyssa's eyes met Dev's. Then, to his surprise, she grinned. "Actually, I'm disordered."

"My locker is disordered," said Aidan, "you are clinically insane."

"You didn't tell him?" Lyssa said to Dev, as though her behavior in Dr. Kimani's class were something she and Dev openly acknowledged and discussed on a regular basis.

"No."

She shrugged and turned the music back up. A car sped by them, blasting its horn. Dev checked out the minivan's speedometer. Forty miles an hour.

"I'm fine with the word 'crazy,' though," shouted Lyssa, agreeably, over the pounding bass. "Some people aren't."

"Lyssa," said Dev warningly, although he wasn't sure why he wanted to stop her. It was her secret, after all, and Aidan would keep it to himself, Dev didn't doubt that. When Dev looked over at Lyssa, he noticed that her eyelashes were coated with black mascara but were almost white at the roots, and he had to look away. He remembered the day of the fire drill, her body shaking, her impossibly frail arm bone through her sweater. I didn't ask for this, he thought, almost angrily. I don't want to feel this. I don't want to know more than I already know.

"What are we talking about here?" called out Aidan, leaning forward and knocking lightly against the back of Dev's head as though it were a door.

Lyssa turned down the music. Dev's heart sank.

"I have OCD. Obsessive-compulsive disorder."

"Oh, yeah," said Aidan, "my mom has that. She keeps our house crazy clean. Hangs up her clothes by color. Goes ballistic if there's a crumb on the kitchen counter. All that business."

"Oh, please," scoffed Lyssa, "that sounds like OCPD, *if* that. A personality, uh, foible? OCD is an official mental illness. You have to meet these really strict clinical criteria. Like the disordered behavior has to take up more than one hour of any given day. *And* you have to have irrational thoughts and compulsions that you, like, *know* are irrational and still can't stop." Dev stared at Lyssa. She sounded proud of herself. You're not just crazy, he wanted to tell her. You're crazy *and* weird.

"Like what?" asked Aidan.

"Well, a lot of stuff, but mostly? At school? I worry that I might shout out inappropriate stuff right in the middle of class."

"What do you mean?" asked Aidan. It was a legiti-

mate question and his voice was nothing but kind, but
Dev shot Aidan a look that said, "Can it." Aidan made
a confused face and mouthed, "What?"

Lyssa's neck turned red. Oh, great, thought Dev, here
we go. He wished he had on a baseball cap so he could
pull the brim down and disappear under it. Instead, he
slunk in his seat and shifted his gaze out the window.

"Weird, um, sexual stuff. Sometimes. Totally inappropriate stuff that I don't even really think. You don't
want to know."

Dev was so startled by this that he sat up and turned
sideways to look at Aidan. The alarm on Aidan's face
was reassuring. He looked like a person who did not,
in fact, want to know. "No, no, you're right. No need to
lay it all out there."

"So to keep from shouting out, I do these rituals."

Aidan looked more alarmed. Dev noted that his jaw
actually dropped. "Rituals? Like voodoo rituals?"

No one said anything, but then, Dev couldn't help
himself. He knew better than he wanted to know that
Lyssa's disordered mind was no laughing matter, but
before he could stop it, a whoop of laughter was flying
out of his mouth. Lyssa shot him a narrow-eyed glare,
but then she cracked up, too, and within seconds, they
were both totally gone, turning purple and sputtering
out things like "voodoo dolls" and "disemboweling
chickens" between spasms of laughter.

After a few seconds of looking back and forth between Dev and Lyssa, Aidan leaned forward, put a
hand on Lyssa's shoulder, and said with mock seriousness, "Lyssa, I owe you an apology. If I had known you
were clinically insane, I never would have called you
clinically insane."

Lyssa laughed harder, stomped enthusiastically on the accelerator, and said, "No problema, dude. It happens all the time!"

They were on their way to Philadelphia to find a man named Tremain.

Aidan and Lyssa knew about Dev's father theory. Willingly, Dev had given Aidan the whole scoop. Reluctantly, internally kicking himself multiple times, he'd given Lyssa the bare bones.

As soon as Christmas break ended and they were back in school, Dev had told Aidan.

"I don't know why I didn't tell you before," said Dev, eyeing Aidan's face nervously. "I just kind of didn't get around to it before I ended up telling Clare."

Aidan didn't say anything for a few seconds, but as soon as his face broke into a smile, Dev knew everything was all right.

"Dev," said Aidan, holding up two fingers of his right hand, "I have two words for you." He put up the index finger of his left hand. "And one question."

"Oh, great," groaned Dev.

"Feminine." Aidan put down one finger of his right hand. "Wiles." He put down the other.

"Yeah, yeah, yeah," said Dev, embarrassed, "whatever."

"They'll get you every time, man. Feminine wiles will get you *every* time." Aidan shook his head, world weary. "I know from whence I speak."

"You just said 'whence.'"

Aidan waggled his still-upright index finger.

"Okay," sighed Dev, "what's the question?"

"You took your *girl* on the *bus*?"

"Shut up," said Dev, grinning and giving him a shove.

"Okay, okay," said Aidan, straightening his shirt. "Real question: Why do you want to find him?"

Dev stared at Aidan, stumped.

"I mean," Aidan continued, "are you just curious? Just want to check him out? Are you mad at him? Do you want to show him how cool you turned out, *not* that you're cool? Do you want money from him? Do you want him to, you know, *be* your *dad*?"

"I don't know," said Dev, slowly. "I guess I didn't think about why."

"What are you talking about, dude? You're always thinking about why. You're the guy who thinks about why."

"I know. I guess—I guess I was just thinking that whatever my mom's up to with him, she doesn't want me to know. She'd probably just find him and yell at him or talk him into paying for one of those stupid schools and never even tell me about it."

"And?"

"And I guess I thought that that wasn't fair. He's *my* dad."

His face got hot. As soon as he'd said the words, he realized how babyish they sounded. He could tell Aidan thought so, too. For the first time since they'd met each other, Aidan couldn't look him in the eye.

"That's pretty lame, isn't it?" said Dev, grimacing.

Aidan shrugged.

"Okay. What about this? I want to have a say. I don't know what I'd do if I found him, and to tell you the truth, I'm not even sure I want to find him. But when I do think about finding him, I think about seeing him, seeing what he looks like, and then deciding whether to talk to him or not. Whether to tell him or not tell him or, you know, walk away forever. Does that make sense?"

Aidan looked at Dev and nodded. "Yeah. It does."

"And if I do talk to him, I'd say that I don't want to go to one of those schools. No way. I want to stay where I am."

"Good." Aidan put out his fist, and he and Dev bumped knuckles. "So, you want a ride to Philly or what?"

But they ended up having to wait a couple of weeks, and then, two days before they were supposed to go, Aidan met Dev at his locker before first period with a sheepish look on his face.

"What'd you do now?" inquired Dev, amiably.

"I broke up with Maria Winfield."

"I thought you weren't going out with Maria Winfield. Last I heard, you were just *hanging* out with Maria Winfield."

"Hanging out still requires a breakup. Of sorts."

Dev smiled. *Of sorts.*

"So what?" he said. "Why the long face? Last I heard, you didn't actually like her that much."

"Right. Hence the breakup." Aidan winced. "The, uh, problem is that I kind of broke up with her in my car in front of her house for fifteen minutes too long last night."

Dev looked at Aidan.

"You were late getting home," he said finally.

"Yep."

"They took your car keys."

"Yep."

"For how long?"

"Two weeks. I tried to negotiate it into three weeks minus this Saturday, but I got no takers."

"Oh," said Dev. "I appreciate the effort, though."

"Any chance your mom'll lift the moratorium on train riding?"

Right before Christmas, one of Lake's customers had handed her some long-winded story about the customer's fifteen-year-old son ("an honor student," like that mattered) showing up at home in the dead of night reeking of beer with a bloody lip, a torn jacket, an empty wallet, and a warmhearted but impatient cabdriver awaiting his $150 fare. According to the customer, the kid had taken the train into the city to do a little last-minute Christmas shopping and had fallen in with three "bad older boys" in hooded sweatshirts and goatees who'd gotten him drunk and then mugged him on the platform at the Thirtieth Street station before he could hop the train home.

Even though the story was definitely fishy (How many fifteen-year-old boys went combing the boutiques of West Philadelphia for Christmas gifts? Why had the bad boys bothered to get him drunk when three to one seemed like pretty good odds that they could've robbed him sober?) and also probably embellished (If a person were lonely enough to pester a waitress with a story like that during the dinner rush, isn't it likely that they'd throw in a few juicy fabrications?), Lake used it as a tidy illustration of why Dev would ride trains without adult supervision over her dead body.

"I bet you weren't going to let me ride the train even before you heard that story," Dev had told her.

"That's certainly possible," Lake had answered with a noncommittal face. "In any case, ixnay on the rainstay."

Dev grinned wryly at Aidan. "No, I'd say that moratorium's rock solid."

He appreciated that Aidan did not suggest that Dev ride the train anyway and then lie about it. When it came to obeying his mother, Dev was comfortable

(comfortable enough, anyway) with splitting hairs and blurring lines (his mother now let him ride in the car with Aidan on main roads and she had never actually *said* that Dev was not allowed to go to Philadelphia) but uncomfortable with breaking laws that she had explicitly laid down. Dev had never explained this distinction to Aidan, but he seemed to get it without being told.

"It needs to be this Saturday, right?"

"Not really," said Dev, trying to sound nonchalant. "My mom does a double shift one Saturday a month, so we could do it next month."

"Wow," said Aidan, shaking his head. "A month? Sorry, man. And we found him, too, old Ben Tremain. We found his address and everything."

It had been right there in the Philadelphia phone book. Not Benjamin or Benedict. Not Teddy either, but Aidan had pointed out that Teddy might have been a nickname or a middle name or maybe Ben was the nickname. Maybe he was big. Maybe he was gentle.

"No sweat," said Dev. "I bet Ben's not going anywhere. He'll have the same address next month," but he was startled by how dejected he felt. What's your deal, he asked himself. One minute, you don't care if you ever find him; the next minute, you're sinking like a leaky balloon because you have to wait thirty measly days to go look for him. Dev bristled with irritation at himself. A little consistency, asshole. A little consistency would be nice.

Then Dev heard a jangling sound behind him and turned to find Lyssa two feet away, slinking from around the last locker in Dev's row with a self-satisfied expression on her face, shaking something silvery in her hand so fast that Dev couldn't make out what it was.

"Guess what?" she said.

"How long have you been standing there?" demanded Aidan.

Dev felt a whir of concern about what Lyssa had overheard, but then looked at Aidan and shrugged a resigned shrug. A girl who executed umpteen loopy-ass rituals a day in the middle of a high school with next to nobody noticing knew a thing or two about subterfuge. If Lyssa had made it her business to find out his business, there wasn't a lot he could do about it.

"What?" Dev asked Lyssa in a tired voice.

Lyssa stopped the jangling, and let what she was holding dangle in front of Dev and Aidan. Car keys.

"What?" said Dev again.

"I'm free on Saturday," said Lyssa, smiling a half-smug, half-sugary smile, "that's what."

Dev was nervous. Of course he was. As he walked along the city street, every step he took on the busy, occasionally cracked sidewalk was possibly moving him toward not only the man who'd supplied half of Dev's DNA, but also toward what Dev had begun to think of as a geologic period shift. Change. Big, big change. Dev didn't know that much about geology, but he knew that shifts like this were tricky things: they could mean the Cambrian explosion or the K-T extinction; oceans teeming with life or every last dinosaur dead in the mud. He realized the list was playing in his head: Ordovician, Silurian, Devonian, Carboniferous. The list steadied him, but the nervousness was still there, an annoying whine, like a mosquito buzzing in his ear.

But even through his nervousness, through the whine and the reciting (Triassic, Jurassic, Cretaceous . . .) and the name Ben Tremain, Ben Tremain pulsing like a bass line underneath it all, the city was seeping into his consciousness. A tiny used-book store; a man handing out flyers; electric blue daisies in a flower stall; people in café windows reading newspapers, drinking coffee, wearing odd glasses and leather jackets; a mosaic-covered wall, the shards of mirror flashing; restaurants with framed menus outside their doors; steam pouring from a grate; acrid smells, or sweet, or plain bad, drifting and temporary, like passing clouds. Dev had spent zero time in cities. He imagined Darwin in the Galápagos. The farther Dev walked, the more he looked around, paying attention, taking it in.

So that when Aidan asked him, in a low voice, "Hey, Dev, are you, um, noticing the neighborhood?" Dev automatically answered, "Yeah, man. Totally. It's amazing."

Aidan nodded and said, "Sure. Sure it is. But you know where we are, right?"

Dev stopped walking so abruptly that Lyssa, who was walking behind them, bumped into him.

"You mean we're lost?" asked Dev.

"We're lost?" squealed Lyssa. "Aidan, you *said* you knew where we were going. You *said* you had a map of the city tattooed on your brain; you said—and I *quote*—'My internal compass hasn't failed me yet.'"

"Settle down," said Aidan. "We aren't lost. I just wondered if you all had noticed where we are?" He pointed surreptitiously at a large, rainbow-striped flag flying from someone's balcony.

"So what?" said Dev.

Lyssa glanced at the flag and then said, "My mom says decorative flags are tacky."

Aidan shook his head at this, then intoned, in a deep,

radio-announcer voice, "My friends, we are entering the heart of"—he paused dramatically—"the Gayborhood."

Dev and Lyssa stood silently on the sidewalk, letting this soak in, and Dev began to notice a few things he hadn't noticed before. Pairs of women. Pairs of men. The pairs walking together or pushing strollers or holding hands or exchanging sections of the newspaper. As Dev watched, in front of him two men in expensive-looking parkas crossed the street with a tiny Asian boy swinging between them, his red-sneakered feet flying off the ground every few steps.

"Oh," said Dev, quietly.

"Whoa, whoa, whoa. Hold up," said Lyssa, turning to Dev, her pale blue eyes round as quarters, her eyelashes weedy and ink black in the noon sunlight. "Your *dad* is *gay*?"

"Lyssa," said Aidan, and he made a ferocious slicing motion across his throat.

"Is this my dad's—neighborhood?" Dev asked Aidan. "I mean, Ben's neighborhood?"

Aidan nodded to a row of tiny houses a half block away.

"That one, with the red door, across from the Starbucks."

Dev thought for a moment, scrolling through the gay people he'd known. It didn't take long. Mick and Elliot from his mom's restaurant back in California. His sixth-grade gym teacher, Miss Pike. A twelfth-grader at Charter named Patrick Gold who worked at the Teen Hotline, passed out flyers for gay pride marches, and wore T-shirts that said things like GAY IS THE NEW BLACK. What if Dev's dad was gay? What if that was the real reason things hadn't worked out with Lake?

After a few long seconds of trying to imagine having a gay dad and drawing a blank, Dev shrugged.

"You guys drink coffee?" he said.

Dev got hot chocolate. Lyssa got chai. Aidan got a venti caramel macchiato heavy on the vanilla, with whipped cream and an extra shot of espresso. They snagged a table by the window, and as soon as they sat down, Aidan handed over his cell phone and Dev called Ben Tremain.

"Hello," said a man's voice. The voice didn't sound particularly gay to Dev.

"Uh, hi," said Dev, "could I speak to Ben please?"

"Speaking."

Dev hung up.

"It was Ben," he said, "he's home."

"You want to sit here and see if he comes out?" asked Aidan.

Dev nodded.

"Did he sound gay?" asked Lyssa.

"Not really," said Dev, "I don't know."

"Oh, you'd totally know," said Lyssa, tightening her ponytail. "God, it would suck to have a gay dad."

"Shut up, Lyssa," said Aidan.

"Well," said Lyssa, loftily, "I'm sorry, but I just don't believe in it."

"You don't believe in gay people," snickered Aidan. "Like believing in them is *optional*? Like gay people are the Easter bunny?"

"I just think it's not normal," she said primly. "And I think a lot of people would agree."

Dev thought, *Isn't it possible that a person who has to touch her nose eight times before she can get up to sharpen a pencil so that she won't scream out sex*

comments in class is not an expert on normal? He
didn't actually pose this question out loud, but when he
looked over at Aidan, Dev could tell he was thinking
more or less the same thing.

A thought hit Dev. "Hey, Lyssa," he said, and as soon
as he started talking, he wished he'd never started, "I
noticed—I mean you don't seem to be doing all those—
you don't seem to be very, uh, compulsive today." He
blushed. Why had he said that? When he looked up at
Lyssa, her face seemed different, like the usual bright,
haughty tautness had jumped ship. Instead, she looked
exhausted and sad. Dev felt about two inches high.

"Sorry," said Dev, quickly, "it's none of my business."

"Fluvoximine," she said, dully. "I guess it's pretty ef-
fective? I hate it because it makes me clumsy when I
dance, but my parents said that if I don't stay on it, I
have to quit." She paused. Then added, "Which is a
totally retarded idea because ballet is the only good
thing in my whole stupid, fucking life." When she said
it, her voice was vicious, mournful, and scared, all at
the same time.

Abruptly, all three of them averted their gazes,
turning their faces to the window. Dev felt suddenly
ashamed of himself for what he'd thought earlier, back
in the car, that Lyssa should keep her craziness to herself, that having to feel compassion for a messed-up,
hurting person was annoying and unfair. Dev thought
about what good, reassuring, interesting company his
brain had always been. How nightmarish, how abjectly
terrible it must be when the enemy lived inside your
own brain, when the enemy *was* your own brain.

Because Dev was thinking about this, it took a few
seconds for him to realize what he was seeing.

"Look!" he almost yelled. "There he is!"

The man stood on the stoop, framed by the red door, buttoning his black wool coat. Right away, Dev noticed two things about the man: he was extremely short and he looked extremely young.

"Oh, sure that's your dad," said Lyssa, "if he had you when he was ten."

"You can't tell from this far away," said Aidan. "And, you know, if he's gay, he probably takes really good care of himself. Sunscreen, facials, all that stuff."

"He's, like, five feet tall," sneered Lyssa.

"More like five five, I bet," said Dev.

"What are the chances of you having a really short dad?" said Lyssa, her eyebrows raised.

"Not great," Dev had to admit, "but it's possible."

"But hey, hey, you know what?" said Aidan, excitedly. "That might not be Ben. It might be his short, young domestic partner. Ben might still be in the house."

Even though this was Dev's potential dad they were talking about and even though he had not had time to get comfortable with the idea of having a gay dad (he wasn't *un*comfortable, but the jury was definitely still out), there was no way not to chuckle at "short, young domestic partner."

"All right," said Aidan. "Let's move it out. I'll bus the table. You guys follow him."

But that turned out to be unnecessary because the man set off across the street, straight for the Starbucks door. Without thinking about what he would do or say, Dev got up and walked toward the door so that he was standing just to the side of it, his fidgety hands shoved deep into his coat pockets, when the guy walked through it. When he saw him up close, Dev knew

without a doubt that this man was not his father. Lake
had told him that Teddy Tremain had been a couple of
years ahead of her in school, which would make him
well into his thirties. Dev wasn't so great at judging
age, but the guy in the wool coat was somewhere in the
neighborhood of ten years older than Dev, maybe less.
If this was Ben Tremain, he probably wasn't anybody's
dad, and definitely not Dev's. Nope. No way.

As Dev watched, the girl at the Starbucks counter
tilted her head languidly and gave the man the kind of
smirking, eyelashy, intimate smile that not-gay women
only ever smile at not-gay men, at least as far as Dev
knew, which admittedly wasn't all that far. Still, when
the man stared right at the counter girl's eyes, deliberately unbuttoned his coat, and slowly smiled back,
there was no doubt. Any idiot could tell: they were
classic, they were *textbook* two-people-being-not-gay-
together. Dev felt a quick little irrational pang of regret.
Not only was his potential gay father not his father, he
wasn't even gay.

"You're late today, Ben," the girl admonished, "but I
saved you an everything bagel."

"Cool," said the man who was not Dev's father. "This
must be my lucky day."

When Dev got home, he found a note from Lake:

Devvy,
   *I ran home between shifts hoping to catch a
glimpse of my elusive offspring, but no dice. Hope
you and Aidan are up to your usual good, clean,
SAFETY-CONSCIOUS fun. Call the restaurant
to check up on me when you get home. An
insanely large chunk of lasagna is in the fridge.*

*Vinny says you're wasting away. Rafferty's home
this evening if you want company. When it comes
to the lasagna, he might be persuaded to pitch in.
More hugs than you'd EVER allow in person,*
                                          Mom

Dev read the note once, then read it again. It was an
ordinary note. Actually, Dev realized it might not be
ordinary as far as notes to kids from moms went, but as
far as notes from *his* mom went, it was ordinary, which
made what happened when Dev read it for the third
time all the more *extra*ordinary. Because what Dev
did the third time was cry. Dev hadn't cried for a long
time. Months, definitely. Years, maybe. And while he
didn't fall on the ground and howl, he didn't merely do
some insignificant eye rubbing either. By the time Dev
got to the word "safety-conscious," his eyes were burning; by "insanely," they were swimming with tears; by
"Mom," the tears were rolling down his face and there
were faint, puppylike sounds happening in the vicinity
of his Adam's apple. Other times, Dev would have felt
humiliated by all this, but right then, staring down at
the note, at the familiar handwriting, jagged and beautiful at the same time, all Dev felt was confusion and a
kind of wonder.

I'm sad, he thought at first. *How did I get to be so sad?*

But then it dawned on him that what he was feeling
wasn't just pure sadness, but a guilt/sadness compound,
heavy on the guilt. G_2S. He'd lived his entire life with
his mom, and it had been a good life. It *was* a good life,
and the parts that hadn't been good had had nothing to
do with his mom; the bad parts happened *in spite* of
her. But while she was out pulling a double shift, Dev
had spent the day trying to dig up her secrets, trying

to find someone who had, Dev was very sure, never been interested in finding Dev. In fact, by all accounts, Teddy Tremain had never been very interested in Dev at all, not even when they lived in the same house.

Still, Dev missed him. Not all the time or even very often, but now and then, missing would hit Dev, throw him off balance, a sudden, undeniable ache to know his father, how his voice sounded, what his face did when he read the paper or looked at his son. And the missing wasn't fair; it wasn't earned. In fact, the missing, the searching, the imagining were so unfair that when you put them all together, they looked a lot like betrayal. Like Dev wasn't happy with his life. Like Lake wasn't enough.

Dev stood at the kitchen table crying as he hadn't cried in years, steeped in guilt and sorrow, gratitude and love, and understood—not like a dawning, but like a punch in the stomach—that everything his mother had done—leaving home and school and Teddy, working as a waitress when she was smarter than anyone Dev knew, moving across the country and then across the country again, staying up late to discuss evolution, physics, genetics, coming home between shifts, bringing lasagna, leaving notes, telling lies, keeping secrets—every single thing had been for him.

"I'm done," he said out loud. "No more looking. If she wants me to meet him, fine. But I'm done." Saying this felt solemn and official.

After the crying, Dev sat down at the kitchen table, drained and fragile, like an empty glass. After what seemed like a long time, he got up, called the restaurant, left a message with Angie the hostess that he was home, then went into his room and wrote to Clare about his day.

At the end of the e-mail, he wrote, "I'm finished with all that stuff. Let my mom introduce us. Let *him* find *me*. Yeah, right. I don't care, though. I mean, come on, the guy didn't even love me when I was a baby and cute (and I was unbelievably cute). Who needs him?" Then he wrote, "I know what that sounds like. But I don't. I really don't need him. I figured that out once and for all."

Dev thought about knocking on Rafferty's door, but he was too tired to talk, and he knew Rafferty would want to talk. He was turning out to be a nice enough guy, despite the phony-sounding name, but because he was now Lake's boyfriend or whatever, he spent a lot of energy "getting to know" Dev, and that evening, Dev wasn't up for talk, and he absolutely was not up for being known. So he sat with a book about paleontology, an old book he'd read so many times that his exhausted brain could nudge around the familiar ideas without even trying, and he ate the lasagna, demolished it, every last bite, and even with all that food inside him, the delicate empty feeling never went away.

At nine o'clock, he walked into his room to check for Clare's instant message. He'd check it, he'd write back, then he'd go to bed and let himself fall 90 percent asleep the way he always did, leaving 10 percent to listen for the last piece of the night world to fall into place, the all-clear signal, his mother opening the front door. He was so tired that even his bones were tired; he could feel tiredness all along his spine and inside his ears. But then he saw Clare's message, and in the same instant that white light and electricity flooded his brain, his heart stood still in his chest.

"Listen, Dev, if he doesn't love you, it's because he doesn't know you. I know you don't need him to, but if he met you now, he'd definitely love you."

"How do you know?" he wrote back. He shut his eyes, waiting, the buzz of the computer screen suddenly as noisy as a swarm of bees.

Somewhere in Virginia, in a town cradled by hills, in a room Dev had pictured a hundred times, Clare typed out these words with her hands: "Trust me. I know."

THIRTEEN

Cornelia

*W*hen you unexpectedly find yourself a member of a group earmarked for craziness, you can go one of two ways: embrace, indulge, celebrate your newly lunatic identity, or defy it. Because I am in my own puny way a swimmer against the tide and because I've always bristled at the concept of women, pregnant or not, as hormone addled, but mainly because, throughout most of my pregnancy, I simply did not feel all that much crazier than usual, I defied it. I was meticulously sane. I made an extra effort to make sense when I spoke; to not weep over fallen cakes, or at the sight of other people's babies, or at the perfect, ineluctable beauty of a peeled orange; to not rage at the plumber for showing up three hours late. I kept exquisite track of my keys and my appointments. I never got farther than the driveway before discovering I was wearing two different shoes. I only called my husband by the wrong name once.

But as I sat on my front steps, ostensibly enjoying the spring sunshine, like a normal human being, but

inwardly subtracting—my mental finger firmly on
the rewind button—a fourteen-year-old boy back to
a microscopic clump of cells, I had to admit that my
behavior might be falling a weensy bit short of sane.
Sometimes, though, there's a fine line between craziness and bliss, between craziness and absolute clarity,
so fine that if you were the woman I was that morning,
the line might have grown so fine, so transparent and
wispy that you would have ceased to realize it existed
at all.

If you were the woman I was that early spring, safely
tucked into my second trimester like a bird in a nest,
triple screen, nuchal translucency, nausea all behind me,
if you'd seen the early ultrasound (flashing coin, pulsing
star), felt the secret, moth-wing flutters, heard the heartbeat's gallop, you would have walked through your days
looking at people, and thinking, "Somebody's daughter,
somebody's son," as stunned as though you were the first
person to discover it: that people beget other people, that
every person on earth emerged from another person's
body. The UPS man; your neighbor's blond children; the
woman at the gym; sullen-faced skateboard kids in the
supermarket parking lot; your own green-eyed, familiar,
incomparable husband.

It doesn't happen often, at least not to ordinary
people like I am, the awareness of a miracle glowing
just under the skin of the commonplace, and when it
happens, you want to pay attention. I sat there with tentative, early spring all around me, that first scattered
blooming, that first lemon-lime green resting as fragile
as frost on the bushes and trees, and paid attention as
hard as I could. If you were the woman I was, the fourteen-year-old boy mulching your flower beds would not
have escaped your notice. You would have sat on your

front steps in the sun, watching him and imagining the months suspended in fluid and darkness, the arithmetic of the cells, the spiraled genes willing the baby he'd been into being.

As I watched him, Dev took off one of Teo's old work gloves and pushed his hair out of his eyes.

Boom. From that first microscopic second, it was all set down. Encoded. Ordained, I thought, awestruck. *Straight brown hair, long fingers, slate blue eyes.*

I shook my head at myself. Thank God that the kid, smart as he was, wasn't clairvoyant or he would have thrown down his rake and run for the hills.

Then Dev startled me by saying, "So, do you ever, like, picture what he'll look like?" He grinned. "I mean, what *it* will look like. It feels wrong to call it 'it' though."

"I know what you mean," I said, nodding. "We gave up on pronouns a while back. You can call it Penny if you want. That's what we call it. Because Penny looked like a little flashing penny in the first ultrasound. Although you could argue that Penny isn't exactly a gender-neutral name."

"Oh, yeah, it is," said Dev, immediately. "Penny Hardaway. He never really came back after his knee blew out, but he's definitely male."

I laughed. "That's exactly what Teo said. Almost to the word." Then I answered, "I do imagine how Penny will look. A lot. But lately, more than imagining what Penny will be later, I imagine what Penny is now. I wish I could be in there, where the action is." Because I knew that this might sound silly, even though I was deeply serious, I grinned and shrugged.

But Dev just looked thoughtful and then said, "But you *are* there, right? I mean, you're the there where

Penny is." He looked up at me and said, "How cool. To be someone's there," and the hint of wonder in his eyes told me he'd glimpsed the miraculous inside the ordinary, too. From what I knew of Dev, I would have bet my last dollar that this happened to him a lot more often than it happened to the rest of us.

This boy, I thought. Lake is so lucky, Lake is blessed among women to have this boy.

"You're right," I told him, "you got that exactly right."

Then because I could feel the faint burning behind my eyes and in the back of my throat that meant I was on the verge of embarrassing us both into speechlessness, and because I loved talking to Dev and wanted to keep doing it, I hopped to my feet and said, "I'll go grab us both some water."

When I came back, Dev was dumping some more mulch into the flower bed. He thanked me for the water and then drank it the way kids drink, like he'd been wandering in the desert for days. Dev looked down, scooting the velvety, nearly black mulch around with the toe of his sneaker. When he looked up, he said, "Clare told me about Christmas." And I swear the boy's face began to shine. I recognized what I saw there: that a person's name could be infinitely precious, that just saying it could make you feel singled out for glory.

Thus shining, he continued, "How everyone was unbelievably happy when you and Teo told them that you were . . ." He broke off and I watched him ransack his brain for a word less intimate, less everything else, less *pregnant* than "pregnant." Finally, he said, "When you told them about Penny."

"Yep," I said, softly, remembering, "they were pretty happy." And then because I knew he was ready to explode with wanting to, I said, "Tell me what else Clare said."

He stuffed both gloves in his back pocket and sat down on a step a few down from mine, and he started talking in a let-loose, happy way that reminded me of a child on a swing, kicking higher and higher.

"She described everything, how you guys were at the dinner table, all of you. Clare and her mom and her mom's boyfriend Gordon and your parents and Teo's parents and your brothers and your sister Ollie and her boyfriend Edmund and you and Teo, and how when you said it, everything got quiet. The talking and the silverware noise stopped. Time stopped. That's what Clare said." Dev paused, smiling a private, downward smile. "She said it was one of those moments when people stop time."

"It was," I said, "but it didn't last long. You get dragged back into the temporal realm pretty quickly in the Brown house."

"That's what Clare said. She said that it turned into Times Square at midnight on New Year's. Everyone was up out of their seats all at the same time, hugging and kissing and cheering."

"And high-fiving and slapping Teo on the back and saying, 'Well done, dude. Your "boys" came through for you!'"

"Toby, right?"

"Toby *and* Cam," I corrected dryly. "My two little brothers are cut from the same cloth, that cloth being a faded Bob Marley T-shirt."

Dev laughed. "And Ollie. Clare said even Ollie got tears in her eyes and came over and hugged you."

"So hard that she almost cracked a rib," I added.

"Ollie has a good heart beating inside her. She just forgets about it most of the time."

"And your dad just sat there smiling and smiling. Even when he started eating again, he just kept smiling."

And my mother. For the first five seconds after I broke the news, in the stillness that followed, before she had jumped up to seek out bottles of champagne and to rinse and dry each Waterford flute despite the fact that they were, like everything in her house, spotless and dust free, before she'd busied herself with gathering the proper elements of celebration while everyone else just celebrated, my mother had looked at me with a tenderness so raw and burning that I could almost not bear to see it and could almost not bear it when the five seconds ended and she looked away.

"Clare said she'll remember it forever, the way joy poured into the room," said Dev in a quiet voice.

I smiled. My Clare. "Those were her exact words, weren't they?"

"Yeah," said Dev, his eyes meeting mine, "she's always saying stuff like that, isn't she? Stuff that only she would say." And even though neither of us moved, even though the same four feet and twenty years that had separated us seconds before still lay between us, we were suddenly right next to each other, inches apart, bumping elbows in the same small boat of loving Clare.

"Yes," I said.

Dev stood up then. He didn't jump up embarrassed. He didn't break the moment. He just stood up and got back to work, and the moment went on. Neither of us said anything, just remained together in a wide quiet that contained the spring and the rustle of the rake in the mulch and the whine of a distant lawn mower and Clare.

After a few minutes, Dev said, "Lucky Penny. All those people who can't wait for him to show up and be part of the family." Then he caught himself. "Or her." He smiled.

I saw the smile, but I also heard the ache that he couldn't quite keep out of his voice when he said the word "family."

Oh, Clare, I thought automatically and with a nearly oracular certainty, *you need to love this boy.*

This thought, especially the urgency of it, took me off guard, and I knew as well as anyone how odd it was. Clare was fourteen, after all, an eighth-grader. And I should say that I wasn't planning out Clare's future in my head: love, marriage, children. Not exactly, not the nuts and bolts of it. But some things, no matter how unlikely, are just supposed to happen. You know what I mean. Some things just smack of the future and feel part of an overarching rightness. The person-to-be inside me was one of these things. Clare loving Dev was another.

Call it a vision. Intuition. A gut feeling. A revelation. The wish of a hormone-addled, sentimental pregnant woman. Call it whatever you want.

Just do it, Clare. Part command, part prayer. *Just love him back.*

In all ways but one, being pregnant is nothing like contemplating the purchase of a new car.

For most of my life, this bit of wisdom had eluded me because, for most of my life, in addition to being happily or unhappily unpregnant, I'd also been happily, triumphantly carless, but everything you have heard about the suburbs and cars is true: if you live there, you need one. And once you begin to think about buying one, once you've gotten to the stage at which you are contemplating buying a specific make and model, what happens is that you who have never noticed cars at all, for whom Sienna has forever been burnt orange, Sonata a piece of music, Tahoe an elopement destination, Touareg nothing on God's green earth, you begin to see the car everywhere. Volvo station wagons crop up like dandelions on the roadside. Toyota Priuses materialize like worms in spring rain.

I think you see where I'm going with this. When you are pregnant, pregnant women are ubiquitous. I remembered it from the first time: New York City studded with pregnant women, like stars in the firmament, their swaybacked posture, one hand pressed to their lower backs, their secret inward expressions. I would meet their eyes and feel connected to them, and, despite the fact that outwardly, I looked like my same, scrawny self, I believed they sensed it, our identical chosen-ness, our shared participation in biology's best magic trick.

I remembered afterward, too, when I was walking around emptied and heartsick, how they were still there, all around me, every place I went.

So when Toby came walking through my front door one Sunday morning with a very young, black-haired, solemn, and conspicuously pregnant woman, I was so used to the sight of pregnant women that it took a moment for the fact to sink in.

It was nine thirty, and Teo and I were doing what we did every Sunday morning, eating bagels with all the trimmings; drinking coffee (decaf, alas, for me and Penny); and luxuriating together in the big, fat Sunday *New York Times* the way other people luxuriate in hot baths, trading the Week in Review for the magazine, the front page for the book review, sometimes talking, sometimes reading out loud, but mostly existing in a lazy, gorgeous, coffee-and-caper-scented hush.

Teo and I treasured our Sunday mornings. We indulged in the belief that they were the universe's gift to us, that the Fates had conspired to arrange our weekly two hours of beatitude. Even Toby seemed to be in on it. He'd gotten a job as comanager of a ski shop that a college friend (Llewellyn Sparks, otherwise known as—what else?—"my boy Sparky") had opened in Philadelphia, and, Saturdays after work, Toby and Sparky Sparks, those two unlikely instruments of fate, would generally commence carousing in ways that precluded Toby's making the long drive home and necessitated his sleeping on Sparky's sofa or floor or, possibly, given their mutual arrested development, upper bunk.

So when Toby sauntered in with the young woman at what was, by his standards, the crack of dawn, and said, "Yo, family members," my first thought was "No, no, no, I'm right in the middle of the Modern Love column!"

My second thought was "Thank God I'm wearing decent pajamas."

My third thought was "That must be Miranda, and Toby was right about her chocolate brown eyes."

And only then did I get around to "Holy shit, she's pregnant."

Something similar must have happened to Teo because the first thing he said to Toby, right about the time I was reflecting on my pajamas, was "You're early, man. What happened? Philadelphia run out of beer last night?"

But a few seconds later, right after Toby said, with a big, gleeful grin, "Check it out, this is Miranda," I looked at Teo and saw his hand, bagel in tow, frozen midway to his mouth and his face broadcasting such naked shock that I wanted to tell him to get a grip before I realized that my face was doing the same thing.

I yanked myself together, stood up, straightened my pajama top, and began to yammer: "Hey there, Miranda. I'm Cornelia, Toby's sister. I've heard all about you. Well, um, not *all*. Ahem. Not, you know, *everything*." I continued in this manner for some time, and through it all, Miranda eyed me with an expression I recognized instantly, even though I'd last seen it on the faces of Amish families during a sixth-grade field trip to Lancaster, Pennsylvania: a wary, pitying dignity. "You English," Miranda seemed to say, "how do you live as you do?"

I shot Teo a "throw me a lifeline" look, but the man didn't move. Nervously, I gathered my hair and pulled it away from my face even though my hair was so short as to be perpetually off my face and entirely ungatherable. Then I said, lamely but mostly sincerely, "It's so nice to meet you."

Miranda shut her pretty eyes and puffed out a sigh. "He didn't tell you," she said through gritted teeth.

Then in a lightning-quick, thoroughly un-Amish move, she balled up her fist and nailed Toby with a punch to the upper arm.

"Hey!" yelped Toby, but he didn't look upset. His eyes actually had the nerve to twinkle. As a matter of fact, his whole irresponsible body was twinkling. "Surprise!"

"Toby," said Miranda, flatly, not looking at him, "you are an ass."

Toby looked at me. "Oh, yes," I assured him, "you are."

He turned to Teo, who had finally unraveled the mechanics of placing his bagel on his plate and rising to his feet.

"Ass," Teo confirmed.

"Oh, come *on*," averred Toby, jovially. "I was planning on telling you guys. I even thought about doing it at Christmas, doing that knife-tapping-my-glass, 'I have an announcement to make' routine. I just didn't want to, like, steal your thunder."

"For starters," I said in a big-sister tone that would have annoyed even me if it hadn't been so abundantly necessary, "Christmas was three months ago. Surely, there have been a few moments in the past three months when you could have shared the news without stealing anyone's thunder. Furthermore . . ." I had been about to say something like "Furthermore, you cowardly juvenile, you know very well that your announcement would have incited a completely different variety of thunder than your married sister's. Along with lightning, earthquakes, hail, and, possibly, a plague of frogs," but it occurred to me that Miranda might be better off without this bit of information, so I finished with "Furthermore, you're an ass."

"Okay, okay," said Toby, still twinkling, but throwing up his hands in surrender. "My bad. Now that you know, though, is it awesome or what?"

Not a muscle in Miranda's face twitched, but something in her eyes suggested that "awesome" was not the word she would choose, and not merely because it made her pregnancy sound like a new skateboard. I softened. "Of course," I told her, walking over and giving her a hug, "of course it is. The news just caught us off guard." She raised her eyebrows with a tired irony that said "Tell me about it."

Then Teo was next to her with his top-drawer, kindest

smile. "Sorry, Miranda. We're a little dumb on Sunday mornings. Why don't you let me take your coat?"

Miranda pushed Toby firmly away when he tried to help her off with her coat and removed it herself. As she unwound her long gray scarf, her gaze dropped to the cluttered top of our dining room table and one corner of her mouth lifted in fond recognition.

"You figure out the trick to the crossword puzzle yet?" she asked.

"It's a killer," said Teo. "Something to do with First Ladies' maiden names and the periodic table of the elements. We think."

"You sit down," I said to Miranda, pulling out the chair next to mine. "Give us a hand with it."

"Can I get you some coffee?" asked Teo, starting for the kitchen.

Miranda hesitated, then sat down in a grudging manner meant to suggest that, while she did not generally like being taken care of, in the interest of making things go smoothly for all of us, she'd make an exception this morning. But I watched her shoulders relax and saw her look up at Teo with a smile of honest gratitude. Face it, friend, I thought to myself, a little taking care of is just what you need.

"Sure. Thank you," Miranda said, then added, automatically, "Decaf."

Our eyes met, and, for a split second, instead of being two people caught in a desperately and possibly eternally uncomfortable situation, we were simply two pregnant women, smiling the same wry smile.

Miranda was due at the end of May, although, unlike most women, myself included, for whom, despite their doctor's warnings that it's only an approximation (Ollie gave me the unsolicited assurance that the chances of accuracy were roughly 5 percent), the due date is a sacred promise, the holy grail of dates, Miranda was counting on being late.

"May twenty-eighth doesn't really work for me. I need a week or so to regroup after finals. Pack my bag, shift my mind-set, get my brain and body into baby-delivery mode." She didn't just sound hopeful; she gave the impression that the postponement of her child's birth was all arranged. Miranda sat in the passenger seat of my car. She was turned partially away from me, but her profile, with its Isabella Rossellini nose and milky skin, bespoke a cool, almost queenly decisiveness. Even in the oblique, she looked like a girl who was used to getting her way.

Because I'd invited Miranda to stay for an early dinner before remembering that we had next to nothing to eat in the house, she and I were on our way to the small, conveniently located, horrendously expensive gourmet grocery store that Teo had christened Sucker Mart after the day he'd gone there with a list from me and purchased, in a moment of inattention, a $22 bottle of vanilla extract. (For months afterward, every time he bit into a homemade cookie he'd say, "These are the best cookies in the history of the world. Repeat after me: these are the best cookies in the history of the world.")

"I see what you mean," I told her, which wasn't exactly true. I did see what she meant, but I thought she was kidding herself. From where I stood, the movement from exam mode to baby-delivery mode seemed pretty negligible when viewed against the larger backdrop of moving from decades of childless living to a lifetime of motherhood. *Regroup? Pack my bag?* But then I caught a glimpse of Miranda's hands, startlingly young hands, the nails bitten to the quick, a silver ring on one thumb, and felt a rush of compassion. She'd be the mother of a newborn in a matter of weeks, but she was still twenty-three, barely out of college, still at the age when finals are a combination of Mount Everest and the bogeyman, the biggest challenge you can imagine.

We rode along in a moderately awkward silence, but I resisted all my impulses to fill it. I'd done enough yammering for one day. Besides, earlier, something had flashed in her eyes when I'd announced I was off to the store and she'd volunteered to come along, something that told me she wanted to talk. I kept quiet and drove.

Finally, she said, "I guess Toby told you that we're not together anymore." There was a note of what might have been, in someone else's voice, defensiveness, but the uptilt of her chin and her remote eyes turned it into a challenge.

"He said something like that. Not that exactly." I didn't mention her alleged case of "I love you buts" or Toby's confidence that he'd win her back, no sweat, although the next thing she said told me that she knew about the "no sweat" part.

"Of course not," she said, an edge of bitterness in her voice. "He thinks he'll wear me down. Charm me into being in love with him. I'm sorry, but his faith in his own charm can be so galling."

Certainly I could sympathize with this. I'd thought the same thing about Toby myself, too many times to count. I was even willing to acknowledge that Toby's galling faith in his own charm was not even a matter of opinion at this point, but a simple fact. Toby: curly brown hair, blue eyes, size-10 shoe, galling faith in his

own charm. I knew that. Still, I felt a flare of sisterly
indignation when Miranda said it. Because I was not
an experienced enough driver to reconcile these oppos-
ing sentiments while operating an automobile, I didn't
speak until I'd pulled into the Sucker Mart parking lot
and turned off the engine. Then I looked Miranda in
the eye and said, "So you're not in love with him?"

I saw it then: a tiny hesitation, a wobble in Miranda's
self-assurance. Maybe, I thought. Maybe Toby has a
chance. Looking at Miranda off balance, the small,
momentary furrow across her brow, I remembered
something else about Toby's faith in his own charm,
the most galling thing about it: it was usually justified.

"Not"—she paused—"not the way I'd need to be."
Then she clenched her small hands into two frustrated
fists. "He's so *literal*. And limited. This idea of his that
the world is one big playground. The total refusal to see
complications or dark sides. It's so adolescent. Don't
you think?"

"Yes," I answered. I couldn't deny it. Now that she'd
dropped her steely implacability, I found the truth elbowing out sisterly loyalty.

"And you know what else?"

"What?"

"He doesn't know me. I mean, he knows the parts
he wants to know. The sunny parts. But he doesn't
want to know the rest. And trust me, it's not all sunny.
My life . . . ," she said, rapping on her sternum with
one hand, "is *not* a beach."

"Can I ask you something?"

She nodded. When viewed head-on, her face was
vulnerable, pale violet hollows under each Pre-Rapha-
elite eye.

"How did the two of you end up together?"

"You mean why would Toby fall for such a sour-puss?" She sounded glum and arch at the same time.

I didn't reassure her that she wasn't a sourpuss. I said, "No, I don't mean that." It wasn't actually at all obvious to me why Toby would be attracted to Miranda. Not that she wasn't attractive in a dour, whip-smart, imperious way. I could visualize plenty of men being attracted to her, just not my bright-eyed, bushy-tailed brother. But I also understood that what I'd seen of her was far from a complete package, and we hadn't met under the most comfortable of circumstances. The morning hadn't actually been a showcase of my charms either. "What I mean is, why would *you* fall for *him*?"

She shrugged, then stared down at her ragged fingernails.

"Come on," I said, opening my car door, "let's go shop."

In the fish department, as we admired the tuna, Arctic char, wild salmon fillets, and red snapper, displayed like sculpture, a glistening study of pinks, Miranda said, wistfully, "He thinks I'm funny. Hardly anyone thinks I'm funny."

In the bakery section, amid the boules, ficelles, batons, baguettes, bloomers, miches, and twists, all not so much baked, apparently, as lovingly coaxed into being by artisans, she said, "He wakes up happy. Happy is his fallback mode. Who wakes up happy every single morning?"

In the poultry department, right after I told her about the time Teo came home with a chicken and said, "This chicken roamed freely, ate organic whole grains, was given zero antibiotics, and was taught to read before they slaughtered it," she said, "Have you ever seen Toby in the ocean?"

"Yes," I said.

"Surfing, bodysurfing, whatever. The way he just gives his body over to it, free, and so at home in his own skin. That physical joy. You know?"

I knew. "It's the way he does everything. He's always been that way, ever since he was a little boy. You should have seen him sled."

"I just wanted to be close to that."

She was near tears. Her face and her voice were so profoundly woebegone, so flat-out sad, and that's when I knew that Miranda would never love Toby enough. She wouldn't live with him. She wouldn't marry him. If she'd been simply angry with him, or disappointed or frustrated or impatient, he would have had a chance, but what I understood at that moment was that she had tried, that she wanted him and ached for him and would never think of him without longing and regret. But she had *tried* and couldn't love him enough.

Oh, Toby, I thought, *it's over.*

Out loud, I said, "But it's not really over. There's the baby."

Miranda pressed her palms against her eyes hard, as though she were stanching a wound. When she took her hands away, she frowned and gave her head a short, impatient shake. Then she looked at me and said, coldly, "I don't know what your politics are, but until I give birth, I am carrying a fetus, not a baby."

It may have been a low blow, but it hit its mark, and, instantly, helplessly, I fluffed up into full-blown, pupils-dilated defensive mode, like a threatened cat. It was all I could do not to hiss and bat Miranda with one clawed foot, and I wanted to whip out my pro-choice résumé, to explain that those were my politics, too, from way back, that I'd been active in my college's branch of NOW, that while she was sitting in algebra (or pre-algebra) class, I'd been doing clinic defense, walking frightened women into Planned Parenthood through hordes of yelling antichoice protestors. Yes, Teo and I allowed ourselves to call Penny "our baby," but that was purely personal, a way to negotiate the unknown, a way to bond, a show of faith. In my defensive state, it even flashed into my head to tell her about the miscarriage, an impulse so appallingly wrong that it brought me back to myself in a flash. I gave Miranda a neutral "Of course."

Then she said, "Anyway. I think I'm going to give the baby up." She stopped. Her mouth tightened. "Not *up*. That's a stupid phrase. Over. To people who are ready to be parents."

For a few seconds, I could not comprehend what she meant. I stood staring at her, struggling to understand, gripping the handle of the grocery cart so hard that pain shot up the backs of my hands. I let go.

"Adoption." Miranda threw the word like a stone. "It's a good thing."

She picked up a spelt loaf, examined it, then tossed it into the cart.

"Oh, don't look like that," she told me, angrily, but her eyes were pleading. "I am twenty-three years old. I'm not ready to be a mother. I want a life." She pointed a finger at me. "And you know Toby has absolutely no business being someone's father."

She turned on her heel and started walking. Less than two hours ago, I'd been eating bagels and reading the newspaper. Now I was watching my brother's life fall to pieces in the middle of Sucker Mart. I placed a hand on my belly. "Breathe," I told myself, "handle this." I left the cart where it was and followed her.

"Miranda." I kept my voice low, even though I wanted

to bellow until jars fell off shelves. "Does Toby know about this?"

She didn't answer. I didn't exactly grab her, but I slid my hand around her upper arm so that she would stop walking.

"What?" She swung around to face me and hissed, "Toby is the manager of a ski shop, and it's *the* best job he's ever had. He doesn't take anything seriously. Nothing. He talks about marriage like it's this totally great luau we should go to. You think he'd make a good father? Honestly?"

"How far have you gotten with this?"

"Let's just say I've looked into it."

"And Toby doesn't know."

"Not yet."

I didn't know if Toby would be a good father or not. Frankly, it was a hard thing to imagine. But I was pretty sure of one thing. "He won't let you. You can't do it without him, and he won't say yes."

The sadness was back. "I know he'll hate it. I hate it. It's agony. But it makes sense. My brother and his wife adopted a baby from China two years ago. You should see them with her."

"But, Miranda—"

That's as far as I got. I didn't even know what I'd been about to say to her, but before I could go on, she was shouting, "I am *not you,* Cornelia! Not every pregnant woman in the world is *you!*"

The store got so quiet that its discreet and upscale version of Muzak—what sounded like Glenn Gould playing Bach—seemed to get deafeningly loud, and I'm sure that people were staring. But I didn't notice them. My eyes filled with tears.

"You're right." Even though Miranda was practically

vibrating with rage, I took her hand and squeezed it, and she didn't pull away. "I'm sorry."

Later, in the car, I said, gently, "You do need to talk to Toby."

"I know," she said. Then she grinned forlornly. "I had this crazy idea that you might do it for me."

"He'll try to talk you out of it."

"I know that, too," Miranda said, miserably, and then she turned her troubled face away and said, more to the car window than to me, something else. Her voice was so small that I wasn't sure I'd heard her right. I think she said, "Maybe I'm hoping he will."

That night in bed, after I'd told Teo about what had happened at Sucker Mart, I said, shakily, "Miranda says Toby wakes up happy every morning. She says happiness is his fallback mode."

"That sounds about right." I heard the smile in his voice. "He's got other modes, though, probably a few he doesn't even know about yet. He'll get through this."

"Hold on. You're saying there's more to Toby than meets the eye? Still waters run deep?"

Teo chuckled. "I wouldn't call his waters still. But yeah, I'm saying something like that. There's more to almost everyone than meets the eye."

I thought about this, about Toby having hidden reserves of fortitude, humility, reason, seriousness, strength, something other than careless joy. I'd always been the first person to say that Toby needed to grow up. Now that he was about to have to, all I felt was a chilly, spreading sadness that seemed to seep into everything.

"Sometimes, happiness feels so fragile," I said.

"Even ours?"

Teo expected me to say no. I sat up so I could look at him.

"Everybody's," I said, gently.

I thought he would touch my belly, but instead he touched my face. He slid his thumb carefully along my jaw.

"So what do we do about it?" Teo asked.

"You tell me." I had my own ideas, but I needed to hear his. I held my breath.

"Live. Forget that it's fragile. Live like it isn't."

I exhaled, kissed my husband, and found myself remembering Toby cliff diving on a family vacation to California, running full tilt, straight for the edge and over, flinging his body into nothingness with a whoop of exaltation. At the time I'd thought it was pure, arrogant recklessness, the dumbest kind of dumb fun. But what if it was something more? What if cliff diving wasn't as much about recklessness as trust, trust in the air to hold you and the water to cushion your fall? Belief in a benevolent universe. Kierkegaardian theology in action. Maybe, just maybe, it was Toby's version of a leap of faith.

The more you think about the physical world, the more impossible it seems. And I'm not just talking about Dev's brand of physics—string theory, quantum mechanics, all the mind-blowing rest of it. Take something as old hat as sonar. Bodiless, invisible sound traveling, bouncing, entering liquid and coming out with an image you can watch on a screen. A tiny hand splaying against a cheek. A head turning toward you in the dark. A moving picture made of echoes.

The day after Miranda's visit, I had an ultrasound. I'd had them twice before, but this one wasn't planned.

I'd gone in for a regular visit. Blood pressure, weight gain, sugar levels, all fine. No swelling in my ankles. No varicose veins. The tape measure pulled across the arc of my belly gave the right answer: the centimeters matching up with the weeks in the usual, magical way.

Dr. Graham checked for the fetal heartbeat, and I waited for the emphatic thrummings, the beautiful galloping iambs.

And they didn't come. Just empty, anonymous, undersea sounds.

Dr. Graham frowned.

You can imagine what I can hardly stand to remember. A moment to rip out and burn. Airlessness. My body rigid as wood. Fear a mounting screech in my head, an icy black wave towering at the end of the examining table.

Then Dr. Graham slid the monitor to a different part of my belly, and there it was, in the room with me, Penny's blessed assurance: "I am, I am, I am, I am, I am."

Dr. Graham's face relaxed, along with my clenched muscles and the entire clenched world. I shut my eyes in gratitude and sank into the sound, letting the heartbeats rock me like a mother's arms.

When I opened my eyes, Dr. Graham was frowning again, but with proof of Penny reverberating around me, I couldn't care.

She pressed on the base of my belly with her hand. Her frown deepened.

"There's something here," she said.

The "something here" turned out to be something that had been there all along. I'd even seen it just ten weeks before, and at the time it had seemed entirely innocuous, tiny, vaguely egg shaped, and tucked into the lining of my uterus. The obstetric radiologist had pointed it out but said he wasn't worried. He said this kind of thing was very common. He told us it was too small to matter. I'd pushed away the word "tumor"; I'd embraced the word "benign."

But it had grown.

A uterine fibroid, inside the lining, but crowding its way—like an elbowing bully—into the space that rightfully belonged to Penny.

The doctor Dr. Graham sent me to was named John Goode, a name so trustworthy that I decided it canceled out the suspicious blond streaks in his hair and the fact that he looked about sixteen years old. He had excellent posture and a slow, genteel, Deep South accent that made the phrase "submucosal myoma" sound like music.

"What does this mean?" I asked him. "What happens now?"

"Well, we bump you up to high risk, the perk of that being that you'll have a lot more ultrasounds. You'll get a new doc. Also, regular nonstress tests, which are entirely painless. In short, we'll keep a close eye on that baby of yours." It took John Goode a very long time to say all of this, but I hardly heard because my attention got stuck early on, at the words "high risk."

"Why high risk?" I asked him. The question came out more tremulously than I wanted it to. I cleared my throat. "What risks?"

"Well, I should begin by saying that more often than not, women with fibroids do fine. Yours is bigger than we'd like for it to be, but women with fibroids a lot bigger than yours go full term and have deliveries that come off without a hitch."

While this sounded like good news, I could tell by

his voice that he wasn't finished, that there was news ahead that wasn't so good. I waited, wanting Teo. He had left his hospital in Philly as soon as I called, but he hadn't arrived yet, and I wanted him.

"I'll tell you, though, I find the location of yours somewhat concerning. A little too close to the placenta for comfort. If it keeps growing, we could see an abruption, the placenta getting displaced from the uterine wall. I'm not saying I think that'll happen, but it's a risk. A lot of women go full term with a minor abruption. If it's not so minor, well, we might be looking at preterm labor."

"Tell me what to do. No exercise, special diet, bed rest. I'll do it."

John Goode gave me a rueful smile. "Unfortunately, there's nothing you can do to fix it. But the flip side of that is there's nothing you can do to make it worse either. Exercise is fine. You've been doing a beautiful job of taking care of yourself so far. Just keep it up."

He kept talking to me, but my own heartbeat was so loud in my ears that I couldn't really hear him. A sob snagged in my throat. I waited until it subsided. Then I said, "Can I look at the baby again? Please?"

Penny was turned sideways and was more babylike, less space alien in profile. I could see the small, definite ski-jump nose, the noble forehead. As I watched, Penny kicked out a leg, extending one perfect five-toed foot.

"Look at that," said John Goode, softly, "he or she is sucking his or her thumb."

I looked. Penny was. I was somebody's there, and the somebody whose there I was was sucking its thumb.

I am, I am, I am, I am, I am.

I stared and stared at the gray-and-white image, at the precise and fiercely alive being that resided inside my body, and a cooling, silvery peace began to fall upon me like moonlight.

A nurse put her head inside the door and said, "Your husband just called. He's getting on the elevator. He'll be here any minute."

I knew what I'd do when he got here. I would leap. I would stare down doubt and fear and choose joy. I'd point to the stalwart creature on the screen, the one with hands and feet and a face, our brave, thumb-sucking kicker, and I'd tell Teo, "Put your faith in the Penny."

FOURTEEN

$\mathcal{S}$he could have forgiven the infidelity. She would not forgive it because, while Piper detested the role of victim, she had always found solace in justified anger the way other people found solace in liquor or God. But she could have. What she could not forgive was what he had done to her house. Because it had been distinctly *her* house, always, from the first time she and Kyle had walked through it seven years ago.

Piper recalled that day with perfect clarity. Kyle had stood with his hands in his pockets extolling the virtues of old houses to Roxanne, the young realtor with the high-pitched voice and higher-pitched, jutting breasts, as if he hadn't spent the last two weeks campaigning on behalf of Presidential Oaks, a new subdivision distinguished by a nearly complete absence of trees, oaks or otherwise, and by the fact that every model home bore the name of a different U.S. president. Kyle's particular favorite had been the Kennedy, naturally, and he'd gone on endlessly about the grand foyer and the five walk-in closets in precisely the tone of voice he was now using to sing the praises of "original wainscoting" and wide-plank floors.

"That's crown molding, genius," Piper had muttered. "And those boobs wouldn't fool a six-year-old."

But Roxanne's and Kyle's voices had faded along with Piper's annoyance, as Piper shifted from merely looking at the house to actually seeing it. Ruthless, efficient, her mind excised from the living room the current owners' exasperating modern furniture, the leather-and-metal sofas, the glass tabletops, and the stupid geometric lamps. It yanked off framed posters and garish paintings, and smoothed café-au-lait-colored paint over the mottled gold, Venetian plaster-effect walls of the dining room. In the kitchen, Piper issued approval to the oak cabinets and stainless-steel appliances; vowed to fight the owners for the iron pot rack over the island, on the grounds that it was not furniture but an intrinsic part of the room; and placed the whimsical backsplash of black-and-white tile in the "don't-love-but-can-live-with" category. By the time Kyle and Roxanne caught up with her, Piper was mentally hanging periwinkle curtains with dime-size white polka dots in what she knew would be the bedroom of her first, as-yet-unconceived child and the house was irrevocably and, she believed, eternally hers.

But Kyle had ruined it. Somehow, in leaving the house, he had infiltrated it. Piper recalled a newspaper article she'd read years ago about toxic mold, how it had silently, secretly taken over a family's home, creeping into the walls, the floors, the pink lungs of the children. Although Piper's house looked the same as it always had, Kyle had insinuated himself into every room, like rot, like poison, so that she could barely stand to be inside it. She hated him for that. It shocked her that he could accomplish such a thing: turn something she loved and owned into something repulsive. Even back before the problems began, when they were like any other married couple, she would have scoffed at the idea that he possessed that kind of power.

But Piper could not enter the master bathroom without remembering the morning after Elizabeth's funeral, Kyle's voice telling her about the woman, the words exiting the hole of his mouth.

The funeral had been easier than she had expected. In the car on the way there, on a hill about a mile from the church, there'd been a bad minute when Piper had been overtaken by the sensation of free fall, as though the car had hit ice and gone into a tractionless, hockey-puck slide. She'd pressed her hand to her stomach, and Kyle had said, "You doing okay?" A question irrelevant for so many reasons that Piper wanted to laugh.

But at the funeral, she did do okay. The funeral was a production, a play complete with costumes, stage directions, a musical score, a simple script. You stood on your mark, you said your lines. *This is why people have funerals,* Piper had thought. *Because we all know what to do at them.* She looked around her at the social moment, at the people in dark clothes shaking hands and sitting in their places. *How convenient,* she thought, gratefully, in what turned out to be the day's single rush of emotion, *that this is what we do with death. How lucky.*

Afterward, at the reception brunch, she had grown brisk and brittle, turning sideways to edge through the crowd, consulting repeatedly, tersely with the country club's director regarding the unforgivably runny Hollandaise, the browning petal edges of several white lilies, the malfunctioning spout of a silver coffee urn. She glared at one guest's loosened tie so pointedly that he spilled his drink tightening it. Her neck ached; her smile was a fissure in her face. She felt like a secret service agent and a high school principal.

Her one soft moment was for Tom, when she met his eyes and he mouthed, "Almost over," and smiled. She raised her eyebrows in a way that meant "My thoughts exactly," and gave him a discreet, heartfelt thumbs-up.

Cornelia and Teo had come, Cornelia in an unexpectedly appropriate charcoal wool jersey dress, jewel necked, A line, and just below the knee. Black suede pumps with a slim Mary Jane strap.

Just before they'd left, Cornelia had touched Piper's arm and Piper had whirled around, steeling herself for yet another "I'm sorry for your loss," but Cornelia's voice was all firm kindness and no pity when she said, "I'll take Meredith and Carter tomorrow morning. Around eight thirty." It was clearly not a request, but before she could be annoyed by such presumptuousness, Piper found her fingers around Cornelia's hand, holding on, found a thank-you caught at the base of her throat, found her head nodding yes.

The next morning, with the children gone and Kyle at work, Piper realized with her entire body that she was alone for the first time in months. There was nothing else she should be doing, no child waiting just outside the door. Piper had lived for so long inside the small chalk circle of Elizabeth's dying, like a figurine in a snow globe, and as she stood naked, the bathroom tile cooling the soles of her feet, her world widened around her, stretched out on every side, dizzyingly large, frighteningly empty.

In the center of this space, Piper began to assess her condition. Gingerly, starting with her feet, she ran the flats of her hands over her body, impersonally, taking stock. Her legs needed waxing; there was a dull, slight pain in her left knee, her hip bones were sharp, her stomach flat but soft. She took a breast in each hand, strummed fingers over her ribs. Tension burned between her shoulder blades, inside her neck and jaw. Probably she'd been grinding her teeth in her sleep again. A pain began just above her left eye and radiated upward, then down the back of her head. It was a pain she recognized from other times: a sinus infection, pretty far along, too. The glands under her jaw were actually swollen. How, she marveled, had she been sick without knowing it?

What started as an assessment turned out to be a reclaiming, and in the end, it wasn't the small changes in her body, but its familiarity that undid her, that sent grief barreling into her like an assailant who'd been waiting in the shadows. Grief that was not for Emma and Peter or for Tom or Astrid, that was not even for Elizabeth, but that belonged wholly to Piper. A fact: Piper was embodied, and Elizabeth was not. Piper stood reeling, her hands pressed to the center of her chest, pain flooding her body, pouring down her limbs.

Afterward, as the bathwater clattered into the tub, she thought, with incredulity, how she had not known that sorrow could make your body hurt, and then, as she lay in the tub, the hot water up to her chin, she understood, with equal incredulity, that she felt better. Not happier, but more normal. Found, like an object washed up on a beach.

"You're here," she whispered, "you're still here."

Finally alone with her sadness and her living body, Piper closed her eyes.

There was a click and a ripple of air and Kyle was in the room.

"It's the kids' pediatrician," he barked.

Piper didn't move, just opened her eyes to stare at him. He was jacketless, his shirtsleeves rolled up as though he were preparing to street fight or scrub a pot.

"A knock would have been nice," she said, finally. "And what the hell happened to work?"

"You won't listen to me. Ever," he said. "I had to catch you when you weren't expecting it." His voice managed to be querulous and triumphant at the same time.

"You pretended to go to work? What did you do, drive around the block until Cornelia came for the kids?"

"As a matter of fact, I drove to Dunkin' Donuts for some breakfast. Not that it's any of your business."

"A second breakfast? You ate breakfast before you left. An English muffin. Whole grain."

Kyle's chest heaved in a protracted sigh. "Did you even hear what I said? It's the kids' pediatrician. We're in love. We've been together for over two years."

Piper leaned her head back against the edge of the tub to laugh.

"What's so goddamn funny?" demanded Kyle.

"You're trying to tell me that you've spent the last two years fucking Leo Feldman?" It felt good, it felt *heavenly,* to say "fuck," to use the verb form, no less. Heavenly, like a huge bite of chocolate cake.

"What?" Outraged and disbelieving, his hands on his hips, his cheeks puffed out, Kyle looked exactly like a pitcher in a baseball game who thinks he got a bad call. Kyle loved baseball, but Piper found the players ugly and ridiculous, with their fat bottoms and their spitting and their mouths full of God knows what. Kyle looked like he was about to rip off his cap and throw it to the ground.

"You've gained some weight, haven't you?" she told him, narrowing her eyes. "I hadn't noticed. Those pants could stand to be let out a tad in the seat."

Kyle's red face got redder. He spluttered, "I know what you're doing, Piper. You're taking over. You're trivializing. This conversation is not about the size of my ass. Or about Leo Feldman, whoever the hell that is. It's about me and Colleen."

Colleen. A flash of reddish hair and brown eyes. Light orange eyebrows.

"Colleen Mullins? The nurse at Candlewood Pediatrics?" said Piper. "Did she tell you she was a doctor?"

Decent, maybe even dewy skin, very white teeth, but a small droop beneath the chin, a wattle in the making. With the back of one finger, Piper tapped the taut spot between her own chin and neck.

"She's a nurse practitioner, Piper. She has a goddamn master's degree, and she sees her own patients, who call her, by the way, Dr. Mullins."

"Our children's pediatrician is Dr. Leo Feldman," Piper said coolly, "M.D."

Confusion clouded Kyle's face. "But I took Carter in when he had the ear infection. That's when I met her."

"Newsflash: Carter has had a dozen ear infections. If you'd taken your children to the doctor more than once in their collective lives, you would know that while Dr. Feldman is their actual doctor, when he's not available, other doctors fill in, and, when none of the real doctors is available, they see Nurse Mullins. Who has apparently been passing herself off as my children's doctor to their father."

"No," protested Kyle. "We just don't talk about the kids that much."

"Really?" said Piper, corrosively. She noted with some weariness that she was angry again. The twenty minutes she had spent alone in the bathroom had been the first sustained anger-free period she had experienced in a very long time, but at the mention of her children, the anger came boiling back. "How civilized of you, to keep them out of your sordid affair. Or maybe you just forget your children exist when you're with Nurse Colleen?"

Piper expected Kyle to yell some more, to stomp around and rage, his eyes bulging. But Kyle's face turned sad and open. Abruptly, he sat down on the bathroom floor, his hands limp in his lap, his trouser legs riding up to show the skin above his carefully pulled-up socks. Kyle was particular about his socks. It was something he and Piper shared. Oh, no, Piper told herself, no going soft over a pair of Wolford cotton/wool blends or over the sight of your husband splayed on the floor like a hurting child.

"I love my kids," he explained, quietly, "but I love Colleen, too. I want her. I can't tell you how much. I belong to her. I can't live here anymore. Please try to understand."

As soon as he'd finished talking, the light in the room seemed to sharpen, and Piper lay in the tub with the stark, wretched fact of her own nakedness. Because she did understand. The honesty in his voice was unmistakable. This was not some sloppy fling, a ludicrous mistake for her to clean up. Kyle was in love. He would leave his family. His children would grow up the children of divorce, which could not happen. Piper would be a divorced woman, which she could not be. None of it could be happening, but it was. Oh, God. She was naked in a room with a man who would leave her. Piper shuddered and sat up, pulling her legs tightly against her chest.

"Get out," she whispered, and then corrected herself. "Leave the bathroom, please."

"Piper, we need to settle things."

Piper gazed bleakly at him over the peaks of her own knees.

"Don't do this," she said, pleading.

Kyle met her eyes. "Oh, Pipe," he said, "if only I could help it."

It was the first Monday in March, exactly a week after Kyle had moved out the last of his belongings, that Piper and her children spent the night at the Donahue house for the first time.

At least, that was how it felt to Piper. It wasn't literally true. They had spent the night there before, during Elizabeth's three days of dying, but it was impossible for Piper to think about those days as existing within the ordinary flow of time and events. Those three days were exempt; they counted too much to count. Anyway, back then, the house had not been, in Piper's mind, the Donahue house, but Elizabeth's house. And Kyle had been there, too. They had been two families together, keeping vigil.

Piper tried to tell herself that she had not meant for it to happen. Then she told herself that, for God's sake, it was no big deal, a one-time thing. But even the next morning, hurrying home in the pearl gray, gathering light, she knew: she had made it happen; it was a big deal; it would happen again.

Tom had had a business dinner, and Ginny had her

grandchildren for the weekend, so Piper had brought Meredith and Carter over to spend the evening with Peter and Emma. She fed them organic chicken nuggets, peas, and the sticky instant mashed potatoes that Ginny had introduced to them and that Emma adored. They cut flower-shaped cookies from dough Piper had made earlier that day and decorated them with colored sugar, the two little children making a mess, pressing their tongues to the sugar on the table, Emma and Carter sprinkling with heartbreaking carefulness.

Sweet, serious Emma, potty trained since age two, had begun to wet her pants at school. The first time it happened, she'd hid it from her teachers, and when Piper picked her up at the end of the day, Emma had turned mutely around to show Piper her sodden red corduroy pants, cold and sticking to her legs. The bewilderment on the child's face was even more painful to see than the shame. Piper lifted Emma into her arms, kissed her, and said, "No worries, Em-girl. We'll pop you into a warm bath, just as soon as I get you home."

For a few long seconds, Emma held Piper's gaze with an expression that said, "How did this happen to us?" so clearly that Piper could hear the words inside her head. Then Emma smiled slowly and said, "You'll pop me? Like Pop-Tarts."

"Like popcorn!" added Carter.

"Exactly," said Piper, with an ache in her chest.

After that, Tom put a Ziploc bag full of clean clothes in Emma's backpack, and almost every day, Emma came home wearing them, her wet clothes sealed away inside the plastic bag.

Tom told Piper that Peter would wake up, now and

then, in the middle of the night, sobbing and asking for his mother, but during the day, he seemed fine. Gradually, though, Piper began to see how he clung to her, scrambling onto her lap as soon as she sat down, wrapping his arms around her leg as she stood at the kitchen counter. He'd always been a child who stuck close. My remora, Elizabeth had called him, my fat little barnacle.

Once Meredith had pushed him and said hotly, "She's my mommy, not your mommy."

"My mommy died," said Peter, without hesitation, looking from one face to the next, as though reminding them all.

Piper had been about to scold Meredith when Tom stopped her with a glance. Later, he told Piper, "It only makes sense that she'd feel that way sometimes. But the kids are good for each other."

Piper knew they were, as she watched them together, all four on the giant armchair listening to Danny Kaye tell the story of Tubby the Tuba, an album Elizabeth had loved as a kid, draped over each other with the gorgeous indifference of children who haven't yet learned that it matters where one body ends and the next begins.

She put them to bed, Meredith in Peter's new toddler bed, Peter in his crib, Emma and Carter in Emma's double bed. It was something she'd done many times, both before and after Elizabeth had died. She'd put the children to bed, Tom would come home, Piper would go back to her house and then walk over early, around the time the kids would be waking up. The children were all good sleepers, and it was a good system. It worked.

Only on this particular night in early March, the idea of going home to her house was unbearable. Just

picturing herself removing her clothes and lying down
in her own bed made Piper's stomach churn and her
head pound, but even so, she hadn't known up until
the last few seconds what she would do. Until she
heard Tom's car in the driveway, she was just a woman
lying on the sunroom sofa reading a book, but as soon
as the headlights swung their way into the room, as
though on cue, Piper placed the open book on her
chest, one hand resting limply on its spine, turned her
face toward the back of the sofa, and pretended to be
asleep.

She heard Tom open the kitchen door, shut it behind
him, and then for a few seconds, she heard nothing, no
footsteps, no thud of his briefcase on the tabletop, and
she imagined Tom standing in his dimly lit kitchen,
feeling the stillness leaning in from every side.

In the seconds that she listened to Tom walk toward
the sunroom, there was still time for Piper to change her
mind, but she didn't, not when she heard him pause at
the door, heard the faint creak of the doorjamb as he
rested his shoulder against it, heard the soft half chuckle
that meant he was smiling at the sight of her, not even
after he turned and walked upstairs. She deepened her
breathing, kept her eyes still under their lids, settled into
the game of feigning sleep, just as she'd done countless
times as a child. Deliberately, she relaxed her forehead,
smoothing out the space between her brows. She remembered her mother's mocking voice chilling the air
around her bed. "I know you're faking, Piper. No one
frowns like that when they're asleep." The forehead was
the dead giveaway, the detail most people forgot.

By the time Tom had reentered the room, Piper's
imitation of sleep was so complete, she had almost
fooled herself. Gently, Tom slid the book out from

under Piper's hand, then he lay a blanket over her, one that Piper, without opening her eyes, recognized as the goldenrod-colored one that Elizabeth had ordered from the Garnet Hill catalog and that she kept in the trunk at the foot of the guest room bed. The blanket smelled faintly of cedar. Through all of this, Piper stayed motionless, and then something happened that made her fling open her eyes and sit up so fast that the blanket slid onto the floor in a heap.

It was nothing. Nothing. Just the back of Tom's hand brushing her neck as he pulled the blanket up over her shoulders, a touch so small and accidental it should have gone unnoticed. It should have been relegated immediately to the discard pile of meaningless events, and Piper would swear forever afterward that the touch *had* been meaningless. To her abstract, conscious, voluntary mind or whatever they called the part of a person that typically assigned meanings to things, the touch meant nothing.

It was all her body's doing. In the space between one breath and the next, her nerve endings had seized the touch and run with it, driving its tingling heat along her network of internal telegraph lines and straight into every hidden peak or tip her body held. Piper could taste the touch on her tongue, and when she opened her mouth, the touch came out as a single, ragged note: "Oh." Piper shot upright, her face flaming, one hand jammed against her chest, the other against the flat place between her hip bones.

"Jesus God," said Tom, jumping back, aghast, "I didn't mean to scare you."

Piper just stared at him, helpless, waiting for everything burgeoning to subside, for her heart to stop beating too much blood into all the wrong places. Jesus

God is right, she thought, and then, unaccountably, she was laughing, a big, loose, Julia Roberts blast of a laugh that rang and rang inside the sunroom, inside her own ears. You have lost it, she thought. After all these years, the old bod was asserting itself; it had decided to have a mind of its own. Great fucking timing, she told it. And she laughed harder.

Tom smiled in a confused way, never taking his eyes off Piper, backed up until his legs hit the seat of the armchair behind him, placed a hand on each arm of the chair, and lowered himself into it.

Piper pressed her palm to her mouth in an effort to force the laughter back. "Tom," she gasped out, giggling, "come on. That's the way people look at a crazy person."

Tom smiled. He had changed into gray sweatpants, a T-shirt, and wore shearling, moccasin-shaped slippers. Piper remembered Elizabeth teasing Tom about his aversion to being barefoot indoors, no matter what the weather. "Winter, spring, summer, and fall!" she'd sung at him, and he'd looked down at his feet and said, good-naturedly, "I wouldn't call it an aversion. A disinclination, maybe."

"Yeah, I guess it is," he said now. "But you've probably earned a little crazy time."

She rolled her eyes. "Kyle, you mean. His big exit."

"Kyle and everything else." Kyle and Elizabeth he meant. Elizabeth first, and then Kyle.

"He hired a professional packer, did I tell you that? For the wine cellar. A man showed up at my house with boxes and a roll of bubble wrap."

"You're kidding," said Tom. "Did you tell him to help himself to a bottle of Château Latour?"

Piper snickered. "And canned goods. Kyle packed

those himself. I went to the pantry for tuna fish, and the case from Costco was gone. Tuna fish, refried beans, cling peaches." God knows Kyle could keep the cling peaches, his favorite since childhood. White-trash food, Piper had thought scornfully every time he ate them. Just picturing the orange slices, flabby and flesh-like, crowded into all that gluey juice made Piper gag.

"Not that I gave them tuna fish much, not more than once a month. Because of the mercury. But how was I married to a man who would steal his kids' tuna fish?"

Tom shook his head in disgust. Then he said, wryly, "I knew that at least, about the mercury. It's always a relief when I realize I know something about how to take care of the kids."

"You're doing great," Piper told him. She meant it. For years, Tom had brought the same distracted geniality to parenting as the rest of the dads they knew. But in the past six months, he had undergone a process that Piper could only think of as, despite her distaste for any term with even a whiff of spirituality about it, a deepening. It wasn't that he loved his children more than before. All the fathers Piper knew loved their kids, Tom included, Kyle included.

But Tom had developed into a father who was *attuned* to his children. She'd seen it on his face at the playground. He might be talking with another parent, but, all the while, part of him was alert to the sound of his children's individual voices, was listening for shifts in the general tenor of the playground noise that meant trouble. Piper had once watched a Discovery Channel show with the kids about the African desert or, possibly, the Australian outback, some impossibly foreign place, and suddenly there had been a tiny fox on the screen. The fox stood perfectly still, poised, except for its large, triangular ears, which swiveled around, sometimes each in a different direction, a posture of dogged and fine-tuned attentiveness Piper recognized immediately and that she had, until Tom's transformation, associated exclusively with mothers.

Tom listened to his children when they talked, carefully searching their faces for fear or sadness (both of which Piper knew he often found). He was learning to read them, just as mothers learned to read their newborns' various cries, discerning hunger from sorrow, anger from tiredness, loneliness from pain. He wasn't an expert yet; he made plenty of mistakes, but he was getting there. He was trying.

"Thank you," Tom told Piper, sincerely, "I hope so. But we were talking about you and Kyle."

Piper said, "I feel selfish complaining to you of all people about my stupid marriage." Saying this startled Piper a bit because while she had, very occasionally, felt selfish before, selfishness was so out of keeping with her view of herself that she had never admitted it to anyone. While her senses had fallen more or less back into place, she still felt a slight interior reverberation from Tom's touch. Good Lord, is this how it would be now? Would she just feel and say *anything*? She wondered, drearily, if this happened to all newly separated women, then realized that even though she would have died before asking another such woman, it was depressing to think that she didn't know a single one.

"Don't feel selfish. Especially with me." With a groan, Tom leaned back in his chair, his legs stretching out, his hands locked on the top of his head. "Man, I feel like all I've done for a year is talk about my problems. So go ahead and talk. Talk about it all you want."

Piper raised an eyebrow. "Really?"

"Really. And I promise to try not to do that thing men do, the solve-it-instead-of-listening thing. Elizabeth hated that."

Piper laughed. "Are you kidding? I do the same thing. She hated it in me, too."

So Piper began to talk, not the guarded, flippant talking she'd done with Kate on the subject ("leave it to Kyle to pick a pasty-faced trophy wife with a double chin just so everyone will think he really loves her"), and not the emotion-laced, naked talk of talk shows, not confession, but a kind of straight talk that was new to her. Direct, honest, but unadorned and detached, like the voice-over in a historical documentary.

Calmly, setting down fact after fact, Piper told Tom about the bathroom breakup scene, including Kyle's socks and the way the water turned cold when he told her he was in love with Colleen Mullins. She told him about telling Meredith that Daddy was going to live somewhere else, the excitement in her daughter's voice when she said, "Will there be puppies there?" And about her house, how every room screamed failure and tawdriness, how she secretly wished a contained, efficient fire would burn the place to the ground while she was picking the kids up from school.

True to his word, Tom listened. He asked two or three questions, leaned forward once in concern, but never tried to solve anything (what was there to solve?), never acted angry or amazed by Kyle's betrayals (she wanted neither anger nor amazement, not that night anyway), and never, thank God, touched her.

They talked for almost two hours. It seemed a much shorter length of time to Piper, although afterward, she realized she was sleepy.

Just after Piper had refused his offer of the guest

room, just before Tom went upstairs, Tom said, "You guys stay here whenever you want, okay? I mean it."

"We couldn't," demurred Piper, although just then she couldn't think of a single reason why. Later, she'd think of plenty, but at that moment, she was drawing a complete blank.

"Why not?" he said, with mild impatience. He raked his hair with his fingers. "You know, it wouldn't be us doing you a favor. More like the other way around."

"What do you mean?"

His blue eyes were tired in his long, sharply angled, tired face. "I mean that I like it when you're all here. Emma and Peter do, too. It feels more . . . normal."

"Oh," said Piper, blinking, "okay." Then she added, "Nice talking to you, Tom."

"Likewise, Pipe."

She turned out the light, and, very quickly, wrapped in the smell of cedar, she fell asleep.

As soon as the first trace of light glazed the sky and filtered through the overgrown rhododendrons outside the sunroom windows, Piper sat up, abruptly, wide awake, panic in her throat, her hands flying upward into her rumpled hair.

"Look at you," she scolded, "just look at you."

She scrubbed a forefinger across her unbrushed teeth, yanked on her shoes, shrugged on her coat, and rushed home so quickly and so weighted down with regret that she was panting by the time she opened her front door. As soon as she'd shut it behind her, she ran to the bathroom, taking the stairs two at a time, and brushed her teeth.

It wasn't until she had changed her clothes and was making coffee that she began to realize what she did not regret. She did not regret the conversation with Tom, not even when she recalled describing to him the moment in the tub, gooseflesh pebbling her skin under the harsh light.

As she poured milk into her coffee, she realized that she did not even regret spending the night at the Donahue house. Or, more accurately, she realized that she harbored no *personal* regret for having done it. How could she? Even now, sitting on her own sofa with her coffee, her legs tucked under her, she loathed being at home. She put down her mug and ran her hands over her arms, wiping off the invisible film of wrongness that seemed to coat everything. From where she sat, she could see the yawn of the empty wicker basket that used to hold Kyle's golf magazines. Of course she didn't regret spending the night at the Donahues'. In her personal opinion, it had been a very good idea.

However, when she saw past her personal opinion and thought about the opinions of others, she felt regret drop into her stomach like lead. Shit. Shit. Shit.

When Tom had said that their being there felt normal, she hadn't disagreed, but now she wanted to. She wanted to knock some sense into the man. She considered marching straight over there, even though he was probably asleep and the kids wouldn't be up for a good two hours, to tell him that whatever he thought, most people would not find it at all normal for a newly separated woman (and just then the term seemed especially apt, as though she were pulled into pieces and scattered on the living room rug) to sleep over at the home of a recently bereaved man and his family.

"You are a *widower,* asshole." Piper said it out loud to the empty room in a poisonous voice. "So it's fine for you. No one would blame *you.* But guess who gets to be the desperate, abandoned, conniving slut down the street taking advantage of her dead best friend's husband? That"—she stabbed a finger into her chest—"would be me!"

After this outburst, she finished her coffee, then after some thought, went to the garage, found a stepladder and some tools, and set about removing the window treatments from the living room windows, the awful pleated swags and heavy drapes, the one decorating choice she had allowed her husband to make. Using a screwdriver, she even removed the brackets holding the carved gold-finished wooden poles with their elaborate pinecone finials (Who did Kyle think he was? Napoleon?) and considered using the poles as firewood (she could just feel the ax in her hand, although they probably didn't own one; Kyle outsourced all manual labor, chopping included), but instead shoved the whole mess into two garbage cans and put them out at the curb.

By the time she got to Tom's, he was making waffles for the kids and, although she felt a little shy for the first few minutes she was there, Piper didn't feel like yelling at him anymore.

It wasn't until she lay awake in her own bed that night that she went back to the touch. Tom's fingers brushing her neck and her body's reaction. Did she regret it? Stupid question. How could you regret what you didn't make happen? It would be like regretting getting rained on, she decided. Whatever she'd felt on the sofa had been completely involuntary, but what to call what she'd felt on the sofa? Oh, for shit's sake, say it, she thought. Lust. Of *course,* lust. Lust like a house on fire.

She looked around at her Anjou green bedroom walls, imagined them going up in flames, and half laughed, half moaned, "Piper Truitt, you've lost your marbles." But someplace in her psyche, a few levels down from the laughing, moaning, regretful, discombobulated level, she acknowledged with a shiver of wonder that the experience, from pretending to sleep to naming the feeling on the sofa, was the bravest thing she'd ever done.

Still, as she turned off her bedroom light, her last thought was that it could have been anyone who set her off. For what seemed like forever, she had been touched by men—Kyle, her hairdresser, her dentist—in entirely predictable ways. When was the last time she'd been caught off guard by a man's hand on her skin? It wasn't Tom, specifically. *Tom?* Please. It could have been anyone.

They spent the night again the following week. Then twice the next week. On the third week, they established what would become a routine: Monday, Wednesday, Friday nights. This was also the week that Piper left a toothbrush for herself in a drawer of the vanity in the first-floor bathroom, but it wasn't until the following week, after forgetting her pajamas and sleeping in her jeans and a starchy white shirt, that Piper left a pair of sweatpants and a loose T-shirt in the downstairs linen closet, clothes that were assuredly not pajamas, that were merely pajamalike. She continued, despite Tom's cajoling, to sleep on the sunroom sofa.

On Thursday morning of the fourth week, as Piper was leaning over to tie her sneakers, preparing for her crack of dawn departure, she heard footsteps, and said, still tying, "You're up early." Then she peered through her veil of hair to find two small bare feet on the floor in front of her. Piper nearly jumped out of her skin.

"Carter! Sweet pea."

"I heard you cough," explained Carter. He pitched himself onto her, his head whapping her squarely in the chest, his arms around her neck. At some point in the past couple of months, the child had turned into a freight train. He loosened his grip just enough to grin up at her with his tiny, square, tile white, symmetrical teeth. Ever ahead of the pack, Emma had lost her first tooth a week ago and refused to put it under her pillow. Instead, she had tucked it into the very back of her ballerina jewelry box "to keep for Mommy."

"I *knew* it was you," squealed Carter. "You sleeped over, too?"

When asked a direct question, Piper was fundamentally incapable of lying to her children. It was not that she believed in a strict adherence to the truth—she played the Santa Claus/tooth fairy/Easter bunny game like everybody else—it was that when caught in the clear blue beam of their gaze and *asked,* lying felt so utterly counterintuitive that she never managed to eke one out. The only time she'd come close was when Carter asked where Elizabeth went after she died, and, without hesitating, Piper had answered, "Heaven," but because Piper was not 100 percent convinced that this wasn't the case, her answer was not 100 percent a lie. So now, instead of answering, she began to tickle Carter's neck, his favorite tickle spot, and said, "What are you doing up so early, early bird? Catching worms?"

"Catching Mommy!" cried Carter, which made Piper give a long, silent, ironic groan. Carter wriggled away and flopped sideways onto the sofa, burying his face in the pillow that Tom had insisted Piper use. He looked up with his nose wrinkled and exclaimed with glee, "The pillow smells like Mommy!"

The next night, surrounded by yelping, leaping chil-

dren, Piper carried her toothbrush and her non-paja-
mas up to the guest room, where she would sleep that
night and the Monday, Wednesday, and Friday nights
to come, but to which she never retired until after
all of them, including Tom, had gone to bed. Picturing herself and Tom climbing the stairs together and
then saying good night in the hallway embarrassed her
beyond measure. But sleeping in the guest room put her
within earshot of the children. It made absolute sense.

In fact, what made the enterprise of spending nights
at the Donahues' possible for Piper, despite her newly
discovered underground wellspring of bravery, was its
sheer practicality. That and the fact that it made the
children feel safe. More than safe. Happy. Although at
first the happiness made Piper anxious.

"Do you think we're interfering with some kind of
natural mourning process?" she'd asked Tom during
one of their nighttime conversations. Unaccustomed to
admitting self-doubt, Piper felt shaky asking the question. Her voice actually shook. She cleared her throat.

"You mean, are we making their lives too stable?"

"Of course not," she snapped. "Children's lives
can't be too stable." Maybe that was what she meant,
though. Piper herself experienced Elizabeth's absence
as a ragged hole, a wound in the universe. Every single
day, there were moments when she felt nearly crazy
with missing her. It had happened just that evening,
when she slid her hand into Elizabeth's oven mitt. "I
just mean that maybe we're distracting them from what
they've lost. I don't want them to get slammed by it
someday because they never faced it."

"We talk about her," said Tom, meaning Elizabeth.
This was true. They talked about her a lot. Emma had
taken her mother at her word when she'd told her she

would always be with her. "Mommy's watching you eat your broccoli, Peter," she'd said the other day. "She's proud of you."

"They all know what they've lost." Tom's voice was quiet. "And they'll probably get slammed by it anyway, probably over and over again."

This is what the grief books they read said. Graduations, weddings, the births of children, death casting a shadow across every joyful event. The thought made Piper sick to her stomach.

"Anyway, Elizabeth would approve," said Piper. She'd imagined Elizabeth cheering her on as she walked up the stairs to the guest room. Whatever the kids need, she would have told Piper, and to hell with anyone who thinks differently.

"Oh, yeah," agreed Tom, "Elizabeth was an iconoclast from way back." As soon as he said it, Piper realized it was true. Piper had always scorned people who defied public opinion (she had always *been* public opinion), while all the while her best friend had been one of those people. Maybe that's what I love most about her, she thought now. Loved. Love.

Tom was grinning now. "Elizabeth would approve. Kyle I'm not so sure about."

"Fuck Kyle," said Piper, vehemently.

Tom shot out an incredulous laugh. "You say 'fuck'?"

"Of course not," said Piper. Then she smiled.

But if Piper was not quite the person she used to be, she also was not different enough to approve of their situation quite as unreservedly as Elizabeth would have. She never mentioned it to a soul, including Ginny, who must have had her suspicions, and she maintained her habit of getting up and out of there early, walking home in the grainy morning light to shower and change her clothes before most of the world was up. Strolling alone through the crisp air, away from Tom's house, on the sidewalks of her neighborhood where she had every right to be, with each step, Piper felt lighter, more blameless.

One morning, she ran into Cornelia. It was a dim, chilly morning and Piper was remembering the conversation she'd had with Tom the night before. A woman at work had asked him if Peter and Emma had gone to their mother's funeral. When he'd told her they hadn't, she'd pursed her lips, frowned with her eyebrows, nodded, and said, "Interesting move."

"Like we were playing fucking chess," spat Tom to Piper. But Piper had seen something else in Tom's eyes, under the anger, a hauntedness she understood. They had made the decision together, along with Astrid, to honor Elizabeth's request—her "vote" she'd called it—to keep the children home, but sometimes Piper wondered, too, if they had made a mistake. The children had been with Elizabeth almost until the very end. They had watched her die. They had lit candles and made good-bye-I-love-you cards and told stories and sung songs the evening before the funeral. They had said their good-byes. Still, Piper wondered.

Lost in these thoughts, she didn't see Cornelia until she was almost on top of her. All in black, Cornelia was balanced on her left leg like a flamingo, pulling on her right foot in what Piper recognized as a quadriceps stretch, and when Piper gave a startled "Hey," Cornelia yelped, "Holy Moses!" and almost fell over. The two women gaped at each other.

"Holy Moses?" said Piper, skeptically, and Cornelia laughed.

"I didn't expect to see anyone."

"What are you doing out at this hour?" Shit, thought Piper. Now why had she thrown that question of all questions out there for anyone to get their hands on?

"Teo's been working like a fiend lately, and I've been missing him," explained Cornelia. "So I decided we should go for a walk together, a little warm-up before his real morning run. I can use the exercise. But the man's legs are the length of my entire body." She smiled ruefully at Piper. "I petered out early on." She swept one hand through the air. "Teo's out there somewhere. Runs his wife into the ground and takes off like a jackrabbit."

Piper noticed the way Cornelia said she missed Teo, without a trace of sheepishness or theatricality, as though it were a natural thing to tell someone. Piper tried to remember what it was like to miss Kyle, not to be impatient at his lateness, not to miss having a husband like everyone else, but to miss Kyle, specifically.

"Oh," she said suddenly. She took a step back and eyed Cornelia. "You're due when? August?"

"July," said Cornelia shyly. "You could tell? Even through my jacket?" Piper recognized her tone: the honest delight under the pretend dismay.

"You're showing, sure, but actually it was your lips. The lips are a dead giveaway."

"Really?" squeaked Cornelia.

"Every pregnant woman has lips like Brigitte Bardot."

Cornelia tapped ruminatively on her lips with two fingers. "Ooh la la, I think you're right."

Admit it, Piper said to herself, you like her.

"Congratulations," said Piper, with a catch in her voice, and then her arms were around Cornelia, who hugged her back.

"Thanks, Piper."

Oh, why not? Why the hell not? "Kyle moved out."

"I know," said Cornelia.

"Oh," said Piper. "I guess everyone's heard by now."

"I didn't hear, not the way you mean. I'm not exactly a person who hears things." There was a tiny note of bitterness in her voice. "Unless it's from Teo, who is oblivious to gossip. Or my friend Lake, who hears less than I do."

"So how did you know?" asked Piper.

Cornelia lowered her eyes and rubbed the bridge of her nose in a delicate gesture of embarrassment. "Um. He told us, actually. He came over to ask Teo for a hand with some boxes of books, and he just told us."

Piper snorted. "Kyle's an idiot packer. I bet he put every book he owns into a washing-machine box and then expected to carry it to the car."

"At least twenty-four hours afterward, Teo was still clutching his back and claiming to be a mere shadow of his former self," Cornelia said, grinning, "so I'd say that's pretty accurate."

"Cornelia, if you want to get some exercise, forget walking at the crack of dawn. Why don't you come with me to step class? I did it up until my thirty-ninth week both times."

Cornelia looked doubtful. "What if I don't know how?"

"Hello? That's why they call it a class?" said Piper, with her hands on her hips. "It's a cinch. Come on. I'll pick you up tomorrow at nine." She resisted an urge to advise Cornelia on appropriate step-class attire. The world wouldn't end if she wore the wrong thing, would it?

After a pause, Cornelia smiled. "Why not? I mean, apart from all the obvious reasons, most of which involve my falling flat on my face."

"You'll be fine," said Piper, firmly. She smiled back. "You'll get back up."

As Piper walked up the steps to her front door, she realized that Cornelia was the first person who had talked to her about Kyle leaving without offering Piper sympathy. Maybe she knew that sympathy was useless and patronizing and made Piper want to slap people. Something about Cornelia made you believe that she'd know a thing like that.

Then Piper realized that Cornelia hadn't asked her what she was doing out at that hour. It was a question anyone would ask. But maybe Cornelia just wasn't the nosy type.

Later, as Piper stood under the shower, an alternative reason came to her like a thunderclap: maybe Cornelia hadn't asked because Cornelia already knew. Piper stood under the bitingly hot water, her pulse going haywire, but then, from out of nowhere, like a snapshot dropped in her lap, she saw Cornelia with Elizabeth, laughing at the black-and-white movie, and she understood that there was nothing to worry about. Piper, who knew better than anyone that women friends were untrustworthy, had trusted Elizabeth. And she could trust Cornelia, too. She felt it in her bones.

"Since when did you get so intuitive?" she asked herself with disgust. Even the *word* "intuitive" set her teeth on edge, always had. But after a moment she answered, "Since now."

There was a step in Piper's spot.

They had arrived early so that Piper could go over a few fundamentals with Cornelia and had found, as Piper had anticipated, an empty studio, empty except for the step that Piper would never in a thousand years have anticipated and which felt like a well-placed jab, a charley horse to the psyche.

Piper had been taking this step class for three straight years with near-perfect attendance, even during Elizabeth's illness, far longer than any other member of the class. Everyone knew that Piper always put her step in the same place, in the front row, just left of center. No divisions in the mirror on the wall interfered with Piper's view of herself. She was not close to a speaker. Her spot was, in every regard, perfection, and so patently hers that she no longer even bothered to get there early to claim it. If she had thought about it, Piper would have assumed that, on the few days when she'd been absent, the spot had been left open, out of respect for her.

But here was someone else's step, stretched out like a teal-and-black leer on its two sets of risers, with someone else's towel and water bottle placed not beside it, but, in a glaring act of insolence, on top of it.

"Is something wrong?" asked Cornelia, following Piper's gaze. "Because we can go if something's wrong."

Piper turned in a way that made her hair bounce. "Oh no, lady," she scolded, "you're not getting out of it that easily." She cocked her head in the direction of the step, and said, crisply, "There's just such a thing as exercise etiquette, but sometimes newbies take a while to catch on. That's been my spot for three years." She gave a crisp little laugh. "And that's three exercise-class years, which is equivalent to about thirty regular years."

"Great," groaned Cornelia.

The step turned out not to belong to a newbie at

all, but to Margot Cleary, a not very interesting, pro-
nouncedly pear-shaped, peripheral member of Piper's
circle whose daughter Tansy was in Carter's class at
Tallyrand and whose lip augmentation had created a
very minor buzz a few months before. Now, as she
wiggled her fingers and gave Piper a saccharine smile,
her mouth seemed composed of two slabs of glistening
organ meat. Even Cornelia noticed, pooching out her
own lips and throwing a quizzical look Piper's way.

Piper made an injection motion with her fingers,
while stage-whispering "Gore-Tex," which sent Cornelia into a silent fit of laughter that warmed Piper's
heart. It was a bonding moment as old as the hills:
two women sharing a laugh at the expense of another
woman who richly deserved it. But this feeling didn't
quite dispel the cold dread that had been stealing over
Piper since the first second she saw Margot's step in
her spot.

After class, as the room emptied of people, Piper told
Cornelia, "Awesome job, superstar. Not a single face
fall." Cornelia hadn't taken to it like a fish to water the
way Piper had her first time, but she was light on her
feet and tried very, very hard.

"It was fun," said Cornelia, then she laughed and
said, "theoretically."

"Meaning?" Piper felt an itch of impatience. Cornelia and her quirky remarks.

"Meaning it was a fun activity, and I can see how, in
time, I might actually have fun doing it."

After processing this explanation, Piper was surprised to find that she knew exactly what Cornelia
meant. She was about to tell her so when Piper caught
a glimpse in the mirror of Margot Cleary approaching

her from behind. Piper spun lightly around, a frosty smile in place, prepared to accept Margot's apology with the appropriate stony graciousness.

Margot crossed her arms over her chest. A painfully thin woman named Erin Gustafson, another minor, far-flung light in Piper's social firmament, skittered up to stand next to Margot. Ever since Kate had told her the rumor that Erin suffered from trichophagia, a disorder involving the compulsive eating of one's own hair, Piper found it impossible to look at Erin except out of the corner of her eye.

"Piper," began Margot, "this is a bit awkward, but it really has to be said."

Piper raised her eyebrows, waiting.

"I mean, I wouldn't normally say anything, but when my child gets involved, well"—she gave a faux-flustered pause—"it's just gone too far."

A warning went off in Piper's head, but she said calmly, "Margot, I have no idea what you're talking about."

"Don't you?" asked Erin. Her voice was as thin and dry as her hair.

Margot cleared her throat. "Tansy came home yesterday with quite a story. Apparently, Carter announced that since Kyle left you, you've been sleeping at Tom Donahue's. Apparently, it's a regular thing."

As if in slow motion, Margot's words slammed into Piper, one by one. Oh, God. Oh, God, it was over. Everyone would know. *Everyone will know, everyone will know,* the phrase spiraled crazily through her head.

"If you want to expose your own children to your disgusting behavior, that's your choice, but what about mine? How do you think that sounded to Tansy: Carter's mommy playing sleepover with Emma's daddy?"

"Fun?" Cornelia's voice was as clear as a chime. All three women stared at her.

The expression on Cornelia's face was pleasantly inquisitive, but her body in her black bike shorts and tank top was arrow straight and taut with contained energy. Despite the fact that she was both child sized and sporting a glued-on soccer ball of a pregnant belly, Cornelia looked positively scary.

"Your daughter's in Carter's class, so she must be, what? Four? Five?"

"Five and three quarters." Margot's face turned red. "She has a late birthday, so we held her back last year."

Cornelia merely looked at Margot.

"Voluntarily," added Margot.

Cornelia waited a few more seconds before continuing. "As I was saying, I can't imagine that a five-year-old, even one almost six, unless she'd been exposed to some pretty adult ideas, ideas completely inappropriate for a child her age, would find the notion of a two-family sleepover anything but fun."

Through the haze of her own panic, Piper could see Margot piecing together what Cornelia meant. Finally, Margot burst out with, "Tansy is as pure as the driven snow! She doesn't even see commercials. PBS Kids *only*!"

"Then I'm not sure I see the problem," said Cornelia with sweet bemusement.

"The problem," Margot said, gathering self-righteous steam, "the problem is that Elizabeth Donahue's body is hardly cold yet, and her so-called best friend is fooling around with her husband!"

Piper just stood there, blood pounding in her ears, wishing Margot Cleary would disappear, burst into flames. But even that wouldn't help. Piper knew with doomed certainty that seconds after Tansy had told her story, Margot had flipped open her cell phone to call everyone they knew.

"And," inserted Erin, nastily, "it doesn't take much imagination to figure out that it probably started before Elizabeth was even dead."

"'Not much, perhaps, but just of a certain kind,'" said Cornelia.

"What?" spat Margot.

"Nothing," said Cornelia. "I'm wondering, though, if you might be interested in Tom yourself?"

Margot went from red to pale, except for her mouth, which remained a moist scarlet. Lip gloss at aerobics, thought Piper fleetingly, how pathetic is that? "You're insane," gasped Margot.

"Well, if you're not interested in Tom yourself, then how is the nature of his relationship with Piper any of your business? Why in the world would you care, much less get so excessively angry?"

Margot looked like she might burst at the seams. Her lips began to twitch, thickly, but no sound came out. Two red slugs, thought Piper, red slugs mating. Somehow the sight of them steadied Piper.

"Go home, Margot," said Piper, in a tired voice, "it's time to go."

Margot glared at Piper with vicious little badger eyes, growled, "You make me sick," and left.

Erin stood there, her scarecrow body panting. Piper gave her a brief sideways glance.

"Oh, for God's sake, Erin. Go. You look like you're about to cough up a fucking hair ball."

* * *

Inside her car, in the parking lot of the gym, Piper lost it. She dropped her head onto the steering wheel and sobbed.

After a few minutes, Cornelia didn't touch her, but said, compassionately, "Piper."

"I'm sorry," said Piper, sobbing, not looking up, "you just have no idea what a disaster this is for me. They will tell everyone I know. Everyone. I'm ruined."

"You're not ruined," said Cornelia.

Piper turned to Cornelia. "I didn't sleep with him. I mean, we sleep there sometimes because I hate my goddamn, fucking house and the kids want to be together, but I don't sleep with Tom."

"You don't have to explain. It doesn't matter," said Cornelia, in a manner that made Piper believe she really meant it.

"You're right." Piper ripped off her headband and shook out her hair. "It doesn't matter because the truth doesn't matter. Effectively, I'm sleeping with him. Period. Oh, Cornelia, you don't know what these people are like."

"Maybe you don't," ventured Cornelia. "Maybe they aren't as bad as you think."

Piper gave a bitter, barking laugh. "Of course I know what they're like. I *trained* them! Megan, Liddy, Allie, Parvee, Kate, all the rest." She paused. "Well, maybe not Kate. But everyone else."

"But, Piper, who cares? If they're anything like those two women back there, who cares what they think?"

Piper turned on Cornelia, screeching, "That's easy for you to say. When you're nobody, it's easy not to care what people think."

Silence.

"Cornelia," Piper began, "I didn't mean that. I—"

Cornelia cut her off by snapping, "Hey, Piper, here's a radical idea: be true to yourself."

Piper stared at Cornelia, flabbergasted. Then she sat back in her seat with the blue sky and the cars and the green verge of grass outside the car windows, considering what Cornelia had said.

The truly strange thing was that it *was* a radical idea: be true to yourself. Piper had heard those words a hundred times without ever knowing what they meant, and now they seemed to be layered with meaning and speaking directly to Piper. She took the words apart, put them back together, unpacked them like a box. *Be true to yourself.* If she didn't do it, who would? Not Kyle. Not even Elizabeth, who had left her. *Be true.* How had she gotten the idea that she wasn't allowed?

Then she looked at Cornelia and said, "You and your New Age mumbo jumbo."

A smile made its radiant way across Cornelia's face, a certain kind of smile that Piper recognized, although she hadn't seen it in a long time. "Thatta girl!" said the smile. Cornelia put out a hand and moved a piece of Piper's hair back into place.

"Everything still sucks," grumbled Piper. "Royally."

"I know," said Cornelia, still smiling.

Piper slid her headband back in place, started her car, and drove them home.

FIFTEEN

Somewhere, something incredible is waiting to be known.

—CARL SAGAN

It hadn't been easy, separating the "Rafferty" from the "Pleat." It hadn't required mental nuclear fission, maybe, but it had not been easy and it hadn't happened overnight either because for a long time, in Dev's mind, those two names (and their pseudonymous effect) had been a single entity, a two-word, nominal joke. Setup: Rafferty. Punch line: Pleat.

Even after Dev had begun to like Rafferty, after the two names were no longer glued together with a sneer and after Rafferty had asked Dev to call him Rafferty instead of Mr. Pleat, the names stayed inseparable. Calling Rafferty by both names, if only inside his own head (he tried to avoid calling him anything at all aloud), kept a small, necessary space between Dev and the man who was so obviously, so *blatantly* in love with Dev's mom.

Not that Rafferty went the moony, Hallmark cards,

gooey compliments route, which would have most assuredly earned him Lake's everlasting contempt. In
fact, while his name might sound exceptionally fake,
the man himself turned out to be exceptionally genuine, sincere, but in a good way, a way that put him
several cuts above corniness. Dev had never even seen
Rafferty and his mom kiss, although he was sure they
had. But there was something about Rafferty's face
whenever he looked at Lake, something about the way
he'd pick her hand up off a tabletop and hold it between
the two of his that made Dev look away fast but also
made him positive that, while Rafferty might not stand
outside serenading her the way one old boyfriend had,
he would, without question or hesitation, throw himself
in front of a bullet train to save her life.

Dev wasn't uncomfortable in some lame, babyish,
nauseatingly creepy *Oedipus Rex* way with a man being
in love with his mom. But Dev knew Lake, and he was
also beginning to know about being in love, and he
understood that, despite the fairly substantial handful
of boyfriends she'd had over the years, Dev had never,
ever, not once, not even for five minutes seen Lake in
love. In a state of grudging, ironic, distracted semiaf-
fection, yes. But not in love. Consequently, for months,
Dev took care to keep Rafferty at a safe, double-named
distance so that when the guy got his heart smashed,
Dev wouldn't get hit by the flying debris.

But then Lake changed. One Saturday in April, Dev
and Rafferty were playing chess outside, each sitting
on his respective deck with the chessboard balanced on
the flat rail between them, when Dev glanced up to find
Lake, who had come home between shifts without their
knowing it, watching them through the sliding glass
door. Dev smiled at her, but she didn't see him because

her eyes were on Rafferty. It was Rafferty's move, and he was doing the remarkable, only occasionally annoying thing he always did when he played chess, which was to talk. His eyes were scanning the board, and Dev could practically see his brain clicking away, considering and discarding move after move, while in one, long, continuous stream of words, he told Dev the not uninteresting story of the summer when he was seventeen and built a racing bike from scratch.

Dev sat watching his mother watch Rafferty, thinking she was probably doing the same thing he was doing, marveling at the guy's wacky multitasking abilities (he was a decent chess player, too), when he noticed with alarm that, even though her mouth was smiling, his mother's eyes were filling with tears. As he watched, her face changed and changed again, softened and shifted, and she was suddenly giving Rafferty what Dev could only describe as the fullest look he'd ever seen on anybody's face, a look that included sadness, hope, and—there was no getting around it, even though Dev tried—desire, all of it adding up, unmistakably, to love.

Dev turned back to the chessboard, his embarrassment turning first to relief and then to bona fide happiness. Lake loved Rafferty. Somehow, it felt like a victory for all of them.

So by the time Rafferty took Dev to see the house he was renovating, Rafferty had been Rafferty, both out loud and inside Dev's head, for over a month.

The house sat on the frayed, green edge where the suburbs began to diffuse and give way to countryside. A white clapboard house with a front porch and big trees in the right-side yard, the original farmhouse of a cornfield-turned-subdivision, the glassy new homes

("The guys who sell them always call them 'homes,'" Rafferty had told Dev. "Subliminal advertising at its least subliminal") glinting just beyond the back fence.

"Generally, when I renovate a house," Rafferty explained as he opened the front door, "I have to juggle three things: what the clients want, what the clients think they're supposed to want, and what the house wants."

"What do you mean, what the house wants?" Sometimes, pretty often even, Rafferty said intriguing things.

"Like this room," began Rafferty, walking through what Dev supposed was the living room, to one so tiny and dim that it was more an alcove than a room and was lined from floor to ceiling with new, built-in shelves. "People think they need light, light, light. A lot of folks would want to cut in a bigger window, add a French door, maybe get rid of one or two of those big trees outside. Some people would even knock out this wall and incorporate the room into the larger living space. And, yeah, light's important, but it isn't everything. This is a house that wants to hang on to its small, quiet pockets. It respects a person's privacy."

Dev looked around, smelling the clean, sawdusty, fresh-paint smell of the place. "I like this room," he said finally. "The sun coming through the green leaves makes you sort of feel like you're underwater." His imagination sketched in a deep chair and a brass floor lamp curling over it. "It'd make a great place to read, I think."

"Me, too," said Rafferty. He smiled at Dev.

"So this house is for you, right?"

They walked to the kitchen in the back of the house, a square, unexpectedly modern room, with silvery appliances and an island with its own sink. Dev slid his hand across a countertop of weathered-looking, sand-colored stone.

"Jerusalem stone," said Rafferty. "Needs more upkeep than some people want, but I like it." He smiled a wistful smile, not at Dev, but at the room, the cabinets and stone floor and the place where a table would stand one day. "Yeah, this one's for me. I started on it a while ago."

His voice had an ache in it, so Dev said, tentatively, "For your wife, I guess. And Molly."

"Molly, yeah," said Rafferty. "But when I bought it, I already knew Gretchen would leave. She hadn't said so, but I could tell."

He sounded so sure. Dev wondered how you could be sure of something like that, and also how you could watch TV or run errands or eat dinner—do anything ordinary—with a person, knowing that they wouldn't be around for long, that your life without them was lurking around the next corner. Wasn't at least the *possibility* of forever the whole point of everything?

"Well, it'll still be Molly's house, right?"

"Sure. Summers," said Rafferty, "holidays. Occasional long weekends, maybe. Buddy's transfer to Florida is supposed to last three years, then, supposedly, they'll be back in the area. We'll see."

"Buddy?" Gretchen's soon-to-be second husband. "Sounds like a dog in a kids' book. A basset hound, maybe."

Rafferty laughed. "Well, he sure didn't turn out to be my buddy, did he?" Rafferty stopped laughing. "But maybe things happen for the best. Not Molly moving a thousand miles away, which stinks no matter how you look at it. But, you know, I met your mom." Dev knew Lake made Rafferty happy, but his voice didn't sound happy as he said this. It sounded fogged over with loneliness.

"Were you, like, thinking my mom and I would move in here?" Even though he knew he probably should feel nervous about asking this question, Dev didn't. Something about Rafferty made it easy to talk without weighing what you wanted to say beforehand. Rafferty hesitated, but he didn't act startled or as if Dev had overstepped.

"I would really like for that to happen," Rafferty said, finally, "but I don't think it will."

"Did you ask her?"

"No. I mean, I plan to, someday soon. I'll just put it out there. But every time we start moving in the direction of that question, she starts talking about how she doesn't know how long you two will be sticking around."

Dev's stomach dropped a couple of inches. Ever since the trip to Philadelphia when he'd sworn off looking for his father, he'd almost forgotten his theory, that it included squeezing money out of his dad and taking off for one of those rich, seedy, sunbaked towns so he could learn how to maximize his potential and take over the world. He hadn't really forgotten. The idea stewed on some obscure back burner in his brain, and now and then he caught a whiff of it, but he'd gotten good at ignoring it, at pretending that all the things about his life that he liked—Aidan, Cornelia, Teo, Clare (who would arrive before long to spend a spectacularly huge chunk of the summer with Teo and Cornelia), his school, their house—were permanent fixtures, solid. Rafferty, too.

Even Lake behaved as though they were staying, planting dahlia and calla lily bulbs with Rafferty, flowers that wouldn't bloom for months, granting permission for Dev to try out for basketball in the fall, once he had a year of high school under his belt. He'd even checked the mail one day and found a packet of information from the University of Pennsylvania's College of General Studies. Maybe Lake had shelved her plan to leave and had just been putting Rafferty off, nervous about committing herself and Dev to something as big as moving in. Or maybe she still planned to grab the money and run, but was doing some pretending of her own.

Dev didn't know if Lake had found Teddy Tremain yet, but he suspected that she hadn't because even though she'd never said anything much worse about him than that he was an overgrown baby, it had always been completely clear to Dev that she did not want the man in their lives, especially in Dev's life. If she had found him and asked him for the money, whether he had said yes or no, Dev was certain she would have packed up and yanked Dev out of this town just as abruptly as she'd yanked him (however willingly he'd gone) out of California.

"Well, if anyone needs a house that respects privacy, it's Lake." Dev told Rafferty this in a dry voice and with a sly look, and Rafferty laughed, but Dev hoped he understood what Dev was trying to say. Something like "If Lake ever does decide to move us in here, it's okay with me."

Rafferty walked Dev through the rest of the house, pointing out the original glass doorknobs and the original old-fashioned keyholes, the kind people looked through in movies; something called tongue-and-groove boards in the floor; a ball-foot tub big enough for a lounging hippopotamus, but Dev was only halfway listening. What Rafferty had said about Lake had tugged something into the light, a fantasy Dev had caught himself unreeling just once, before shoving it into an obscure corner of his imagination where it had lain inert for months.

In this fantasy, Lake met Teddy Tremain again, but he was a changed Teddy Tremain, older and wiser, a full-fledged adult with a fascinating job, a house close to Liberty Charter, and a love of bike riding and basketball, but with a hole at the center of his otherwise great life, a distinctly Dev-and-Lake-shaped hole. In the fantasy, Lake asked Dev for permission to marry Teddy, and Dev said no problem, and together, they stepped into the hole and filled it. Dev knew this to be a supremely pathetic fantasy, childish and futile. What made it worse was the real longing it sent blazing through Dev's chest, like a comet.

Rafferty was gesturing toward a rectangular skylight in the sloped bathroom ceiling, explaining how he'd placed it so that morning sun would slant across you as you showered. Dev thought, drearily, how Rafferty would always have this, at least; even if he lost Lake, he'd have this house, a job that he loved. Maybe he would be okay.

Then Dev was struck by another thought, and for the first time in a long time, "Rafferty" and "Pleat" slammed up against each other in a nomenclatural fender bender that jarred loose one major "what if." What if it *was* an alias? What if he and Lake were just testing the waters, making sure Dev liked Rafferty before they revealed his true identity? He gave Rafferty a surreptitious once-over: the right age, blue eyes, straight medium brown hair, maybe five ten, attached earlobes (Dev's were unattached, but so were Lake's, so no problem there), no widow's peak or cleft chin (ditto Dev). Nothing obvious to cancel him out on the basis of phenotype. But come on, Dev told himself, no way, don't be a jerk. It was just the pathetic fantasy messing with his mind.

But he asked anyway. Astronomically long shot or not, what could it hurt? Quickly, before he had time to seriously contemplate this question, Dev asked.

"Hey, Rafferty, um, you know so much about farmhouses. Where did you say you grew up again? Iowa?"

As usual, Rafferty didn't miss a beat. "I don't know if I ever did say, but nope. Wrong belt. Iowa's corn; I'm Bible. Roswell, Georgia, outside Atlanta." As soon as Rafferty said this, Dev noticed two things about his voice: it contained a blurry-edged, protracted quality, a drawl that Dev realized had been there all along, and it held the ring of truth. The frail soap bubble of hope, which Dev could have kicked himself for setting afloat in the first place, popped with a splat.

How is it that he kept getting suckered into this? Into feeling like he had lost something he hadn't even had? This time, he felt like Rafferty had lost something, too, which made even less sense, but which helped somehow, being disappointed for someone else instead of just for himself.

After a few seconds, Dev swallowed hard and smiled. "Anyway," he told Rafferty, "it's a really, really great house."

A couple of days later, when the phone call came from Lyssa's father telling Dev that she had taken "a hazardous number of her mother's sleeping pills" and would reside in "a state-of-the-art behavioral-health inpatient facility" (that was how her father talked, like he was reading from an official press release) two hours away for an as-yet-undetermined number of weeks, Dev had seen Lyssa's number on the caller ID and had strongly considered not picking up the phone, a fact he would feel guilty about almost immediately.

His guilt expanded exponentially when Lyssa's father explained that while he himself would have preferred to keep this in the family, Lyssa had requested specifically that he telephone Dev and Aidan Weeks because they were her two "best buds" at school, and she was hoping that once she was allowed to receive phone calls at the facility, they would give her a call.

But both of these jabs to Dev's conscience ended up feeling like mere pinpricks in comparison to the third.

It wasn't often that Dev became a complete bumbling idiot, if only because, when treading unfamiliar, heavily potholed, potentially idiocy-inducing ground, Dev usually managed to keep his lips zipped. But the terrain of Lyssa's hazardous pill ingestion and consequent hospitalization was like nothing Dev had ever set foot on, was roughly equivalent, in terms of unfamiliarity, to the surface of Mercury, and just about as hot.

When Lyssa's father finally finished his calm, rehearsed-sounding speech and Dev had a chance to get a word in, here's what he said: "I'm sorry. I just don't understand why she would do that. I saw her, like, three days ago and she was fine." He paused. "Well, fine for Lyssa, which I know isn't all that fine. But she seemed like herself, like she wouldn't do this."

"I don't know how much you know about Lyssa's mental health, but she is a fragile young woman. She suffers from multiple anxiety disorders, obsessive-compulsive disorder among them," replied Mr. Sorenson, in a pleasant, detached, information-delivering manner, as though he were describing *anything*. "The monarch butterfly," intoned a voice in Dev's head, "migrates close to two thousand miles in a single season. The average ant can carry twenty times its own weight." Who the hell called their own daughter "young woman"?

"And she's gotten physically unhealthy as well, increasingly physically unhealthy, dangerously underweight, which is why we insisted she quit ballet."

By the time this bit of information had clicked into place for Dev, Mr. Sorenson had glided well past it. When it did click, Dev forgot he was talking to an adult and cut in with "Wait, you made her *quit ballet*?"

"That's correct."

And then Dev said it, didn't even really say it because it wasn't even really a word, just a sound: "Ohh-hhhhh." But even as the sound stretched itself out into the empty air between the two telephone receivers, he heard everything it contained and he knew Lyssa's father heard it, too. "I get it now," the sound said. "If you made her quit the one thing that made her want to live inside her messed-up body, then it makes total sense that she would try to kill herself."

Dev spent the silence that followed wishing like crazy that he could turn back time or snatch the "Oh" out of the air and shove it back down his own throat.

When Mr. Sorenson spoke again, the press-secretary tone was gone, as though it had never been. He didn't even sound mad, which is what Dev expected. His voice was plain anguished, a terrible sound to hear.

"We didn't know! Our girl was turning into a skeleton. She was going off her meds because of the damn dancing. And we didn't hear her when she said it was the only thing that made her happy. Who could believe that about their child? Seventeen years old with only one good thing in her life?"

What a nightmare, thought Dev, to be somebody's father.

"Mr. Sorenson?" Dev said carefully. "You wouldn't have made her quit if you knew. Anyone could see that. You were trying to help her."

He meant what he said, but he felt dishonest saying it. Who did Dev think he was, consoling Lyssa's dad when Dev wasn't even sure, most of the time, that he liked her? Consoling under false pretenses. It made Dev feel like a criminal.

"We were. God help us, we screwed up, but all we want is for her to be happy. For her life to be good." Then he said, "Maybe you can tell her that when you talk to her. I'm sure it will mean a lot coming from you. Could you do that, Dev?"

"Definitely," promised Dev. What else could he do but promise? "I will definitely tell her that."

For a while after Dev hung up the phone, after his pulse slowed down, he felt basically normal.

"So, okay," he said to himself. "So they found her in time, and she's getting help, so it'll be okay."

And because he realized that he was starving, he walked into the kitchen and made himself his double-decker specialty sandwich—bread, jelly, bread, peanut butter, bread—found a bag of barbecue potato chips, and sat down to eat. Midway through the sandwich and one-third of the way through the bag of chips, the "Lyssa will be okay" certainty and the normal feeling began to be edged out, like a fast-motion eclipse, by an image of her putting the pills into her mouth and swallowing them. There had to be a moment in there when

Lyssa had felt the pills, smooth and clicking, on her tongue and could have spit them out, the whole gravelly mouthful, and she had let the moment go by. That's what Dev couldn't get over: she had let the moment go by. She had barreled right past it and had swallowed, swallowed *on purpose,* in order to die.

Even though Dev knew death to be a biological fact, he couldn't imagine really doing it. He couldn't imagine *anyone* really doing it, let alone himself, let alone on purpose, and he figured that was the way it was supposed to be: people living their palpable lives in their reliable, breathing bodies, and death unimaginable, a nonfactor. But Lyssa had been able to see it: body dead, life over. She had wanted it, and that made no sense, no evolutionary sense, no any kind of sense.

Dev called his mom at the restaurant because that was the first thing he thought of to do, even though he knew the way she worked: when he got upset, she got worried, and when she got worried, she got mad. The only wild cards were how mad and at who; this time it was extremely and Mr. Sorenson. "That man's got no business burdening a fourteen-year-old kid with his family's problems"; "I'm sorry about Lyssa, I really am, but you need to just put this out of your head, Devvy, go out and shoot some baskets, ride your bike"; "If we weren't slammed right now, I'd call that man and tell him how little I appreciate his complete lack of judgment"; and so forth.

This response wasn't particularly helpful on its face, and it definitely didn't answer his question of how Lyssa could want to die, but listening to it, Dev felt a little better. His mom was his mom was his mom. And when he hung up, he realized that while he might not be ready to put Lyssa out of his head, riding his bike

and shooting hoops were good ideas, genius ideas actually, so he stuffed a ball into his backpack and took off.

But when it came time to turn right toward the playground and courts, Dev kept going straight, into Aidan's
neighborhood, flying past pool-table lawn after pool-
table lawn, then out the other side because even though
he knew he would talk the entire mess over with Aidan
before long, he didn't want to just yet. Pretty soon, he was
almost to Cornelia and Teo's house, and then he swooped
left down their driveway and then he was knocking on
their door, and even though he wasn't entirely sure what
had brought him there—something different from the
spontaneous, homing-pigeon instinct that had made him
call his mother, but not that different—as soon as Teo
opened the door, Dev knew he had made the right call.

They went to the playground and shot hoops in the
sun, and for half an hour, that was all Dev wanted. Teo
was good. Not as quick as Dev, but almost ("You age
from the feet up," said Teo, "consider yourself warned"),
and what he lacked in speed he made up for in unpredictability. A tricky, short-burst player who went left
when you would have bet your last frigging dollar he'd
go right. But overall their games were similar. They
were both a little overly ambitious, had fast hands and
uncanny peripheral vision and were even built along
more or less the same lines: broad shouldered in an
angular, skinny-guy way, tall and loose limbed.

At one point, Teo made a ridiculous shot, a crazy-
impossible fall-away, and Dev shouted, "Sweet!" He
meant all of it: the shot, the slap of their sneakers on the
blacktop, his T-shirt swishing around his torso, the outrageously blue sky, the new, cut-grass tang of summer
in the air. And he thought that maybe he wouldn't tell
Teo about Lyssa after all, that playing ball was enough.

But when they took a break, flopping on the grass and twisting open their water bottles, Dev went ahead and told, about Lyssa and her OCD, about the phone call and what came after, Dev sitting at the kitchen table, trying and failing to comprehend how Lyssa could consider her options and choose to go from being a living body to a dead one.

"I mean, unless you believe in reincarnation, which I don't think Lyssa is the type to believe in, and even if you believe in heaven or whatever, this is *it,* your one, like, terrestrial shot, and she threw it away. No matter how bad things are, how're you going to throw away your one shot?"

Teo held the ball between his hands, rotating it thoughtfully, as if he might find an answer for Dev on the other side of it. When he spoke, he didn't sound like a doctor talking but just like an ordinary person. He said, "It's hard to say what was happening inside her head. Her brain doesn't function quite like most people's to begin with and maybe, under a lot of stress, she just lost the ability to hope."

Dev pondered this, hope as an ability. In Dev's experience, hope was something your brain just went ahead and did, even sometimes against its own better judgment. *Hope is the thing with feathers.* They'd read that in English too long ago for Dev to remember the rest. Emily Dickinson, who was one wild thinker. He made a mental note to go back and take another look.

"I guess that's what's so hard for me to get, the no hope. To think that, of all the potential scenarios out there, there's not a single good one? It just seems like we—human beings—know so much, but it's nothing compared to what we don't know. The universe surprises us, right? That's just what it does. So how could she be so one hundred percent positive that nothing good would happen? Because she would have to be totally positive, wouldn't she? To do what she did."

Teo looked up and squinted out across the playground, thinking. "You'd think so. But maybe she didn't think it all the way through. Her mind might have been moving too fast or have been too disorganized. Maybe she wasn't even really thinking about death, but just about ending how bad she felt right at that particular moment."

Dev considered this. "So if someone had been there, right at that particular moment to help her calm down and think straight, maybe she wouldn't have gone through with it. I feel like I'd give anything if I could have been there and stopped her."

Teo nodded.

"But you know what? Not because she's my friend. Because the crazy thing is that I'm not even sure she is my friend." He hesitated, then said, "I don't like being around her all that much, to tell you the truth. She makes me nervous."

Teo smiled. "Yeah, I can see how she might."

"Sometimes, and I know how mean this is, I even feel resentful. Like, why did she choose me to be comfortable with, or whatever? Why couldn't she have just left me alone?"

Why had he said that? Dev sat with his elbows on his knees, staring down at the stony dirt and the tufts of grass. He liked Teo and Cornelia, a lot. They were the easiest adults to be around he'd ever met, even easier to be around than Rafferty because they were happy. You could tell how much they enjoyed living their particular lives, and Dev really, really wanted them to like him, which made showing Teo the weaseliest, whiniest,

meanest aspects of his personality, the parts he showed
almost nobody, a highly counterproductive thing to do.
Stupid ass, he told himself. Stu. Pid. Ass.

But Teo just pointed out, in his regular voice, "You
haven't told her to leave you alone, though. Even though
you could have."

Dev looked up, startled. "I guess I could have." He
shook his head in disbelief. "How come I never thought
of that? That's weird, isn't it?"

"Not so weird," said Teo, and the frank approval, the
straight-up *liking* in his eyes when he said this made Dev
feel sort of shy, but at the same time, great, better than
he'd felt even during the ball playing.

Teo grinned at Dev. "I guess Lyssa's one of those surprises you were talking about. The universe throwing
you a curveball. Maybe it'll all make sense someday."

"Or not," joked Dev. Then he leaned back to face the
radiant, wide-open sky. "Thanks a lot, Universe," he
said.

The phone call that would change everything happened
on the last day of school, and although, following the
phone call, it would be a while before Dev could appreciate its ironies or joke about them with anyone, once
he could, it would strike him as pretty freaking apt that
the phone call of his life (okay, so he was only fourteen,
but if this phone call wasn't the phone call of his life, he
didn't want to know) was actually a *missed* phone call.

"The bell tolled for thee," Aidan would say, "but you
were too busy scraping dog shit off thy shoes to get it."

Which was basically what happened, and by the
time Dev got through the front door, dropped his overstuffed, ten-ton backpack (gym clothes, notebooks,
yearbook, random last-day-of-school detritus) in the

hallway, and got to the phone, it had stopped ringing and was sitting there, mute, no message light blinking. Ordinarily, Dev would have just picked up the phone and called Lake without even bothering to check the caller ID, since whenever she wasn't at home when he got back from school, she employed her spooky mind-reading skills to call him within four minutes after he walked through the door, but in addition to treading on dog shit, Dev was also treading on a cushion of start-of-summer, Clare-imminence air, so he checked. On the off chance that it was Clare wanting to celebrate the last day of school via telephone with Dev, even though he knew Clare's school had gotten out four days earlier, he checked.

It wasn't Clare. If it had been Clare, the name on the screen would have been HOBBES, V C (Clare's mother's name was Viviana Clare, a fact that pleased Dev, primarily because anything having to do with Clare pleased him, but also because it was a cool name) followed by a number with the area code 434, but even though he knew this, for a crazy, sentimental second or two he thought maybe it *was* Clare, calling out to him, because what it said on the screen was this: DEVEROUX.

For several bewildered seconds, all Dev could do was stare at the phone, then he shrugged and said, "Nutty," turned around to walk away, made it about four feet before curiosity got the best of him, turned around again, grabbed the phone, and called DEVEROUX back.

A woman answered, picked up after half a ring, and instead of saying hello, said, "Ronnie?" in such a hopeful voice that Dev sort of hated to set her straight.

Feeling vaguely dumb, he said, "Uh, no. I think you must have just called me by mistake. I saw the name on the caller ID and, well, my name's actually, weirdly enough, Deveroux, uh, Tremain, so I figured I'd call back." Dev paused, the dumb feeling snowballing at warp speed. "And, you know, *see*."

The woman didn't say, "See what?" which would have been a perfectly legitimate question to which Dev had no ready answer, or "Oh, that's okay," or "What a fascinating coincidence, Deveroux," or even, "Jeez, a person can't even dial a number wrong these days without some yappy kid wasting her time." For what felt like ages, she didn't say anything at all. Then, she said, "Oh, oh, oh," and, to Dev's abject horror, the woman burst into tears.

After a few seconds, still crying, she said, "The day Ronnie told me she named you that, I just stood in my vegetable garden and cried. I was that relieved. I figured if she really hated me, she wouldn't have given her son my name."

Dev had no idea what this meant, but his heart was starting to pound anyway. Pay attention, he told himself without knowing why.

The woman kept talking. Talking and talking, the words tumbling out fast.

"And to think you called because of the name. I almost didn't change it, and it caused a scandal, I can promise you that. But I did my duty. I stayed married to him, even though I thought about leaving a thousand times, running off to find you and Ronnie and get her to forgive me. But when he died, I just didn't want the name anymore. I always loved my old name. Laura Deveroux. I thought it sounded like a star out of one of those old movies my mom and I loved to watch together. So I took it back. It's only been since last December, kind of a Christmas present to myself."

Find you and Ronnie. Inside Dev, a light was beginning to dawn, a pale, fragile glow, distant and deep, like the light from a bioluminescent fish in an underground cave.

"Ronnie?" he said. The name came out in all but a whisper.

"Oh, I'm sorry, honey. I can't seem to remember that. She's still Ronnie to me."

She said, "Here I am rambling on and on."

Then, she said, gently, "I'm your grandmother, Dev, and I have missed you since the day you were born."

Laura Deveroux. Up until last December, Laura Larrabee, wife of Guy Larrabee.

His grandmother. His *grandmother*.

Lake's mother. More accurately, Ronnie's mother, since that's who Lake had been until the day she took off, pregnant, leaving behind her parents, her name, and every single other thing that belonged to her apart from some clothes, the tangle of DNA that was Dev, and Teddy Tremain, who didn't belong to her all that much, apparently, since she'd left him, too, before long, shed him and a whole life, like a snake sheds its skin: Veronica Lake Larrabee.

Apart from the fact that his grandfather had died last fall, none of this was anything Dev didn't already know. He even knew that Lake's first name was Veronica, although he didn't really connect it with her and hadn't thought about it in years. But he found that it didn't matter what he had known before. Now that the information was coming from his actual grandmother, who was probably sitting in some room, her kitchen probably, in her actual house in Iowa, it stunned him. His mother had left and never gone back. She had left her parents behind forever. What a breathtakingly enormous and final thing to do.

But *had* she left them behind?

"Hold on," said Dev. "You know our number. She talks to you?"

"Not very often." Laura's voice began to tremble again. Even shaky, her voice was much younger sounding than Dev would have expected. She didn't sound like somebody's grandmother. The words bounced around the interior of his skull, echoing: *Somebody's grandmother.* His.

"Not so often as I wish she would. And only me, never Guy. She hung up if he answered. But he wouldn't have talked to her anyway, and that's a very sad fact. I didn't even know you all had moved until she called me last fall to say she saw Guy's obituary in the newspaper."

"She gets an Iowa newspaper? I don't think so. I never saw it."

"Ohio, honey. And no, she reads it on her computer." Ohio.

"Right," said Dev after a beat. "I meant Ohio."

"Blake's Tavern, Ohio," said his grandmother.

"Right," Dev repeated. "Do you know . . . I mean, did Lake tell you why we moved here?"

"Something about a school for you. She says you're a brilliant student, which does not surprise me at all. Not at all."

"That's all she said? That's the only reason she gave?"

"Sure, Dev. Why, honey? Were you thinking there was more to it?"

"I don't know," said Dev. Then he just said it. Why shouldn't he say it? His mother whom he trusted had lied to him about Iowa. He had lived with the lie of

Iowa like a little jar of poison for as long as he could remember. How could she let him live like that? In a surge of anger, he threw it out like a rock into a pond. "I think we're here looking for Teddy."

But it didn't make a splash. At least, not the one Dev had expected.

"Teddy Tremain? Why, Dev, Teddy Tremain's right here in Blake's Tavern, not two miles down the road from me. He's been here for going on ten years now. Lake's known that all along."

Slowly, Dev walked into the living room and sat down on the floor, thumping his back against the sofa, an unspooling sensation inside his stomach. They were not here to find his father after all. He had been wrong about everything, all this time.

"Teddy took over his father's heating and air-conditioning business. He's got three boys of his own now."

Of his own.

"He's a nice young man, just like always, which is, I guess, why Ronnie picked him to run off with."

One sentence, one *word* in one sentence clanging like a wrong note, and there Dev was: on the edge of a vertiginous cliff, his legs shaking. All he had to do was ignore it, the one word, call it a slip of the tongue. Or he could hang up, push a button, and leave the woman on the other end of the line, never go back. Her own daughter had done it. But even as these possibilities spun through Dev's head, he acknowledged with some bitterness that they weren't really possibilities. You couldn't change who you were. He was the guy who doesn't let it drop, the guy who *asks,* even if the truth might fall on him like a ton of bricks.

In a thin voice he didn't recognize, Dev asked, "What do you mean, picked?" Right after he said it, he pressed the speaker button on the phone, set it on the rug, a few feet away, then squeezed his eyes shut.

When his grandmother spoke next, her voice filled the room. She told him this: "To run off with and marry. After that older boy she was so crazy about at Princeton left her high and dry. Found out she was pregnant, dropped her flat, and went on his merry way, to law school or medical school, something. The bum."

He started to say, "You mean Brown," to correct her, but the words never made it out. She wasn't wrong. He was the one who was wrong. The one who didn't know anything at all.

Dev could not believe it, how quickly his life had become one of those Escher drawings in which everything seems to fit together and make sense but in which everything is impossible: water flowing up a flat plain; stairs you climb down and up at the same time; a boy sitting, oblivious, sleeping with his knees tucked in, on a ceiling. His father was not his father. His mother who never lied to him was a liar.

His grandmother kept talking, but Dev wasn't listening because he was connecting dots. He didn't really mean to connect them or even want to connect them. It was as though he were sitting on the rug with his palms pressed against his eyes, watching as a picture emerged all on its own, emerged and then grew more detailed by the second, until there it was: a man with a basketball, a tall, lean, long-armed man in an old, loose, gray T-shirt, threadbare and coming apart at the neck.

Orange basketball. Orange letters across the front of the gray shirt.

Princeton.

Teo.

SIXTEEN

Cornelia

Technically speaking, I was not the last person in my family to learn how to swim. Out of the four children and two adults who comprise my family of origin, I was fourth, technically, but only because Cam was in utero and Toby was barely a year old, a good ten months away from being certifiably pool safe. (I jest not; the certificate is pressed between the pages of his meticulously maintained baby book, which also contains the list of words he was able to speak at the time: "no" and "ta," a version of "helicopter" so truncated it seems more like evidence of maternal wishful thinking than of true linguistic prowess, wouldn't you agree?)

I was six when I learned. While I would not say that I am obsessed with this particular subject, I've done quite a bit of research on it, casual, unobsessed research spanning close to three decades, and my results seem to indicate that, in many families, perhaps even in the vast majority of families, at least among non-island-dwelling peoples, six is a very reasonable age at which to learn to swim. *Many* young children are afraid of being submerged in water. One might even argue, if one were, say, cornered by a gaggle of teasing family members, that the fear of being submerged in water is, at the very least, understandable, and at the very most, evidence of an uncommonly fine-tuned survival instinct. In any case, in most families, there is nothing whatsoever shameful about six.

Needless to say, I did not grow up in most families, but in a family of veritable otters, streamlined and bearing, year-round, for years, an odd, silvery cast to their hair and the faint smell of chemicals. My father, a backstroke specialist, swam at the college level and has a box of medals to prove it. Ollie, of course, began competing at age four, qualified for the Junior Olympics in three events at the mind-numbingly prodigious age of seven and three-quarters, only giving the sport up at age sixteen, after profound agonizing, in order to become a full-time tennis star and future valedictorian. In addition to his much-vaunted ability to conquer the ocean waves, Toby still holds the two-hundred-yard individual medley record at our country club pool, where Cam became the youngest lifeguard and swimming instructor in said pool's history. Even my tiny, manicured, late-middle-age mother still manages to squeeze in, between her endless philanthropic duties, garden club meetings, golf, tennis, and anal-retentive housekeeping, about 250 laps per week.

In such a family, six was late. Six was *unthinkably* late and cause for, depending on the family member, gentle ribbing, constructive criticism, firm encouragement, and scathing ridicule.

When I finally learned, it was not from the instructors at the Westerly Family Swim School, who had taught not only my siblings, but over half the kids in town and their parents before them. Westerly was a hallowed institution, a kind of fundamentalist church of swim lessons that promised—what else?—salvation, not only from drowning but from a life devoid of confidence and self-respect, and although they approached the second oldest Brown child with the same benign ruthlessness that had proved so successful not only for them but for missionaries throughout history, I was intractable, a lost soul.

My baffled parents gave it the old college try as well, in tandem and individually, even going so far at one point as to bribe me with the plastic model of Misty of Chincoteague that I desired over all other objects in the world. No dice.

When I finally learned, it was from Teo Sandoval, age eight and a half.

It was mid-July, which meant that I had spent a full six weeks in various permutations of pool pariahdom: reading Laura Ingalls books on a lounge chair, playing solitary card games on a beach towel, or dangling my feet in the water watching kids two-thirds my age play Marco Polo and sharks and minnows with glee. On this particular afternoon, I was doing the leg-dangling routine, sitting in my favorite spot, almost directly below the lifeguard stand where the other kids (i.e., Ollie and her henchgirls) would be less likely to taunt me or splash water in my eyes.

I'm not sure how it happened. One minute Teo was cannonballing off the diving board with the other older boys, each dive preceded by a Tarzan yell, each ending with a simultaneous rocketlike surfacing and hair-flinging jerk of the head, and the next minute, he was sitting next to me, saying, "Not to be mean or anything, but you're missing the whole point of summer."

I shrugged. "So?"

"So, I bet I can teach you how to swim by the end of the day."

He did not. It took six days, like Creation, but the miracle isn't that I learned. After all, I was not uncoordinated. I was a decent soccer player and a crackerjack Chinese jump roper. The miracle is that I ever let him teach me in the first place, that I allowed my three-and-a-half-foot tall, water-wingless body to be coaxed off dry land into four feet of water, held up by nothing more than the skinny brown arms of a rising fourth-grader.

We negotiated the terms first, of course. He promised me that there would be no surprises. He would not dunk my head underwater when I was least expecting it, and he would not, no matter what, let go of me, even if he was certain beyond a shadow of a doubt that I was ready. And because he had never lied to me before, had never, to my knowledge, lied to anyone (although I should jump in and say that the child Teo was not a saint; lying just wasn't one of his vices and still isn't), I believed him.

But the promises alone don't explain the draining away of the fear, fear that usually defied all rational thinking and snapped me up in its jaws like a great white the second I hit water. The simple, peculiar truth is that with Teo's hands on me, I was not afraid. By the end of the first day, I could float on my back, one of his hands under my shoulders, the other against my knobby lumbar vertebrae; by the end of the third, I could dog-paddle, his hand propping my solar plexus; on the fifth day, for the first time ever, voluntarily, I put my face in the water, eyes open, and on the sixth day, at my solemn request and in what still ranks as one of the bravest moments of my life, he let go, and I swam, joy-fully, like a birthday goldfish wriggling out of a Ziploc bag, a distance of ten feet, from Teo's arms to the side of the pool.

When I was no longer six years old, when I was a grown woman whose belief in the possibility of safety, while far from shattered, had suffered the inevitable hard hit or two, Teo's touch did not displace fear as ab-solutely as it once had. But it was still true that his skin on mine worked a kind of instant, inexplicable, possibly chemical magic. When he touched me, the world fell into alignment—a laying on of hands, a chiropractic of the soul—the threat of drowning evaporated, and hope cast its light. I know this sounds dramatic, but what would you have me do about it? Some things *are* dramatic. Put it this way if you prefer: under Teo's touch, I could be-lieve in happy endings. Or middles. Or beginnings.

At the start of my thirty-second week, when Dr. Helena Oliver, our high-risk obstetrician, slid the ul-trasound wand over the slippery slope of my comically mountainous abdomen, Teo took my hand and pressed into it the usual minor miracle, the infusion of hope. And even though the doctor gave us the very last thing I expected her to give us (the thing she and other doc-tors had taken meticulous care *not* to give us no matter how ardently I asked for it), namely, the unequivocal assurance that our shiny Penny was out of the woods, I was jubilant, soaring, incandescent with gratitude, but not stunned. Of course our baby would be fine. Of course.

"I'm very pleased with how things look in there," said Dr. Oliver, her eyes on the screen. "The baby's on the small side, but not concerningly small, perfectly

developed, and your uterus has stretched in such a way
that the fibroid is not threatening the placenta at all."

"Way to go, uterus," whispered Teo, addressing my
belly, his mouth lifting at the corners in a smile so
gentle it hurt to see it.

"So we're out of the woods?" I asked. My eyes filled
with tears. Infusion of hope or not, sometimes you just
need to hear a thing said.

"The baby is out of the woods," clarified Dr. Oliver,
and then she went on about possible risks to the mother
(the mother!) during delivery, but I had stopped listening. The baby was okay. The baby was gorgeously, radi-
antly okay. The planets swung serenely in their orbits,
the ocean tides rose and fell, my uterus had stretched, I
held Teo's hand, and all was right with the world.

Afterward, in the parking garage, as Teo began to
open my car door, he changed his mind, turned, fell
against me, and pressed his face into the side of my
neck.

"I know," I whispered, twining my fingers in his hair,
feeling his eyelashes, the architecture of his face, his
warm skin, and from within the hilly country my body
had become, the seismic shift of tiny limbs. Of course
I knew. It took away my breath, too, how we could take
up so little space and yet contain it all, the vast demands, the amplitude of love.

When Teo dropped me off at home, we kissed inside
the car like two teenagers, until my mouth felt bruised.
Then I went inside and called first my mother, then Teo's
mother, Ingrid, then my friend Linny, letting the joy of
these three good women rain down on me, dancing in it
Gene Kelly fashion, clicking my heels, twirling giddily

around lampposts. After that, I went into Penny's room
to spend a little time alone with my full heart. It was
a pretty room, cucumber green, with white furniture,
a quilt from Ingrid, my grandmother's rocking chair, a
dresser full of soft clothes. One of my holy places, every
last thing in it chosen with love. I folded and unfolded,
pressed tiny pajamas and featherlight blankets against
my cheeks. If I had been an only slightly different
person, I would have fallen to my knees on the white
flokati rug Ollie had found for Penny on a trip to Greece.
Instead, I rocked in the rocker with my eyes shut, breathing prayers of thanksgiving into the hush.

Afterward, I craved company. Actually, to be specific, I craved Piper's company, and you don't need to
tell me how crazy that sounds. But like Emily Dickinson says, "The soul selects its own society," and, apparently, the soul, at least my soul, plays by its own
inscrutable rules, because it wasn't the first time I had
wanted Piper. In fact, in her own thorny, generous, improbable way, Piper was becoming as indispensable a
friend as I had ever had.

But she wasn't home, not at home and not at Tom's
house (she had just two days ago given me permission
to call her there, jotting down the number on a piece
of personalized notebook paper with her name and a
pink-petaled daisy in the bottom-right-hand corner,
ripping it out and handing it to me with a jaunty non-
chalance so studied and so clearly proclaiming, "I have
nothing to hide," that it gave my heart a twinge). Due to
my admittedly old-ladyish uneasiness with cell phone
culture (you know what I mean, it blurs the boundaries
between the public/private realms, discourages quiet
introspection, results in abominable driving, fills the

world with silly noises, et cetera), I try not to pester people when they're not at home, but I broke my own rule and had started to dial Piper's cell number when I remembered that she had an appointment that afternoon for several, thankfully unspecified forms of waxing. Although I am not a waxer myself (when I told Piper this, she gave me the sort of look you'd give someone who claimed not to brush her teeth), I could imagine that even a hotshot cell phone user like Piper would prefer not to have a conversation while hair was being systematically ripped from her body.

In my current two-local-friends existence, that left Lake. "The elusive Lake," Teo called her, or sometimes "your imaginary friend." He was referring to the fact that, in all the months I had known her and that we had known Dev, he had never met her, had only even spoken to her on the phone a handful of times, but Lake was elusive in other ways as well. She was elusive when she was in the same room with me, as I've described, and sometimes, in flashes so fleeting and inexplicable that I could never be sure they had really happened, I thought Teo might be right about the imaginary friend part, too. A barbed glance, an icy pause, a shift in tone of voice, and I would wonder if Lake considered me a friend at all.

But mostly, she was lovely: droll, sly, smart, and affectionate. And mostly, she seemed to think I was lovely, too, so I called her. It was two o'clock. She would be nearly finished with her shift at Vincente's.

As soon as the hostess handed Lake the phone, she demanded, "Are you hungry?"

"Did Vinny tell you to ask me that?" Despite the many plates of pasta I had annihilated in his presence,

Vinny labored under the misapprehension that I was
scandalously underfed. "A nibbler," he would accuse,
with hurt in his eyes, "a guinea pig!"

"Who else?" said Lake.

"That baby is crying for some pasta!" Vinny shouted
in the background. "Don't be a stingy mama!"

"No pasta," I told Lake, groaning, "no garlic."

"Ah," she said, sagely, "you've entered the indiges-
tion stage. The diminished-appetite stage."

"Diminished appetite?" shouted Vinny in horror.

"Tell him that's what happens when someone does
headstands on your digestive system all day long."

Lake laughed and said, "Come over and tell him
yourself."

Once we were sipping our coffees—mine, in a sad
oxymoron, a decaf cappuccino—and spooning in the
heavenly crema caramella gelato Vinny had forced
upon us, I told her my good news about Penny. I hadn't
been sure if I would because while Lake was happy to
discuss pregnancy as a general, physical phenomenon,
the few times I'd ventured into the realm of the personal and emotional, she had clapped shut like a clam.
The last time this had happened, after I'd told her
about Teo confessing his secret wish that Penny would
be a girl ("I wouldn't be disappointed with a boy," he'd
quickly clarified, "are you kidding? a son? But right
now I'd say it's sixty-forty, girl"), I'd sworn off disclos-
ing anything close to my heart. But I decided that if
Lake could not rejoice in Penny's emergence from the
woods, it was best to know that now and walk away
from her forever.

I told her, and she didn't say a word, just leaned over,
placed one long hand on either side of my face and

kept them there for a few seconds, giving me a smile of sweet, undiluted gladness.

"Thank you," I told her.

After she took her hands away, I said, "Now, you tell me something."

"Like what?"

"Like anything," I said. "Something about you. How is . . ." I smiled mischievously, then finished, "Dev?"

Lake laughed. "Dev, huh? Dev is Dev. Cutting grass with Aidan, playing basketball, riding his bike, reading his head off, and awaiting the second coming of Clare. I don't feel like I see him that much, to tell you the truth. He's outside a lot and getting a little distant and teen-agery on me, which I suppose had to happen. But he's fine." She gave me a narrow-eyed, knowing look. "Next question."

"What do you mean?" I said, innocently.

"Rafferty's good. Working a lot."

"Oh, working a lot. That's what I was wondering about, his work."

"All right." She made an exasperated sound. "Rafferty's doing what he always does: muddying the waters, stirring the pot, driving me up the frigging wall."

"Elaborate," I instructed.

"He's just so *sure* of everything."

"About being in love with you."

"For starters. He loves me. He loves Dev. He wants us to all move together to his pretty white house and live happily ever after."

"The rat bastard."

"And you know what? Fine, *fine,* let him be sure, but he has to be so *open* about it? He can't just keep it to himself?"

"An honest man. The nerve."

"Men are supposed to toy with you, am I right? Play games? Get cagey every time someone mentions the word 'commitment'?"

"That's what you want?"

She swirled her spoon through the melted ice cream and sighed. "That's what I know. I don't know what I want."

"Do you love him?"

"Don't ask that like the answer to it is the answer to everything," she snapped.

I eyed her, sipping my cappuccino.

"Okay, okay, yes, I love him. I can't help it." Then she added, in a small, forlorn, un-Lake-like voice, "The trouble is, he's too good for me. And don't say he's not, because he is."

"He probably thinks the same thing about you. People in love feel that way all the time, like they don't know what they've done to deserve each other."

"Is that how you feel?" asked Lake, raising one eloquent eyebrow. "Like you don't deserve . . . Teo?"

For some reason, this question caught me off guard. Maybe it was the unexpected shift from her life to mine or the almost imperceptible chill that blew through our conversation like a draft. I didn't want her disappearing on me, so I trod lightly with my answer, honestly, but lightly.

I gave her an okay-you-caught-me look, and said, "No, I guess not. I definitely feel lucky." Blessed is what I really meant. Chosen. Consecrated. (I know, I know, but you try it someday, being honest about love without sounding extravagant or self-important; love *is* extravagant; it makes you important; I can't help that any more than you can.) I left it at lucky and moved on. "But deserving or not deserving doesn't seem to have anything to do with me and Teo. We just"—I hesitated, then tried to undercut the rest with an apologetic shrug—"belong to each other."

"I can believe that," said Lake, pensively, but with no chilliness at all. "You're two nice people who belong together. And maybe what I mean is that even though I want Rafferty, he belongs with someone else."

"Why?"

A long, prickly silence ensued, during which Lake began to change before my eyes, and even though I knew I should have been used to these abrupt transmutations, these hairpin turns, they made me dizzy every time. Now it was awful to watch the way Lake grew smaller and more slumped. The energy seemed to be draining out of her, even out of the kinetic corkscrews of her hair, but when her eyes finally met mine, I was unprepared for the misery I saw there.

"I have made a god-awful mess of my life," she said, desolately. "And other people's."

"Lake," I said, putting my hand on top of hers, "what is it? What's wrong?"

She stared at me. I watched her face, her deep breaths, and I understood that Lake, who seemed fearless, was afraid. She was gathering her courage, moving, step by trepid step, toward something big and scary, and she was taking me with her.

But we never got there. At least, I don't think we did because what she said next was serious and profound, but it was not a revelation. It was something I've known since the first week I met her. She squeezed my hand, let go, and said, slapping the words down one by one, like playing cards, "Everything was for Dev."

So that was it: the old sorrows. I exhaled, getting my

bearings like someone who's felt the rush of the traffic on her face and then stepped back onto the curb. "But you told Rafferty about all of that, right? Brown, your parents. He knows."

Lake shook her head. "He doesn't know the half of it. No one does."

"So tell him. He's a father. He'll understand."

"I was trying to make a good world for Dev, but I screwed up a *lot*. I crossed too many lines. Rafferty might understand the motivation, but there are mistakes even he won't be able to forgive."

"I bet he will."

"I hope so," she said, but there wasn't a trace of hope in her voice. She scanned my face with her piercing blue eyes, and I was unprepared for what she said next, in the same lost-cause tone. "I hope you will, too, Cornelia."

"Me?" I tried to imagine regret so voluminous that it extended to people you hadn't even hurt.

Lake sat very still and I had that feeling again, as though we stood on the brink of something momentous, but then all she did was smile a lopsided, dispirited smile and say, "Everyone."

Later that day, as I sat in the Donahue kitchen talking to Piper, I had the unexpected experience of recalling, in full-color, lurid detail, an episode from *Star Trek,* the original series. I say "unexpected" for a host of reasons, not least among them the fact that for most of my life, *Star Trek,* original and otherwise, had existed, if it had existed at all, as an amorphous smudge on the farthest-flung periphery of my consciousness. In fact, I lived a blissful thirty-two years without ever watching a single episode, and then, on a gray Saturday in February, all of that changed.

Teo was laid low by an upper respiratory infection and had languished on the couch all day enduring myriad symptoms, including fever, sore throat, seemingly ceaseless complaining, and a harsh and primitive cough, like the call of a pterodactyl. While ibuprofen, chocolate milk shakes, and constant attention seemed to offer him some relief, it wasn't until his feverish channel surfing hit pay dirt in the form of a Trekathon (not, obviously, my word) that he truly took a turn for the better. He asked me to watch with him, and because he's a hard man to refuse, avalanche-inducing cough notwithstanding, and because playing nursemaid had worn me to a frazzle, I plopped myself down and watched, first skeptically, then with increasing, and increasingly morbid, fascination.

In the kitchen with Piper, the episode that came back to me was one (of many, I suspect) involving a parallel universe in which every major character has a doppelgänger with an evil heart and disastrous fashion sense. Despite the wanton torture, the massacre and assassination plots, the goatees, hip-hugging sashes, and biceps-baring gold vests, there is the suggestion that the mirror crew members bear core similarities to the real ones, that the good Spock (whom I kept calling Dr. Spock, much to Teo's disgust, and who would, on twenty-first-century planet earth, be diagnosed with Asperger's syndrome so fast it would make his pointy-eared head spin) and the bad Spock are not as different as they seem, that they are merely products of their radically different environments: there, but for the grace of God, go I, off to commit genocide in a terrible outfit.

Transitioning so quickly from Lake at Vincente's to Piper in the Donahues' showplace kitchen was not unlike slipping from one universe to the next, but this thought did not come to me right away. When I arrived, Piper was ferociously slapping kosher salt onto a large, probably free-range, probably vegetarian chicken and didn't stop until I began to tell her about Penny. After I'd finished talking, she raised a finger, said, "One sec," and proceeded to soap and scrub her hands with such verve and thoroughness that for two crazy seconds, I thought she might be planning to snap on gloves and deliver Penny herself. When she was sufficiently sterile, she walked around the counter and, expertly sidestepping my belly, enfolded me in a breathtaking hug.

When she had stopped hugging but was still gently holding on to my upper arms, Piper explained, "Salmonella. You can't be too careful." But I wasn't fooled. I'd seen her swipe her fingers under her eyes before she'd turned from the sink. While I didn't doubt that Piper was a meticulous hand washer by nature, I knew she'd been buying time, getting her pesky emotions under control. If you had told me six months ago that Piper Truitt would be shedding tears of joy for me, I would have sent you home, your tail between your legs, my derisive laughter ringing in your ears.

But even with the tearful moment safely behind her, it was clear from the way she gritted her perfect teeth and began to viciously attack a bulb of elephant garlic that Piper's emotions were a long way from being in check.

"Piper?" I said, tentatively.

"What?"

"Is something wrong?"

Piper dislodged a giant clove of garlic and placed it on the cutting board, fire in her eyes and a Henckels chef's knife flashing in her hand. When she brought her fist down on the flat side of the knife, the unshakable granite counter shook, and when she lifted the knife to survey her handiwork—the clove smashed beyond all recognition—the satisfaction on her face was out-and-out scary.

Picking out the papery clove covering, she made her lips into a tight line and shook her head.

"It's Tom," she growled, at last.

"What about Tom?"

Piper put one fisted hand on one cocked hip and pointed the knife at me.

"Guess," she demanded, "guess what he said to me this morning."

I liked Tom. He was funny and sweet, and if you caught him in the right light, he bore a mild resemblance to Gary Cooper in *Mr. Deeds Goes to Town.* I tried to think of what he could have said to make Piper so furious.

"That you should've waxed *weeks* ago."

But Piper would not allow the mood to be lightened.

"He said, 'I've been thinking. Why don't we just do this? You put your house on the market and the three of you move in with us.'" Piper gestured madly with the knife as she said this.

"Wow," I said.

Piper glowered. "Wow is right. Wow is the understatement of the century." Two stabs in the air, one for each "Wow."

"Piper, could you put that knife down?"

She glared at the knife as though it had leaped into her hand of its own annoying accord and set it on the cutting board.

"So is he suggesting . . ." I paused. The question had to be asked, but very, very carefully. "Is he thinking that the two of you will alter the, um, platonic nature of your relationship if you agree to . . . cohabitate?"

Piper spat out a caustic laugh. "Don't be insane, Cornelia. I've had enough lunatic talk for one day."

"Sorry. So, what did you tell him? That he was a lunatic for suggesting you move in?"

Piper's face lost a little of its scorn. "Well, no," she said, in a quieter voice, "I thanked him for the offer, but told him he was being naïve. Families don't just shack up together. That's not how the world works."

"Actually, I think most of the world does work that way."

"I'm talking about the *civilized* world, Cornelia, not rain forest people with plates in their lips."

(I know. I'd wondered it many times myself: how Piper had lived thirty-five years without learning that you are *not allowed to say things like this*.)

"Are you just worrying about what people will think?"

"Just?" Piper drew herself up. "I have to live in this town, and so do my kids, and I'm already being shunned by most of it." She shook her head in disgust. "Shunned! Like an Amish woman who forgot to wear her stinking bonnet."

I suppressed a smile. "That wasn't a trivializing 'just.'"

"What?" I could tell by Piper's grimace that "That wasn't a trivializing 'just'" fell into the category of "Quirky Turns of Phrase Uttered by Cornelia That Bug the Shit out of Piper." The trouble was that I never knew which phrases fell into that category until I saw the grimace, by which time it was too late. The other trouble was that I didn't really care.

"By 'just' I meant is that your *only* worry, the single thing standing between you and doing it."

Piper's head gave a son-of-a-gun shake. "You. You and Tom."

"Me and Tom what?"

"I knew you'd agree with him."

I could see Piper scanning her piles of vegetables, considering what to brutalize next.

"I didn't say I agreed with him."

"Tom thinks you just *do* things." She gave a frustrated whinny. "He's so damn *sure* of everything."

As soon as she said it, I heard Lake's huskier, but no less peevish, voice saying the same words, minus the expletive, which was rather funny given the fact that not long ago, when it came to slinging around expletives, I'd have put my money on Lake over Piper every time. And that's when the *Star Trek* episode came hurtling, unbidden, out of the blue, to squeal to a stop in the forefront of my brain. Two women, one blond, one brunette, both stymied by a kind and decent man's unbewildered offer of a home. Two sides of the same coin. I could hear the *Star Trek* voice-over man saying those words (actually, I can't *swear* it wasn't the *Twilight Zone* voice-over man), although I would've bet that he couldn't tell you any more than I could which was the pure-hearted friend and which the cold-blooded knockoff.

I amused myself, briefly, with the image of Piper sporting a bouffant shag and a two-piece polyester starship suit, then said, "You didn't answer my question. Is worrying about what people will say the only thing stopping you from moving in?"

Piper's cerulean eyes bored into me for a few seconds, then she tidied her impeccably tidy bob with one pink-tipped hand, and said, pertly, "Cornelia. Just for the record? Being friends with you does not mean I have decided to go bohemian."

I laughed. "Thanks for clearing that up."

"Now, for God's sake, let's talk about something else."

I considered telling her about the uncanny resemblance Lake's life was suddenly bearing to Piper's own, but I knew the information would go over like a ton of bricks. No matter how many cordial, albeit accidental, encounters she and Lake had had, they had done nothing to lessen the sting of the ancient Piper/Viper remark. In fact, in a nimble, if waspish, riposte, Piper had dubbed Lake, doubtless for all eternity, "Snake."

"Toby moves out tomorrow," I said.

Piper frowned. "And in with that ridiculous Miranda, I hope."

I sighed. "No, Piper. Into an apartment just a few buildings away from hers, as I'm pretty sure I told you. Twice. At least."

"I thought she might have come to her senses and decided to give her baby a decent home."

"The baby will have a decent home."

"Two homes, you mean," said Piper, scornfully. "They'll pass it back and forth like a football."

"They'll raise the baby together, but in two separate residences, yes, although Miranda's agreed to let Toby sleep on her pull-out couch for the first few weeks."

"How sweet of her," said Piper, acidly. "Make someone else get up in the middle of the night."

I smiled. "Toby says getting up in the middle of the night with his baby will be totally cool. The best thing to ever happen to him. More fun than a zillion miles of double-black diamond runs. And so forth."

"I'm not sure 'fun' is the word, but he's right about the best-thing-ever part," said Piper, "although he might not know it at four in the morning." Then she added, "I hope Miranda realizes that Toby can't actually nurse the baby. I hope she also knows that not nursing for the first six months is the same as flushing the baby's immune system and fifty IQ points right down the toilet."

"As you know, Miranda is planning to nurse. I get the sense that she mostly wants Toby there for moral support. I think she's scared."

Piper pinched up her face, as though Miranda's fear were a fly in her soup. "Whatever. As long as Toby's happy."

"He's deliriously happy about the baby, happy in a deeper, bigger way than he's ever been happy before. And with Toby, that's saying something. But he's sad about Miranda. I've never seen him so sad."

"Well, she's an idiot not to marry him."

"She doesn't love him," I reminded Piper.

"Of course she loves him."

"Not everyone sees him the way you do," I teased. Despite Toby's haphazard grooming and rampant goofiness, Piper had liked him instantly, and ever since the day he had straightened the training wheels on Emma's new bike, the boy could do no wrong.

Piper threw a piece of red bell pepper at me. "And so what if she doesn't think she loves him? Has she noticed that she's pregnant with his child?"

"Their child," I corrected.

"Exactly. If two people are raising children together, they should live together, whether they're in love or not. Running back and forth between houses makes absolutely no sense." From the prim, self-satisfied face Piper made, the face that used to make me crazy back when I couldn't stand her, it was clear that her two Freudian slips had slipped right past her notice.

"Children?" I said, wide-eyed and as sweet as sugar. "Houses?"

After a befuddled interlude, Piper froze, a hot blush creeping up her neck and staining her face. Instead of replying, she snatched up the knife and a peeled potato and began to hack.

Without looking up, she said, "You know the worst part about it? What people would say about Tom."

"What do you mean?" What I was thinking was that whatever they would say about Tom, it was nothing compared to what they would say about Piper.

"They'll say that he's desperate to have someone take care of his kids, like he doesn't know how to handle them, which is complete crap." I noted but refrained from mentioning Piper's use of the contraction "they'll," as in "they will," as opposed to "they'd" as in "they would."

"Do you think Megan's husband bothers to read about the nutritional needs of children? Or Kate's? Or Parvee's?"

"No?" I guessed.

"They wouldn't recognize the food pyramid if it bit 'em on the ass. I can tell you that. Tom is so far above the rest of the men in this town that they couldn't spot him if they used a fucking telescope." She put the knife down and looked at me. "And you know what else?"

"What?"

"He talks."

"He does?"

I felt a moment's confusion. With two words, Piper had shifted from discussing Tom as father to Tom as man. It took me just a couple of blank eye blinks to get oriented again, but Piper must have seen my confusion because she explained, "Teo probably talks. But, newsflash: most men don't know how to have a conversation, at least not about anything important."

"I've heard something like that."

"Well, it's true. But Tom says what's on his mind, like it's just the normal thing to do. I find myself telling him things I never even told Elizabeth."

As soon as she said Elizabeth's name, Piper's eyes filled with tears. She pressed the back of her hand to her mouth, and stood that way for a long time, and, then, I saw it: further evidence supporting my parallel-universe theory, a theory that suddenly wasn't funny anymore.

I had asked Lake if she loved Rafferty, and as I watched Piper stand there, Lake's answer came back to me, the part when she said, "yes," followed by the part when she said, "I can't help it."

I wondered if Piper realized how she felt. I didn't think so. But she would. She had to. Nothing would be more terrible than if she never admitted it to herself. Even so, a tiny protective part of me hoped that she wouldn't. Piper worked so hard to keep her universe in balance. I could imagine the information that she loved Tom blasting through it like a supernova, sending it wobbling like a broken top across the black infinity of space.

Jasper Gregory Bloom-Brown, eight pounds, eleven ounces, pushed his rosy, bellowing way into the world on a glorious June morning ten days post due date, straight into the waiting arms of Tobias Randolph Brown, his father, and amid the undulcet strains of the University of Colorado fight song, which Toby had caused everyone, from the nurses to the obstetrician to Miranda, to commence singing the moment Jasper crowned.

I wasn't there, but Teo and I arrived a couple of hours later bearing hot pink peonies, chocolate cigars, a bottle of effervescent grape juice, and the shared, but very slender hope that, in addition to the baby, the birth experience would have delivered Miranda the realization that my little brother was the man of her dreams. At first, I thought perhaps it had. When we arrived, the two of them were sitting side by side in the hospital bed, murmuring to the pink-and-blue cocoon in Miranda's arms. They were smiling and their faces bore the identical mix of exhaustion and radiance. As soon as Toby saw us, he called out, "Yo! Aunt Cornelia! Uncle Teo!" Then he grinned from ear to ear and said, "You gotta see this."

Jasper was a big, fat, fantabulous feast of a baby, with cloud gray eyes and black curls peeking out from beneath a tiny blue watch cap.

"Good hat," said Teo. "He looks like a very short lobsterman."

"Little guy aced his APGAR," crowed Toby. "Blew that puppy right out of the water."

"And see his eyelashes?" cooed Miranda. "A lot of babies don't even really have them."

I started to say that Toby had. I couldn't tell if I remembered them directly or only remembered the hospital photo of them, black feathers poking out around his squinched newborn eyes. But I wasn't sure if Miranda would welcome this news or not, so I just said, "They are delicious. *He* is delicious."

He was. Somehow, Jasper had leaped past the fragile, otherworldly creature stage and gone straight to being one of those babies you want to chew on.

Teo smiled at Miranda. "And look at you. You look like you could do this every day."

"Oh, yeah," said Miranda, "piece of cake."

"She was so hard core," said Toby exuberantly. "The doctor would say, 'Why don't you take a minute?' and Miranda would ignore him and push like crazy. You should've seen her focus. Total Lance Armstrong."

Miranda's laugh was the loosest, most openly happy sound I'd ever heard her make. It shimmered in the funny-smelling hospital room air.

"You weren't so bad yourself. You made me laugh during transition labor. How many doulas could do that?" She reached for Toby's hand.

"I'd do it again in a second," said Toby, quietly. He brushed a kiss over Miranda's knuckles. "You just let me know."

I dropped my gaze to the tiny person in my arms, feeling superfluous. We were all superfluous just then, me, Teo, even Jasper. The moment belonged to Toby and Miranda. I looked into Jasper's serious, slightly crossed eyes, and prayed, to him, I think, "Let her love him. Please. Just let her change her mind." But when I looked up, the broken expression in my brother's eyes told me that however immense the past twelve hours had been for them both, the experience hadn't been enough to push Miranda over the edge and into love with Toby. I knew, too, as Toby must also have known, that if the past twelve hours hadn't done it, nothing would.

Carefully, I handed Teo the baby, walked around the bed, and put my arms around my brother.

"Jasper is dazzling," I whispered in his ear. "And I love you, sweet boy."

I felt him hanging on to me. When he let go, I straightened up and told Miranda, "We'll let you get some rest."

"Come back, though, okay? Later?" she said.

"Sure," said Teo. "We'll bring dinner."

"Oh, thank God," said Miranda, throwing back her head. "I haven't eaten in eons."

A dashing young doctor looking precisely like a dashing young doctor in a television show about dashing young doctors knocked on the open door of the recovery room. I saw Miranda straighten the neckline of her hospital gown.

"Hey, there. Sorry to interrupt," said the doctor, and then, to Miranda, "I'm Dr. Hirsch. Alec Hirsch. I'm the attending taking over for Dr. Smythe. How are you feeling?"

"I'm feeling like the next person who palpates my abdomen gets the crap beat out of him," sang Miranda, as saucy as a bluejay.

Toby eyed Dr. Alec Hirsch, who was flashing teeth that made his white coat look downright ecru.

"I think that's a good sign," said the doctor.

"We were discussing her first meal as a mother," said Teo. "So what'll it be?"

"A chicken-cutlet sandwich from Tony Luke's, with broccoli rabe and sharp provolone. Extra huge," shot back Miranda, so fast we all laughed. She smiled demurely. "Please."

Teo and I walked back to the hotel room we'd reserved for the night, and made the ultra-subdued, highly choreographed variety of love we made these days. "It's all I can manage," I had explained to him apologetically, a few weeks earlier. "Otherwise, I'm haunted by visions of you wrestling with a deranged beach ball. But it's just provisional, I promise you that."

"A stopgap measure," Teo had replied, a gleam in his eyes. "So to speak."

That evening, when we got back to the hospital, Teo

ran into a radiologist he knew from New York, and I
made my way to Miranda and Toby's room alone. As I
walked in, I heard a shower running and saw Toby sitting on the edge of Miranda's otherwise empty bed, his
back to me. His shoulders in his blue-and-white-striped
T-shirt were hunched, and his shaggy curls covered the
back of his neck, and for an accordion-like instant, time
compressed, and I was in the room with Toby, seven
years old. I was his big sister, watching him cry silently,
the way he'd always done, as though if he didn't make
a sound, it didn't really count. Not wanting to embarrass him—and when Toby was a kid, crying set him on
fire with mortification—I simply stood there. Then, in
the space of one breath, time expanded, and Toby was
a man again, a new father, and I was flying across the
room, calling out, "Toby! What is it? Something happened to Jasper?"

But Jasper was there, in Toby's arms, hatless and per-
plexed and adorable, and Toby was wiping his own wet
face with the corner of his blanket.

"Jasper's great," said Toby. "I just . . ." He broke off.

"Tobe?" I sat down next to him on the bed. "Honey?
Is it Miranda?"

He shook his head. Without taking his eyes off his
baby, he said in a hoarse voice, "It's just that this, right
here: this room, this day, Jasper. This is my *life*."

"Oh, Toby. It's a lot to take in. It makes sense that
you're feeling overwhelmed."

He smiled at me. "But that's the thing. I'm not."

"You're not?"

"I mean, yeah, it's big. It's colossal. But I *get* it. I
belong right where I am. That's an amazing feeling."

I smiled. "But you always seem that way. You always
have. Like wherever you are, you're at home."

Toby nodded, thoughtfully. "I know. I thought that, too. But I was wrong." His eyes started to fill again, and he rubbed them with his forefinger and thumb. He took his hand away and beamed at me. "I'm Jasper's dad, and it's like that's who I was all this time, but I didn't know it because he wasn't born yet."

He bent down, put his face next to the baby's face, and I watched them breathe the same air, Jasper and his father. My brother, transfigured by love.

"And now he's here," I said, softly.

In a cloud of steam, Miranda emerged from the bathroom, stepping gingerly, wearing a white robe, a towel wrapped around her head.

"Hey," she said.

"And now you're here," said Toby. He was talking to his son.

SEVENTEEN

Earth's the right place for love:
I don't know where it's likely to go better.
— ROBERT FROST

*W*hen you considered the whole of human history, which Dev knew was a speck, a subatomic particle in an atom of a microbe on a flea clinging to the colossal breathing animal of the cosmos, which was itself a speck floating on the endlessly deep, endlessly long river of spacetime blah blah blah, the event was tiny. The event was *quantum*. But what was also true was that it had happened, just as surely, just as *much* as anything (the big bang, anything) had ever happened, and, in Dev's private, unscientific opinion, more.

Dev kissed Clare.

Dev kissed Clare, although he realized that it might be just as accurate to say that Clare kissed Dev, because he was pretty sure that the movement of her face toward his was dead-on symmetrical in both timing and speed with his toward hers, making the kiss one of the most precisely synchronized acts ever to occur on planet Earth. Even so, Dev had wanted to kiss Clare and, without hesitating, had kissed her, a fact that was hugely important to Dev later, after everything that would happen in the twenty-four hours following the kiss had happened, even more important, though only a fraction, than the miraculous fact that Clare had kissed him. Why it was more important was a little hazy for Dev, but it had something to do with having been, for that one, pure, green, blue, brown, and gold cut-grass-smelling moment, a person who trusts his own instincts, a person—a man—who has a say in the way his life turns out.

The kiss was perfect. It was perfect not only because of everything that was part of it, but because of everything that wasn't. Dev had spent the past week in a weird state of frenzied inertia, scrupulously avoiding his mother and trying unsuccessfully to ignore the boa constrictor of lies and truth that had been tightening its grip on him ever since his grandmother's phone call. But even before the kiss, at the heart-stopping second he saw Clare walking toward him on her own legs, her own feet denting the grass across Mrs. Finney's backyard, the boa constrictor fell away like a husk, just disappeared, the way all bad things are supposed to disappear in the presence of something entirely good, but usually don't.

Dev had known she was coming. They had planned it, that Dev would be working in Cornelia and Teo's neighborhood on the morning Clare arrived, that she would find him there. There even seemed to be some collusion on the part of fate because Mrs. Finney hadn't just hired Dev to cut her grass, she had hired him to take care of her yard for two full weeks so that she could visit her daughter, who had broken her ankle falling off a ladder and needed help taking care of her kids. While Dev knew that viewing someone else's crap luck as a convenient little piece of your personal grand plan was plain cold-blooded, he had thought about it and was almost positive that a cracked bone was his limit; if anything worse had taken Mrs. Finney to Boston, Dev wouldn't have felt anything but bad. But no matter how you sliced it, when it came to seeing Clare for the first time in months, more alone was better than less, and completely alone in a pocket of green leaves and grass and yellow sun was flat-out transcendent.

Despite the plan, though, despite the fact that through close to two hours of mowing, pruning, and watering, all of Dev was waiting for Clare, down to his fingertips and the hairs on the back of his neck and the valleys of his lungs where the air never quite seemed to reach no matter how hard he breathed it in, when she finally arrived, he wasn't ready. He was standing in the sun watching the water from the hose arc rainbows over a patch of delphiniums so ferociously blue that he could still see the color with his eyes shut, when something, a sound or a shift in the molecules of the air, made him look over his shoulder, and there she was, shimmering against the drapery of green like a hologram or a mirage.

He almost dropped the hose, and then he looked down at his hand holding it, wanting to turn it off, to stop the noise and glitter of the water before his overloaded senses collapsed into chaos, but having no idea how. "Lift your thumb," ordered a faint, tinny voice inside his head, "and don't be a bonehead." When he turned back to Clare, she was maybe six feet away, not a hologram or a mirage, but not exactly Clare either, a girl with a short khaki skirt and swinging hair and long brown legs, the kind of girl you wanted to look at for-ever but could never actually talk to. Dev only managed to look for a few seconds because he was distracted by his heart, which had turned into a woodpecker inside his chest and was banging away at his sternum. You are an idiot, he told himself. You are standing here frozen like a five-foot-eleven asshole garden gnome.

When he looked up again, she was next to him and had coalesced completely into herself, Clare made manifest, regarding him from under her long, straight brows and smiling not only with her mouth, it seemed to Dev, but with her black eyelashes and the angles of her shoulders, and all the layers of brown inside her eyes.

"Hey," she said.

"Hey." It was like trying to stare at the sun. Dev dropped his gaze to the defunct hose, tossed the hose onto the grass, and wiped his hand on his shorts, but when he looked back at Clare, the idea of shaking her hand like she was the freaking president or somebody's dad seemed totally insane. A hug was obviously the way to go, the only drawback being that if that much of him touched that much of her, his brain would explode. Still, not touching her was the most insane idea of all. Dev wished there were a leaf in Clare's hair so that he could pull it out, and because this was, hands down, the corniest wish he'd ever wished in his life (and he'd wished some pretty corny things over the last seven months), he grinned and shook his head in disbelief.

"What?" asked Clare.

"I just—" said Dev. He shook his head again. "I just can't believe you're here."

"I can't either."

"And the really weird thing is that I kind of don't know what to do."

"Me, either. But you're glad, right?" She blushed but kept her eyes on his. "I mean, I'm glad."

"Glad?" Dev pretended to think about it.

Clare laughed, and Dev's lungs pulled in their first real breath of the day. It had to be over eighty degrees out, but the air in Dev's chest felt cool and sweet, almost Alpine. So maybe this is how we do it, he thought with relief. Joke around like normal human beings.

Clare lifted her hand to slide her hair behind her ear and something sparkled, and, reflexively, Dev reached out and caught her hand on its way down, lightly, just letting it fall into his palm. Clare gave a small gasp, and the two of them stood still for a split second, looking at her hand, before Dev said, "What's this?"

"Looks like a hand," said Clare.

"Ha-ha," said Dev. He touched the bracelet on her wrist, silver, with a single charm, a bird. "This."

"An eighth-grade graduation gift from my mom," said Clare, "It's a—" She paused.

"Sparrow," finished Dev, quietly. Clare-o the sparrow, Clare's father's name for her, the man who had left when she was two and died before he and Clare had really gotten to know each other.

"Right," said Clare, and the tiny catch of sadness in her voice unlatched something in Dev so that all the things he had stored up about Clare from their months of e-mailing—what hurt her and made her happy; the stuff she'd lost and hoped for; every small, interesting idea, everything funny and sad and specific and real—came rushing out to attach themselves to the girl who stood next to Dev in Mrs. Finney's backyard. When he looked into her eyes next, he gave a start of recognition. He held her pretty hand—smooth on the outside, rough on the inside from field hockey and tennis—and saw the Clare he knew, the one who had figured out how to make her father part of her life, to love him even though he was dead and had never really, as far as she could tell, loved her.

There you are, Dev thought, and it was suddenly the easiest thing in the world to keep holding Clare's hand, walk with her over to the shade of Mrs. Finney's back steps, and sit down beside her.

They talked, about the wacky, brilliant Emily Dickinson poems they'd decided to read and discuss together ("Pretty geeky?" Dev had asked, after proposing the poetry plan; "Absolutely," Clare had agreed, happily), about Lyssa in the hospital, and Clare's mother's engagement, and how a full month stretched out before them, clean and open, like new snow. They sat so close that their legs touched. Clare smelled like white soap and mint and something buttery, like caramel, although Dev wondered if he was just imagining that part because of the color of her skin.

Dev loved talking to Clare, but all the time they talked, he looked at her and wondered what he had wondered before, about museum guards and Inuits: how you got used to so much beauty or if you ever did. Like how a person could just go about his ordinary life—salmon fishing, dogsled driving, or whatever— with the northern lights hanging in the sky above his head.

Because you saturated sight, and I had no more eyes, Dev thought, suddenly, so that when he leaned in to kiss Clare, they were still there, Emily's odd words and the giant, blazing curtains of auroral light, but two seconds in, and Dev wasn't thinking about them anymore. He wasn't thinking at all, really, was just aware of Clare's mouth against his mouth, her cheek against his hand,

and it wasn't like the meeting of solar wind and a magnetic field or like electron entanglement or like a binary star or like any theory of relativity, special or general. There was matter, and there was energy, and something definitely happened to time, but Einstein was nowhere in sight, and it wasn't like anything else in the world.

After the kiss, they spent a few taut, silent seconds with their eyes locked, and just when it all threatened to feel like too much, Clare's face blossomed into a total reflection of how Dev felt: happy in a little-kid, verging-on-goofy way. Dev had to laugh at his own weirdness. He had just performed what could be considered the most adult act of his life so far, and here he was, feeling like a ten-year-old kid who had just gotten off an awesome roller coaster. Weirder still was that it didn't seem weird, at all. It seemed like exactly the right way to feel.

"Well, that was pretty great," Clare said, knocking her shoulder against Dev's.

"You think?" he said, knocking her back.

"What do you think?" she demanded.

Dev scratched his head, then said, "I think it definitely did not suck."

"Thanks," said Clare, rolling her eyes. "Remind me why I missed you so much."

He gathered a handful of her hair and tugged. He couldn't stop smiling.

"I missed you, too."

"Good."

"But being away from you isn't that bad."

"That's nice, Dev."

"No, I mean that being away from you isn't as much like being away from a person as being away from most people is. If you get what I mean."

Clare tilted her head, one finger on her chin, considering this. "I think I do. Which is kind of scary."

"But you know what?"

"Being with me is better?" She leaned forward, menacingly, until their foreheads were touching. "Choose your words carefully."

"Yes."

"Good choice."

With Clare's mouth this close to his, it was impossible not to strongly consider kissing her again, even though Dev suspected that asking for anything more at this point might be interpreted (by God, the universe, whoever presided over these things) as a lack of appreciation for what had already happened, and Dev felt appreciative in every bone of his body. Still, Clare's hair hung in glossy, sunlit curtains on either side of her face and the tips of their noses were almost touching, and the *right thereness* of Clare seemed to have a gravitational pull of its own (and, of course, technically, Clare *did* have such a pull, if you believed Sir Isaac Newton), and Dev was just beginning to question who he was to argue with gravity when Clare said, "I'm supposed to be inviting you to lunch."

Dev leaned back a few inches. "What?"

"I had strict instructions from Teo and Cornelia to bring you home for lunch. But I got distracted."

Dev smiled at this, but as soon as Clare said Teo's name, the perfect moment ended, rounded itself off and detached itself, like a bubble from a wand, so that it floated a little distance away, self-contained and separate. Dev would find out later, and soon, that it wasn't like a bubble at all. The memory of the kiss would turn out to be more like a marble, shining, rock hard, and durable, so that what would amaze Dev the most about that day was not how fast a good thing could go bad, but how a good thing could get tumbled around in a god-awful mess of confusion and anger, but stay clean and pure and whole in his mind. Something for him to keep.

For now, Clare was still there, and Dev was still happy, but Dev's secret had slid between them, so that now Dev saw Clare the way he'd been seeing everyone for days, as if he were looking at her through a pane of glass.

He would tell her. He hated having a secret from her, and at least three times over the past week, he had even gotten as far as sitting down at his computer and beginning the e-mail. "Hey, Clare," he'd written, "I figured something out about my dad," or "I don't know the right way to say this," or "Here's my latest theory," even though he didn't really consider it just a theory anymore. Dev had known that he could hit delete, bail out on the e-mail at any time, and probably would, but, still, he never could bring himself to get any further than the opening sentence. Dev was scared and not just of telling Clare. He was other things besides scared, too, and he hadn't even come close to sorting out everything he felt, but he saw it straight ahead, inches away, the point of no return, the end of life as he knew it, and he was scared the way he hadn't been scared in years and years, the kind of scared that made you want to put your hands over your ears, squeeze your eyes shut, and wait for it to be over.

"We should probably go," Clare was saying. "Toby'll be there any minute with his new baby."

"No," said Dev, more sharply than he meant to. "I mean, I can't. My mom."

"Shoot," said Clare, crestfallen. "I thought this was one of the Saturdays she worked."

"She does," said Dev, "but when she comes home between shifts, she wants me to be there." This was not technically a lie, and there was no way he could sit down at a table with Teo and Cornelia and act like everything was normal, but in the beam of Clare's guileless brown gaze, Dev felt like a world-class jerk. I'm sorry, he thought, I'm sorry, I'm sorry, I'm sorry.

"I'm sorry," he said, squeezing Clare's hand. "But, hey, can you come over later?"

Clare brightened.

"Aidan's coming over, and there's, like, this thing I want to tell you both."

"Oh." Clare looked startled, then she smiled. "Okay, Mr. Mysterious. I bet I could come over for a little while before dinner. I need to meet my friend Aidan in the flesh, don't I?"

Dev laughed. The last time Clare had called, Aidan had insisted on talking to her. And talking to her and talking to her and talking to her.

Clare stood up, pulling Dev up after her. When they stood face-to-face, she hugged him.

"Oh, Dev," she whispered. Then, she smiled. Then, she was gone.

Dev began at the beginning. He hadn't planned to. He had planned to begin with the phone call from his grandmother, and beginning at the beginning—with his mother, who never went to Brown, at Brown—meant covering ground he had already covered with both Aidan and Clare, but he needed to walk them through his process, step by step (and that's how it seemed, like a journey, a trek through the freaking Amazon with squawking monkeys swinging by and poison-dart frogs stuck to every tree), so that they could understand. Maybe more than that, he needed his friends to be with him amid all the lies and truth because he felt alone. It was funny how, until this past year, Dev had felt alone basically all the time without caring much or even really noticing, but now alone hurt. Alone felt a lot like lost.

He was nervous, at first, but only until he remembered who Aidan and Clare were, that, as they sat listening (and he loved their identical careful, leaning-in, dark-eyed, serious listening), they were themselves, people Dev knew and who knew him, people he loved and who loved him, although none of them had ever said the word "love." It was the same kind of remembering that had happened earlier that day with Clare's bracelet and her voice saying, "Right," and somewhere in the back of Dev's brain, a thought flickered, that maybe this would be the key to dealing with everything that would come: to hold people (Teo, Lake, Cornelia) in his mind in their entirety, to resist every impulse to turn them into ideas, to keep them specific no matter what.

But that thought could wait. Dev had a story to tell.

When he got to the part about the phone call, the telling got hard. Just thinking about that day still made Dev feel beat up and sad. After he had exchanged promises with his grandmother—she would not tell his mother she'd talked to Dev; Dev would call her again soon—and hung up, Dev had started to shake like something out of *The Call of the Wild,* like he was freezing to death, and he'd pulled his knees to his chest and put his head down, but the shaking hadn't stopped. Each lie his mother had told him felt raw, sticky, like a burn, and for the rest of the week, he'd done everything he could not to be alone with her because every single ordinary thing she did or said made him realize even more how

much he had lost. The mother he had lived with for fourteen years was gone, and even though she had never truly
been the person he'd thought she was, she had been that
person to him. He missed her. He hated her for taking
herself away from him, but he missed her more than he
hated her, and he hated that, too.

Dev was sitting on the living room rug, and now, as
he started to slowly re-create the phone call for Clare
and Aidan, he realized he'd pulled up his legs and
wrapped his arms around them as though the shaking
might come back, and, fleetingly, he felt mad enough
to punch something. He didn't want to be this person,
vulnerable and folded in on himself and afraid. Before
this, he'd been strong. He'd been *happy*. Disgustedly,
he unfolded his arms and leaned back on them, stretching out his legs like a guy on the sidelines of a pickup
game or a kid just hanging out with his friends.

He had already told them about the basketball playing, Teo in his ratty Princeton T-shirt, and, maybe because this seemed like an aside more than a vital part
of the story, they both spoke for the first time since Dev
had started talking. Clare had said, smiling, "Whenever
people mention Teo's wardrobe choices, Cornelia says
this quote from William James, 'Wisdom is knowing
what to ignore.'" Then she'd added, proudly, "But, yep,
that's Teo: Princeton, then Stanford medical school."
Aidan had shaken his head sympathetically and said,
"If only the guy were good looking, he might have a
chance in this world." And part of Dev had wanted to
stop right there, just leave the rest alone, but the weight
of needing to tell them sat in his chest like cement. Just
do it, he told himself, do it fast.

He did. Quickly, in a flat voice, the way some kids
read out loud in class, Dev recounted the conversation.

There was no need to point out Lake's lies. He watched each one register on Clare's and Aidan's faces; he felt each one knock the wind out of him all over again. Iowa, Teddy, Brown. Dev looked at his friends, their surprise and sympathy deepening, their worry for him growing bigger the longer he talked, and it occurred to him that probably in the history of the world, no one had ever loved two people as much as he loved them. He held their gaze all through the part about Teddy and his family ("three boys of his own") living in Blake's Tavern, even through the part when his grandmother said Lake had picked Teddy, and Dev had asked, "What do you mean, picked?"

Then Dev stopped. His mouth felt like a desert. He looked straight at Clare, swallowed hard, and began, "Clare. Please."

"What, Dev?" she said. "What can I do?"

Please don't get hurt, he wanted to say. Please don't freak out. And then he thought, *Please don't hate Teo,* which surprised him because why should he worry about Teo? But Dev just dropped his head, stared at his knees, and told the rest.

When no one said anything, he looked up. Aidan's and Clare's faces hadn't changed.

Aidan said, "Yo, I know it looks bad for your mom, but I bet she just wanted to leave that old life behind."

Clare nodded and said, "I bet she started telling people all that stuff before you were even born, and by the time you got old enough to ask questions, that was the story she was used to. Maybe she didn't really *decide* to lie to you."

Dev stared at them, confused. No one was freaking out. They were consoling him about Lake, both of them. How had that happened?

A grin shot across Aidan's face. "Dude, you have a grandma! Pretty cool, right?"

"Yeah," said Dev, uncertainly.

There was a short silence. Then, Clare said, softly, "So what now? There's this new guy out there some-where, right?"

"You think you'll look for him?" asked Aidan. "I know you said you were done with that, but we were looking for the wrong guy. It's, like, your dad could be right next door."

They both sat there, waiting for Dev's answer. His stomach clenched. Oh, no. Oh, *shit*. They didn't get it. He had laid everything out for them, and they hadn't figured it out. It's because of Teo, Dev understood. In their minds, Teo was so not a guy who could do what Dev's father had done that they couldn't even see what was right in front of them.

Dev took a deep breath. "No. Listen. He's not right next door, but I know where he is. So do you. Think about it."

Then Aidan blinked and it was like someone hit a switch and threw a spotlight on his face. He stuck both hands on the top of his head and blew out a silent whistle.

"Princeton," said Aidan. "The guy was going to med school. Aw, man."

Dev nodded.

"So hold up, this is not a coincidence, right? Your mom made friends with Cornelia on purpose to, what? Like, check them out?"

"That's what I think," said Dev, but he wasn't look-ing at Aidan anymore. He was watching Clare shake her head and sink back into the sofa cushions, farther and farther back, with a look on her face that told him that no matter how far she backed away from Dev, it wouldn't be far enough.

Dev stood up. "Clare."

Clare's wide, blazing eyes broke Dev's heart.

"You're wrong." She said the words through gritted teeth.

"Clare," Dev said, pleading, "I know it sounds crazy, but it makes sense."

"You are wrong," she repeated.

He took a step toward her, and she put up her hand.

"Don't." Then she was on her feet, breathing hard. "Teo would never do that. You don't know him. He would never get a girl pregnant and then leave her, just dump her like she was nothing."

"I thought about that," said Dev, gently. "But this was a long time ago. He was, like, a kid. He was on his way to med school."

Clare leaned toward him, her fists clenched at her sides. "Never. He would never do it." She turned her back and started to cry. Dev watched her shoulders quake and put out his hand to stop them, but the second he touched her, she wheeled around.

"You just want to belong to them," she hissed. "Your mother's a liar and your father didn't want you, and you think you can just take Teo and Cornelia away."

Dev stumbled backward, as though she'd hit him. He had known Clare would be upset, but it had never even occurred to him that she would be mad *at him*. How could he have been so stupid as to worry about her hating Teo? Tears covered Clare's face, and she was seething with rage—he could almost feel it, coming off her like heat—and she didn't hate Teo. She hated him.

"He would never keep a secret like that from Cornelia," gasped Clare. "*Penny* is Teo's baby."

Clare looked down at the floor, trying to stop crying, to bring her breathing back to normal. When she looked up at Dev, her eyes held a balance of anger and sadness that was worse than the awful rage, worse than anything Dev had ever seen.

"How could you *do* this?" she asked him.

"Wait," said Dev. He would try to explain, even though he knew it was too late, even though he had already lost her. "This is something that happened to me. I just put the pieces together because they were there. I didn't want any of it to happen. I didn't do this."

"You still think you're right? Did you ever think that *maybe* you could be wrong about something?" She turned to Aidan. "Will you take me home? Please."

Aidan looked from Dev to Clare, then nodded. Clare turned her back. Aidan squeezed Dev's shoulder on his way out. Then there was the terrible sound of the front door slamming, and Dev was alone.

In the end, it seemed easiest just to get on his bike. Dev didn't want to do anything, had zero desire to act at all, but sitting around the house with a stomachache, staring at walls, felt too pathetic and too much like waiting, either for something good that would never happen—an e-mail, a phone call, Clare at the door, God showing up with his beard and sandals to say, "Just kidding"—or for the big, unknown *next*, the fallout, the equal and opposite reaction—about which, uncharacteristically, Dev was too anxious to even feel curious.

So he pumped up his tires, jammed on his helmet,

and took off toward the steepest hills in town. It turned
out to be the right move. Between the mean heat of the
sun, the weekend traffic, and his burning leg muscles,
Dev had no energy for real thinking. Clare showed up
a few times inside his head with her sorrowful, furious
eyes, but Dev shook her away and kept moving.

When he got home, the sun squatted low and orange
in the sky, Dev was stiff, drenched in sweat, and thirst-
ier than he'd ever been in his life. He poured out and
gulped down glass after glass of water, thinking nothing but "replenish," a lush, wet word he had always
liked, a semi-onomatopoeia. Thinking the word was
like riding his bike, a way of getting the old Dev back,
not the one he'd been before that morning, but the one
he'd been back in California, when solitude was business as usual, his best bet.

But his heartbeat when he saw the message light
blinking told him that he had a long way to go, or, even
worse, that the distance between the past and present
Devs was cavernous, unbridgeable, even if he traveled
at light speed.

There was no voice mail from Clare. There was
one from Aidan, saying he was coming over tomorrow after breakfast, and one from Lake. Dev held the
phone away from his ear, but he could still hear Lake's
rasping, familiar voice, checking in, teasing him about
Clare, telling him she would see him tonight, signing
off with "Miss you, Devvy." For a hard few seconds,
Dev thought that message would be his undoing, the
last straw, but he squeezed his eyes shut and told himself, "No, no, no, no, no," until the tide rising under
his ribs subsided, so that it turned out not to be the last
straw after all. Dev figured that it had to be the next-

to-last, though, the penultimate straw, so even though it
was eight thirty and even though Dev had not skipped
a meal in forever, he cut his losses, chose the most
abstract, challenging, least-connected-to-the-human-
world book he owned (one on chaos theory, dense and
bristling with math), and went to bed.

He didn't want to see his mother, so he read for a
while and turned off the light. In the dark, the blowup
with Clare came back to him, not once, but over and
over, like waves on a beach, cresting and crashing, so
that when Lake came into his room and said his name,
he was wide awake and had to hold himself still and
force his breathing to slow until she went away. All
night, he felt restless and strange, almost hallucinatory,
as if he had a fever, and then, maybe an hour before
the sun came up, he searched around for the memory
of Mrs. Finney's yard, found it, and let himself move
through it in slow, almost real, time, until he was remembering Clare's hug, how her arms around him
had felt amazing and, at the same time, natural, even
familiar, and right at that second, he allowed himself
to consider, for the very first time, the possibility that
she wasn't gone for good. Maybe she didn't hate him.
Maybe she would remember who he was, and maybe
she would come back.

When Aidan showed up, Dev was pretending not to be
watching his mother. He was sitting on the sofa with
his chaos-theory book, chomping his way through his
third brioche from the bag Rafferty had brought over
that morning, but over the edge of his book, he was
watching Lake. She sat with Rafferty at the little glass-
topped table on the back deck drinking iced coffee,

barefoot, in a long, loose, faded blue cotton dress with her hair knotted and twisted and stuck through with chopsticks, and she appeared 100 percent relaxed, an uncommon state for Lake, historically speaking, but one Dev had seen her in a lot lately.

I wonder if she loved him, thought Dev, meaning Teo. He wondered if Lake had ever sat, laughing, with one foot casually resting on Teo's knee. He wondered if they'd ever made a world out of just their two selves and their small, familiar touches and their conversation. It didn't matter, of course, but Dev wondered anyway.

He was still wondering and watching when Aidan knocked, and, at the sound, he jumped up so fast that his book went flying. He felt as if he'd been caught shoplifting or cheating on a test, neither of which he'd ever actually done in real life.

"Come in," he shouted, picking up the book and putting it on the coffee table.

To Dev's vast relief, Aidan didn't give Dev any searching looks or approach him like Dev might spontaneously combust, the way some people would have. He walked in and his eyes went straight to the white paper bakery bag.

"What?" asked Aidan, pointing. "Doughnuts, bagels, what? I haven't eaten since breakfast."

"It's eight forty-five," said Dev.

"Like I said," said Aidan.

Dev tossed Aidan a brioche, which he handily caught and then held close to his face, squinting.

"A bun in a hat," he said, finally. "Great."

"It's a brioche, from some new French bakery down the street."

Aidan bit the topknot off the brioche and with his

mouth full said, "Who are you, Josephine Baker?" which made Dev laugh a creaky laugh, the first one in what felt like decades.

Aidan sat on the rug, polishing off the rest of the brioche.

"So, you ready to spring Lyssa out of the insane asylum?"

"Tomorrow, right?" said Dev, although he'd completely forgotten about this. "And I don't think you're supposed to call it that."

Aidan shrugged. "I'm looking forward to the car ride more than anything. Two hours with Mr. and Mrs. Sorenson."

Dev had talked to Lyssa in the hospital twice and had been surprised both times by how normal she sounded. Lyssa-normal, but still, she hadn't sounded drugged or depressed or like someone who would swallow a bottle of pills. During the second conversation, she'd even been chewing gum, which Dev had found especially reassuring. Lyssa had made him promise that he and Aidan would be there on the day she got discharged.

"Some people bring gifts," she had said, her gum cracking away, "flowers and whatnot. But don't go overboard."

Now, Dev asked Aidan, "Did you get her a present?"

"My mom ordered her flowers. They can be from both of us. And I thought we could throw in a copy of *The Bell Jar.*"

"Nice," said Dev. "Why do you think she wants us to come?"

"She likes us. I think she needs us."

"She must be desperate if she needs us."

"Well, she *did* try to commit suicide," Aidan pointed out.

Dev laughed again and this time it sounded less like the laugh of a ninety-year-old man than the first laugh had.

Then Aidan brushed the crumbs off his shirt and looked Dev in the eye. "She didn't say anything. On the ride home. Not that you asked."

"Nothing?"

"Thank you. And she said I seemed like a very nice person."

"Maybe you should ask her out."

"Who says I didn't?"

"She didn't say she hates me?"

"Look. She was mad, okay? She was, like, startled. But no woman flies that far off the handle unless she has some strong feelings for you."

"Hatred is a strong feeling," said Dev, but he felt hope pop its head up fast, like a Whac-a-Mole, and he didn't try to crush it.

"Trust me. That girl is smitten."

Dev winced. "Please tell me you're quoting your great-aunt Gertrude."

"Hold on. 'Smitten' is a cool word."

"You know it rhymes with kitten, right?"

Aidan made a face as if he were about to ask Dev something.

"What?" asked Dev.

"Never mind. You probably don't want to talk about it."

"When does that stop you?"

"You're right. Okay, so I get that you're shaken up." Aidan darted a glance out the sliding glass door. "Your mom lying. The whole paternal-discovery thing. Clare going totally ballistic."

"Thanks for listing all that."

"But have you thought about—" Aidan shook his head. "Probably not. Forget it."

"Just say it."

"Well, there's a silver-lining factor, right? I mean, Teo. Did you ever consider that, dadwise, he might be pretty awesome?"

Dev didn't answer right away. "I guess. Yeah. But I didn't spend a lot of time on it. He has a family, you know? He has, like, this perfect life. And he never tried to find me."

"He might have. Your mom changed her name when she married Teddy."

"Come on," said Dev. "There are private investigators. There's the Internet. Anyone can find anyone."

"So maybe he didn't try. That doesn't mean he wouldn't be glad to see you now. You're an okay kid."

"Thanks."

"Seriously. You're not that bright, but you don't totally suck at basketball." Aidan dropped the joking tone, and said, "Are you planning to, uh, mention this to your mom anytime soon? If I were you, I probably would have, like, staged a major confrontation as soon as I found out."

Dev groaned. "I know. I thought I'd do that, too, and then, I just didn't. I mean, yeah, I know I have to talk to her about it, but it's like I want to sometimes and other times, I just want to forget the whole thing. Because it's hard to picture how it would work. What? Teo and Lake would, like, raise me together? She'd call him and say, 'Uh, Dev won't do his homework. Could you come talk to him?' I don't think so."

"I don't either because you *love* homework." Aidan shrugged. "I don't know, but maybe you guys could work it out."

"Probably not. I've been thinking that my mom and I

should just leave. It would suck to leave, but maybe we should. Rafferty could come with us, maybe."

Before Aidan could start talking Dev out of this idea, someone knocked at the door, and Dev's stupid heart started pounding for about the thirty thousandth time in twenty-four hours.

"You look," said Dev, hoarsely. "Sneak over and look out the peephole, and tell me if it's her."

Aidan ducked and headed for the door. When he put his eye to the peephole, Dev heard him whisper, "Holy shit."

"It's Clare," said Dev.

Aidan turned toward him with saucer eyes and said, "It's all of them."

EIGHTEEN

Cornelia

*H*ere is how I remember it.

The glass bowl of fruit salad is cool between my hands. Aidan opens the door, and we step through it and Dev's face is all wrong, aghast. Nothing moves but his gray-blue eyes; they dart from me to Teo to Clare to Aidan.

"Are we—early?" I ask.

Dev opens his mouth, but nothing comes out.

Aidan says, "Sort of." I know he isn't making a joke. He is simply the kind of boy who answers when an adult asks a question.

Then, there is the shoosh of the sliding glass door opening and Lake steps through, talking to someone over her shoulder.

"Wait till you hear the rest. You won't be—" She turns, sees us, and stops walking, as though she has smacked into an invisible wall. Her eyes find Teo and widen with what looks like (but could not be; how could it be?) fear.

For a few seconds, the six of us stand, caught in stasis, the air charged with confusion and shock, Teo, Clare, and I frozen with our hands full, like the magi in a wooden nativity. Champagne, stargazer lilies, fruit salad.

Then Teo's voice says this: "Ronnie?"

I turn my head to look at my husband, who is looking at Lake.

Before Lake can correct him, Clare's voice, tremulous and wire thin, says, "You *know* her?"

A Braxton Hicks contraction begins to tighten its grip around my middle. It has been happening for weeks, my body's rehearsals for the big event. Aidan takes the fruit salad out of my hands.

I catch my breath and say, "Clare. Teo. Did you dip into the champagne on the way over or what? This"—I make a flourish with my hand in Lake's direction—"is Lake."

"Hold on," says Teo, still looking at Lake, "Ronnie Larrabee, right? We went to college together."

I smile apologetically at Lake. "Teo. Honey," I say, with exaggerated slowness, "you're mistaken. Lake's name is Lake, and she went to Brown, where you did not go. Lake, please tell this delusional man what's what."

Somewhere in the middle of this, a sound like a sob breaks from the direction of Clare. Her face is stricken. Her hand is over her mouth.

"Hey," I say to Clare, confused, and suddenly, a voice is slicing the air, a voice so shot through with bitterness that I almost don't recognize it.

"Go ahead, Mom. Tell us what's what. How you went to Brown and you're from Iowa and my dad's name is Teddy Tremain."

Automatically, Teo reaches for me, his hand circling my wrist, and I know he understands what I understand: something terrible is happening.

Lake moans, presses a hand to the center of her body, and wilts, her eyes on her son's furious face. "Oh, Devvy. How did you—?"

"How did I what, Mom?" I know that the sound of his voice is breaking his mother's heart, because he isn't even my child and it is breaking mine.

Then Dev rips his glare from his mother and turns it on Teo. "What about you, Teo?" He almost spits the name, which makes no sense at all. Oh, no, I think, no, and then Clare is saying it, yelling it.

"No! Dev, stop!"

"Why don't you tell us how you know my mom, Teo?" Dev is starting to cry now, slapping away tears, and I feel a rush of sympathy for him because it is awful to be fourteen and crying in front of a roomful of people.

I put my hand over Teo's, the one that holds my wrist, and look up at his baffled face. "Teo?"

"We dated. Toward the end of my senior year. For a little while. That's all."

Dev shakes his head. "That is not all. Tell me the rest."

"That's enough, Dev," says Lake.

"No, Mom. It's not enough. Don't you get it? I need to hear the rest."

Then Clare's arms are around me, and she is saying she is sorry. "I shouldn't have brought you here. Let's go home. Please." She begins to pull on my arm.

I shake her off and say, "Look. Someone needs to tell me what's going on."

"Mom," demands Dev (how can this be Dev?), turning the word into a harsh bark.

After an empty moment, Lake draws in a breath and says, drearily, "Okay, Dev. Okay." She turns to me, then. "Teo's right. We knew each other at Princeton. We dated for maybe three weeks."

"Why," I ask Lake, "did you never tell me that?"

Another Braxton Hicks starts its slow squeeze, and Clare sets the lilies on the floor and brings a chair from the dining room. I want to stay standing, with everyone else, but heavily, as deliberately as a Galápagos tortoise—it is the way I do everything these days—I lower myself into the chair.

"Don't stop, Mom," orders Dev, but I can tell his anger is faltering, is being diluted with other emotions. "Tell the rest. Tell me why you broke up."

Lake straightens and, in a Piper-like gesture, smooths her raucous hair.

"I don't know if I'd call it breaking up. We weren't really together enough to break up. But we did go our separate ways. For the usual reasons. We weren't well matched. He was graduating."

"What else?" Dev raises his voice. "Say it? Would someone just say it?"

"Oh, God," breathes Lake.

"Teo," says Dev, desperation in his eyes.

Teo's voice is gentle. "Dev, I don't know what you're asking for."

"Deveroux," says Lake, "we will talk about this later." She addresses the rest of us. "Please. I need some time alone with my son."

I see Dev's hands clench into fists. *"Whose son, Mom?"*

I get short of breath then, air a shallow, sideways knifing in my chest. The lilies lie on the floor near my feet, their mouths gaping, their odor snaking into the air. You love the smell of lilies, I remind myself as I am lifted on a swell of nausea.

Lake shakes her head at Dev. "Not now. Later. I promise."

"Dev," begs Clare.

With eyes like furnaces, Dev watches Clare cry, then scans the other faces in the room.

"Look at all of you. Is it so terrible? Will the fucking world end? Am I that bad?"

"Is what so terrible?" I ask him.

"I'm sorry, Cornelia," he says.

Dev wipes his face, then takes a step toward Teo. He swallows hard.

"You got her pregnant, and you just walked away from us like it wasn't your problem. Like we were nothing. And you never tried to find me, ever."

Colors burn too brightly, and as my heart races, the rest of the world goes into slow motion, and all I can see is Teo's face shifting, in a series of minute permutations, from stymied to stunned. He shakes his head slowly, slowly, slowly.

"No. That's not right," Teo says.

Dev says, "Say it, Mom. Is Teo my father?"

I don't want the answer, but I am staring at Dev's face, and I don't have to hear the answer to know it. My entire abdomen is rigid, and I feel faint, but not so faint that I don't see what I cannot believe I haven't seen before: the shape of Dev's eyes, his cheekbones, his smile, all the resemblances to the face I know better than any face in the world.

We all wait until in a whisper, Lake answers her son (*Whose son?*), "Yes."

I close my eyes, thinking, breathe breathe breathe. "Teo."

Teo crouches next to me, cradling my cheek, then sliding his hand to the side of my neck to feel my pulse. "Cornelia. Sweet girl. Is it labor?"

"I don't think so." Teo's face is there, the slant of his eyebrows, the lightly etched parentheses around his mouth, every plane and angle achingly familiar and so beautiful, and I see nothing else. I focus on his green eyes, and wish upon them the way people wish upon shooting stars and dandelion clocks. It is not a brave wish. *Belong to me,* I think. I rest a finger on the dip in his upper lip, then lift it away. "Teo, tell me what all of this means."

"Breathe," says Teo in the voice he uses when we're alone, "it'll be all right. Just give me some deep breaths."

Clare sounds faraway. "I only did it because I wanted to show Dev he was wrong. I'm so, so, so sorry."

"We'll let these people go home now, Dev. And you and your mom can talk." It is Rafferty, who has appeared from out of nowhere.

"Were you planning to lie to me for my entire life?" Dev asks Lake.

"Let me talk to you," Lake pleads. "Devvy, I'll tell you everything."

"You know what?" Dev says, raw panic rising in his voice. "I don't want to be here anymore. I don't want any of you. My grandmother said I could live with her. Laura Deveroux. In *Ohio.* I'm gone."

Dev moves fast toward the door, and that's when it happens, the thing that, afterward, I will keep seeing happen: Teo jumping to his feet, turning his back in his white polo shirt, going after Dev, leaving me gasping and sick. Leaving Penny. Dev yanks open the door and runs, and Teo would have run after him. I know he would have. But suddenly he is head to head with Lake. Lake is what stops him.

"Excuse me," says Aidan, shoving past them both. I hear him shouting Dev's name, then the sound of one car door, another car door, then the engine, starting up, roaring away.

I watch Teo's back stiffen. "You told him I knew?"

"I didn't tell him anything. But lies. He's right. I told him so many lies," says Lake.

I cannot stand to see it, Lake and Teo, discussing their child. Blood pounds in my temples, and I make a sound, "Oh." Teo turns. I see the blank look, then see him remembering that I am there. I see Teo remembering his pregnant wife.

"I need to go home," I tell him, "I can't process this. I need to go home."

"Okay. Of course." Teo moves toward me and puts out his hand. "We'll go home."

"No!" I shrink back, one arm across the curve of my stomach, pulling Penny back, too.

And it is as if he has been bitten by a snake. He drops his hand. In thirty years, I have never seen Teo look so hurt, and it is wretched, impossible. But, I can't be with him just then. I love him; I am lost without him, but I can't ride next to him in the car.

"I'm sorry. I just can't." I swallow. "And, anyway, you need to talk to Lake."

"I'll drive you," says Rafferty. He puts out both his hands and helps me out of the chair. Even though there is no way on earth I am going home without my husband, when Rafferty opens the door, I take Clare's hand, and the three of us leave Lake and Teo alone to

reckon with their past and with the incalculable everything that lies between them.

I was so sure I needed to be alone. Through the silent
car ride and the endlessly long walk from Rafferty's
car to my front door, I felt like a person underwater, my
lungs bursting, frantic to break the surface and emerge
into a still, dry solitude. I had it planned: a kind but
perfunctory collection of sentences for Clare ("I love
you. None of this is your fault. I need to be alone for
a little while now") and then a mad dash for the bedroom, shut door, drawn blinds, closed eyes. Cut off and
floating, like an astronaut in an escape pod. I believed
that utter aloneness was my only hope, but when I
turned to Clare to issue the perfunctory sentences and
saw the stark misery on her face, I got what I *really*
needed, a shot of empathy—my only hope—and just in
the nick of time.

We sat together, her legs tucked in, her head on
my shoulder, and after her apologies to me had spun
themselves out, despite all my assurances that she was
blameless, I said, "Tell me what happened with Dev."

She described their months of e-mails and phone
calls, about seeing him in Mrs. Finney's backyard. Yes,
Clare was fourteen years old, still part child, but the
thing that cut its jagged, yearning way across her voice
was love.

"You know what he said? He said that being away
from me is less like being away from a person than
being away from other people is. I don't know anyone
else who would say something like that. And he was
right. When we were apart, I missed him all the time,
but he didn't feel faraway. He felt closer than the kids
at school."

She lifted her head and looked at me. "It's like with you and Teo, when I'm in Virginia and you're here. Exactly the same." She dropped her eyes. "Well, pretty much the same."

"Certain people are like that, I guess. They're together no matter where they are. They just belong to each other."

Her eyes filled with tears. "Except not anymore. I ruined it."

"Oh, Clare. Don't say that. It's not the kind of thing you can ruin." Less than an hour ago, I would have bet my life on this. You still can, I told myself fiercely, you still would.

"You don't know how mean I was. Dev trusted me, and I was horrible to him. But he was only telling me what his grandmother told him. About Teo knowing."

"Maybe that's what Lake told her mother." It was so hard to say Lake's name, but not impossible. I was in no way ready to discuss any of this, but in the context of being there for Clare, I could do it, and this realization filled me with relief.

"I told him that he just wanted to claim you and Teo because his own family was a mess. I know I made him feel awful. And I'm so sorry. I should never have said that because that's exactly how I felt when my family was a mess. Back when I met you guys. I wanted to belong to you, too."

"I know, honey. You didn't mean to hurt Dev."

Clare shook her head. "No, I did. Or maybe not. I just wanted it all to be a lie. I was scared." She wiped her eyes, and said in a small voice, "And maybe, just for a second, I was jealous. Because you and Teo are mine."

"Nothing will change that."

"I know that now, but right then, I guess I wasn't

really thinking straight. I couldn't stand what he'd said about Teo knowing and walking away. Teo would never do that."

"No."

She fixed the light of her brown eyes on me. "And that's what really matters, right? That the part about Teo knowing was a lie."

I couldn't answer. Instead, I looped Clare's hair behind one ear and kissed her cheek. Her damp lashes flared in starry spikes around her eyes. She moved away from me a little, stretched out her brown legs, and stood up, a long streamer of a girl, unfurling. Oh, Clare, I thought, you are so grown up, and the pang of sadness I felt became the engine of a train, pulling all the other sadnesses after it. Teo is the father of another woman's child, I thought. Teo has a son with Lake. All this time, every second, Teo and Lake have had a son.

"That's what makes me believe that everything will work out in the end." Clare's smile dawned, sweet and winsome and brave. "Because if Teo is Teo, then nothing can be that bad. And he is. He's the same man we've always known."

It was my cue. Don't you think I know that? It was my moment to rally, to grin and say, "You bet he is, kid!" I should have risen up in glory, lip stiff, head high, Jean Arthur wisecracks tripping off my tongue, arrow straight and backed by a radiant sky, and believe me, I have wanted to be the scrappy heroine as much as anyone. But when the occasion presented itself, with Clare standing above me, her faith as resplendent as a full-blown trumpet flower, I did not rise to it. I did not shine or seize the day or set an example for others. I remained on my sofa, broken and small, sadness pulling me down and down and down. I squeezed Clare's hand and said, "Thank you, honey." It was a cop-out, a botched line, wrong, wrong, wrong, and the worst part was that I was too tired to care.

I wish I could tell you that things got better after that. Things? That *I* got better after that. I wish I could tell you that I spent the hours before Teo came home to me wrestling my fears and jealousies into the ground or engaged in a cool, Socratic dialogue with my best self, so that by the time he stood in the doorway of Penny's room, his hands in his pockets, his face crossed with wonder, weariness, sorrow, and other emotions I could only imagine, I greeted him with a brave heart and a tranquil mind.

But if I learned anything from this whole experience (and I learned plenty), it's that, when it comes to scrappy heroism, I am not the quickest study in the world. I am not the slowest, either, I don't imagine. It took approximately forty-eight hours, fifty-six, if you count sleep time, although neither Teo nor I did much sleeping. For fifty-six hours, I dragged the two of us through a mire of misery. I was petty and frightened, mean and reptilian, for which I will never stop being sorry, and even when the turnaround came, there was no radiant backdrop, no triumphant music.

What saved me from myself? Nothing extraordinary, no stunning revelation or near-death experience. What saved me is what saves most people. You know what I'm talking about. The usual.

Teo found me in Penny's room, rocking in my grandmother's chair and reading Penny a book in what I hoped was a soothing voice. I was trying to be a serene ecosystem, to quiet my slamming heart, modulate my breathing, stem the flow of adrenaline or epinephrine or plain bad energy, whatever my poor Penny had likely been swimming in for far too many hours.

And it was very nearly working. The room was dim except for the sunlight leaking around the edges of the closed curtains; apart from my voice and the homey creak of the rocker, the house was still; and the book was one I'd loved for years and years, the story of a bat who wants to be a poet. The bat reads his poem to a chipmunk, and I read it to Penny, a poem that starts with a birth, shifts into moonlight, and ends, like everything for children, with sleep: "'All the bright day, as the mother sleeps, / She folds her wings about her sleeping child.'"

I read this, and just after I said the word "child," a tiny, round, pearl gray, illuminated space opened up in the day, and my sadness began to subside, and this lasted maybe a minute. What ended it was a series of sounds that, until that moment, had only ever made me happy, tires on asphalt, a key in the door, a step on the stairs, the sounds of Teo coming home.

He didn't speak at first, merely stood in the doorway watching me. For an ungainly moment, I was overcome with shyness, but I knew that every second I spent not looking at him hurt him, so I looked, and there he was. My tense, tired man, his bones under his skin, his complicated eyes.

Listen: I never see my husband from a distance, ever; I experience him as human every single time. It sounds like nothing, the way that I'm explaining it, but I am with him differently than I am with other people. Immediacy comprises most of how I love him. Total immersion. What I want you to understand is that this didn't change, not as I sat in Penny's room searching his face, not through the fifty-six hours of hell I was about to put him through. I loved him the way I always love him, the whole time, and I can't figure out if this makes my behavior more egregious or less, but in any case, I'm not asking for forgiveness. I just wanted you to know.

As I watched him watch me, I saw his face clear, like a cloud lifting, and he smiled with just the corners of his eyes, and said, "Two weeks."

I slid my hand over the great, taut curve of my belly and nodded.

Teo said, "Cornelia," and it amazed me, as it always amazes me, how he can make my name hold so much.

"It's true, isn't it?" I said, which brought the cloud back down, but I had to ask.

"Yes."

He walked across the room and sat on the floor near the rocking chair.

"I liked our life the way it was when we woke up this morning," I told him. "I loved everything about it."

My hand lay palm down on my belly, and with one finger, Teo traced around it, dipping carefully into the valleys between each finger, like a kindergartner drawing an outline with a crayon, a way to touch me and Penny at the same time. Then he turned my hand over and pressed two fingers to my pulse point.

"Is it beating?" I asked.

"I love you," he said, and smiled, "for your beauty." It was a private joke, one dating from the very beginning of our being in love, and I knew what he was telling me, that the important parts of our lives hadn't changed and wouldn't change, and for one, split, crossroads second, there was a chance for me to be good, to avert pain and suffering, to believe him. But I didn't take that chance because suddenly I was furious. Fury hit me like a hurricane, and I reeled.

Through gritted teeth, I eked out, "You *love* me? That's it?"

Teo has always been a man who fights fire with quiet, and he didn't say anything now, just removed his fingers from my wrist, rested his elbows on his bent knees, his hands loosely clasped, and never took his eyes off mine.

"I won't share you," I told him, "I don't know how to share you."

"I don't know how to do any of this."

I realized that I had expected him to say he was sorry, although it was unclear even to me exactly what he had to be sorry for. The fact that he didn't say it made me angrier.

"Tell me about you and Ronnie. In college."

"You need that? Now?"

"Tell me." I glanced around our baby's green-and-white room. "But not in here."

"It's not that sordid, Cornelia."

"Where's Clare?"

"Reading in the hammock. She called Toby. She wants to stay with him for a few days, to give us a chance to be—alone." The word "alone" swayed under a load of irony. I wasn't the only one who could get mad.

"She feels terrible about this," said Teo.

"I know. But none of it is *her* fault."

I got up and walked into our bedroom, where the sight of our bed made me want to throw myself down on it and wail, but I just lowered myself into the armchair. It was not a comfortable chair, too deep for me, so that I couldn't lean back and still rest my feet on the ground, but it was the only chair in the room. Teo sat on the bed, his back against the headboard, and despite my rage, I ached for the distance between our two bodies.

"Tell me."

"Jesus, Cornelia. I met her at a party."

"Tell me."

Teo's eyes said, "Please, don't do this." Then, when I didn't say anything else, he shifted his tone into neutral.

"We were in the basement of some eating club. I was leaving because people were way too drunk, and anyone could tell it would end badly. She was leaving at the same time, and we talked on our way out. Her friends were still inside, so I walked her back to her dorm room. When we got there, we drank a cup of coffee."

"Did you spend the night?"

Teo gave me a cold stare. "No. We saw each other a handful of times, but it never got serious. I was a senior. I guess I was already halfway out the door."

"So it was, what? A fling?"

"It was *college*. Remember college? How does this help?"

I drew myself as upright as I could, under the circumstances. "The roof just got blown off of my life because a woman from your past showed up and pretended to be my friend, *cultivated* a friendship with me deliberately. She stalked us. You know that, right? And now she is screwing up the world I had ready for my baby, so I would really like to know precisely what I'm dealing with here."

"But these questions. Why do you need to know about our relationship? You think she wants me? She wants to get back together, after fourteen, fifteen years? That's crazy."

Our relationship.

"How would I know what she wants? She lied to me every time she opened her mouth. I don't honestly think that I'm the one who's crazy here, but I'm sorry for putting you in the position of having to defend her."

Teo shook his head. "Stop this, Cornelia."

"Finish your story."

"We dated, if you can call it that."

"You slept together. Obviously."

"We spent two, maybe three nights together."

"Consecutive nights?"

"Are you really asking me that?"

"So what happened?"

"Nothing happened. To tell you the truth, I don't remember it that clearly, but I think I just told her that I felt like it wasn't going anywhere."

"Why?"

"She was smart and interesting, but not, as it turned out, in a way that actually interested me. She was angry and sort of—dislocated. And sad. And I just didn't like her that much."

"In other words, you had meaningless sex with her and then dumped her." Even through my haze of anger, I knew this was going too far.

"Yes!" Teo said this so loudly, I jumped. "I'm an asshole, okay? Is that what you want to hear? So it wasn't a shining moment. So I fooled around with someone I couldn't see a future with. Did you never do that? I was twenty-two. But, hey, it looks like I'm going to be made to take responsibility for my actions, so you can feel good about that."

His anger was so justified that it blew mine out like

a birthday candle. He was right; there was no reason for me to know all of this. He had been answering my questions in good faith, when all I'd been doing was punishing him.

"I'm sorry, Teo. I get mad when I get scared. Forgive me."

Without meeting my eyes, Teo said, quietly, "I know you're scared. I hate it that this is hurting you, and I will do whatever I can to help you. But you know what?"

"What?"

"This is happening to me, too."

Shame engulfed me, then, because until Teo stated this very obvious fact, it hadn't been obvious to me at all. I got up from the chair and sat down on the bed a few feet from him. I was too ashamed to touch him.

"I didn't even ask you how you felt," I said, bleakly. "Oh, Teo."

Finally, he looked at me, with a ghost of a smile. "You still could."

"How do you feel?" I shivered and wrapped my arms around myself. Maybe that's why I hadn't asked. I was afraid to know the answer.

"You know the way you looked at me when I said I'd take you home?"

"Oh, God. I'm sorry for that, too. I was—beside myself."

"You looked at me like you didn't know me. Like I'd turned into someone else."

I started to apologize again, and he reached out and put his hand over mine on the bed. "It's okay. I only bring it up because that's how I felt when I found out, like I didn't know who I was."

"Do you feel like that still?"

He hesitated, then smiled. "I know I'm the guy who loves you, which is a lot to know."

"Good." I knew he wasn't finished. Just stop there, I thought. That's everything.

"But all this time, I've had a son. A *son*." A shimmer of awe slid across his face.

"Don't say that," I whispered, harshly, the world blurring with tears.

"How can I not say it?" His voice hardened. "She should have told me."

"What would you have done?"

"I don't know, but she should have given me the chance to figure it out."

I pressed my hands to the sides of my head. "No, no, no."

"I need you. I need to be able to talk to you about this."

"I can't hear you wanting a different life. I won't listen."

Teo grabbed both of my hands and held them in his. "A different life? Cornelia. Look at me." Reluctantly, I looked. "Do you really think I could ever not want you and our baby?"

It was a low moment, a desolate, howling-wind moment. I heard wolves at the door. Because the question wasn't sarcastic. It wasn't rhetorical. That this man I had loved my entire life was asking me this, with urgency and seriousness, scared me as nothing else that day had scared me. For a few dizzy seconds, our life felt so provisional, pieced together out of plywood and glue.

"How did we get here?" I asked Teo.

"Answer me." He tightened his grip on my hands. His face flushed in the manner it always did: twin dark pink swatches burning down the centers of his cheeks, from the top of his cheekbones to a centimeter above his jawline. A memory flew at me: Dev's face, flushing in precisely that way.

"No. You love us. I know that." I pulled my hands away. "But I just want things to be the way they were. I want you to want that, too. And you don't, do you?"

"But things can't go back to the way they were."

"Of course they can't. But I want us to be together in *wanting* them to."

It was a petulant, childish thing to want. I see that now. Maybe I even saw that then, but it didn't make me want it any less.

Teo took a long time to answer. Finally, he said, carefully, "Listen. I love the life we woke up with, too. And I don't know how to be anyone's father except Penny's. But I missed out on Dev's entire childhood, and I can never change that. Is it so bad for me to feel like I've lost something?"

Remember, fifty-six hours. Just because I wasn't mad at Teo anymore didn't mean I was about to exhibit a shred of nobility.

"You should feel what you feel," I said, turning my face, "but right now, I can't hear about it."

Teo stood up and walked out of the room. I didn't watch, but I closed my eyes and saw him anyway: his back in his white shirt, moving away.

After this, we entered a kind of fugue state. Time crawled. Day bled into night. Teo and I coexisted in a muffled, airless stupor. He got someone to cover for him at work. We didn't answer our home phone. We marked time in none of the ordinary ways; mealtimes dissolved, clocks went blank. We lived under lockdown. Inmates, contagious ward patients, bugs in a jar.

This gray isolation was punctuated only twice, early on, the first time by Toby when he came to pick up Clare. While Clare got her duffel bag, Toby grinned nervously, shifting his weight from foot to foot like a boxer.

"No offense, but you guys look like the walking dead."

"It's been a rough day," said Teo.

"Crisis mode, huh?"

"You could say that."

"Clare can tell you about it," I said. "But, Toby, if you could resist sharing it with the rest of the family?"

"Oh, yeah, gotcha. Total discretion. Because, not that you and Teo are fighting, but if you are? Mom would totally take his side. Dad, too, probably."

"Thanks, Tobe," said Teo.

"Dad would not," I said. "And we're not exactly fighting."

"Cool," said Toby.

Clare came down the stairs with her bag. I smiled at her. She hugged me, and then Teo.

"Don't worry," I told her. "We'll work it out."

I felt Teo's eyes on me as I said this.

"Man, am I glad to hear you say that," hooted Toby. He swiped the back of his hand across his forehead in mock relief. "Phew. I mean, look, no pressure or anything? But relationshipwise, you guys are, like, the benchmark. Everest. The Taj-freaking-Mahal. The *apex* to which the rest of us aspire."

"That's not pressure," said Teo.

"Do you really want to go with this incorrigible?" I asked Clare.

"Don't worry," she said, smiling a wan smile, "I'll keep an eye on him."

Toby and Clare walked out the door, but before it completely shut behind them, Toby came back and clamped me in a wrestling-hold hug.

"Seriously," he whispered in my ear, "you need anything, you tell me."

Tears were rising in my throat, so I just gripped his shoulders and nodded.

Toby stepped back and smiled at both of us. "Par example, if you need me to kick his ass, I'll do it." He hooked his thumb at Teo, who shook his head and smiled. To Teo, Toby added, "Or vice versa."

"I wouldn't tangle with her if I were you," said Teo, wryly.

Toby balled his right hand into a fist and pounded his chest. "Big love, kids," he said, and left.

The second visitor was Piper. She arrived at seven P.M. on the dot, a vision in eye-blue Nike running shorts and teeth-white sneakers, ready for our evening walk, about which I had completely forgotten.

I considered hiding out, waiting for her to leave, but I knew she could see both of our cars in the driveway, and Piper was an undeniable force, a steamroller. She would knock on that door until the crack of doom. I opened it, and although I had just opened it for Toby a few hours earlier, I felt like Boo Radley or a vampire, knocked backward by sunlight.

"Good God," gasped Piper, recoiling, "you look terrible."

"Hi, Pipe. Nice to see you, too. I'm sorry, but I really can't go walking tonight."

"Tell me about it. Walking? You look like you should be hooked up to an IV."

I had to smile at this.

"Teo and I have sort of been through the wringer

today. I'll tell you about it, later. We're having some—problems."

Piper shot me a skeptical look. "Problem problems or you-and-Teo problems?"

"Meaning?"

"Meaning you have a problem by regular standards or by glitch-in-your-perfect-marriage-that-no-one-else-would-even-notice standards."

I considered this. "Regular," I said, finally. "Global. Galactic."

Her demeanor softened. "Oh. Well, I'm sorry to hear that. Can I help?"

"No, but thanks. We just have to muddle through it right now."

"I see." She hesitated, then said, "Just don't—" She broke off, which moved me. I knew that eventually she would say whatever she had to say, no matter how cutting, but her second thinking, as partial as it was, stood as a testament to how far we'd come.

"What?"

"Just don't do anything stupid, Cornelia."

"I appreciate the support."

"I support you. I do. A hundred and ten percent. But any idiot can see that you and Teo are something special. Destined." She made a disgusted face and flicked her hand a few times, as though the word "destined" were a cloud of gnats. "Whatever. You know what I mean. If you guys can't make it work, there is no hope for the rest of us."

First, Toby. Now, Piper. For the years we had been together, I had lived easily inside the shine of my and Teo's reputed specialness. But suddenly, it felt a little smothering.

"Everest," I said, blandly.

"What?"

"Toby told me more or less the same thing."

"Well, good for him. Now do yourself a favor, and listen to us."

Left alone, Teo and I wandered foggily around our house, each bubble wrapped in our own separate broodings, but bumping into each other now and then, mainly to exchange words that only deepened our unhappiness.

Some examples follow. Supply your own details and modifiers and tones of voice. When in doubt, go caustic.

In the living room:

"I'm only circling the wagons, Teo."

"I know you are. I guess I'm wondering who gets to be inside the circle and who gets thrown to the wolves."

At the kitchen table:

"Why now? Why did Lake hunt you down now, after all these years?"

"You know about Dev's rough year and all that testing he had done. She wanted money to send him to a special school. But it was more than that."

"She told you it was more than that or you just intuited it?"

"I didn't intuit it because she's a stranger to me. Remember? We don't have an unspoken connection. She told me. It hit her all at once that it was a mistake, cutting Dev off from everyone, taking him to that town. She panicked. She felt like she was blowing it. She wanted help."

"So she stalked you. Correction: she stalked me in order to, later, stalk you. Preliminary stalking. Laying-the-groundwork-for-further-stalking stalking. Right?"

"Why ask me? You've got it all figured out."

In Teo's study:

"Let's just leave. Run away. Please, Teo."

"You don't mean that."

"If Clare hadn't gotten us over there, you still wouldn't know."

"But I do know. So do you."

"She's got Rafferty now. She's not alone anymore. Let's just go away and raise our baby, and pretend this never happened."

"You want me to walk out, be the person Dev accused me of being."

"He's lived without you for this long. He'll be all right."

"You wouldn't love me if I were that person."

"I would!"

Silence from Teo.

"What you really mean is that you wouldn't love *me* if I were *this* person."

"I love you because I know you're not."

In the dining room:

"What are you going to do, Teo?"

"What am I going to do. What is *Teo* going to do. What is *Teo's* plan of action. That's the question at hand, right?"

"What do you mean?"

"I mean, what the hell happened to 'we'?"

Silence from me.

"I got us into this mess, so how am I going to get us out of it? Is that how it is?"

"That's not what I meant."

"Are you sure?"

"No."

There was all of that. All of the above. And also this. In the bedroom:

Teo behind me, one hand resting on my shoulder, the other on my belly. Me leaning back into his chest. Feeling our baby move, feeling him feel our baby move.

And this.

In the kitchen:

"Remember the summer we played touch football every single night, all of us?"

"Even in the rain."

"Remember when you left for college and I wouldn't say good-bye?"

"Yes."

"It was because I didn't want you to see me cry."

"I knew that was why."

"Remember when you taught me how to swim? Remember the first Christmas we spent with Clare?"

"Cornelia. I remember everything."

He slept downstairs on the sofa. Not because we couldn't bear to be close to each other, but because sleeping in the same bed, our bed, with so much pending, so much unresolved between us was unthinkable.

On the second night, before I went upstairs, this happened.

Teo said, in a heartsick, ragged voice, "I know this isn't what you bargained for when you married me. I wouldn't blame you if you left."

I didn't answer. I hardly heard. The dismal sentence added itself to the general dismal hum of everything we'd said to each other that day. I trudged up the stairs without another word and went to bed, and even though the sky outside was still light, I fell into a pit of bone-deep exhausted sleep. Two hours later, I shot out of this sleep like a woman shot out of a cannon, panting, my pillow soaked, my body shaking, my heart sledgehammering under my ribs. I wanted to fly out of bed, but I was so heavy. I was waterlogged and drowning. I thought my clomping down the stairs would have woken anyone, but Teo must have been as bone tired as I had been because when I got to him, he was still asleep.

The streetlight sifting through the living room curtains carved shadows into my husband's face, painted his goldenness over in grays and whites, and the stillness of him shot me through with icy fear. Teo looked dead. I wanted to fall on him like rain, wash away every unkindness, everything from the last fifty-six hours that hadn't looked like love. Softly, I kissed his neck, his temples, the center of his chest, the palms of his hands.

"Wake up," I whispered, "Teo, wake up."

"You're here?" His voice was hoarse in the dark and only half awake.

"You're not allowed to think I'd leave you. You hear me? Or that I wouldn't have married you if I had known. I'm sorry. I love you so much, and still, I made you feel that way."

"Cor." He ran his fingers over my face. "I'm sorry, too. I missed you."

"I left you alone with everything. But I won't do that anymore. I promise."

For a little while, we became nothing but being together. Hands and breath. Gravity and weightlessness. Murmuring and mouths and skin.

"I want to see you in the light," he said, finally. His mouth on mine, he reached backward for the lamp and turned it on.

"Checking to see if I'm really who I said I was?" I asked.

"I was pretty sure it was you. My beautiful wife."

"I'm enormous," I reminded him.

He smiled. "If this were a movie, you'd go into labor right now."

"Well, thank God it's not, then. Because I have a new question for you. For both of us."

"Okay."

"What are we going to do?" As soon as I said it, I understood its power, this single, simple question, what I had spent the last two days stumbling toward. I asked the question, and what had frightened me so much was suddenly no longer a threat. It was something for us to do together, to make part of us. Teo was right. Everything turned on the word "we," a synonym for love, the thing that saves us all.

"I don't know. But we'll work it out."

"I need to tell you something," I said. "In the interest of full disclosure."

"Uh-oh." His eyes grew serious. "Tell me."

"I love you. I'm not afraid of losing you, and I'm not going anywhere. But I'm still sad. I wanted this baby to be your first child. And now Penny's only your first child with me."

"Only? Only has zero to do with us and Penny. My first child with you. You and me with a *baby*?" Teo graced me with the loveliest, most can't-believe-my-luck smile I had ever beheld. "It's everything. You know that." He pulled my face toward his and kissed me again. "I'm sad, too. None of this is what I'd expected to happen, either. But can I tell you one thing I've figured out?"

I nodded.

"Don't pull away, all right?"

"I won't."

"If you think: Lake and Teo have a child together, it's hard. I can't tell you how hard it is for me. But instead of thinking about it that way, think this: Dev."

I absorbed what Teo said, and then, nervously, slowly, I took the first unsteady steps toward letting in what I'd been trying so desperately to block out: Dev talking about poetry, raking mulch, saying, "How cool. To be someone's there." Dev's sudden smile. Thoughts shooting like meteors across his blue eyes. The longing in his voice when he talked about family, about Penny being born into all that waiting love.

But there stood Lake, a shadow in the background.

All of my life, love had trumped sadness and anger. It had been that kind of a life. Let it continue, I prayed. Let me do the right thing.

To Teo, I said, "I promise you I'll try."

NINETEEN

What knocked the wind out of Piper was not the guilt or the panic or the worry about what people would say if they knew. It was not even the shame she felt on the days (rarer and rarer) when Elizabeth was everywhere, in the drooping branches of her favorite lilac bush, in the four black slots of the toaster, staring out from the faces of Emma and Peter, punctuating the very air of Tom's house in now-you-see-it-now-you-don't gleams, like fireflies or phosphorus. Instead, it was how all of that, even the shame, even Elizabeth's face, could fade into the background, leaving Piper with the stark truth of just how good it felt to *want* someone again.

And she did want him. It was impossible not to acknowledge this. She could have no sooner denied being hot in the sun (hot in the sun in *Africa*) or being thirsty or feeling pain when she banged her shin on something sharp. His body, the presence of his body, cut a path through hers like a roaring tornado. Not always, of course, not every single second. God, no. There would be no living with that, and she was busy, after all, cooking and feeding, tidying and organizing, and when

they were all six together, she was nearly always being
clung to, climbed up, kissed, needed and needed and
needed, always by people other than Tom. But then she
would slide an egg onto his plate, he would pour her a
cup of coffee or reach for the remote control or loosen
his tie (Oh God, that sideways tug), and she would find
herself swept up, engulfed, possessed, stampeded by
desire.

Even when Piper was not deliberately being true to
herself, she knew that she wanted him. When she was
being true to herself, when she sat alone and tried to
answer the question "What do you really, really, really
feel?" which took painstaking effort, still, effort, focus,
and some cross between courage and recklessness,
what she knew was that as exhilarating as it was to
want him, to want *anyone* after so many years, ordinary lust was the least of it. Call it extraordinary lust,
she thought. On the occasions when she stripped away
everything except the truth of her feelings, she called
it love.

She wanted to tell Cornelia. When Cornelia knocked
on Tom's kitchen door that morning, Piper's first
thought was that she would tell Cornelia how, just two
hours ago, in that very kitchen, Piper had experienced
a kind of envy she had forgotten existed, envy of his
wrists for being attached to his hands, of his hands for
being his, of his shirt for containing his chest, and his
cell phone for being slipped into the pocket of his pants.
After he had left for work, she had leaned against the
refrigerator and thought, rapturously, miserably, Jesus
God, I have lost my mind.

But Piper didn't tell Cornelia this because Cornelia
needed to talk, to tell a story so bizarre, so unsettling, so
juicy that the old Piper would have been nearly swoon-

ing with delight at the thought of passing it on. The old Piper would have already been formulating the words that she would use, the order of telling, the insertion of asides or details or pregnant (so to speak—ha!) pauses. As Piper listened to Cornelia, she was aware of an odd sensation, a kind of tender incredulity at not wanting to do any of these things, at wanting to do nothing that would give this pretty, weary-eyed woman with her exposed, vulnerable neck and her delicate hands clasped on the table more pain.

They talked and talked.

Finally, Piper said, viciously, "Snake. You must want to rip her hair out."

"I did. I still do, sometimes." Cornelia gave a tired smile. "She's got a lot of hair."

"It's insane, the amount of hair that woman has," said Piper.

"She called me."

"Well, I certainly hope you didn't talk to her."

"She's going to be in our lives, Piper," sighed Cornelia. "At least it looks that way. I couldn't not talk to her."

"Did she apologize at least?"

"A little, but I think she wants understanding more than she wants forgiveness."

"Typical."

"And the thing is that I do understand, some of it anyway. She got more than she bargained for by moving here, although I'm not sure what she bargained for. I don't think she's sure; I don't think she thought it all the way through. She wanted to be in control of everything, though. She wanted to scope Teo out, decide whether or not to tell him about Dev, decide what to take from Teo, decide whether to go or stay. But nothing worked out the way she thought it would. She came here in a blind panic, bearing the full weight of Dev's unhappiness in school, of what she saw as her own failure as a mother. But then the unexpected happened."

"Dev found out that his mother is a lying sack of shit."

Cornelia smiled again. "Well, I guess that *was* unexpected, but that's not what I mean. I mean they got happy. *Without* Teo, their lives got better. Dev fell in love with school; he has friends here; his teachers love him. And Lake fell in love with Rafferty. She said that lately she would have given anything if they could have just lived here forever without telling us about Dev, but she'd trapped herself, painted herself into a corner."

"Because she made friends with you, and you're Teo's wife."

"Yes. And she tangled up Dev's lives with ours. And with Clare's. It was just a matter of time before she and Teo ended up in the same place and it all came tumbling out."

"Even if she didn't know you, that would have happened eventually. It's a very small town." Piper grimaced. "As I have reason to know."

Cornelia unclasped her hands, rested them on Piper's arm for a few seconds, then clasped them again.

"So she was in a bind. She couldn't stay and she couldn't stand the thought of leaving."

"Cry me a river."

Cornelia dropped her eyes. "So here's what I asked her."

"Go ahead."

"I don't know why I wanted to know. Maybe because I felt my anger at her fading and I wanted to stay mad."

"Damn right."

"I asked her if she came here with the idea of taking him, not just for Dev, but for herself."

Piper snorted. "Duh."

Cornelia blinked.

"Have you *seen* your husband?"

"Oh," said Cornelia, dismissively, "you mean the looks thing."

"No. I mean generosity, kindness, humor, blah blah blah. Financial stability. And looks. Of *course*. You don't forget a face like that, even fifteen years later. Not to mention the body."

Cornelia widened her big eyes and grinned. "Why, Piper Truitt!"

Piper shrugged. "If you like tall and lean. And green eyes."

Cornelia leaned toward Piper. "I'm guessing you prefer blue."

Even though this could have meant anything, Piper understood immediately what it did mean.

Piper did not blush or smooth her hair or panic or deny. In this instant, she was more than not ashamed. How strange, she thought, to feel proud, as though just being in love with a man—not having him or getting him to fall in love with her—were an accomplishment all by itself, something to dignify her life. She had never loved a man like this and hadn't known that it was possible. With a start, she realized that it was how she loved her kids.

"We'll save that for another time," said Piper, finally. "So what did she say? Snake."

"She got huffy, at first. She said that she could've told him she was pregnant, all those years ago. He was so nice, she said, that he might have tried to be with her, even though he obviously didn't want to. Which is why she didn't tell him." Cornelia paused, lost in thought, her face tensing, then said, "But then she admitted that it had crossed her mind, when she came out here to find him. Not a plan, really. Just a little bit of—hope. That they'd meet again and something would spring up between them."

"Happily ever after," said Piper, acidly. "What stopped her from trying?"

"If you can believe her," Cornelia said, quietly, two coins of red appearing on her cheeks, "I did."

"The fact that Teo had a wife?"

"No. She assumed he'd have a wife. But Lake got more than she bargained for with me, too. She liked me, she says, against her better judgment."

"Oh, that's such bullshit," said Piper. "She *liked* you? Please."

"I don't know, Piper. Stranger things have happened." Cornelia's eyes twinkled. "Like *you* liking me."

"You're right. That is strange," Piper said.

Cornelia smiled, then her eyes grew thoughtful. "You know what I keep thinking? It doesn't make sense, but I keep thinking that none of this can be happening because Teo and I have always been together. How could he have a child with another woman when he and I have been together all our lives?"

Piper's first impulse was to correct Cornelia, to point out that of course they hadn't always been together. They had gone to different colleges, lived in different cities. Sure, they'd kept in touch, probably seen each other now and then. Still, there was a lot of unaccounted-for time drifting around out there. But because she realized that Cornelia actually knew these facts, Piper thought past her first impulse and tried to understand what Cornelia really meant.

"You mean that's how it feels."

"Yes. It's easy to feel like real life has only happened

when we've been together, but then this happens, and I see that it's *all* real. I'm just one part of Teo's story." Cornelia shivered.

"An important part. And anyway, that's not such a bad thing, is it? You wouldn't want to be some second-cousin bumpkin couple on some mountaintop who spent every second together and then got married when you were fourteen, would you?"

The sparkle came back to Cornelia's face, and Piper felt a little thrill of victory. "No, I guess not."

"What happens next? What will you and Teo do about Dev?"

Cornelia drew a deep breath and tapped her fingertips noiselessly on the table. "We decided to take our cues from Dev. Try to do whatever he needs us to do. We called him, but he was staying at Aidan's house. He's home now, Lake says. But he hasn't called us back, yet."

"Letting him call the shots is a good way to begin, anyway. But remember that he's a kid. He might not know what's good for him."

Simultaneously, Cornelia squeezed her eyes shut and pressed her hands together as though she were praying. "I wish I were sure that I could do this." When she opened them, her eyes were wet.

"You can."

"Oh, I can love Dev. I know that. And I will do whatever needs doing. I'm talking about happiness. I don't know if I can be happy with Dev in our lives as Teo's son." She lifted her hands to her face and wiped her eyes. "It's just that I had a vision of how my life would be. I've had visions before that never came to pass, and I was better off for getting thrown for a loop. But this. It's hard to let go of my idea of family, just Teo and me and our little baby."

Piper felt her heart opening, felt affection flowing out of her toward Cornelia, so she made her voice brisk and businesslike. "Of course, you can be happy. Look at me. I had my picture-perfect life, and my husband left me for a red-haired, weak-chinned nurse; I'm practically living with my dead friend's family; no one in town speaks to me, with the exception of Kate and you, but I'm fine. My life is real for the first time in ages. If you'd told me a year ago that all those things would happen and I'd still be fine, I would have told you you were crazy." Piper felt her throat tightening, but she drew her lips into a thin line and said, tersely, "And a lot of why I'm fine has to do with you, knowing you. So don't be ridiculous."

A few minutes later, as Cornelia was leaving, she rested her hand briefly against Piper's cheek. The way she touched people, marveled Piper, like touching was easy.

"You look great, you know," said Cornelia.

"Oh, well, when it comes to being pretty, I run circles around every woman in that old crowd of mine, always have. Not that that's hard to do."

Cornelia laughed. "Beauty is the best revenge. But I meant that you look happy. Whatever is happening with—him, it suits you."

"Nothing's happening. Not happening-happening. I just feel—" She stopped.

"Well, that's something happening," observed Cornelia.

That night was the second night of the Hanro nightgown, which would not in itself have been significant necessarily, but it was also the first night following the first *morning* of the Hanro nightgown, and that was very significant indeed. Not that Piper was blaming the night-

gown itself. It wasn't even that sexy, being ankle length,
cotton, and snow white to boot. But it had vermicelli-
thin straps and, in particular spots, it clung to her body
like rain. Still, no one in her right mind could blame a
nightgown for anything, and only in her lowest moments
was Piper *blaming* anything or anyone at all. She had
spotted it in the Garnet Hill catalog, in the section she
usually blew past without a glance, and, without weighing the pros and cons, she had picked up the phone and
ordered it, even springing for, in a last-second, unana-
lyzed burst of urgency, overnight shipping.

It wasn't like anyone would see it, anyway, she had
told herself. When she spent the night at Tom's house,
her habit was to remain in her clothes until just before
she got into bed and then to change out of her pajamas
before going downstairs for breakfast, and even on the
two occasions when she and Tom had seen each other
after lights-out (once Tom's car alarm had gone off; another time, Peter had walked out into the hallway and
vomited, uproariously), her pajamas had been no great
shakes, a baggy T-shirt, a pair of baggy shorts.

But the first morning after the first night that she had
worn the Hanro nightgown, Piper had gotten up as usual,
chosen her clothes for the day, and then had simply failed
to put them on. What's the big deal, she had chided herself, but then, biting her bottom lip, she had reached into
the closet and slipped on a thin blue cardigan, which
hadn't covered up much of anything but which had reassured her anyway. When Tom came downstairs, Piper
was already in the kitchen, slicing strawberries into the
kids' cereal bowls. "Morning, Pipe," he'd said, in his
regular morning voice, but Piper knew that he'd noticed
the nightgown because of how thoroughly he appeared

not to notice. Despite the children screaming with delight at the sight of her "dressed up," Tom never said a word.

After he left for work, Piper stood at the kitchen window, looking at the two empty chairs in which she and Tom had sat the evening before, drinking gin and tonics, with the insects whirring in the trees and the kids hurtling through the lazy fan of the sprinkler. They had talked, as they always talked, and now Piper wondered if what they had said to each other, and what had passed between them in the intervals of not speaking, had been part of her decision to come downstairs in the nightgown.

With Cornelia's permission, Piper had told him about Cornelia and Teo, and they had been discussing whether or not Dev would be able to forgive his mother or at least to understand why she had done what she'd done.

Piper had run the lime around the edge of her glass and said, "I think I'm starting to understand why my mom did what she did."

"You mean running away with the guy from the farmers' market."

"And before that. Wearing bikinis, smoking, dancing around the living room like a teenager with her friend Marybeth. I hated her for all of it."

"Maybe you sensed that she would leave."

"Maybe. And, don't get me wrong, I still think she handled things badly. She didn't just leave my dad, she left us. What mother leaves her children?"

"She did try to make amends, though, right? Later?"

"I guess, but it was too little, too late. Even now, she calls me twice, three times a year? But I think I understand her *reasons* for doing what she did. She decided to choose happiness, a real life, even though it meant breaking all the rules she'd ever lived by."

With vehemence and a blue, unvarnished look, one that blurred the yard around them into a single emerald streak, muffled the buzzing, chiming music of the insects and children's squeals almost into silence, and made Piper lose her breath, Tom had said, "Good for her."

That night, Piper and Tom walked upstairs together, as they often did, and said an ordinary "good night," but then Piper didn't enter the guest room, turn on the light, and shut the door behind her. Feeling fully awake, but moving like someone in a trance, Piper glided through the guest room in the dark, headed straight to the bathroom, took off her clothes, brushed her teeth (brushed her teeth *naked,* her breasts falling softly forward as she leaned over the sink), then lifted the nightgown from the hook on the back of the door and slipped it over her head.

When she opened the door of the bathroom, she could hear Tom's footsteps in the hall, the creak of one bedroom door, then another, as Tom checked on the kids. Piper didn't think. She walked in the direction of the room's large, bare window, but a few feet from it, she stopped and simply stood there, poised between two rectangles, the window with its moon and the open door behind her. She felt pale and brushed with light, front and back. She felt pliant and slender, a white birch tree, a filament at the center of a lily. She waited.

Behind her, Tom said, "Piper?"

Without turning around, she said, "Hey. What's that moon called, the one that's almost full?"

His hand was on her waist, his mouth on the curve of

her shoulder. She closed her eyes at the feel of his un-
shaven chin; she tilted back her head, pressed her back
into his chest. He slid his other hand under her breast,
the place where a shadow would fall if her breast was
bare, and then the nightgown strap dropped down her
arm, and her breast was bare except for his fingers
moving lightly over it. Piper turned around in Tom's
arms and kissed him as though it were the very last
time, her last chance to kiss anyone, their mouths tast-
ing like mint, and all the while Tom's hand was tugging
the nightgown higher, up the side of her body, the air
cool on her legs, and a voice said, "We can't," and, goddamn it if it wasn't her voice, and everything stopped.

They stood against each other, panting. Piper slid the
strap back into place; then, Tom took her hand and led
her to the edge of the bed, where they sat, shoulder to
shoulder.

"It's you," he said, "specifically. It's not just because
I'm lonely. In case you were wondering."

"Thanks. It's you, too."

"Would it make any difference if I told you that she
was planning to divorce me, before she got sick?"

"I knew about that," said Piper, noticing how even
now it was easy to talk to him, "and it does make some
difference, but I guess not enough." She let go of his
hand and pushed her hands through her hair. "You
were right about her being an iconoclast. She would
have been all for me moving in here with my kids.
Anything for the kids. But no woman would be okay
with her best friend and her husband . . ."

Tom didn't say anything. She listened to his breathing and thought how even this was pretty good, just
sitting here with him.

"I don't feel like her husband now. I feel like I used to be her husband. I loved her, but I don't belong to her anymore."

"Maybe I still do. I'm sorry."

Tom looked past Piper, out the window. "Gibbons," he said, "gibbous."

"That's right," said Piper, turning to look. "Waxing gibbous, waning gibbous. I'm not sure if it's waxing or waning."

"Well, it was definitely waxing there for a while," said Tom with a grin in his voice.

Piper batted his shoulder and laughed.

"So what do we do now?" she asked.

"I don't think we should pretend it never happened."

"I don't either."

"And I sure as hell don't want you and the kids to stop staying here."

Piper's eyes burned. Quietly, she said, "Well. Thank God for that."

"Why don't we try just, you know, acknowledging this, and keep on like we were?"

No way, she thought, will it be that easy. Aloud, she agreed, "The way we were was good."

"Yeah," said Tom. "Not quite as good as *that*." He gestured to the spot in the room where they'd stood together.

Piper smiled.

"What if I," began Tom slowly, "tested the waters. Now and then."

The word no wouldn't come. Finally, Piper said, "Fair enough."

Alone in bed, Piper felt purely awake, tingly, alert to all the parts of her body at once. She felt as though she should be glowing under the silken cotton of the sheet, emitting a blurred halo of radiance, like a streetlamp in mist. Alive, she thought. I feel alive.

She remembered the day that Elizabeth had told her about Mike, the yoga guy, about the hot hand-holding and four kisses. Piper hadn't fully understood why Elizabeth had wanted her to have this information, something about keeping it in storage in case Tom needed to know that Elizabeth hadn't been faithful. But what if Elizabeth hadn't meant the information to be for Tom at all? What if it was her way of giving Piper permission to be with him after Elizabeth was gone?

It was a tantalizing notion, and for a few beautiful seconds, Piper allowed herself to believe it, but then, quick and vicious, like a person stomping on a bug, Piper crushed the thought. Ha. Dream on, idiot. There could be no wriggling out, no whitewashing, or turning a blind eye. For Elizabeth, Tom and Piper together would be betrayal, pure and simple. Unforgivable.

But the night pulsed vibrantly on and the alive, radiant sensation persisted, and, eventually, a tiny, frail, parachute seed of an idea drifted into Piper's head. She dismissed the idea before it could take root, but it would be borne back to her again and again: that perhaps one of the disadvantages of the dead is that, no matter who they were or how much anyone had loved them, they do not get the last word.

TWENTY

You are brave and good. —CLARE HOBBES

*F*or two days and two nights, Dev's brain went on vacation, a thing that his brain had not, to his knowledge, done before (and if his brain didn't know about something his brain had done, could it actually be said to have done it?—this was as weighty a question as Dev's vacationing brain deigned to consider), and what Dev discovered was that, while he knew it couldn't last forever, he liked it. He could see how you could get used to the not-thinking, the haphazard floating through days, your brain lounging around like a tourist in a loud shirt, grasping nothing heavier than a magazine and a drink (umbrellaed, water beaded, pineapple hanging off its rim like an elephant ear), lulled by the sound of seagulls and ocean waves.

As soon as Dev had run out of his house, away from the assortment of dazed and freaked-out people that was too collectively unwieldy to be anybody's family, after his dazzling sheen of rage had dimmed and he felt deflated and lost, Dev found that thinking about what had happened was a very bad idea, like climbing up a mountain in an avalanche. Even thinking about thinking about it was dangerous and ill-advised, so he channeled all the energy he usually spent on pondering, untangling, and sorting into the total refusal to ponder, untangle, and sort.

He shot baskets with Aidan without thinking about shooting baskets with Teo. He worked in Mrs. Finney's yard without thinking about kissing Clare. He ate everything Mrs. Weeks put in front of him—barbecued chicken and buttered corn and bright, fat slices of tomato—without recalling the way his own mother's face settled unconsciously into something like bliss whenever she watched Dev eat what she'd cooked.

Even picking up Lyssa at the inpatient facility was okay, a welcome distraction. It was not so much good to see her (because she really was at least ten different varieties of annoying; that hadn't changed) as it was good to see her looking good, to see her wagging her head to the music in the car, earrings swinging, ponytail tossing like a pompom at a pep rally. Even though Mr. Sorenson had been careful to warn them that OCD was a disorder from which few sufferers (he actually used the word "sufferers," which on top of being almost impossible to pronounce, also seemed like one of the last labels you'd want to slap on your kid) ever recover completely, Lyssa seemed more relaxed to Dev. Her face had lost some of that tightrope-walker look, and when the Sorensons dropped Dev and Aidan off in front of Aidan's house, and Lyssa leaned out the window to say, "Thanks, guys," there was something quiet and real behind her eyes, so that when she followed up with, "How 'bout if I come by tomorrow?" neither boy had the heart to say no.

But if the days were easy for Dev, one unscrutinized moment gliding into the next, the nights were hard. At night, he didn't exactly think, but it was as if all the unthought thoughts and unfelt feelings morphed into a dense, jellyfishlike creature that beached itself on his chest. On the second night at Aidan's house, in an effort to prevent the creature from smothering him, Dev propped himself up with pillows and read one of Aidan's books, a thriller about a forensic scientist, until he fell asleep.

The next morning, at what Dev could have sworn was five A.M., although it turned out to be nine, he awoke to the sound of Aidan entering the room, clearing his throat extravagantly, and remarking, "Thomas Jefferson slept sitting up."

Dev didn't open his eyes. "Good for him," he grumbled.

"I learned that during one of the Weeks family's famous edifying vacations. That's why his bed was so short."

"Fascinating."

"Most people see those old-school beds in those old-school historic homes and assume that they're short because the people were smaller back then. But at six two and a half, TJ ranks as our third-tallest president. James Madison, on the other hand, was a whole different story."

Dev raised his eyelids a couple of millimeters. "Are you right on the verge of shutting up?"

Aidan took a hit from his towering glass of orange

juice, then scratched his head in a way that meant he was about to spring something on Dev.

"Listen up. I realize that you're currently not dealing with the maternity/paternity/shocking revelation issues in your life right now."

Dev groaned. "Yeah. And?"

"Not 'and.' 'But.'"

"That's just great."

"*But* your mom just called. She's on her way over to drop off your bike and some clothes and whatever. My mom wondered if you might want to talk to her."

"No thanks. I'm still on vacation from her."

"Got it."

But the truth was that the vacation had had its legs kicked out from under it the second Aidan had mentioned Lake, and even though Dev proceeded to go casually about his normal morning business, he knew that he was moving as slowly as he could (brushing his teeth for so long that Aidan had knocked on the bathroom door with predictions about irreparable dental damage) so that he would still be upstairs when she arrived.

The harder he pretended not to wait, the harder he waited, his ears straining for the sound of the Honda pulling into the big circular driveway, and when she finally got there, no way was he setting foot downstairs, but he heard her talking. He couldn't make out any words, and didn't want to, but he recognized the pitch and frequency, the particular way her voice rearranged the air in the house, the way he would recognize his own face in a mirror, and when he heard the front door slam, he positioned himself, in spite of himself, near the upstairs hall window and watched Lake walk to the car. Her walk, her hair, her green T-shirt, the *outline* of her were so familiar to Dev, matched up so completely with the mother he had carried around in his mind, conscious and unconscious, since forever, that for a moment, pure recognition crowded out everything else, and Dev began to make a beeline for the stairs so that he could run out and catch her before she left.

He stopped himself, of course, but the sight of her had rocked everything loose inside Dev so that a few minutes later, just before Lyssa was scheduled to arrive, Dev asked Aidan if he would mind meeting her outside and bringing her up to speed before she came in.

"We could, like, maybe talk about it or something?" Dev felt his face turning red. "But giving Lyssa a play-by-play sounds like about as much fun as . . ." He was at a loss.

"Scrubbing the enamel off your teeth?" suggested Aidan. "No problem, man. Meet you out back in a few."

Dev made himself two bagel-and-peanut-butter sandwiches, took them outside, and sat down to enjoy the elaborate tapestry of blooming, buzzing, birdsong, turquoise water, and pristine grass that was the Weeks backyard. Whenever Dev sat back there, he could totally see the point of becoming a millionaire. Even the dragonflies seemed better than your typical dragonflies, stitching through the air on their miniature stained-glass-window wings. He bit into his sandwich and let himself relax into the ease and abundance around him, become part of the picture. But as soon as Dev saw Aidan and Lyssa walking toward him, the easefulness was replaced by a queasy embarrassment at the part freak show, part pity party his life had become, until Lyssa struck a melodramatic pose and intoned, "Dev

Tremain, international man of mystery," in a dopey voice that instantly made Dev feel normal.

"Hey, Lyssa."

Lyssa plopped into a chair next to Dev, lifted her black movie-star sunglasses, and surveyed her surroundings.

"This is so *InStyle* magazine it's not even funny." She dropped the glasses back onto her nose and turned her attention to Dev. "So how cool is it that your dad's not gay?"

"I'll assume that's a rhetorical question," said Dev.

"Actually, according to Aidan here, the guy's a total hetero hottie."

"Well, maybe I can fix you up with him," said Dev, then he gave Aidan a quizzical look. "You *said* that?"

"Lyssa, no offense, but do you think you might have missed the general thrust of our conversation?" Aidan rolled his eyes. "I *said* in *passing* that you even kind of look like the guy, if you, you know, subtract the extreme handsomeness."

"Thanks, Aidan," said Dev.

"So, what, you're, like, camping out in the 'Kennedy compound.'" Lyssa wobbled her head from side to side and made fluttery quotation marks in the air with her fingers. "In a state of total decision avoidance?" With one index finger, she began twisting her ponytail like a crazy person dialing a rotary phone over and over and over.

"Great," growled Dev. "Therapy speak. Just what was missing."

Lyssa smirked and twirled her hair faster. Her legs were crossed and she began to vibrate her dangling foot so fast that the table shook.

"Would you cool it with the constant motion?" said

Dev. "It's like hanging out with a flock of freaking hummingbirds."

Lyssa didn't change a thing, just said, coolly, "Inaction inertia is no way to live, my friend."

"It's temporary," said Dev. "Just until I figure out how to exist in the same house as my pathologically lying mom."

"She's still your mom," said Aidan, abruptly.

Dev shot him a look.

Aidan shifted uncomfortably in his chair. "Not that you shouldn't be mad. You should. Definitely. But until this stuff came up, your mom was cool, right? She inspired serious mom envy in, like, everyone."

"So?"

"So I'm just saying that, yeah, she messed up big-time, but that doesn't X out all the cool stuff she's done."

"Whose side are you on?" As soon as Dev asked this, he wished he hadn't.

"Yours, man. All the way."

"Yeah, I know."

Lyssa slid her glasses on top of her head and leaned toward him. "You want some words of wisdom?"

The incompatibility of wisdom and Lyssa was so complete that Dev studiously avoided Aidan's eyes so that he wouldn't burst out laughing. With his peripheral vision, Dev could see Aidan studiously avoiding Dev's eyes as well.

"Okay," said Dev, "shoot."

"We think our parents are in charge, right? Like they know what they're doing? But the truth is, they're making it up as they go along, just like we are. Just like everyone. If we judge them by their worst mistakes, they're all, like, gargantuan failures. Maybe you should try judging your mom by her intentions, by whether she, like, loves you and is doing her best."

Dev just sat there. Then he looked at Aidan, who shrugged and raised his eyebrows in a "Who knew?" expression.

"Lyssa," said Dev, "that really was pretty wise."

Lyssa shrugged, picked up Dev's bagel, and took a bite. With her mouth full, she said, "So go home already."

He wasn't sure what he had expected. That she would be brisk and sure of herself, probably. ("Have a seat, Deveroux. Time to clear the air.") Or affectionate and wry. ("This mess your old mom's gotten you into makes string theory look like a piece of cake, huh, Devvy?") Or cool and unemotional, methodically laying out her acts and motives like a defense attorney. But what he had never expected was that she would be broken. Hollow-eyed and slow-moving. Uncertain and as droopy as an unwatered plant, perpetually on the verge of tears. The opposite of herself.

Because the sight of her scared him, he decided to believe, at first, that she was faking, going for the sympathy vote, so that when she looked up from the corner of the sofa (where she sat doing what—no book, no phone, television off, not even a glass of iced tea), and asked, "What can I say to you?" in a small, small, dust-mote-sized voice, Dev dropped into a chair across the room from her and gave her an injured, sarcastic, "How am I supposed to know?"

Lake's eyes flooded with tears, but she just sat looking at Dev, not wiping her eyes or turning her face, crying without will or energy, crying as though she just leaked tears, like a broken faucet, instead of being a person who almost never cried at all.

"Do you hate me?" she asked him.

"That's not a fair question," said Dev. "It's not either/

or. If I say no, that doesn't mean everything is fine."

The tears kept slithering down her face.

Dev remembered what Lyssa had said to him about intentions, and he asked, "Why?"

"Why what?"

"Why everything. What else?" He didn't want her to cry harder but he felt impatient. Where was the quick, sharp-tongued mother when he needed her? "Why did you do what you did?"

For a long time, she didn't answer. Finally, she pulled the neck of her T-shirt up and wiped her face. Thank God, thought Dev.

"For so long, I swear I thought we were better off separate from the past. I lied to you to protect you."

"From what?"

"From people who never wanted you to be born, I guess. I hated everyone who didn't want you the way I wanted you."

"But he didn't know. Teo."

"No, I never told him. He didn't love me. I couldn't take the chance that he'd stay with us out of a sense of obligation."

This struck Dev as unjust, but he decided to let it go. Let Teo deal with that one.

"But you could have told me the truth about it all, once you decided to move out here. Did that even occur to you? You just stuck me in the car and drove me across the country, like a pet dog or something. Why didn't you tell me?"

"I had to find out what they were like. I thought I had to, anyway. I hadn't seen Teo since we were both kids. What if I told you and you got excited to meet him and he turned out to be no good?"

"Then I would have been disappointed. So what? A lot of people are disappointed by their parents."

Lake flinched at this, and Dev held his breath, but she didn't start crying again.

"What if he was dangerous?" she asked.

"I thought about that. But at some point you must have decided that he wasn't because you sent me over there, right? By myself? That's the worst part."

"What? You think I put you in danger? Dev, I really believed—"

"No. You let me get to know them, you let me *like* them, under false pretenses. I hate that. It's like you made liars out of all of us."

"You're right." Lake said, nodding. "That was a bad decision. Once I had checked them out, I should have told you who they were. I guess I wanted to see how you reacted to him, both of them, before you knew about—the connection. And I wanted them to see how great you were—how great you are—before I told them who you were."

Anger surged in Dev's chest, but he was still freaked out by her lost, dilated eyes, so he kept his voice low. "You treated us like a science experiment, or like, like puppets. You wanted to manipulate everything. Don't you know that you can't do that to people, Mom?"

To Dev's horror, Lake cupped her hand over her mouth and began to sob.

"I'm sorry," said Dev, drawing back, "but I need to tell you what I think."

Lake shook her head and worked to catch her breath. At last, she said in a ramshackle voice, "It's just that you called me 'Mom.'"

"Oh," said Dev, but this was more than he could stand.

He jumped to his feet, needing to get away from this defeated woman who was nothing like his mother, and mumbling something about his room, he walked out.

He lay down on his bed and pulled his pillow up around his ears, but he could hear Lake crying again, hard, and the sound made him feel doomed, like the sound of her crying was the sound of the end of the world, so he got up to find her.

She sat at the kitchen table, her head on her crossed arms, her shoulders heaving, and Dev felt a flare of anger at her for turning things around so that he was comforting her, but more than he was angry, more than anything else, he wanted her to stop crying and feel better. He pulled out the chair next to hers and sat down.

"Please stop, Mom."

Her face was still buried in her arms when she said, "I have lost all of you. Cornelia. Rafferty. You, most of all."

"Rafferty?"

Lake raised her head. "He couldn't stomach the lies, and why should he? His ex-wife lied to him and now I have. He says he needs time apart, to think, but I don't believe he'll be back."

Dev looked at his mother, at her trembling jaw and her train-wreck eyes. He breathed in and tried to clear his head of anger, annoyance, fear, everything that might stop him from saying what he needed to say. He searched inside himself for kindness and found it, right where it always was.

"You haven't lost me. I'm here, right?"

Lake's face went perfectly still. "Can you forgive me?"

"Mom, this isn't a one-conversation deal. It'll take a while to fix, don't you think?"

"Yes, I know it will. But I just wonder if you think a time will come when you can forgive me."

"I don't know." Dev shrugged. "Probably. Knowing me."

His mother's smile seemed to sweep through the room like the beam from a lighthouse.

"But I have to say this, okay?"

Lake nodded.

"I don't know if I can ever trust you. Forgiving is different from trusting."

"I will never lie to you again, Dev, not even to protect you. I swear to God."

Dev didn't nod. He couldn't say okay because really, everything wasn't okay, and if he didn't trust her—and he didn't—then how could he believe what she had just said?

But he could say this: "What happened, it doesn't erase everything else."

"What do you mean?"

"You've been—" He stopped. "As my mom, you've done a lot of right things, more than I can count. The bad stuff is there and it isn't going away, but it just sort of sits alongside the rest. It doesn't cancel the rest out."

The gratitude on her face was too much. He knew she wanted to touch him or wanted him to touch her, would settle for any kind of touch, no matter how slight, but her desperation just made him feel worse, especially because he couldn't do what she wanted.

"I'm pretty tired," he said.

Lake sat up straighter and gave him an only partway brokenhearted smile. "All right. You go to bed, then, Devvy."

At nine o'clock, Dev sat down at his desk to find an instant message from Clare. Staring at the words across the glow of his computer screen, Dev believed he knew how Galileo must have felt discovering the moons of Jupiter.

"I am so sorry for all the terrible things I said to you, Dev. Most people would not want to hear from me and wouldn't even read this, and I'm afraid that you might feel that way, but I also know that you aren't like most people. So I have to think there's a chance that you will want to and a chance that you would read this, and even if you don't, I just need to write it because it would be very, very wrong having those terrible, mean things be the last words I say to you. I was scared and jealous, and I felt like you were stealing something from me, even though I know that you would never, ever do that. I'm sorry. I see now that what you did was so brave. That's what I want to say most of all. You are brave and good. I feel like I've known you all my life. Longer than that. I hope one of these days I get to do more than just miss you, Dev. (It makes me feel better just to write your name.) Love, Clare."

Love, thought Dev. Love. He rested two fingers against the word on the screen.

"I'm here, Clare," began Dev, "and it makes me feel better to write your name, too."

Later, as Dev lay in bed thinking about nothing but Clare, he heard his mother talking and walked out into the hallway to listen. She wasn't crying, but her voice was tremulous, rippled over with unhappiness. Shit, what now? thought Dev, leaning his back against the wall. He closed his eyes, listening, concentrating, trying to fill in the silences that were the other side of the conversation.

"Of course he likes them, Mom. They're good people."

["Why do you say that like it's a bad thing? Don't you want him to like them?"]

"Of course I want him to like them. I want whatever makes him happy. But that doesn't mean it isn't hard. It's been just the two of us all these years. How can I share him now?"

["I thought you said you would do whatever Dev wants. Don't you think he deserves to have a relationship with his father?"]

"Yeah, Mom, I think he and Teo deserve to know each other, and I'm not saying I won't let that happen. I'm only saying it'll hurt. A lot." Lake's voice became almost savage with unhappiness. "What if he wants to live with them?"

["You don't really think he would want that, do you?"]

"I don't know. He might. He doesn't trust me anymore." Lake began crying again, quietly this time. "You know what I wish for? Some distance. Physical distance. Not that much, a few hours maybe? I want to be the full-time parent, and I know that's selfish, but it kills me to think of losing him. I mean it. It would kill me."

As Dev and Clare stood on the front steps of Cornelia and Teo's house, just before Clare put her hand on the knob and pushed the door open, Dev almost refused to go through with it. His heart was thudding, nervousness was twisting itself into Gordian knots inside his stomach, and he strongly considered grabbing Clare's hand and taking off for whatever place there was in the world (and Dev had little faith, at this point, that such a place existed) where his life wouldn't feel like one momentous moment after the next. A place where crossing the threshold of a house was an ordinary, undramatic act, symbolic of nothing. Dev looked down at his sneakers. He wanted to be a kid in sneakers, period. Was that so much to ask?

But when they did cross over and were standing inside the front hallway of the house, the foyer or vestibule or whatever the heck it was called (and Dev busied himself for a few seconds, searching for the proper word), it seemed briefly (for maybe twenty heartbeats) that the moment might be unmomentous after all. Teo and Cornelia weren't standing just inside the door, serious faced and poised in attitudes of anticipation like characters in a movie. Instead, they were clattering around in other parts of the house, and just as Clare reached for Dev's hand and squeezed it, Cornelia called out from the kitchen, "Guys, is that you?" (because their coming there was not a surprise, no more surprises), and she appeared with a dish towel in her hand, just before Teo kind of trotted down the stairs in a way that was normal and fast and unceremonious.

Okay, thought Dev, maybe it'll be fine, maybe it'll be normal. But when they were all four standing in the front hall together, Dev felt their connections web-spinning through the air between them, drawing them together with sticky threads: you're my father, you're my father's wife, my stepmother (*stepmother?*), pregnant with my half brother or half sister (although weirdly, this was the least complicated part and gave Dev a pure jolt of joy every time he thought about it: my brother, my sister), and you're the girl I love (it's true) who is like a daughter to my father and my father's wife, which makes you kind of a sister although no way are you my sister, are you kidding?

Dev was out of breath and couldn't think of what to say beyond "Get me out of here," which would have been entirely inappropriate, obviously, and maybe no one else could either because for a long time, lifetimes, eons, at least ten seconds, no one spoke a word.

Then a grin cut across Teo's face, and he said, "So, Dev, how's your summer so far?"

Dev could have flopped backward onto the ground, the way he did after an especially long bike ride, he was that relieved, that exhausted, but he just grinned back, shrugged, and said, "Pretty uneventful."

Then he looked at Cornelia, who was folding the dish towel into a tiny square, and asked, "How's Penny?"

"Huge," said Cornelia, "and preparing for arrival, which really can't come soon enough, in my opinion." Her tone was chipper and joking, but there was so much gentleness in her eyes when she looked at Dev that he felt his own eyes start to sting in a dangerous way. He swallowed and looked at the floor, and suddenly, Cornelia was there, her hand on his arm, smiling up at him.

"We all got thrown for a loop, didn't we?" she said, softly.

All Dev could do was nod.

"You most of all," she finished, and this was so surprising, was such a nice thing to say, especially to a guy who had shown up in her life like a spy or a grenade that, even though she was an adult and Dev wasn't particularly a kisser, Dev leaned down (she was so small) and kissed her cheek.

"Now, why don't you come in?" she said. "Let me feed you something."

Dev said, "Uh, I don't think I'll stay. I mean, not this time."

After a beat, Teo said, "Then, next time."

"Yeah," said Dev, and he glanced at Clare. "And there will definitely be a next time. If that's all right, I mean."

Teo smiled. "A next time sounds great."

"But I wanted to say something."

He looked at Clare again, and saw that her eyes were filling up with tears, but she smiled encouragingly.

"Go ahead, Dev," she said.

"Well, I know you guys must be really mad at my mom. I would be if I were you. I'm pretty mad myself, actually. But she's, like, my mom, you know?"

Teo nodded.

"Of course she is," said Cornelia.

"And she's a mess, right now. She feels bad about what she did, I promise she does."

"She told us," said Teo.

"The thing is, she's scared of losing me, and I can't really stand for her to be scared of that. She deserves a lot of things, but not that." He paused. "So I've been thinking—and I haven't even told her this—but I've been thinking that maybe we should live somewhere . . . else."

Dev saw Teo's face tense.

Cornelia said, "Oh, Dev."

Then Teo took a few steps toward Dev, stopped, and put his hands in his pockets as though he didn't know what else to do with them. Dev saw that Teo was choked up, his jaw clenching and unclenching, and for the first time, it occurred to Dev that maybe, for Teo, Dev wasn't just an intrusion or even a situation to accept and handle with grace. Maybe Teo *wanted* to be his father. With wonder, Dev felt the sere, brown, vacant-lot piece of himself that had been waiting for his father to want him mist over with green, like a yard in springtime.

Clare made a hurt sound, ran over to Teo, and put her arms around him. "Not that far away. And not forever," she said. "He doesn't mean he'll never come here."

"Yeah?" said Teo, looking over Clare's head at Dev. His eyes were green.

My father, thought Dev.

"Maybe I'll come a lot, if that's okay," he said.

"We won't," Teo said slowly, "try to talk you out of leaving."

Cornelia said, "But—" and Teo said, "Cornelia," as though he were reminding her of something.

Teo went on, "But we want you here. Whenever you want to be here. Even when you don't. Always. Okay?"

"Okay." Dev smiled at Teo, then at Cornelia. "Thanks. I should go now, I guess."

Dev turned around. Then he turned back and told Teo, "I used to look for you."

"You did?"

Dev nodded. "I'm glad it's you." He couldn't say "father," yet. "Out of all those people who were the right age or in the right place or whatever, I'm glad he turned out to be you."

Teo's gaze moved over Dev's face, from his forehead to his eyes to his chin, not as though he were searching for resemblances, but more like he was learning Dev's face, part by part. His eyes ended up looking squarely into Dev's eyes and he smiled.

"So am I."

TWENTY-ONE

Cornelia

$\mathcal{C}$hildbirth is old hat, the oldest around, a story told over and over, so I will try not to give you a blow-by-blow (or breath-snatching-squeeze-by-breath-snatching-squeeze) account of my personal childbirth experience from the moment my water broke and gushed straight through the seat of my cane chair in the Thai restaurant Teo and I had gone to with Piper and Tom (although the look on Piper's face would make a pretty great story all by itself) to the second my baby broke like a seal, almond eyed and slick, from the anonymous ocean my body had become.

But I wanted to say something about pain. Because even though I had absolutely no use for it at the time, and, in fact, would have traded minor body parts to be rid of it (an offer I made to every medical type who entered my line of sight during labor; no takers), pain turned out to be instructive later in a way that would change the lives of everyone. Not everyone-everyone, of course, but my everyone, the people I've been given (and God knows it hasn't always been my choice), the ones who are mine to love.

"In labor," they say. *In.* As though pain were a room or water or fog. In deep, I named it "a wilderness of pain," and you don't have to tell me that, in the wide universe of metaphors, "a wilderness of pain" shines dimly if it shines at all. Still, it was a metaphor created by me, Cornelia Brown, a metaphor maker from way back (I can't help it; my brain just *will* yank dissimilar items up by their roots and knot them together, no matter how much they or anyone else protests), so, while in labor, I said it over and over, sometimes aloud, mostly not, to remind myself of myself. Lost in pain, in hopes of locating the Cornelia I knew, I shot my little piece of figurative language up like a flare.

What I should confess right now is that I didn't plan on pain. Are you kidding? I planned on spending the easy, breezy, early hours of labor in the comfort of my own home, with a sweetly nervous, watch-checking Teo by my side, and with *Holiday* (followed by *The Awful Truth,* followed by *My Favorite Wife* because if you have to endure escalating uterine contractions, why not endure them with Cary Grant?) in the DVD player, and then, once things began to get dicey, taking a leisurely drive to the hospital and putting in my demand for an epidural immediately, long before I really needed it (per Piper's instructions), and spending the rest of labor happily pain free, only to push heroically, albeit briefly, when the time for pushing arrived.

What I got was: small, internal unsnapping; whoosh of amniotic fluid; a plate of gai pad prik resting untouched, but for one heavenly bite, on the table in front of me. Which would have been fine, *was* fine, really, and which, in addition to allowing Piper the opportunity to make a hilariously horrified face, also allowed her, once she had sufficiently recovered, to note with intense satisfaction her now-seemingly-proven theory (which my doctor husband had, with an annoying air of authority, dismissed as pure mythology) that there was nothing like spicy food to jump-start labor.

But when we got to the hospital, when the hitherto-unknown-to-me doctor who examined me cheerily informed us that Piper was wrong, not even Teo had the heart to gloat. My body had thrown us a curveball (apparently under the outrageous misapprehension that when it came to curveballs, Teo and I were overdue) because while my membranes had certainly ruptured, my cervix was closed as tight as the proverbial drum. He suggested that we try to move things in an un-drumlike direction by jogging around the corridors of the hospital.

As soon as he'd left the room, a nurse who looked so much like Angela Lansbury in *Gaslight* it was plain creepy but who was really quite nice, told us how the last couple she'd seen in our situation had eschewed jogging in favor of the nipple-stimulation route ("It took two hours, and her husband's fingers would probably have fallen right off if he hadn't been so distracted by game three of the NBA championships, but if you're not the jogging type . . ."), a suggestion that caused Teo to begin exercising his fingers in the manner of a maestro preparing to play Rachmaninoff's Piano Concerto no. 2.

We jogged. Nothing.

We took a breather, then jogged some more. Nothing.

We jogged endlessly. I eked out a decent handful of jumping jacks and made one wildly unfruitful attempt at a squat thrust.

Just as Teo was recommencing his finger warm-ups,

Dr. Mary Follows, on whom I had actually set eyes before (my beloved Dr. Oliver had the nerve to be at another hospital, delivering someone else's baby, but had promised to be with us soon), arrived on the scene, recommending that we chemically induce labor now.

"Once your membranes are ruptured, there's a chance of infection, so we could wait maybe a little longer, but not much."

Teo's fingers played an imaginary scale.

I told Dr. Follows, "Now is fine."

She told us that when I got to five centimeters and we were sure labor was in full swing, the epidural was mine all mine.

"You'll go at about a centimeter an hour. We don't want to check you much more than we already have because of the risk of infection, so I'll be back in a few hours. Buzz if you need anything!"

Shortly thereafter, I entered the aforementioned wilderness. I won't describe it in detail, mainly because I can't. For much of it, I was pretty out to lunch (a very bad lunch served by small red imps in hell). Teo talked to me until I ordered him to stop. He held my hand and ran his fingers up and down my forearm until I ordered him to cease all touching (he maintains that I emphasized this request by biting him on the thumb). He watched television with me until I told him that if he didn't switch the damn thing off, I would rise up and shove it down his throat.

The important part, the part that would matter afterward, was how small I became at the end, pain paring off parts of me until I was all but gone, a tiny black comma on an immense white page. Fear went, then intelligence, worry, courage, and charm (as Teo can attest). Complex emotions evaporated. Humor van-

ished as though it had never been. My every neuro-
sis went up in smoke, along with most of the English
language, leaving me with nothing but a sound loop
of *baby, Teo, baby, Teo, baby, baby, baby* playing in
my head.

Yes, pain is abominable, a nightmare, but pain re-
veals, when we've had to throw all else overboard,
what is left in our personal sinking boat.

"I love our baby," I told Teo, eyes closed, teeth set,
"I love you."

Teo jumped out of his seat. "That's it. I'm getting the
doctor."

As it turned out, in the space of time it should have
taken my chemically enhanced cervix to dilate from
zero centimeters to three, I'd gone the whole nine yards,
zero to ten. Later, Toby would theorize that this might
have had something to do with my having "the metabolism of a pygmy shrew," and even though Teo would
muddy this theory's waters with scientific talk about
the variable number and sensitivity of receptors in the
uterus and so forth, my usually science-minded sister
turned a deaf ear to Teo and snatched Toby's theory up
with glee: my unfair allotment of metabolism coming
back, at long last, to bite me on the ass.

"You poor girl," said Dr. Oliver, who was there at
last, "you skipped the easy part and went straight for
transition labor."

"Time for the epidural," I said, between contractions.
When neither Dr. Oliver nor Teo met my eyes, I said it
loudly, "Time for the epidural."

"Ten centimeters, sweet girl," said Teo, apologetically.

"Epidural," I shouted.

"But, Cornelia, here's the good news," said Dr.
Oliver, brightly. "It's time to push."

* * *

What struck me about the rest of it was how little I mattered. A vehicle, a means, someone else's act of becoming. If that sounds like a complaint, it isn't one. All I'm saying is that, from the very first push, I saw to what end I labored, not delivery, depositing a gift to me and Teo on the doorstep of our lives, but *deliverance,* the baby freed, pushed loose and streaming, like God, into the world.

The first time I looked at the face of my child, I didn't think "my child." I made no claims. Transported by awe to someplace way past tenderness, I was courteous and grave, one fierce creature greeting another, newly arrived. Then Teo said, "Our daughter, Cor, our little girl," and—wham—I bought the complete package: tenderness, yes; devotion and longing, euphoria and despair; ache and work and rage and boundless gratitude. My girl and I got it backward, backward and right. She did the claiming. I was delivered, unto her. "You are mine," she cried, her hands reaching for my face, and nothing was ever more true.

Too soon, they took her.

"She's beautiful," I told them, "she's perfect."

"She is," agreed Dr. Oliver, "but I'm not crazy about her breathing. Or her color."

"You think it's the blood?" asked Teo.

"What blood?" I said.

"Your blood," said Dr. Oliver, nodding. "Fibroids are very vascular. We'll suction her out, clean her up, and bring her back as soon as we can. And we'll get you into a real room where you can get some rest, Cornelia. You deserve it."

When they took her, my arms and hands felt empty in an entirely new way.

Teo kissed me and told me that I was a star, an angel, the love of his life.

"Cornelia and Teo," I said to him, "with a *baby*."

He smiled. "Who would ever have thought."

"I miss her."

"She'll be back." Teo's eyes got cloudy and he rested his forehead against my shoulder. "It was hard to see you hurt like that."

"I know it was."

"You were so quiet."

"I promise to scream next time."

We sat that way until a nurse came with a wheelchair to take me to my room. When we got there, we called Toby and Clare. We called my parents and Teo's parents and Linny. The joy we generated was intoxicating.

"She should be here," I said to Teo.

"I'll go find her."

"Good."

"You'll be all right by yourself?"

"I'm fine."

"I love you. You sure?"

"I love you. Go."

Five minutes after he walked out, the pain came back.

Hemorrhage. Even the word is ugly, thick, messy with its silent second *h,* containing rage.

I don't remember much. Contractions and contractions and contractions, time expanding each time I contracted to a hot, red point. Teo back and saying, viciously, "If she says it's not just cramping, it's not just cramping!" Talk of an ultrasound. A wheelchair, an attempt to stand, a warm, wet rush, the bottom dropping out of everything. Then, nothing.

A brief coming to, someone asking me to say my name.

"Am I dying?" I asked.

"Absolutely not," scoffed a nurse whom I would cherish for all of my days.

A shift from stretcher to table.

Round lights burned like moons and then went out.

I saw them before they saw me: Teo in a chair beside my bed, feeding our daughter with a dropper.

I made an infinitesimal move to lift my head, but was stopped by a wedge of ax-blow headache. I waited for the static to clear, then looked again. Teo, his long fingers around the dropper, our pink-faced girl, as singular as a snowflake but durable, Rose Brown Sandoval, eating to beat the band. And then, just like that, I was there and not there, transported hours backward into the worst part of the wilderness, but floating above it, seeing myself reduced to my least common denominator, everything ripped away but my last, best thing, my connection to the people who belong to me, of whom Teo and Rose are just the beginning or the middle (it's hard to tell, connections radiating in every direction like beams of light), but never the end.

Out-of-body experiences, even partial ones composed mostly of memory, don't happen every day. Mine was enough to transmute doubt into certainty, hesitation into urgency, a burden into a blessing.

Teo glanced up and saw me, a galaxy in his eyes, a universe.

"Cor."

"Teo, call him." When you have a revelation, there isn't a moment to lose.

"Who?"

"Dev. Tell him to come and meet his sister."

Teo's eyes misted over, and to hide it, he bent down and kissed Rose's round and glorious head. He stood up and placed her in her transparent bassinet, then took out his cell phone.

"And, Teo, when they get here, say it."

"What should I say?"

"Whatever it takes. Anything. Promise anything. I will, too. Anything it takes to make them change their minds. Whatever it takes to make them stay."

EPILOGUE

TEN MONTHS LATER

Cornelia

*W*e are all here, in our backyard, noisy under the tulip tree and the wash of blue sky and the white party tent we rented for the day of our baby's christening. I say "our baby," mine and Teo's, but really Rose is everybody's baby. She walks through the party the way she walks through the world, making her headlong, wobbling way, not brushing a pants leg or grabbing a skirt for balance without a palm resting on her warm head or someone kneeling to greet her, eye to eye. Now that she's mobile, if she's held, she won't stay for long, except with Toby, who lifts her only to toss her—flying child against the bright sky—or tickle her or turn her upside down, her pink skirt flopping to bell around her head, like the belled blossoms of the tulip tree, as though she is just another living bloom in springtime, which of course she is. Lucky baby.

We are all lucky today. It is one of the days when we

make it look easy, and trust me when I tell you that we have our hard days, too. Hard weeks. But I've found that if you insist on goodwill, if everyone insists on it together, goodwill comes. I've found that love can be a decision. Forgiveness, too.

Clare and Dev are radiant against the white backs of the Adirondack chairs. Dev is stretching out his long legs so that Rose can climb them, scramble up them like a squirrel, and all the children are like squirrels, scurrying past, crisscrossing through the forest of adults. Jasper on all fours, Emma, Peter, Carter, Meredith with her hands full of cookies, Rafferty's daughter, Molly (newly back in Lake's life, Rafferty keeps to the edge of the crowd, uncertain if he's there to stay). The children are loud: piping, screeching, chattering like jays. Ollie's baby is due next month; he will add his voice to the rest. She sits under the white tent, feigning grumpiness the way she always does when she's happy, a demeanor she'll drop once she and Dev get started talking science, unraveling the sticky mysteries of genes.

Now Rose zigzags toward me, throws her pretty arms around my leg, and allows me to lift her. With the weight of her against my hip, with her face near mine, I am perfectly balanced, as firmly planted on the earth as I had ever hoped to be. My baby has my nose and chin, but the rest of her face is Teo's, his eyes, his forehead, his smile, which are also Dev's eyes, forehead, and smile. The resemblances don't stop there. She has Toby's daring and Piper's imperiousness, Clare's sweetness and my father's laugh, Ingrid Sandoval's glamour and my mother's straight back, my temper and Lake's stubbornness. She spots something else she wants and begins to wriggle in my arms. I put her down and she is off.

Piper unlinks her arm from Tom's (she's told me how she cannot stop touching him, her hand on his forearm, his shirt collar, a finger hooked around a belt loop; "It's ridiculous. It'll drive the poor man crazy," she said, not believing it for a second) and walks toward me across the yard, her Delft blue eyes matching the scarf around her neck, not a wrinkle in her linen dress. Last week, she and Tom put both their houses on the market, and put a bid on another one in our neighborhood.

"Were you tempted to leave town?" I'd asked her. "Start fresh someplace else?"

"Hell, no," she'd scoffed.

Now she says, "I think we know the real reason Lake decided not to move." Her tone is pure Piper, approving and disapproving at the same time. "That woman is head over heels for your little girl."

It's true. Love can be a decision, but Lake did not decide to fall in love with Rose. She was ambushed, swamped. I saw it on her face in the hospital. "A total body slam," as my poetic brother would say. I will never forget that morning: Dev holding his sister, time standing still. None of us was going anywhere.

Lake is winding one of Rose's silvery curls around her finger (the blondness, the curls, are a genetic improbability, Ollie tells me, and likely won't be around for long, temporary gifts, babyhood's sleights of hand). It's a thing that Lake has given me and I have given her: permission to love each other's children, a free pass. She reserves her territoriality, her assertions of parental primacy, for Teo, who for all his quietude and kindness, can be as fierce as anyone. What saves them every time, what drives them into truces, compromises, and listening, is Dev, tall, brave boy, who wants them both, wants them with his father's generosity and his mother's grit, and a deep, smart, sweet-souled decency that is uniquely his.

Teo presses his lips to the back of my neck, then whispers, "Isn't she beautiful?" and I know the "she" he means. For my husband, there is one she. One he, too. This morning, under the dim, soaring ceiling of the church, I heard Dev tell Rose, "Let's find Dad." He caught my eye after he said it, and his shy smile lit the room. "I call him that all the time in my head now," he told me. I will tell this to Teo tonight, in bed, where we'll be alone but for our houseful of people, people in every room: Clare, Viviana, Clare's new father Gordon, Teo's parents, my parents, Rose sleeping her fragrant sleep a few feet away. "We'll get hotel rooms," everyone had offered, but we told them all, "No. Stay."

Sometimes, I think I would like to have us under one roof, all of us, everybody here, which makes no sense, of course. No house is big enough to hold us, with all of our tensions, all our wariness and histories. But imagine the nights, those separate breathings, everyone within my reach and safe, everyone together.

I stand here on this spring day in the center of my life. Chaos, din, and beauty. For a moment, I am still. Then "Cornelia," cuts across the noise, and because one of them is calling me, I go.

ACKNOWLEDGMENTS

I am so grateful to the following people:

Brilliant agent and true friend Jennifer Carlson, whose instincts, heart, and good sense never stop amazing me;

My editor, Laurie Chittenden, kind, tenacious, and wise, for making me feel that my books and I were born under a lucky star;

Everyone at Morrow, especially Lisa Gallagher, Lynn Grady, Will Hinton, Tavia Kowalchuck, Debbie Stier, Sharyn Rosenblum, Dee Dee DeBartlo, Emily Fink, and Mike Brennan;

Susan Davis, Dan Fertel, Annie Pilson (seeker of blooming hydrangeas, mellow light, and the perfect shot), and my sister Kristina de los Santos, the sharp and generous early readers without whom I could not do, with additional thanks to Michael Pilson, Rebecca Schamess, and Molly Spruance;

Phineas Pilson, who now talks a blue streak but who inspired the toddler version of Toby Brown;

Andrea Nakayama and Sara Clay Goodman, who so generously corresponded with me regarding illness and hospice care; Drs. Dan Fertel and Arturo de los Santos, for help with all things medical; and Rebecca Kraus, for the aspirin bottle story;

My parents, Arturo and Mary de los Santos, whose love and support mean everything to me;

And those to whom it is my shining luck to belong: my children Charles and Annabel Teague, fierce, funny, and smart, and my husband, David Teague, whose many gifts include changing the way time moves.

**Read on for an excerpt
from Marisa de los Santos' next novel,**

Falling Together

A new novel from the
New York Times *bestselling author of*
Love Walked In *and* **Belong To Me**

What pulled three dear friends apart is
the very thing that brings them together
years later.

It has been years since Pen, Cat, and Will
have seen one another. Much has changed
in each of their lives, but on the eve of a
reunion Pen and Will receive a mysterious
email from Cat asking for their help.

An emotionally precise novel about
friendship, family, and love that will pull
you through a maze of questions to a surprising and deeply fulfilling conclusion.

What would you do if an old friend
needed you, but it meant turning your new
life upside down?

$\mathcal{P}$en would not use the word "summoned" when she told Jamie about the email later that night. Additionally, she would not say that the email dropped like a bowling ball into the pit of her stomach, and at the same time fell over her like a shining wave, sending arcs of sea spray up to flash in the sun, even though that is precisely how it felt.

Across from Jamie at dinner, forkful of rabbit halfway to her mouth, Pen would cock an eyebrow, cop a dry tone, and say, "Leave it to me to get the email of my life while wedged between Self-Help and True Crime, listening to Eleanor Rex, M.D., recount her career as a paid dominatrix."

The truth is that Pen was not giving Dr. Rex her full attention, even though she should have been. She liked Eleanor. She liked her Louise Brooks bob, her large, smoky laugh, and her impeccable manners. In the nine hours she had spent driving Eleanor around to radio interviews, stock signings, and an appearance at an upscale but vampire-den-looking private club called Marquis, Pen had come to view the dominatrix gig—no sex but a lot of mean talk and costumes—as an utterly valid and even sort of nifty way to put oneself through medical school. Even if she hadn't, she should have been listening. As a general rule, she listened to all of her authors. It was part of the job.

But this evening, Pen was unusually tired. She stood with her head tilted back against the bookstore wall, her ears only half hearing a description of how to single-handedly lace oneself into a leather corset ("There's an implement involved," she told Jamie later. "There always is," he said.), her eyes only half seeing the otherwise lovely store's horrible ceiling, paste-gray and pocked as the moon, while the weary rest of her began to fold itself up and give into its own weight like a bat at dawn.

Yesterday, Pen's daughter Augusta had come home from school with a late spring cold, and Pen had recognized, her heart sinking, that they were in for a rocky ride. Augusta's sleep, disordered in the best of circumstances, could be tipped over the edge and into chaos by any little thing. To make matters worse, it was her first illness since Pen had purged their apartment of children's cold medicine following newly issued, scarily worded warnings that it might be harmful to kids under the age of six. When Jamie got home at 2:00 AM, he had found Augusta cocooned in a quilt on the sofa, wide awake, coughing noisily but decorously into the crook of her arm the way she had been taught to do in school, and a pale, wild-haired Pen staring into the medicine cabinet like a woman staring into the abyss.

"I hate the FDA," Pen had spat, viciously. "And don't tell me I don't."

"I would never tell you that," said Jamie, backing up, "Noooo way."

In the bookstore, Eleanor's voice grew fainter and fainter, and Pen was so completely on the verge of sliding down the wall and curling up on the hardwood floor that she was planning it—how she would tuck her knees under her skirt, rest her head on a very large paperback book, possibly some sort of manual—when she felt her phone vibrate against her ribcage. Jamie, a sucker for gadgets, had given her the phone just a few days earlier, a "smartphone" he'd called it, and he had since realized what Pen had known the second he'd handed it to her, that it was far, far smarter than she required or deserved.

A hummingbird, Pen marveled through her sleep fog, *in my purse.*

A second later, she thought, *Augusta,* and then, *Oh no*, and her heart began to do a hummingbird thrum of its own. Generally, Pen's girl was as healthy as a horse, and her cold had been of the messy but aimless variety. But anything could happen. A couple of months ago, Pen had sent Augusta to her father's house for the weekend and, apparently seconds after Augusta had stepped over his threshold, her flimsy sore throat had flared like a brush fire into a serious case of strep.

"Pustules all over her tonsils," his wife Tanya had hissed, *"Pustules. Everywhere!* And you never *noticed*? I've got news for you, lady: strep can turn into rheumatic fever. Just. Like. That."

Anything could happen with children. No one had to tell Pen this. Anything could happen with anything. Pen didn't even bother to check the message before she was punching in her home phone number and snaking her way through the small crowd of people who had gathered at the back of the store to hear Eleanor. In every bookstore audience, there were those who stood on the fringes instead of taking a seat, even when seats were plentiful, folks Pen called "lurkers." Usually, this label was both unkind and unjust, simple snideness on her part, but in the case of Eleanor's lurkers, perhaps not so much.

One ring and Jamie picked up.

"Jamie," Pen whispered frantically into the phone, "What? Fever? Pustules? What? Just tell me."

"You," Jamie told her calmly, "are insane."

Pen breathed, and her eyes filled with tears of relief. She swiped at them with her finger.

"Well, you *called*," she said, clearing her throat, "Naturally, I was worried."

"I called?" There was a brief pause and then Jamie said, "You didn't check the voicemail, did you? You didn't even check the *number* of the person calling, even though it was right there on the screen. Just hauled off and called me in a panic like a crazy person."

All true, but Pen was not going to say that to Jamie, so instead she said, "Not that many people have this number, Jamie. It's new, remember? You and Amelie and Patrick and Mom and Augusta's school. The school is closed; Mom's in Tibet or wherever the hell; Patrick never calls in the evenings; and I just talked to Amelie twenty minutes ago. That leaves you."

There was a small silence as Jamie considered this, then he said, a sly note sliding into his voice, "Let me ask you this."

"No," Pen said, "Whatever it is, no."

"Did your phone even ring?"

"It didn't ring," Pen corrected, "I'm in a bookstore. It whirred."

"Repeatedly? Or once? One long whir?"

"Who knows? Could've been one whir. Maybe. So *what*?" She gave her phone an accusatory look.

Jamie groaned. "Email." He enunciated the word as though it were composed of three distinct syllables. "Didn't we go over this? Check your email, Penelope. We're fine. Augusta's fine. No fever and she ate like a champ. We had a long, and I'm talking about crazy-long, dance contest, and then she conked."

Pen swiped at her eyes again. "Oh. Well, thanks. Sorry."

Quietly, Jamie said, "The world doesn't spin out of control the second you turn your back, Pen."

Oh yes it does. That's exactly what it does. You know that as well as I do. Pen thought this, but she didn't say it.

Jamie sighed. "Listen, if she busts out in pustules, I promise you'll be the first to know."

After she hung up, Pen almost didn't check her email. She glared at her phone and stuffed it into her handbag. Contrary to what Jamie probably thought, she knew how to check it, but anyone who needed urgently to reach her would call, and the mere thought of pecking out an answer on the phone's microscopic keyboard made her fingers inflate to the size of baseball bats. Besides, she needed to get back to Eleanor.

Pen was walking toward the rows of chairs, when she heard someone ask, "So I know you're, like, retired? But do you ever, you know, make an exception if the guy's, like, really special? Like really cool or whatever?" The person's voice had an unfinished, squawking quality: a boy, about twelve-years old, thirteen at the outside. He was talking to Eleanor. Pen winced, stopped in her tracks, and there, in the heart of the Animals and Pet

Care section, she checked her email. The new one was
from Glad2behere, an unfamiliar moniker but one that
struck Pen as cheerful. *Good for you*, she thought.

> Dear Pen,
>   *I know it's been forever, but I need you. Please
> come to the reunion. I'll find you there. I'm sorry
> for everything.*
>
> > > Love,
> > > Cat

Pen did not draw a blank or have a moment of confusion or have to read the message twice. She didn't
think, *Cat who?* There was only one Cat. What she
did was sit down on the floor between the shelves of
books, shut her eyes, and press the cell phone to her
sternum, against her galloping heart. Out of the blue
sky and after more than six years of waiting—because
no matter how hard she had tried not to wait, that is
exactly what she'd been doing—Pen had been summoned. As soon as the merry-go-round inside her head
slowed its whirling and jangling enough for her to think
anything, she thought, *Oh, Cat*, followed by, *Finally*.

Cat would begin it: "We met cute."

"No," Pen would correct. "We met terrifying."

"And hostile," Will would add.

"I wouldn't say 'hostile,'" Pen would say.

"You were yelling," Will would remind her. "And
swearing."

"And pushing," Cat would add. "Although not that
hard."

"How would you know?" Pen would demand. "And I
wasn't the only one swearing."

"I *know*," Cat would insist. "You were hostile. *I* was cute."

"You were terrifying," Will would correct.

"Through no fault of your own," Pen would concede.

"But cute," Cat would assert. "Nevertheless."

And no one would disagree.

This was the way they told their story.

It was the fourth day of the first week of their first year of college, immediately following a lecture on *Beowulf*.

Weeks afterward, when their friendship had become an ageless and immovable fact, Will would remark that he had noticed Pen during the lecture, specifically the way her hair had looked all of a piece, a glossy brown object hanging next to her face as she tilted her head to write.

"God," Cat would say, grimacing. "Don't tell me you were checking her out. Don't tell me that Pen piqued your sexual interest. Because the thought of that is just nauseating."

"Thank you," Pen would say.

"Nope," Will would assure them. "It was just that hair. It was so brushed that it didn't even look like hair. Who has hair that brushed?"

"No one," Cat would reply. "No one has hair that brushed. And no one cries over *Beowulf*. No one but Pen."

Pen had not cried exactly, not out-and-out cried, not during the lecture anyway. She had cried the night before when she had gotten to the part about Beowulf's death. It wasn't so much the death itself, since Beowulf had never, during the hours she'd spent reading the poem, felt particularly real to her. Instead, it was the moment immediately following his death, a still and private moment near the end of an epic's worth of action and fighting, appearing suddenly and taking Pen off guard. The smoke cleared, and there was Wiglaf, the youngest of Beowulf's warriors, exhausted and blood-spattered and out of options, sprinkling water on the face of his dead king to wake him up.

During the lecture, Pen had waited for the professor to cover this moment, its bottomless sadness, but he had not even mentioned it. Still, while he spoke in cool tones about Beowulf's death marking the beginning of the end of an entire civilization, Pen had envisioned the boy's cupped hands full of water and had not burst into sobs, thank God, but had felt her eyes flood with tears. Her embarrassment at displaying emotion in front of what appeared to be hundreds of strangers was compounded by the fact that she was wearing mascara for the second time in her life. Her high school boyfriend, Mitchy Wooten, had liked her lashes "plain," but he had abruptly broken up with her fewer than twenty-four hours before they'd left for their respective colleges. Mascara was part of the new, college Pen, but as her dampened eyelashes began to gum, Pen vowed to throw the stuff away forever, a vow she would keep.

However, before its absolute exit from her life, the mascara had a role to play because when the professor ended the lecture a half-hour early so that the class could break into small groups and meet with their respective teaching assistants, Pen did not go directly to her assigned classroom. Instead she wandered through the belly of the old, neo-classical, externally gracious, internally dank building in search of a bathroom in which to repair her smeary eyes. It took some time, but she found one, and as soon as she opened the door, she found Cat.

The bathroom was tiny, just two stalls, one sink, a

paper towel dispenser, a trashcan, and a large radiator. Lying on the scarred black and white tiles, face-
up, her head jammed against the radiator, was a small
girl in big trouble. Pen did not immediately identify the
exact kind of trouble because the second she opened
the door, the scene slammed into her senses, scattering
them: a spill of black hair, limbs in terrible motion, a
rigid face, a gasping, prolonged moan, a banging, banging, banging.

Pen yelped and fell back against the paper towel dispenser. For a few seconds, her hands flapped stupidly.
Then, she squatted down and took hold of the girl's thin
ankles. She had expected them to stop moving, but they
bucked inside her hands like two animals.

"Oh, God," Pen squeaked, "It's okay, it's okay, it's
okay." But it wasn't.

Pen leaped up, wheeled around, and shoved open the
bathroom door.

"Help," she said, not as loudly as she'd meant to. She
saw a sweatshirt, grabbed it, and pulled it into the bathroom. Inside the sweatshirt was a boy.

"Shit," the boy said breathlessly and with what Pen
would later discover was a relatively rare display of
profanity, "She's seizing."

"Of course she is!" Pen shrieked, even though, before
the boy said it, she had not hit upon a name for what the
girl on the floor was doing, "We have to call 9–1–1!"

"Wait," said the boy.

"Wait?" squealed Pen.

"She's got one of those bracelets."

"A bracelet? Are you insane?"

The boy *was* insane she decided. Insane and useless.
She yanked open the zipper of her backpack, fished
wildly inside it, and snatched out a pen.

The boy pulled off his sweatshirt.

"Oh, great. Are you *getting warm*?" yelled Pen. "Are you a tad *uncomfortable*?" She pushed past the boy and leaned over the girl.

"What are you doing with that pen?" demanded the boy.

"You're supposed to put something in her mouth, so she doesn't swallow her tongue."

To Pen's amazement, he grabbed the pen out of her hand.

"That's a myth, the tongue thing," he snapped, "You'll hurt her."

Pen launched into a rant about the boy not being a doctor, damn it, and about how everyone knew the tongue thing was true and about how he needed to return her pen right now, this second, but the rant petered out before it really got started because what the boy did next was drop to his knees and tuck the sweatshirt under the girl's head, placing part of the shirt on the floor, part of it between her head and the radiator. It was among the most restrained and gentle gestures Pen had ever seen.

"Look," the boy said softly. "She's stopping."

Pen and the boy stayed still, waiting, and in a few seconds the noise emptied out of the room and was replaced by an opalescent quiet.

Eventually, the girl's eyes batted open. She looked from the boy to Pen, bewildered. She turned her head to the side, looked at the base of the sink, and groaned.

"Oh bloody hell," she said hoarsely. "Give me a minute, okay?"

"Sure," said the boy, and Pen added, ridiculously, like a person on TV, "Take all the time you need."

Minutes passed. The girl might have fallen asleep, she lay so still. Her blouse was gauzy and peacock blue, scattered with yellow flowers. Pen caught sight of her own reflection in the mirror and gave a start at how haggard she looked, before she realized it was mostly because of the smudged mascara. Surreptitiously, she touched her forefingers to her tongue and rubbed under each eye. It helped a little.

When the girl opened her eyes again, she said, "So, tell me who you are."

Relief and the sudden sound of the girl's clear voice sent Pen's adrenaline flowing again.

"Pen," she said. "Penelope, actually. Calloway. My grandmother's name. Penelope, I mean. Not Calloway. She was my mother's mother, so you know, different last name." The words hopped out one by one, flip flip flip, like goldfish out of a bowl. Pen sighed.

The girl smiled, and Pen noted that the smile managed to look exhausted and sparkling at the same time. "Got it," the girl said.

The boy wiped his hand on his gray T-shirt and held it out.

"Will Wadsworth," he said.

The girl's eyes widened.

"Get the hell out of here!" she cried.

Will froze for a second, then put his outstretched hand on the back of his head and rubbed. When Pen looked at him, she saw that under his tan, his cheeks were turning red. "Oh, right," he said. "Yeah, yeah. Sure. No problem."

He started to stand, made a slight move in the direction of the sweatshirt, still underneath the girl's head, then seemed to change his mind.

"So, uh, I'm glad you're okay and all," he said and turned sideways to squeeze past Pen and head for the door.

Pen giggled, a slightly hysterical sound, and Will Wadsworth turned toward her, startled.

"What?" he said.

"I don't think she meant for you to really get the hell out," Pen told him, still giggling. "I think it was an expression of incredulity. Disbelief."

"I know what 'incredulity' means." Will looked at the girl on the floor. "Yeah?" he asked.

The girl smiled again. "It was the name!" she sang out, "Will Wordsworth! Like the poet!"

"Uh, it's Wadsworth, actually," said Will, his face relaxing, "Like the other poet."

The girl laughed, a chiming sound, and said, "Well, you sure know how to make a first impression."

Will crouched down next to Cat, his elbows on his knees.

"When *I* first met *you*," he pointed out, "You were having a grand mal seizure."

The girl laughed again and sat up, her back against the radiator. She hooked her tangled hair behind her ears with her fingers, a snappy movement.

"Tonic-clonic," she told them, inscrutably but with great charm, her black eyes twinkling. "And I'm Cat."

When Cat, Pen, and Will emerged, in that order, from the over-conditioned air of the English department building and stood blinking in the sudden sunlight, Pen stood and looked out at the saturated greens of the grass and trees, the white columns blazing against the red brick of the buildings, the cobalt sky stretched tight as a tarp overhead. Ever since she had arrived at the university, she had walked around, heavy ("like a soaking wet pathetic tea bag" she'd emailed her mother) and dull, missing her parents every waking second and also in her sleep. She had watched the other new arrivals, resenting the pact of eager chipperness they all seemed to have signed. Now, standing between Cat and Will, a veil lifted; she felt engulfed by the electric beauty of everything around her. She gasped. It was a loud gasp.

"I *know*," moaned Cat. "The *heat*! Ugh."

"It's like walking through Jell-O. Hot Jell-O," observed Will, shedding the sweatshirt he had put back on only minutes before.

Pen peeled off her red cardigan sweater and said, "It really is awful, isn't it?" But she didn't feel awful. She tipped her face to the sun and smiled.

Will carried Cat's backpack. He offered to carry Cat herself.

"Not to be a jerk or anything," he said to Cat, slowly, "But do you think you can make it walking? Because I can carry you, no problem."

Cat looked at Pen and rolled her eyes. "God, that was jerky, wasn't it? What an offer."

Pen peered at Will. "Do you know what 'jerk' *means*?"

Will laughed. "Okay, okay. Just answer the question. Carry or no carry?"

"No," said Cat, thoughtfully. "I used to be one of those small people who liked to be carried. Up on people's shoulders usually. I'd also sit in laps. But I'm done with all that."

"Gave it up for college?" asked Pen.

"Exactly."

"I gave up not wearing mascara, but then just a little while ago, I gave up wearing it."

"Good choice. With your kind of eyelashes," said Cat, squinting at Pen, "mascara just muddies the waters."

"Good choice to you, too," said Pen, and the three of them, Will and Pen with Cat in between, set off together, amid the people, under the bright sky, and straight into the whites, greens, reds, and blues of the day.

That evening, they ate a cheese pizza on the lawn in front of Pen's dormitory. Plain cheese was Pen's favorite kind of pizza; she found it pure and unencumbered. But in the argument that preceded the placing of the pizza order, Pen had not advocated for cheese. As Jamie had pointed out to her for years, it was a boring preference, reflecting underdeveloped, kindergarten-like taste. So she kept quiet about cheese and let Will and Cat battle it out to a stalemate.

"Forget it," Will said, finally. "I'd rather have no toppings at all than eat anchovies."

"She did have a little bit of a rough day," Pen reminded him, "Maybe you could tough it out this once?"

"No chance."

"Hatred of little fish is a reflection of a little mind," said Cat, primly. "But fine. No toppings. Cheese me, man. Let's do it."

They ate, slathered in citronella and sitting atop Pen's bedspread on the cropped, prickly lawn. Late summer life—young and gold-edged—crackled around them: footballs and Frisbees cutting parabolas into the sky, club music undulating out of someone's window into the humid air, and it seemed to Pen that she, Will, and Cat were part of the action and also separate from it, so that when Will leaned back on his elbows and laughed, the sound rang through the quiet the three of them had made at the same time that it was just another noise.

"Tell us what's funny," Pen ordered.

"'Are you *getting warm*?'" said Will. He shook his head in amazement.

Pen put her pizza slice down and covered her face with her hands.

"Oh no," she said from behind the hands. "I was a nightmare, wasn't I? Totally inept and screeching."

"Oh, yeah."

"What are you talking about?" demanded Cat. "No fair you two knowing something I don't know."

"That's what she said," explained Will. "In the bathroom. When I took off my sweatshirt."

"Oh God," said Cat to Pen. "You said that?"

"I was a little freaked out, Cat."

"You were *enraged*," corrected Will.

"That's what happens when I get freaked out," said Pen, truthfully. "I get enraged."

"And hurl insults," added Will.

"I'm sorry," said Pen. She looked at his face in the fading light and realized that ever since she had met these two people, she'd been too busy at first and then too comfortable later to really notice what they looked like. Will's hair was wavy, but the rest of him was all straight lines: straight eyebrows, a straight mouth, his cheekbones two arrows pointing to the straight line of his nose. Even his eyes were somehow straight. It was a good face, but severe. When he smiled, though, with his straight, straight teeth, everything softened and lit up.

He smiled and said, "No problem. It got pretty scary there for a while."

"Wait! I don't think I thanked you guys, did I?" cried Cat. "Oh God, I didn't!"

Pen looked at her, too, and found that she was bird-boned and broad-faced, not pretty in an ordinary way, but a joy to look at. Her delicate brown hands danced when she talked. She knee-walked over to throw her arms first around Pen's neck, then Will's, planting kisses on their foreheads.

"That doesn't usually happen," she said. "The tonic-clonic thing. Grand mal. I haven't had one in eons. But I got thrown off last night."

"How?" asked Pen.

Cat wrinkled her nose. "Ooh, well, a little party happened in my dorm, I guess."

"You drank?" asked Will, then quickly added, "Not that you shouldn't. I meant does drinking do it?"

"I don't know if it was the drinking exactly. I think it was more of a triangulation."

"Like in trigonometry?" asked Pen.

"Of course not," said Cat. "I hate math. As in three things." She counted them on her fingers, "I drank three beers, even though I hate beer. I stayed up too late. And I forgot to take my medicine."

"So maybe you shouldn't do that anymore," ventured Will. "You think?"

"I definitely shouldn't," said Cat, nodding. "But I probably will."

Then she reached out, grabbed one of their hands in each of hers, and squeezed. "Thank the Lord in heaven you didn't call an authority figure. Or 9–1–1! Gosh, that would've been bad."

Even in the heat, Pen felt her face grow hot, as her own voice yelling about calling 9–1–1 echoed in her head. In a flash, she pictured the ambulance screaming up to the building, Cat being slid into it like a batch of cookies, the hordes of gaping undergrads, Cat known forever after as the girl who mysteriously malfunctioned in the English building. Pen shot a don't-rat-me-out-please look in Will's direction, but he was already talking.

"It was pretty stupid of us not to, given the fact that we didn't know what was wrong with you. A kid at my high school had epilepsy, so I sort of thought the seizure would be over fast. But we didn't know for sure."

Pen smiled her thanks at him. She wasn't ready to tell Cat the whole story, yet, but she knew that she would tell her before long. Maybe tomorrow. Maybe the day after that. There was plenty of time. She watched the sunset settle itself into dark pink and apricot layers behind the faraway trees.

"Your bed's going to smell like citronella for weeks," remarked Will.

"I don't mind," said Pen.

At Avon Books, we know your passion for romance—once you finish one of our novels, you find yourself wanting more.

May we tempt you with . . .

- **Excerpts** from our upcoming releases.

- Entertaining **extras**, including authors' personal photo albums and book lists.

- Behind-the-scenes **scoop** on your favorite characters and series.

- **Sweepstakes** for the chance to win free books, romantic getaways, and other fun prizes.

- Writing **tips** from our authors and editors.

- **Blog** with our authors and find out why they love to write romance.

- **Exclusive content** that's not contained within the pages of our novels.

Join us at
www.avonbooks.com

AVON

An Imprint of HarperCollins*Publishers*
www.avonromance.com

Available wherever books are sold or please call 1-800-331-3761 to order.